If I Were Beautiful

Devon Hartford

COPYRIGHT NOTICE

Want to find out about my next book before everyone else and get free novellas not available anywhere else? Then sign up for my mailing list!

Sign up here:

www.devonhartford.com/newsletter-31

DEDICATION

To JC. The Love Jug is still a secret.

If I Were Beautiful

Will the Nerd Girl get her Bad Boy?

#1 bestselling author Devon Hartford brings you another hot contemporary romance with a mystical twist.

A sizzling modern take on Cinderella

Nerdy Jane Johnson has tried every beauty tip and trick known to woman, but none of them ever made men notice her.
Until now.
For the first time in her life, something is working. She doesn't recognize herself in the mirror. She has literally transformed from nerdy and plain to downright beautiful.
Before her inexplicable transformation, Jane couldn't get a date to save her life. Now she has a date every night of the week.

The bad boy or the billionaire?

Gorgeous eligible men are now throwing themselves at Jane. They're even fighting over her, actual fist fights to win her affection. It's a drama drenched love triangle in the making.
It all seems too good to be true.
The only question on Jane's mind is whether or not her newfound beauty is going to last or if it's some cruel trick of fate that will fade away as quickly as it appeared.
Because everybody knows, when something seems too good to be true, it probably is.

***If I Were Beautiful is a saucy standalone romance with an HEA.

Chapter 1

The funny thing about love is, you never know when or where you'll find it.

You can go from a dating drought to raining men in the blink of an eye. But we all know, when you're waiting for the drought to end, it sometimes feels like it never will…

"You are a shameless con artist, Chelsea," I hissed in my sister's ear.

"Relax, Jane. It's not like I took you to a strip club."

"I would rather do that than this," I grumbled, looking around the crowded bar section of ReaXion, a trendy eatery in the heart of Melrose. "I don't know how you ever thought speed dating would be a good idea."

Chelsea and I sat side by side at a row of tables along the wall with the other women daters. The men milled about in the bar section, awaiting the first bell and the first round of speed dates, which was two minutes away according to the big digital timer at the front of the room. Personally, I was two seconds away from dying of a panic attack.

I hated dating.

Surprised, Chelsea said, "Are you serious about the strip club? Because if you are, we can leave right now. Hunk-O-Mania is like five minutes from here." Chelsea had been boy crazy since she was five and hadn't let up for the last twenty-six years, but I never thought she'd pick a strip joint fantasy over a real date, no matter how speedy. She was just as single as I was. Unlike me, she was great at dating. It was one of her favorite things. Not mine. Men in general were a basic frustration in my life.

"Hunk-O-Mania?" I scowled. "Did you just make that up?"

"No. It's a real place."

"That you've been to a thousand times," I joked.

"Once," she smirked. "I've only been to Hunk-O-Mania once, and that was in college. But if you want, we'll go the next time I'm in town." Chelsea lived in San Francisco and was flying out tomorrow morning, but she'd be back soon. She flew down to Los Angeles for work on a monthly basis and always stayed at my apartment when she did.

"Can we go now?" I groaned.

"To where? Hunk-O-Mania?"

"No. Any place except here."

"The guys at Hunk-O-Mania are hot, Jane."

"How hot?" I wasn't even interested. I was just looking for an excuse to leave.

"Channing Tatum hot. Matt Bomer hot. Joe Manganiello hot. Alex Pettyfer—"

"Chelz, you're listing the cast of Magic Mike. I guarantee you, those guys don't work at a place called Hunk-O-Mania. The guys who work there probably look like Homer Simpson or Peter Griffin from Family Guy. Beer guts galore and receding or nonexistent hairlines."

"They don't look like fat cartoon men," she snickered and held up her iPhone, showing me a photo of a row of beefy shirtless guys with rock hard chests and washboard abs posing on a stage.

"See?" I giggled. "Homer Simpson. That one guy in the middle with the cleft chin looks exactly like Glenn Quagmire."

"Yeah, right. We'll go after speed dating."

"Chelz! I'm not going to Hunk-O—"

The first bell rang and two dozen men made their way to the tables.

"Hush, Jane! Here come the real men." She patted my thigh beneath the table. "We'll go sample the fantasy men at Hunk-O-Mania after speed dating."

"What about dinner?" I whined. "With my beloved sister who I now hate?"

"We have reservations in the restaurant for after." ReaXion was well known for their good food, but I'd never eaten here. "Try to have fun, Jay-Jay."

I grumbled, "What about speed dating could possibly be fun?"

She didn't answer because her date had already sat down at her table and was busy introducing himself.

The man who sat in front of me wore a navy blazer over a dress shirt and was average height with average looks. Charlie Hunnam he was not. He had a bit of a pinched face, but it was nice enough. He was the kind of guy you would never notice in a crowded room. At least he was quick with a warm firm handshake. His hand was damp, but I wasn't one to judge.

"Hey. I'm Mike. What's your name?" He sounded as nervous as I was.

"Jane," I smiled.

Mike smoothed his slacks under the table. "You ever do this before?"

"What, date a man?" I joked. "No, not really." It was half true. At twenty-nine, I had limited experience with men and dating. My relationship with Aaron Gross had lasted less than a year and a half before he disappeared. Yes, disappeared. He just stopped answering my phone calls and texts one day. Later I found out he'd moved to Wisconsin for a job. He never even told me. With Harvey Pews, we'd barely made it to six months when he admitted he was seeing someone else. The whole time. And he wanted to be with her exclusively. *Good luck with that,* I'd said before never speaking to him again. Other than those two losers, there wasn't much to talk about beyond a handful of random bad dates over the years.

Mike gave me a strange look. "Are you okay?"

"Sorry, I just…" I tittered.

"Uh… yeah…" he chuckled nervously, not knowing what to say. He spun a spare drink coaster absently on the table top, which seemed to capture his interest far more than I did. Great. He was probably counting the minutes until the next bell. Luckily, he had only four to go before he'd never have to see me again.

I couldn't believe my first speed date was crashing and burning after less than sixty seconds. Awkward! Now I didn't know what to say either. *Why did I have to open with such a stupid joke?*

He said, "Uh, I think we're supposed to ask each other the basics. So, Jane, tell me about you. When was the last time you jumped out of an airplane?"

"How is that the basics?" I chuckled uncertainly.

He just shrugged in response, not making this any easier.

"Uh, you mean, like skydiving?"

He grinned, "Yeah."

"Oh, I've never gone skydiving."

"You? Come on, Jane. You have extreme sports written all over you."

I couldn't decide if he was joking with me or making fun of me. Experience would lead me to believe it was the latter. I grimaced, "Never jumped out of an airplane before, Mike. Sorry." Now I was so uncomfortable I'd willingly jump out of the nearest one, sans parachute, if it meant I could get out of speed dating. I really needed to kill Chelsea later.

Mike's eyes searched mine. His were a pretty light blue.

Mine were shrunken by my big glasses, which I hated. Because of my strong prescription, I couldn't wear contacts. So I was stuck wearing magnifying glasses ever since I was six. I pushed them up my nose and giggled nervously.

Mike suddenly smiled. A genuine smile. "Um, okay. So, you're not into extreme sports. How about un-extreme sports?" Those light blue eyes of his twinkled with amusement. He was trying and I appreciated that.

I giggled, "What, like sewing? Is that an un-extreme sport?"

"Sure. Sewing. Or knitting. Maybe baking?" Between his bright eyes and bright smile, Mike was more than cute enough for me. Despite our rocky start, I sensed a bit of chemistry.

I grinned hopefully, "I definitely bake. The way I do it is in no way extreme. But I can bake a pretty mean chocolate cake."

"Whoa, not too mean," he chuckled. "Not like devil's food cake or anything dangerous like that, I hope. That might disqualify you."

"No," I half-laughed, "nothing dangerous. I only bake angel food cakes."

"Oh, good. I don't think I could date a woman who bakes Satan's food cake."

"Wait, are you serious?"

"No," he chuckled, a big smile on his face.

"Okay, just to be safe, I promise I'll never bake you any Satan's food cake. Or demon's food cake either."

"Is that a thing?"

"No," I giggled. "What about chocolate in general? Is chocolate too extreme for you, or will you eat something basic like brownies? I've always thought of brownies as the most innocent of all the baked desserts."

"Depends how rich they are," he winked.

"Wow, Mike. Are you a food prude? I bet you don't like hot sauce or anything too spicy either."

"Actually, I'm a huge Sriracha fan. Put it on just about everything."

"Do you put it on brownies? Are you that dangerous, Mike? Or just a poser?"

"Never on brownies. But it goes great with dark chocolate."

"Really?"

"Yeah," he nodded enthusiastically. "If you like hot sauce and chocolate, you'll probably like them together."

"I'll have to try that some time. I might actually like it."

"I can't bake any for you, but I can buy you a bar. Is buying too extreme?"

"No, buying is fine," I laughed. I was really starting to like Mike. Those blue eyes of his were making my heart race. I looked away, starting to blush. He chuckled nervously. If I wasn't mistaken, he liked me too.

"So, Jane, what other un-extreme sports do you enjoy? I mean, what is the *least* extreme thing you like to do?"

"Hmmm. Let me think. Breathe?"

Mike's face glowed with amusement. "I think that takes the cake, Jane. That is possibly the least extreme thing I can think of. Well, except maybe… No. Breathing is definitely the winner. Well played. High five." He held up his palm and I slapped it.

Wow oh wow. I hadn't realized it before, but Mike was actually very cute. I would be thrilled to date a guy like Mike.

And Mike was smiling at me warmly.

We were officially having a moment.

A moment I wanted to last for at least another four hours. Why had I ever doubted Chelsea? Speed dating was the perfect idea.

CLING-A-LING-A-LING!!!

"Time's up! That's five minutes!" The woman who was MCing the evening said over the microphone while ringing a hand bell. "Gentlemen, please shift one seat to your right."

I scribbled a note on my scorecard about Mike's light blue eyes and un-extreme dating. I would definitely be requesting his contact information later.

I hoped he requested mine.

Something told me he would.

I smiled to myself as the next guy sat down.

This guy was much cuter than Mike, but not nearly as interested. His name was Tyler and he had dusty blond hair, a surfer tan, and perfect teeth. After giving me a two second look and half-hearted hello, he refused to make eye contact. His knee bounced under the table constantly, wobbling the table and shaking our drinks. He was practically refusing to talk. I kept asking him questions, but I felt like I was interviewing a two-year-old. I was the only one trying to make conversation.

"So, Tyler. What did you say you did again?"

He tossed back the last of his Jack & Coke and looked over his shoulder toward the bar. "Wonder if I can get a refill?"

"What, now?"

He shrugged and tilted his glass, swallowing an ice cube, which he proceeded to crunch loudly while looking around at the other speed daters. He was doing everything he could to avoid conversation.

If he checks his phone, I swear I'll—

He pulled his phone out of his pocket and thumbed the screen.

I leaned my forehead into my palm and groaned. "Why don't you go get your drink, Tyler."

He gave me a look that said, *We cool?*

I gave him a scowl that said, *You're not, but you can go get your drink now, little boy.*

He stood up and clicked his tongue. "B R B."

"Take your time, Tyler." I folded my arms across my chest and glared at him as he walked to the bar.

Beside me, Chelsea said to Mike, who was her current date, "Just a second." She leaned against me and whispered, "What just happened?"

"Tyler needed a refill," I grumbled.

"Tyler is a leaky douche."

"Leaky?" I giggled.

"Yes, leaky. Forget about him. Try to relax before the next date." She turned back to Mike and smiled, "Sorry."

Mike leaned over the table and said, "Are you okay?" It was so sweet he cared.

I sighed, "I'm fine."

Mike winked, "Do you want me to go kick his ass?" Tyler was twice Mike's size so he was probably joking, but I appreciated the sentiment.

"No, that's okay. I think I can handle it."

Mike grinned, "So *you'll* kick his ass?"

I laughed. "Yeah. But I'll kick his balls first."

"You might be a bit more extreme than I gave you credit for, Jane. I like that."

"Thanks. But you should be focusing on your date with my sister."

Mike's head swiveled between me and Chelsea. "She's your sister?"

"Yeah, she's my sister." I waited for what usually came next: whenever the men I knew discovered my sister looked like a supermodel, they forgot I existed. Unlike me, Chelsea was tall, had long flowing blonde hair, and a perfect body. And no glasses. If she hadn't been so damn smart, she probably would've gone into modeling. But she was, and she thought modeling was stupid, so she went into marketing.

Mike's eyes bulged as he looked at both of us.

Fabulous. He was about to lose all interest in me.

He rubbed his hands together craftily. "What a pleasant surprise."

I rolled my eyes and smirked at him. Mike was a leaky douche, just like Tyler.

Mike turned to Chelz. "So, Chelsea. Tell me everything I need to know about Jane. What's her favorite food? Her favorite restaurant? Does she have any food allergies I should avoid? And what does she like to do for fun besides Satanic baking?"

Chelsea laughed, "Satanic baking?"

"Never mind that. Just tell me what I need to know to get a second date with your sister."

Okay, so Mike was nothing like every other guy who'd met my sister after meeting me.

Chelsea smiled at me and mouthed the words, "I like this guy."

Me too.

I was listening intently while Chelsea started naming off my likes and dislikes.

"Hold on," Mike said to her and turned to glare at me, "Don't listen, Jane. I want everything your sister tells me to be a surprise."

"Yeah, Jane," she said. "This is a private conversation." She waved her hand at me. "Go kick your date in the balls or something."

I laughed to myself and gave them their space. Two minutes later, the hostess rang the bell and the men got up to switch.

Chelsea nudged me and whispered, "Mike is great. I really like him for you."

"I know, right?"

"But you've got a ton more dates before the night is over. Who knows what the evening will bring?"

"Right."

"And you should take your glasses off. You look better without them." She reached up and slid them off my face before I could stop her.

"Wait! I can't see!" It was true. Her face was now a hazy blur.

"See with your heart not your eyes."

"Are you kidding? Eyes are the windows to the soul! Give me back my windows!" I grabbed for them.

She slid them in her purse. "You can have your windows back after speed dating. Now pay attention. Your next date is waiting and he looks like a keeper."

Chapter 2

I turned to face a tall hazy broad-shouldered blur.

"Hey. I'm Zack." He sat down in front of me.

"Jane." I squinted, trying to see what he looked like. An abstract Picasso painting, that's what. For all I knew, he was missing all his front teeth, had two noses, three eyeballs, and four ears. Stupid Chelsea. I couldn't see a thing. "Sorry, this crazy woman next to me just stole my glasses and I can't really see you."

"You want me to steal them back?" Zack offered.

"Would you?" I chuckled.

Chelsea leaned against me and said to Zack, "I'm her sister. I'll give them back later." She went back to Tyler, who I realized she was now ignoring by busily thumbing through her iPhone, giving him a taste of his own medicine.

I smiled at that.

Zack said to me, "She's your sister?" Same thing every time.

"Yeah, yeah," I sighed. "She was adopted."

"Oh, really?"

"No. I was adopted."

"Really?"

I rolled my eyes, realizing I was getting bitchy. Blame rude Tyler. Also blame my gorgeous sister. "No," I sighed, "neither of us are adopted. Can we talk about something else? Tell me about you."

"I'm really boring," he chuckled. Was he trying to find an excuse to stop talking or was I assuming the worst? It was hard to say because I had no idea what Zack looked like. If he was cute, I'd say he wasn't interested. If he looked like a donkey, maybe he was. The only thing I had to go on was his voice. It had a nice crisp manly rasp that I liked.

"You don't sound boring, Zack. Your voice has a sparkle to it."

"Sparkle? Must be all the firecrackers I ate for lunch. I've been burping sparklers all day."

I giggled. "See? You're not boring."

"Trust me, I win awards for boring." There was that cute raspy voice again.

"I will put cash money on the table that my job is more boring than yours." I pulled my purse out and laid a twenty dollar bill on the wood, or what I thought was a twenty because it was so blurry I wasn't really sure.

"Twenty bucks? Damn, you don't mess around. I like that in a woman."

"What, women who don't make messes? That sounds somehow sexist, Zack," I joked.

"Not at all. Who likes a mess? Besides Oscar the Grouch, I mean?"

"Pigpen from the Peanuts."

"Ahhh, Pigpen. You gotta love that guy. No shame whatsoever."

"Exactly." I was partial to men who weren't afraid to show their childish side. "Are you a Peanuts fan, Zack?"

"More of a Snoopy fan. Charlie Brown is a bit of a dweeb and that Lucy Van Pelt is a total bitch."

"Agreed. Are you a bit of a dweeb, Zack?"

"Do you want me to be?" His voice had a soothing warmth.

"I don't know. Maybe?" I shrugged, suddenly blushing. I had no idea what Zack looked like, but I knew I already liked him. I hoped he wasn't too cute or we would never work.

"Anyway, back to this job thing. I promise you, Jane, my job is ten times more boring than yours." Zack pulled out his wallet and laid a bill on top of mine.

"Is that a twenty?"

"It is."

"How do I know for sure? I can't tell without my glasses."

"Guess you're gonna have to gamble I'm telling the truth."

"Okay, tell me the truth. Are you as cute as your voice?"

He laughed. "Ummmm, I don't know. You tell me."

"As blurs go, yours is plenty cute." I liked him even more for his humility. "But the question is, did you put a twenty down or are you hustling me?"

"Both."

"I like the sound of that. Can I be honest, Zack?"

"Go for it."

"I've never been hustled before."

"Then I'll be your first hustler," he chuckled, now sounding nervous but still eager.

"I'm not sure what that means."

"Me neither. But I'll do whatever it takes to get the job done." His innuendo was subtle, but it was there.

"Okay then!" I cleared my throat, my face burning. "I'll see your twenty and raise you another twenty." I put another bill on the pile.

He narrowed his eyes, "Now who's hustling who, Jane?"

"Isn't that a twenty?" I picked up my bill and looked at it closely, but couldn't tell for sure, so I set it back down.

"It is, but I still think you're trying to hustle me."

"Maybe I am," I flashed him a flirty smile.

"I think I better call before the pot gets too hot for either of us to handle." He put another bill on the pile.

"You sure?" The tension between us was definitely charged and increasingly sexual.

"I am. Your job can't possibly be as boring as mine. Little do you know, I've got an ace in the hole."

"Which hole?"

Zack chuckled, genuinely amused. "Are you flirting, Jane?"

"Are you just noticing now?"

"I can be slow on the uptake."

"Somehow I doubt that." But I was loving this.

I may have hated dating when things didn't go well, but I loved it when they did. Like now. "So, Zack." I gestured at our stack of twenties on the table. "Are we really calling this or do you want me to up the stakes?"

"I am a gambling man," he mused.

"And I'm a gambling woman. Here's another twenty." I didn't want to throw away sixty dollars, but I was confident I'd win the bet of who had the worst job.

"Damn, woman. You don't mess around. I'll see your twenty and call." He folded his arms across his chest. "What do you do for a living, Jane?"

I laid my hand over the pile of money. "I'm a night manager at a 95 Cent Store." It was the truth. I dragged the pile of money toward me.

Zack laid his big hand on mine. "Not so fast, little lady." His hand was very warm. He could leave it right where it was all night.

Goosebumps jumped up my arm.

"I have to tell you, Jane, being the night manager at a 99 Cent Store isn't what I'd—"

I cut him off, "95 Cent Store. You're thinking of our competitor. Higher prices. Much nicer stores. Much better merchandise. And much less boring."

He squeezed my hand affectionately.

Liquid lightning crackled through my chest and pooled between my legs. I squeezed my knees together, savoring it. I squinted at Zack, trying to see him better, but he was still just a blur. In my imagination, he looked like a tan version of Michael Fassbender with darker hair and eyebrows. I knew that was unlikely. The real Zack probably did have two noses and four ears, but if that turned out to be true, I'd just take my glasses off whenever he was around.

He said, "I hate to break it to you, sunshine, but this pot is mine."

"Unless someone pays you to watch paint dry, I don't know what you could possibly do that's more boring than what I do."

"I'm a night janitor at an office building downtown."

"Really?"

"Yup. Been doing it six years. Do you have any idea how boring it is? It's the same thing over and over every single night." Okay, so he wasn't a famous actor like Michael Fassbender. But he probably had the right number of eyes and ears. Good enough for me.

"That does sound pretty boring," I laughed, only slightly giddy.

"Yeah. But you aren't."

I was excited to discover he worked the night shift like I did, which meant our schedules were already in sync. I'd learned over the years that working the night shift was rarely conducive to dating.

He still held my hand and I was shaking. He had to be feeling it. And he wasn't pulling away.

Wow, I *really* liked Zack.

CLING-A-LING-A-DING-DING!

"Gentlemen! Please move one seat to your right!"

"Nice meeting you, Zack," I muttered.

His hand was still on mine. "Nice doing business with you, Jane."

"I didn't get to tell you how boring my job is!"

"You can tell me over dinner." He lifted my hand with his and used his other to grab the money. "I'm buying."

I wanted to beg, *When? Now? Can we ditch speed dating and go eat now? I've got reservations for two in the next room!*

Before I could say anything, the next dater was hovering over Zack, so Zack stood and shifted to Chelsea's table.

I didn't bother to scribble any notes on my scorecard about Zack because I couldn't see. And because I would never forget how charming he was. Mike had been fun, but Zack projected a masculine magnetism that swept me away.

While Zack and the other guy were changing seats, Chelsea leaned into me and muttered, "That went well."

I cupped my hand around her ear and whispered, *"Chelz, please don't be interesting with Zack. Or interested. I really like him."*

She muttered in my ear, *"I'll be neither. I came here for you, Jay. I'm not calling any of these guys back."*

"Seriously?"

"Seriously. Now pay attention to this next guy. He's cute."

Chapter 3

"Tonight was a disaster, Chelz! I can't believe you made me do this!" I pulled her by the arm and dragged her from the bar moments after the final bell rang after the final date.

Despite my early successes with Mike and Zack, the rest of the male daters were all duds. I didn't feel any connection with the twenty-odd remaining men. The high I'd felt after talking to Mike and then Zack was long gone. They were gone too. I'm sure they'd forgotten all about me after chatting with all the other women.

Was there anything memorable about a five-foot-nothing nerd girl with thick glasses and bad hair?

I had my glasses back on, so I led the way, dragging Chelsea through the crowded front lobby of ReaXion toward the exit.

Chelsea pulled me to a stop. "What about dinner, Jay? We still have our reservation."

"I just want to get out of here."

"I thought you were hungry?"

"I was two hours ago. Not anymore. Let's go."

"Fine," she sighed and we stumbled out the front doors onto Melrose. The sidewalk was crowded with people going in and out of the various bars, restaurants, and stores along the street.

"Jane! Hold up!" A man's voice called.

I turned and saw someone squeezing past the people waiting outside ReaXion. I whispered to Chelsea, "Who's that?"

"That's Zack."

"Are you kidding?"

"Nope."

Zack was cute. Zack was better than cute. He wasn't Michael Fassbender, but he was nothing to sneeze at. Tall, dark hair, friendly eyes, and a cute smile. A bit quirky with his too big chin, but I could work with quirks.

"Hey, Zack," I said, blushing as he approached.

"Hey, Jane. Hey, Chelsea," he nodded at her politely before reaching into his pocket and pulling out a bunch of twenties. He snapped them between his hands. "I owe you dinner." His eyes were on me. But something told me he was really here for Chelsea. If his gaze moved even a fraction of an inch toward her, I would say no. But it didn't. His eyebrows lifted hopefully and his eyes twinkled right at me.

Me.

"I hear there's a table waiting for us inside," he tipped his head toward Chelsea.

I said, "Did she put you up to this?"

"Dinner was my idea," he said. "She just told me about your reservations."

I glared at her, trying to hide a smile, "You're such a schemer, Chelz."

She frowned, "How is match-making scheming?"

"Please. That's all match-making is."

She shrugged.

"I believe our table is waiting," Zack said, motioning toward the doors.

"What about Chelz? We only have reservations for two. We can't ditch her."

"We'll make it work," he said with absolute confidence. "Let's go." He offered his elbow and I wrapped my hands around it without a second thought.

Despite having three people, the hostess found a spot for us in a corner at a table for two and brought an extra chair and extra silverware for Zack. Chelz and I sat across from each other with Zack on the end. Although it was past ten o'clock at night, we were surrounded by the lively buzz of a packed restaurant: people eating, silverware clinking, animated conversation.

"You guys have fun tonight?" Zack asked, absently adjusting his fork and knife on the table.

I smirked, "If you're like me and you love being treated like a public toilet, then yes, tonight was the highlight of my week."

He chuckled, "Speed dating is like being a toilet?"

"Yep. Nobody wants to spend more than a few minutes dumping their shit on you before moving on and never looking back." Maybe I was a little bit disgruntled after twenty-plus consecutive bad speed dates.

Chelsea grimaced. "Gross."

"I came back for more, Jane," Zack said with a smile.

"Yeah, but that's because you're a janitor. It's your job," I laughed.

He nudged my knee under the table and winked at me, "It's a dirty job, but somebody's gotta do it."

Chelsea shook her head, "There is no way that's not disgusting, you two. Can we change the subject?"

"Sure," Zack smiled at her. "How about you, Chelsea? Did you have fun tonight?"

"I just came for Jane," she shrugged, busy reading her menu. "We wouldn't be here if I hadn't suggested it."

"Suggested?" I snorted, pulling her menu down so I could see her eyes. "How about lied and tricked?"

Chelsea rolled her eyes. "You need to get out more. Now you're having dinner with a cute guy. You're welcome."

Zack laughed, "You two really are sisters, aren't you?"

"I sometimes wonder," I sneered.

"No, we're really sisters," Chelsea said, still reading her menu.

"I can see the family resemblance," Zack said.

I chuckled, "The only family resemblance between a naked mole rat, me, and a lithe gazelle, her, is the fact we're both mammals that have four legs and a tail."

Chelsea rolled her eyes. "You don't look like a mole rat, Jay."

"I have to agree," Zack said.

"You two both need your eyes checked. I'm the blind one with the beady eyes." I pulled my lips back over my teeth and made squeaking high-pitched rat noises.

Chelz swatted my arm and laughed, "Stop, Jay. People are gonna think this place has rats."

I knew it wasn't exactly sexy to act like a mole rat around a cute guy I'd just met, but my fear that Zack was here for Chelsea would not go away. This wouldn't be the first time some guy had flirted with me to get to her. Making dumb jokes distracted me from my self-doubt. The alternative was to sit and stew, growing increasingly worried until I sabotaged the entire dinner by interrogating Zack until he admitted he thought Chelsea was better looking than me and he was only here for her. I'd done it before. Not since high school, but I'd done it.

I scowled to myself, trying to bury the memory.

Despite my worries, I managed to pull myself together and dinner went smoothly. When our check came, Zack insisted on paying. He also insisted on walking us to my Hyundai where it was parked in the residential neighborhood north of Melrose.

"Am I gonna get your contact info tomorrow?" he asked me as we approached my car.

If he was here for Chelsea, he was doing a great job of faking it. "We can exchange info now if you want."

"Sounds great."

We pulled out phones and shared numbers. Chelsea hung back, letting this moment be mine. After, Zack got Chelsea's door, then mine.

When I was behind the wheel, he leaned against my doorframe.

"Thanks for letting me buy you dinner, Jane."

"Thanks for offering, Zack." I meant it.

"We gonna go out again soon?"

"Just give me the word."

"Word." He brushed his knuckle under my chin.

"Uhhhhh…" My skin sizzled where he touched it and my eyelids threatened to flutter.

He smiled, "I'll call you soon. Drive safe." He closed the door and waved as we drove off.

As soon as we turned a corner, Chelsea said, "Zack is so cute. You're perfect for each other."

"He was probably into you, Chelz."

"Don't be so down on yourself, Jay. He was talking to you the whole time. I don't think he said more than three words to me."

"No, he said at least twenty-five," I snarked. "If not fifty. Maybe more."

"Shut up," she laughed. "He liked you, Jay! Couldn't you tell? I could."

"It's just a ruse. Mark my words. At some point, he'll ask for your number."

Chapter 4

"Have a safe flight," I said to Chelsea as we stood on the sidewalk outside Terminal 4 at LAX the next morning. We hugged each other goodbye.

"It was so good to see you again, Jay-Jay." She rubbed my back and pressed her cheek against mine.

"You too." I pulled away. "Where did you get these sunglasses? They make you look like a movie star."

"No they don't," she frowned. With her stylish winter white pant suit, black shoes and black handbag, she looked like she was whisking away to a shopping trip in Paris.

"Yeah, okay," I snorted. Compared to her, I was dressed like a teenage boy. My outfit was my usual casual uniform of jeans and an Old Navy hoodie over a random print T-shirt. Today it was Lumpy Space Princess from Adventure Time.

"You could dress like a movie star too."

"I don't have your fashion budget, Chelz." That was just an excuse. Putting nice clothes on a mole rat didn't make it look like a movie star, so why bother?

"Go to Goodwill in Santa Monica. They always have good clothes for cheap. I bet you could buy an entire outfit for less than twenty bucks."

"Yeah, but I wouldn't look as good as you if I did."

She rolled her eyes, "Jane, would you stop? You've been talking like this since we were kids." Chelsea was in as much denial about her own looks as she was about mine. It was one reason she wasn't a bitch and I loved her for it.

"With good reason," I chuckled, unable to pull myself out of my usual spiral of sinking self-esteem.

"Yeah, well, I'm sick of it. Stop beating up on yourself or I will bitch slap the insecurity right out of you."

I smirked, "Okay, so you can beat me up but I can't beat me up?"

"That's right," she smiled. "As much as I'd love to stay here and kick your ass, I'll miss my flight if I do."

"You're just scared to throw down with your little sister. Especially not in your fancy outfit."

"Ha! You wish. Do you think I care about this outfit? I'll throw down right now." She was joking.

"You can't fight in heels. You'd lose," I chuckled.

She snorted, "I would so own you, you snarky little bitch."

We both laughed as I pulled her bags out of the trunk of my Hyundai and gave her one last hug. "Call me when you're home safe in San Francisco?"

"I will. I want to hear which other guys from last night want to see you again. I really liked Mike."

"You mean the first one I talked to?"

"Yeah."

"You think he was better than Zack?"

"Who cares? The more guys the better, right? That's the whole point of speed dating."

"Right."

"Call me when you find out."

"I will. Hey, are you coming back next month?"

"Probably."

"I already miss you." I meant it and hugged her again.

"Me too." She kissed my cheek. "See you soon!" She wheeled her luggage toward the airport doors, looking every bit like a fashion spread in Vogue magazine as she breezed past a crowd of gawking male passengers and skycaps. She was oblivious to the attention as she turned and blew me a kiss. I caught it and waved goodbye as she walked into the terminal.

I sighed to myself and drove home.

Alone.

I wasn't holding my breath that Mike or Zack or any of the other guys from last night would actually want to see me again. Worse, I had the entire day off to dwell on it.

Ugh.

On the drive home, I called my best friend George Sweet.

"Hey, Jane! What are you doing out of your coffin so early?" George and I had a running joke that I was a vampire because I worked the night shift.

"What do you think, George? I spent the night getting drunk on virgins at a blood rave."

"Oooh! A blood rave! Why didn't you call me?"

"Because you're not a vampire."

"Sadly," he chuffed. George often lamented the fact that vampires weren't real. "Did you dress up as Wesley Snipes from the Blade movies or Buffy the Vampire Slayer?"

"Both," I laughed.

"I hope you have pictures."

"It was a blood rave, George. You know pictures aren't allowed. Blood gets sucked. Virgins are turned. We vampires don't like word getting out."

"That's why you should've invited me," he chuckled, "so I could get turned." George was the only twenty-nine year old virgin I'd ever known who wasn't a virgin by choice, but was defiantly proud of it. He wore his virginity like a reverse badge of honor, like being a loser was something he chose. I think secretly he didn't want to be a virgin but he'd never admit it. One time three years ago, we'd been sitting together under a blanket watching The Nightmare Before Christmas on Halloween. I wanted him to kiss me, but he didn't. I was also pretty sure I wanted to have sex with him. We'd been best friends for nine years. What was not to like about George? When I'd gone to the bathroom to pee, my chest was fluttering with excitement. I decided I would start a tickle fight with him when I came out. Hopefully that would inspire him to kiss me. But when I came out, he was gone. We hadn't even kissed. He didn't call me for a week after that. I thought I'd lost my best friend. Then he did call and acted like it had never happened. I didn't bring it up and we never talked about it afterward. Even today, I could see myself with George. We should've been perfect for each other. He was the Bat-nerd to my Robin-nerd. But I didn't think he could see himself with anybody.

"I would've called," I said, "but Kate Beckinsale wasn't there as Selene from Underworld."

"Oh, then forget it," he snorted. "But the next time you see Selene at one of your vampire parties, call me."

"What if I just see Kate Beckinsale?"

"Mmmm? Nah."

We both laughed.

George was the only male friend I'd ever had who'd never made a move on Chelsea. I sometimes feared he was holding out hope something would happen between them some day, but he'd been around her hundreds of times since I'd met him in college. He and Chelsea were always friendly with each other, but I think after nine years it was safe to assume nothing was going to happen. They were just friends. I think the reality was that George preferred the fantasy women of his comic books, cartoons, and video games over real life women. I sometimes wondered if he was gay but didn't know it, or just afraid to admit it to himself.

He said, "So, how was dinner with Chelsea last night?"

"Dinner? Nuh uh. It wasn't dinner. My lying sister tricked me into going speed dating."

"Speed dating? She should've taken you speed *skating*."

"Skating?"

"Yup."

I shook my head. It was such a George thing to say. I said, "Um, is that a good way to meet guys?"

He laughed. "How should I know? I've never been. But I definitely would've taken you speed skating. That would make a great first date."

I thought it would make a terrible first date, but I suddenly found myself wondering if he was hinting we should go on a first date. No, that was just wishful thinking. We saw each other all the time. He wasn't interested and I was old enough to realize that. But he was still my best friend.

"Hey," I sighed. "What are you doing today? Do you wanna hang out?"

"I'm already hanging out up in Fresno."

"Are you at another Brony convention?" George wasn't a full-fledged Brony, but I always gave him crap about it because he did watch My Little Pony religiously, and had taken me to two Brony conventions.

"No, I'm at my grandma's house. I won't be home until late tonight."

"Oh," I said, disappointment obvious in my voice.

"If you're bored, maybe you should go speed skating."

"Would you go with me?" I felt a rush of hopeful excitement.

"Are you crazy? I don't know how to speed skate. Those skates are like knives. Somebody would end up with their fingers cut off. You shouldn't go either."

Sigh. "Good point. How about roller skating?"

"Fingers crushed under the wheels. So don't ever go roller skating. You've been warned." Now he was joking.

I laughed, "I'll take that under advisement."

"Well, I should probably go. I'm taking Mams to brunch."

"Okay, talk to you later."

I sighed as I drove home alone.

Now I officially had nothing to do today and no one to do it with. I hated spending my days off by myself. There was the slight chance that I'd get a call from Zack or Mike from last night, but I wasn't holding my breath.

<<<<<<<<>>>>>>>

Back at my apartment, I sat on my couch reading a tattered paperback copy of The Girl on the Train. I'd already read it once. Why not read it twice? I had nothing else to do.

Heavy thuds outside caught my attention.

I twisted around and looked out my front window. Because I was on the second story, the balcony walkway outside had a tendency to bounce when people walked along it. I always looked to make sure the rumbling was a person and not an earthquake.

It was a person, but it wasn't someone I recognized. Some big guy holding a huge black chair in his arms. He dropped it outside my front door and my entire apartment shook.

I jumped with fright.

The guy vaulted over his chair and disappeared from view.

What the heck?

Keys jingled in the lock next door. The door creaked open and boots thudded inside.

I yanked my door open to investigate. The big black chair was completely blocking my front door. The back of it was square against my doorframe. If there was a fire or earthquake, I'd be trapped inside.

Was the inconsiderate lout my new neighbor? The apartment next to mine had been vacant for almost a month. Whoever this jerk was, I needed to give him a piece of my mind.

"Excuse me!" I tried to lean my head over the chair so I could see next door, but I was too short to get a good view or climb over it. I tried pushing the chair out of the way, but it banged up against the balcony railing. The only way to move it was to slide it left or right. I tried to budge it, but it was too heavy and I couldn't get any leverage. Maybe yelling would work. "Hey! Your chair is blocking my door!"

Yes, I was irritated.

I waited patiently for a reply but didn't get one.

"Hello?!"

No answer.

Getting more irritated.

"Hey! Are you going to move your chair?! I'm stuck in my apartment!"

I waited, now angry.

Apparently he hadn't heard me. Or didn't care.

What an ass.

I plopped down on my couch and picked up my book.

Ten minutes later, the chair was still blocking my door. Some people. Did they not know the world didn't revolve around them?

Geesh.

I had to pee, so I closed my door and went to the bathroom. While I was peeing, *WHAM!* The entire apartment shook. Had the caveman just broken my door down? It sure sounded like it. If he'd broken anything, Petrak the apartment manager would make me pay for it unless I could prove I wasn't the one who damaged things.

Ass Face had the worst timing.

When I finished in the bathroom and finally opened my front door, the chair was gone.

But Ass Face had left me a present: a huge black skid mark where the chair had obviously slammed against my door. There were also long gouges in the wood. You couldn't miss it if you were blind. Petrak wouldn't miss it either, and he was an angry drunk who had no patience for anyone else's problems.

My blood boiled and my face turned red.

Obviously, Ass Face had no idea who he was dealing with, otherwise he would've taken more care while moving his chair. I stuck my head through the caveman's open front door, ready to yell his face off. But the only thing in the empty front room and kitchen area was that stupid black chair. Where was he? Not here. I had half a mind to get a butcher knife from my kitchen and slash the crap out of it.

"Hello?! Any jerk home?!" I was furious.

No sign of the caveman.

"Hello?!" I wasn't the kind of person to barge into someone else's apartment without permission, but I wasn't above yelling. "Hey! Neighbor! Your chair wrecked my door and left a huge skid mark on it! You need to fix it!" I cringed at the sound of my voice. I probably sounded like a complete bitch, which I wasn't. Ask the people who worked for me at the 95 Cent Store. But come on. Did this guy have no respect for other people's property? "Hey! Are you in here? Anybody home?!" Okay, I was pissed. He was just ignoring me. Like every other guy on the planet. I wasn't worth his time. I wasn't—

"Something wrong?" A bassy voice boomed behind me. It reverberated through my entire body in a pleasurable way that I immediately hated. Hated because it wasn't meant for me. It was meant for women like Chelsea or other qualified supermodels who men didn't ignore this blatantly.

I turned around slowly into a wall of abs.

Shirtless abs. The abs wore a thick leather belt with a huge stainless steel eagle buckle, dark blue jeans, and scuffed up work boots. I was afraid to look up and see what was attached to the abs. I could smell clean man sweat. Make that sex. Man sex. I tried to ignore it. The abs V-ed down to a very bulgy bulge below his eagle belt buckle. Wow oh wow. Did I dare look up? I dared. Because, although these abs alone were worth their weight in gold, the ass face attached to them needed to fix my door.

My eyes crawled up his abs.

A droplet of sweat trickled down between beefy pectoral muscles. To either side, nipple rings dangled from pierced nipples. Razor sharp tattoos sliced across shoulders and down muscled arms. A strong jaw was sand-papered with dark stubble. Full lips. Finely sculpted nose. Blazing blue eyes. Unruly devil-may-care dark hair.

Oh, no.

His ass face was gorgeous. Nothing assy about it.

Mike and Zack from last night had nothing on this guy.

This guy was a certified stud.

I could only stare at him and swoon. Not good.

I couldn't even breathe. My chest was locked tight with fright because I knew this perfect specimen of rugged manhood was now looking directly at my shrunken mole eyes through my window sized glasses. Not the best look for making a good first impression on the sexiest neighbor of all time.

Blaze, I'm calling him Blaze because of his blazing blue eyes, stared down at me, his face an inscrutable stone mask.

God, he was painfully gorgeous.

And very much godlike.

Swoon, swoon, swoon.

This was the moment in the movie when the handsome manwhore took one look at the heartstruck heroine, fell hopelessly in love with her, and changed his whoring ways so they could marry and make beautiful babies and live happily ever after. But the look on Blaze's face did not resemble love at first sight or love at all. It looked more like disgust. No, disinterest. Obviously, he wasn't into female garden gnomes or garden trolls or whatever he thought I was. Heck, for all the interest he was showing me, he might not even know I was standing here.

Was I hurt he clearly wasn't interested?

Or course not.

I was pissed he'd broken my front door. But I did my best to be polite. My glasses had slid down my nose, so I pushed them up. "Um, you ruined my door with your chair."

He frowned, "Who are you?" *Why are you bothering me, you miniature mole creature?*

"I'm your neighbor," I chuckled nervously. "I live next door. You, um, banged your chair against my front door?" I sounded pathetic. I should be lecturing him about gouging it and demanding he pay for it.

He shrugged, his eyes now blazing cold. "And?"

Was that all he could say? Now I was getting mad. "*And*," I mocked sarcastically, "you need to go explain to the manager that you did it."

"Did what?"

"Broke my door!"

Apparently, brains and beauty did not always go together. I folded my arms across my chest defiantly.

He put his hands on his narrow hips casually. After a moment, he glanced over at my front door. "Looks fine to me," he drawled.

"Fine?! That big black gouge wasn't there before you threw your chair against it!"

He arched an eyebrow and stared at me. Translation: *Would you go away, you squat little troll? You're not on my radar. Get it?*

I arched both my eyebrows and wiggled my head. Translation: *Asshole, you need to fix my door!*

He took a longer look at my door and sighed, "I'll take care of it."

I barked, "When?"

His eyes narrowed and he glared at me, "When I get around to it."

"Would you mind telling me when that is?" I was trying to be polite and not run him off. Why? Honestly, I'd never stood this close to a man this hot for this long, and I didn't want him to go away just yet. I had hormones. I wasn't impervious to hot men. Even the ones who are inconsiderate dickholes.

"I said I'll get around to it."

"When is that?" I tried to sound polite, but it came out bitchy.

Blaze broke eye contact. "I've got shit to move. You're in my way."

"What about my door?"

"I'll fix it later."

Was he being nice or was I just wishing?

I know I was wishing he would ask my name. I suspected he was a nice guy under his Ass Face exterior. If he would be the slightest bit polite, I would gladly help him move in his furniture or whatever else he needed to put in his apartment. I would also offer to make lemonade for him or buy him a cold six pack of whichever beer he preferred. And pizza. You always bought pizza when you helped someone move. Yeah, yeah, yeah. I wanted to dote all over Blaze in the hopes that he'd sweep me up in his arms, throw me on the nearest bed (which would be mine) and dote all over every inch of my body.

He made a bro-hand (thumb extended with pinky hooked out) and cocked it over his shoulder. "Move. You're in my way."

Geez. The least he could do was introduce himself and offer to shake hands like a normal person. But no. He was giving me this dismissive bro-hand. So I squared my shoulders and dug my heels in and refused to move, blocking his doorway.

"Really?" He said it with the least amount of interest possible.

I secretly hoped he would manhandle me and throw me out of his way, which would of course require him to get really close and pick me up. Girls could be clever like that. Trick them into fondling you. I'd heard it worked. Maybe not on guys like my friend George. But on guys like Blaze for sure.

Instead, Blaze's face soured with disgust. He turned and walked down the balcony, leaving me standing in front of his open apartment.

"You better fix my door!"

His shirtless muscled back rippled while he walked. The hypnotic dance of his chiseled flesh perfection made me squirm and squeeze my knees together. Did they really make men this hot? Because I'd never seen one before in real life. I wanted him to want me so bad it hurt.

"Hey! You left your door wide open!"

He didn't answer. But he did flip me off.

Like I was an afterthought.

He didn't even turn to face me. Just halfheartedly raised his arm and dismissively flicked his middle finger.

"Dirty butthole!" I hated him even though I still wanted him.

He didn't respond, just kept walking.

"I'm gonna steal all your stuff!" The only thing in his apartment was that stupid black chair.

Blaze didn't slow down. At the end of the balcony, he turned into the stairwell and sauntered downstairs.

Was I heartbroken or hurt?

Neither.

Honestly, I was surprised he'd bothered to talk to me at all.

Not that that made him any less of an ass.

If Chelsea had been here, I'm sure he would've talked to her.

I scowled to myself.

Okay, maybe I was a little hurt.

Chapter 5

Once again, I sat on my couch with my front door open, reading my book, and waiting for Blaze to return.

He didn't.

But I had a bunch of flies buzzing around my apartment.

Stupid Blaze.

An hour later, he still wasn't back, but his front door was still wide open. I guess he wasn't worried about anyone stealing his huge chair. I considered closing his door for him, but I didn't think it was my place. What if he'd left his key inside? I didn't want him getting locked out. He would have to deal with Petrak. Petrak hated it when you lost your key. He also charged you $125 to re-key the lock.

I considered looking around Blaze's apartment for his key, but I wasn't a snoop and I didn't want him to catch me. What would he think of me then? Probably less than he already did.

I'll admit I considered baking a cake for him to make peace. As a neighborly gesture. Since we were going to be sharing a wall, it was the least I could do. But I didn't. I knew from experience that you could shower a guy you liked with attention on a daily basis and he would still ignore you.

Blaze could bake his own damn cake.

I wasn't bitter.

When I realized it was almost one o'clock, I grabbed my iPhone to check my email. I was dying to find out which if any speed daters from last night were interested in me. Mike and Zack hadn't ignored me. They'd both been very interested in me. Maybe some of the other guys were interested too.

I scrolled through and found the email from Extreme Speed Dating LA.

The name reminded me of Mike and all his talk about extreme and un-extreme. I smiled to myself. By the time I finished scanning the email, I was scowling.

I had no matches.

None.

I couldn't believe it.

Two or three, maybe. But none?

What happened to stupid pinch-faced Mike? Was I too extreme for him? Or was he just a liar? Was his Mr. Interested routine all an act? I wasn't sure. Maybe he forgot about me after twenty other dates. Yeah, that was probably it. How could you expect someone to remember you amongst that many other people? I'm sure I just slipped his mind.

(he's not interested)

I sighed.

At least one guy hadn't forgotten me. Zack. I even had his number and he had mine. I really wanted him to call. Sure, he hadn't yet, but we'd just had dinner last night. I couldn't expect him to call today, could I? I could call him, but I didn't want to scare him off by calling too soon. He'd think I was needy. But, after my run in with Butthead Blaze, I did feel worthless and a little bit needy. Not a lot. Just a little. A little bit of man distraction would do wonders for me right now.

I brought up Zack's number in my list of contacts. My finger hovered over the call button. At the last second, I called Chelsea instead. Best to get her advice before I did something I couldn't take back. I called her on FaceTime.

"Hey, Jay. What's up?" Her face filled the screen.

"Are you at a BART station?" BART was the subway in San Francisco.

"Yeah. Lissa and I are going to Berkeley to shop." She turned the phone to face Melissa, who waved.

I'd met Melissa before and liked her. I waved back.

Chelsea turned the phone back to herself. "Did you hear back from the guys last night?"

"No."

"What, did you not get the email?"

"I got the email. It apologized that I didn't get any matches."

"None? What about Mike?"

"That's what I said," I grumbled.

"Well, you've got Zack's number. I liked him."

"That's why I was calling. Should I text him or wait until he texts me?"

"Call him. Leave a voicemail. You're both adults."

"I can't do that. I'll sound desperate."

"So text him."

"When, now?"

"Sure now." It was so easy for Chelsea to act like this. Men chased her. She didn't chase them. She never followed any dating rules either, she just did what she wanted and men still drooled over her. To her credit, she never played hard to get because she *was* hard to get. So many men wanted Chelsea it was ridiculous. But she wanted a husband, not another boyfriend or friend with benefits. She was ready to settle down and start a family, so she was waiting for the right guy to come along.

I said, "Do you really think I should text Zack now?"

"Go for it."

"Okay, I'll do it." I swiped over to the messenger app. My excitement was making me jittery. "What should I say?"

"Anything. Just be yourself." Chelsea was always so encouraging and it set me at ease. "And don't be ironic."

"Okay." I laughed and said what I was typing out loud to Chelsea. "Hey Zack. It's Jane from speed dating." I hit the send button.

"Perfect. Hey, have you talked to Mom or Dad lately?"

"Not in a couple weeks. Why?"

"Mom called today and said you haven't been out to visit her."

"Did you tell her you were just in town and *you* didn't visit either? Pasadena isn't that far from West LA, you know."

"I know," she groaned. "But you know me and Mom are having a thing right now."

"Don't remind me." I rolled my eyes. They were always having a thing. We both knew Mom and Dad held her to much higher standards than they did me, but no one would ever admit it. Consequently, Mom was always disappointed with Chelsea's decisions. I could never figure out why. Chelsea was successful and happy, so what? "You know, you and Mom really oughta—" My phone chimed. "Oh wait! I just got a text from Zack! It says, 'Hey, can you talk right now?' What should I say back?"

"Call him."

"Should I?"

"Yeah. And call me back after."

"Okay." I hung up and dialed Zack.

"Hey, sunshine."

"Hey, Zack." I was giddy that he already had a nickname for me.

"What are you doing?"

"Just chillin. You?"

"Making Sunday plans," he said casually.

"Oh? What kind?" My hands shook with excitement.

"Depends on what you're doing. Are you free later?"

My heart raced. Should I say yes or would that sound desperate? I wished Chelsea was beside me to walk me through this. Screw it. "Yeah, I'm free."

"What do you think about going down to Venice for a stroll on the boardwalk? Weather's nice."

"That sounds great!" I gasped. More calmly, "I mean, sure. Yeah, sure. I could do that."

He chuckled on the other end of the line. "Will it just be you and me, or will Chelsea come along to chaperone like last time?"

That was weird. Even the way he said it was weird, like he wanted her to come with us. And probably not to chaperone. At times like this, I really hated having a hot sister. "Gosh, Zack. I don't know. Do you want me to call her and ask?" He didn't know she was in San Francisco.

"Sure. Why not?" He said it casually, but there was an underlying hint of bullshit I could smell over my iPhone. Amazing how good technology was these days.

I scowled to myself. *Because if you were only interested in me, you wouldn't want her coming along, dumbass.* "Hmmm, let me think, Zack." My sarcasm was clear as day. "Do I want to go out with just you, or should I bring along my hot sister?"

He chuckled nervously but didn't say anything.

I grumbled, "Or maybe I can just have *her* meet you in Venice while I stay home and eat tater tots."

"Tater tots?"

"Shut up, Zack. You're not interested in me, are you?"

He chuckled again, but still said nothing.

"Geez, Zack. Are you that much of a dirty toilet bowl?"

"Ha ha ha."

"Yes you are." I could hear it in his voice. I rolled my eyes. "Why didn't you just ask Chelsea for her number instead of wasting my time?"

"Uhhh…"

"Goodbye, Zack. Don't ever call me because I won't give you my sister's number. Ever. Forget I exist."

I ended the call and immediately dialed Chelz.

"What's the scoop?" She smiled over FaceTime, now on BART. The noise from the train was really loud.

"He was into you, not me!" I sung triumphantly. "You! Not! Me!"

She slumped, her mouth sagging with disappointment. "I'm sorry, Jay. I really thought—"

"NEXT STOP MONTGOMERY STREET. NEXT STOP, MONTGOMERY STREET." It was the train operator on the intercom and the sound drowned Chelsea completely out.

"Forget about Zack," Chelsea said, "Zack is a dick. If you ever bump into him, punch him in the face for me."

"How about I punch him in his dick?"

"Same thing," she winked.

The BART train started braking and turning and it made loud squeals and grinding noises. But I could see Chelsea's beautiful face smiling back at me. I snapped.

"I hate you, Chelsea Johnson! Do you know that?! I hate you because you're beautiful and I hate you because you're nice! And I hate you because you're my sister!" I was trying not to cry. I had no idea if Chelsea had heard my rant over the train squeals, but I didn't really care. I was in too much pain.

When the noise faded, she said, "What did you say? It's really loud in here."

"Nothing." I shook my head and looked away, wanting to hide somewhere and die.

"I'm so sorry about this, Jay. There'll be other guys. I promise. Jay? Are you okay?"

I couldn't look at her for a long time. Suddenly, my anger flared again. "This is all your fault! You know that? You made me go speed dating! You made me! This wouldn't have happened if I'd stayed home!"

"I told you I'm sorry, Jay. I never thought this would happen. I mean, I just wanted you to get out so you could meet some men."

"This always happens, Chelsea! Always!" Now I was crying and smeared a tear across my cheek.

"Oh, Jay. Forget about the assholes of the world. There's plenty of nice guys out there. Guys like George."

"George isn't interested in me, Chelz! He's not interested in anybody!" I was crying hard now.

"You know what I me—"

"NEXT STOP, EMBARCADERO. NEXT STOP… EMBARCADERO."

I grimaced. "I have to go."

"Jay! Wait! Don't hang up! Jay!"

I ended the call and dropped my phone on the couch and walked out my front door with no idea where I was going.

Did it really matter?

I walked for two hours in the LA heat. It was always hot in Los

Angeles, even in February.

At the moment, I had no idea where I was. Somewhere in Brentwood Heights where all the mansions were crammed together on lush tree-lined streets.

I was dying of thirst.

I didn't really care.

LA was having a drought and I was too. A personal drought.

A man drought.

I scowled at myself and pushed my glasses up my nose. They kept sliding down because my face was greasy from all the exertion. Although I'd left my hoodie at home, I was dying in my purple Lumpy Space Princess T-shirt because I'd run out of sweat. My skin was cold and clammy and I was dangerously dehydrated. I was also getting a sunburn on my face and arms.

Good.

Maybe I would die of skin cancer and dehydration all on the same day. Come and get me, Death. Take me to the hereafter. ASAP.

I started turning streets at random, not caring if I got lost.

The mansions got larger and larger. Several had tennis courts and I saw swimming pools in the backyards between the trees. The smell of the chlorinated water reminded me of how thirsty I was. I smacked my dry lips. At one point, I could see The Getty Center high on the hillside that overlooked all of Santa Monica, West LA, and the Pacific Ocean. They had drinking fountains at the museum, but I didn't think I could get there from this side of the mountain.

So I kept walking and turning.

A few streets later, I ended up in a cul de sac. I didn't know if it was the heat, my dehydration, or my frustration, but I suddenly felt nauseous. I nearly collapsed in the shade of several big banana trees planted at the edge of someone's walled off front yard. In this part of Brentwood Heights where everybody had a mansion, everybody also had fences and gates that could only be climbed by fully hydrated ninjas.

I was neither ninja nor hydrated.

Worse, I wasn't sure how much further I could walk and I was starting to worry. I didn't have my phone so there was no one I could call to pick me up. I couldn't even call an Uber car.

When I swallowed, my throat was so scratchy I started coughing. The next thing I knew, I couldn't stop and I started heaving up my guts, but I had nothing to heave. I'd digested my breakfast hours ago so now I was all dried up.

Did anybody have a garden hose? I knew you weren't supposed to drink from hoses because of the toxins, but I didn't care at this point. If it wasn't for all these damn gates, I could easily sneak into someone's yard and steal a drink. Was it possible to die of thirst in the middle of an elite neighborhood because all the rich jerks lived behind walls and security gates and hoarded their water?

It sure seemed like it.

For some reason, that really irritated me. I stood up and walked to the nearest gate. Tall palms and broad leafed tropical shrubs surrounded it. This place looked like a jungle oasis. Plants didn't stay this green without plenty of water. So where was my damn glass? It's not like I needed a gallon.

Just a glass.

I wanted to scream at somebody, anybody. But I wasn't going to scream at the shrubbery.

I looked around frantically until I found a little metal speaker box on a metal pole. Taped to it was a small piece of paper with a hand written note that read: *Press button for estate sale.*

I pressed the button and waited.

Nobody answered. Of course nobody answered. Rich people hated poor people, especially when they were thirsty. Stupid greedy water hoarders.

I was about to walk away when a male voice spoke over the speaker. "Yes?"

"I'm here for the estate sale," I lied.

"You'll need a permit if you parked on the street. Is your car parked nearby?" Could he see me? Yep. Poking from the shrubs above my head was a security camera.

"I walked."

"Walked? From where?" A pause. "Who are you?"

"Who am I?" *Who was this asshole?* "Look, I just need a glass of water. I've been walking around all day in the heat and I think I'm sunburned and I'm going to die of heat stroke if I don't get some water and some shade soon. Can I just come in and get a glass of tap water? I'll pay for it." Rich people loved money.

There was no reply for a long time.

"Hey!" I shouted at the little box. "Be nice, okay? I'm only asking for a *fricking glass of water!*" I tried to shake the speaker box but the metal pole was too sturdy and I couldn't budge it. "You stupid rich asshole!"

I turned to go. Maybe his neighbors were nicer.

The gate buzzed behind me and it rolled across a track, disappearing into a stone wall hidden behind the shrubs. I expected to see a butler walk down the stone lined drive wearing a black tux. A linen napkin would be folded over his forearm and he'd be palming a silver tray that held a tiny shot glass with one swallow of water in it. He'd say "Your water, madam," and he'd stand beside me and scowl while I drank it, like he was doing me a huge favor. Then he'd go without offering seconds or apologizing for calling me madam instead of miss.

Anyway, that didn't happen.

The speaker box said, "Did you want the water or not?"

"Are you a person or a robot?"

"Does it matter?"

"No! Yes! I just—"

"I'm very busy right now. Walk up the drive, someone will get you water and some sunscreen, then you can leave." The speaker box clicked off.

I stared at the box. How rude!

The box clicked on. "I'm going to close the gate now. You'd better come inside. I'm not opening it again." Despite his generosity, something about his tone was extremely irritating.

I wanted to shout, YOU AND YOUR WATER CAN FUCK THE FUCK OFF!!

Instead, I rushed through the gate. It trundled closed behind me as I walked up the drive, which was really a full-fledged road covered in stone pavers. It curved up through the trees and emerged on a huge circular parking area. A tall fountain sat in the center. Life sized winged stone cherubs floated around a bunch of life sized naked stone maidens. The cherubs spat streams of water into the surrounding pool and the maidens poured it from vases. The fountain looked like the kind you'd see in a huge town square somewhere in Europe, not a Brentwood mansion.

Didn't the asshole owner know we were having a drought?

I considered climbing into the fountain and dunking my head in the water and drinking like a wild animal, but I could smell the chlorine and I didn't want to get any sicker. I could splash through the stupid fountain on my way out. If the jerk who owned this place acted any jerkier, I would squat and pee in it.

The parking area held about ten cars and had room for more. BMWs, Mercedes, and Bentleys, or whatever rich people drove when they weren't driving their Ferraris. There was also a Ferrari. And a brand new blue Lamborghini. I had to walk around the back of it to read the logo on the trunk, but it was the real deal. It looked like a blue spaceship.

The huge two story house was old and unkempt. It reminded me of one of those decrepit rundown mansions you saw in movies like *Sunset Boulevard* or *The House on Haunted Hill*. Or maybe that hotel from *The Shining*. I shuddered at the thought. I'm sure whoever lived here was equally creepy.

"Did you want your water or not?" The voice was an irritating baritone that would've been sexy if it didn't sound so impatient with me. The owner of it stood in front of the elaborate wood and leaded glass double front doors. Based on our speaker box conversation, I had expected him to look like a real life version of mean old Mr. Burns from The Simpsons and be wearing a velvet smoking jacket. Instead, he wore a dark sleek three piece suit with a conservative tie and matching pocket handkerchief. The suit looked as expensive as the Lamborghini and way too hot for this weather. Unlike Mr. Burns, this guy was movie star handsome. Early 30s at the oldest. Clean shaven with thick chestnut brown hair swept back in an elegant wave over his flawless features. The suit hugged his broad shoulders and narrow-waisted body. Not a body builder, but clearly a fine physique underneath.

He frowned at me, "I don't have all day."

"Sorry for being dehydrated in your neighborhood. The next time I'm dying of thirst, I'll make sure it's in a poor neighborhood where the people are nicer."

He looked amused. In an angry way. "There's plenty of water in the fountain. You can always drink that."

I scowled, "I considered going for a swim, but I don't want to endorse your wasting of water. We are having a drought, you know."

"Then I guess you don't want my water."

"I knew you were an asshole!"

I wasn't normally like this, but I was extra irritable because of the heat and the dehydration and the way Zack had treated me earlier. And that jerk Blaze, my new neighbor. And this handsome jerk. And that jerk Mike. And my blood sugar was probably low because I'd been walking for hours on an empty stomach.

Rich Guy slid his hands in the pockets of his slacks and glared at me. "Shut up. Get inside. Have a bottle of water. Then you can go. I have business to attend to." He turned and went through the open door, leaving it wide open.

I'm sure he had the air conditioning running full blast in this heat and had no concern for the energy he was wasting by letting all the cool air leak out. Unlike him, I made energy conservation a priority. So I ran up the stone steps and shut the door behind me, but only because I was dehydrated and needed water and wanted to conserve energy.

Not because Rich Guy was impeccably gorgeous.

I didn't care about him.

Once I drank as many bottles of his water as I wanted, I would tell him where to shove the rest of them. And to set his A/C no cooler than 78 degrees because you know an icy asshead like him set it at 70.

Total butt clump with no respect for the environment.

Chapter 6

The grand entrance inside the house was breathtaking.

A patterned marble floor stretched from wall to wall. Twin arched staircases curved around the circular walls. Overhead, an enormous crystal chandelier hung from a cathedral ceiling. I felt bad for whoever had to set up scaffolding so they could dust this place. Centered below the chandelier was an ornate rococo table with a huge flower arrangement of what appeared to be two hundred or more fresh cut roses. I stepped up and sniffed. Yup, they were real.

Apparently, the rich butt clump owner of this place was richer than he was annoying, which I had thought impossible. I shook my head. People with too much money were ridiculous.

Best get my water and get out of here. But I didn't see a butler with a platter and a water glass, or the ridiculously hot owner.

To my right, a twelve foot tall arched mirror was set into the wall. Who needed a mirror that big? A giant? More like a giant ass. Or giant asshead. Make that Mr. Giant Asshead.

Where was he?

And where was my promised water bottle?

There it was.

Behind me on a small folding table stood an opened pack of water bottles. A few had already been removed. I grabbed one and twisted off the cap and guzzled it. I felt better already.

Where was Mr. Giant Asshead?

He sure wasn't hospitable beyond the bare minimum.

Now that I had my water, was it time for me to go?

Well, he had mentioned sunscreen, but I didn't see any on the table. What I did see was a guest book of some sort. Beside it was a glass fishbowl with a few business cards inside. I read several of them. Antique dealers, art collectors, jewelers. Sounded like an estate sale to me.

I'd been to estate sales before. Not at an estate like this. Just regular homes. But they were all the same, right? You walked around, picked out what you liked, then paid for it on your way out.

I probably couldn't afford anything the giant asshead was selling, but he did owe me some sunscreen.

Time to go look for it.

I wandered from room to extravagant room. This place reminded me of those old mansions from the 1930s and 40s you saw in black and white movies, but in full faded color. I doubted the decor had been changed since this place was built. What had probably once been the height of high fashion now seemed worn out and dreary, giving this place an abandoned quality, a pervasive loneliness that seeped from the walls. Whatever grandeur it had had was now long gone.

It was sad, really.

After leaving the drawing room, I found myself in a humongous kitchen. Dusty copper pots hung above an enormous butcher block island. Two gas ranges with eight burners apiece sat side by side against one wall. Ten cooks could work this kitchen. Through the windows, I saw a huge pool surrounded by slate tiles and the backyard garden. They had probably thrown huge parties here back in the day, filling this place with life and laughter, but those days were a distant memory.

In the far corner, a narrow staircase angled upstairs.

Since Asshead was nowhere to be found and I still didn't have my sunscreen, I decided to continue my search. At the top of the stairs, I opened a narrow door and found myself at the end of a long hallway.

The sudden sound of voices startled me.

I dove through the first set of doors I found and listened to the voices. The one doing all the talking was definitely Mr. G.A., but I couldn't make out what he was saying. When the voices faded, I relaxed and looked around.

This gloomy room was obviously the master bedroom. The opulent four poster bed was a dead giveaway. But what really snagged my attention was the mammoth vanity with Hollywood style light bulbs framing the big mirror. I didn't normally like looking at myself more than necessary, but something about that vanity gave me a sense of that old Hollywood magic, the kind where anyone could be glamorous with the right lighting and the right makeup. I sat down on the vanity chair and found the light switch. The bulbs popped on blinding bright.

I pushed my glasses up my nose.

For once, I sort of liked the way I looked.

It had to be the lighting. It washed out my features or something.

If I wanted to go full glamour girl, I needed makeup at the very least. I opened vanity drawers at random. They were filled with old makeup bottles, makeup brushes, antique brass and sterling silver lipstick tubes, bottles of cold cream, perfume, tortoise shell compacts, hairbrushes, and everything else a Hollywood starlet needed to make herself beautiful. I opened some of the bottles and jars. Everything was so old I was afraid to touch it. It probably all had lead in it. Or asbestos. Or talcum powder at the very least.

In other drawers I found plenty of jewelry. Most of it costume but some of it looked really expensive. The pearl necklaces looked real to me, but I wouldn't really know. I felt guilty going through all of it. Makeup was one thing, but I was starting to feel like a thief.

That didn't stop me from trying on some of the elaborate costume necklaces and bracelets. Just for fun. I also dangled a few earrings up to my earlobes.

"You look fabulous, darling," I muttered to myself, shaking my head so the earrings sparkled in the Hollywood lights. I put them back in the drawer with the others. It was probably time for me to go.

But I still needed sunscreen for the walk home.

I opened one more drawer.

Inside was a white jewelry box that was covered in Asian-themed carvings. Very exotic. Dozens of tiny people covered every square inch of the box. If the box had been new, I would've said it was made of plastic. But it looked old and had the creamy look of real ivory.

I'm sure the box alone was worth a fortune.

But what was inside?

I had to find out.

I reached down to pick it up but I hesitated.

Oddly, I had the strange premonition that opening this box was a bad idea.

That was crazy. It was just a jewelry box. I wasn't going to steal anything. I wasn't that kind of person. So what was I worried about? I mean, it wasn't like this was Pandora's box. It didn't look that old. I was fairly confident that all the world's evils were *not* trapped inside. So if I opened it, I wouldn't obliterate all of humanity.

That was just a folk tale.

So I took the box out of the drawer and laid it on my lap.

Then I lifted the lid.

I gasped when I saw what was inside.

Chapter 7

Wow.

The ivory jewelry box was filled with rings.

Diamond rings.

And emerald and ruby and sapphire, and every color of precious stone you could imagine, all set in gold or platinum rings that appeared equally priceless. They were arranged in neat rows on black velvet.

I slapped the lid shut.

I knew what costume jewelry looked like.

This was not costume jewelry.

All the stones were huge. I didn't know much about karats, but I knew there were more karats in this jewelry box than Bugs Bunny could eat in a lifetime.

I opened the lid again.

Why were sparkly things so hypnotic?

Who cared.

I stared.

Despite having a decent paying job at the 95 Cent Store, I wasn't exactly stashing away bundles of cash every month. After paying $1,500 for my one bedroom apartment, more on my car payment, more on insurance, groceries, gas, and every other over-priced LA thing, I hardly had any money left over at the end of the month. I wasn't making much forward progress in my life. Not with men and not with my career. But I could make a lot of forward progress with one of these rings...

Or two.

Or three.

I slammed the lid shut.

No. I wasn't that girl.

It wasn't like I was on the verge of being homeless. I didn't need to stoop to stealing from someone who'd been nice enough to invite me inside his house and give me water, even if he had been 70% rude and only 30% polite.

One more look didn't make me a thief.

I opened the lid.

Wow, wow, wow.

So incredibly sparkly…

Sometimes you could only get a good look with your fingers.

I started picking up rings and examined each one closely, watching them shimmer in the vanity lights. I'd always loved blue sapphires, and one of the rings had a huge blue oval stone. I held it near my ring finger and tried to imagine I was wearing it. It occurred to me it would look better if I actually slipped it on. Just to see it the way it was meant to be seen. I wasn't going to steal it.

I held the ring just above the tip of my ring finger, ready to put it on.

One pressing thought gave me pause.

It was highly unlikely that I'd slide this ring on my finger and it would get stuck, right?

No, that never happened in situations like this.

A lump formed in my throat and I was suddenly convinced Mr. G.A. was standing right behind me, boring a hole on my back with his hateful glare while watching my every move. Shaking with guilt, I slowly twisted around in the vanity chair to look.

I sank with relief.

I was all alone.

I carefully set the ring in the box and put everything away.

I sagged back in the chair and shut my eyes, taking a deep calming breath. My heart was still racing.

"Find anything you like?" Mr. G.A. asked in his imposing baritone.

"Oh!" I nearly jumped through the twelve foot ceiling. "You just scared the crap out of me!" Now my heart was hammering.

He chuckled, flashing his disarmingly adorable dimples. "What are you doing in here?"

"Looking for sunscreen!"

"Are you sure?"

You mean, did I steal your priceless jewelry?

I blurted, "No! I mean yes! Sunscreen! I thought maybe there was some in here!"

He gave me a strange look before walking into the room.

My fear spiked as he approached because I suddenly realized I was clutching something hard and round in my hands. Something that felt suspiciously like a ring.

Shit! How did that get there? I'd put them all away! At least, I thought I had.

I clamped my fingers tightly around it.

If he caught me clutching one of his priceless rings, he'd have me thrown in jail. What was the cutoff between petty theft and grand larceny? I think it was something like $500. Every ring I saw in that box had to be worth a hundred times that. Or a thousand. I cringed and squeezed the ring in my hand as hard as I could and shoved my fists into my crotch. There was no way I would let him see it.

I was not a thief!

It was an accident!

Mr. G.A. pulled up his slacks and sat down on top of the vanity, calling attention to his crotch, which was now inches from my face. Sure, he wore a suit and slacks, but it was RIGHT there and made me forget all about the ring in my hands. For a second. I had to stare. At his crotch. But only for a second. What was I going to do about this ring? I had no idea. My eyes flicked up and met his. I gave him the guiltiest grin ever.

He smirked a dimple at me. His eyes flickered like chocolate diamonds as priceless as the gemstones in the jewelry box. "Something catch your eye?"

"Ha! Ha! Ha!" *Did you mean your crotch or the ring I stole or your eyes or all three?* I tore my eyes away from his. If I looked at them much longer I was going to spill my guts, hand him the ring, and beg his forgiveness.

"Are you okay?" He placed gentle fingers beneath my chin and lifted it an inch so he could examine my face. "I'm starting to worry you have heat stroke like you said."

His touch made my entire face tingle. The only truly handsome man (other than my dad) who'd ever touched me with this much tenderness was my childhood dentist, hot Dr. Becker. Chelz and I used to swoon about him when we were kids. But Dr. Becker's touch never tingled like Mr. G.A.'s touch. I was so nervous I blurted, "Yes! Heat stroke! My brains are addled! From all the heat!"

"Addled? You don't look addled."

"Oh no, I totally am! Addled to the max!" I shook my head and said, "Rattle, rattle, rattle!" I couldn't help but giggle. My glasses slid down my nose, so I pushed them up with a smile. "See? Totally addled." Somehow, his glimmering chocolate gaze made me feel relaxed.

He leaned back on the vanity and planted his hands behind him on the table top, breaking contact with my chin, much to my disappointment. But his face lit up with a friendly smile. "You're too funny." He was genuinely amused.

Why did I suddenly feel incredibly bashful? Oh, because the male runway model in the slick suit was... Was he actually flirting with me?

If he was, it was just out of politeness. But I was still flattered.

"Is there a reason you're squeezing your hands in your lap?"

"Um, I really have to pee?"

"My bad. I'm being completely rude. You can use the bathroom in here." He nodded toward the door in the corner.

I glanced at it. A sense of hope seized me and I shot to my feet. I could easily leave the ring in the bathroom in a medicine cabinet or wherever, and he wouldn't find it until after I was long gone. "Great!"

"One thing before you go."

"Yeah?"

He held out his hand to shake mine. "I don't think I ever caught your name." But he was about to catch me red handed.

I clutched the ring as hard as I could. "Oh, uhh… Jane. I really have to pee. Can we talk after?"

"No. We talk now." He motioned with his hand.

I squeezed my knees together. "I'm going to start leaking any second. You wouldn't want me ruining your rug, would you? It looks expensive."

He stared at me. "Make it quick."

I turned and took a hopeful step toward the bathroom.

"One last thing. Jane." He sounded angry.

I froze in place. "Yeah?"

"Turn around," he commanded.

I did. My heart was racing. There was no way out of this.

He frowned, "What're you hiding in your hands, Jane?"

Caught.

If I dropped the ring, he'd see it fall. I could throw my hands in the air, thus throwing the ring across the room, and shout, "See! Nothing up my sleeve!" But my purple LSP T-shirt didn't even have sleeves, and, with my luck, if I threw the ring it would either hit him in the face or break a window or one of the vanity mirrors or who knew what. But he'd see it for sure.

"Jane. What're you hiding?"

"What did you say your name was again?" I was trying to distract him.

"I didn't." He held out his palm. "Hand it over."

"Hand what over?"

He wagged his fingers. "Now."

My shoulders slumped and I stared at the floor, too embarrassed to look at him. Now I was the giant asshead. "I swear I was just looking. I wasn't going to take anything. It fell out by accident." By *accident*? Wow, that sounded too stupid even for me.

"Show me," he growled.

I unfolded my hands in front of him, cringing, expecting a whipping any second.

"What's that?" he asked.

To my surprise, the ring I held wasn't one of the million karat jewels I'd fondled before he walked in. It was a simple gold band engraved with two hearts. Actually, it looked tarnished, so it wasn't even gold. Probably brass or a cheap alloy. It looked liked the kind of worthless trinkets we sold at the 95 Cent Store in packs of six. It hadn't been in the ivory box and I had no idea where it came from.

His eyebrows lifted casually. "Where'd you find that?"

"I have no idea. I was… Look. I'm going to be absolutely honest with you."

He smirked, "Are you sure?"

I rolled my eyes. "Yes. I promise. Okay, I was trying on some of the necklaces and earrings I found in the vanity, just to see how they looked on me. I kind of got carried away pretending I was a movie star or something. I mean, look at this vanity, right? It forces you to be more glamorous." Did I sound convincing? I thought I did. Did it matter I'd left out the part about looking through the ivory box and pulling the priceless rings out? Of course not.

Did he look convinced? Not really.

I continued, "Anyway. I didn't take anything. I don't know if this ring was stuck to one of the necklaces or what. It must've fallen in my lap without me noticing. I wasn't going to take it. In fact, I'll put it back right now." I stepped around him and set it gingerly on the vanity with a tiny *plink!*

The silence in the room was suddenly overwhelming.

He folded his arms across his suit jacket and glared at me. "How do I know you didn't take anything else?" Why did he have to look so damn handsome while he was interrogating me?

"I didn't!" I pushed my glasses back up my nose for emphasis.

"How do I know you don't have something in your pockets?"

"I promise I don't."

"The only way to know for sure is to strip search you." His eyes darkened dangerously.

"What?!" A wave of electric pleasure zinged through my entire body.

"And check every one of your body cavities by hand."

"My what?" I swallowed hard. "By what?"

"By tongue."

"Did you just say tongue?"

"No."

"No, you said—"

"You heard me, Jane," he growled, his eyes narrowing with a hint of menace.

I gawked at him. Was he serious? He looked damn serious. Now I was getting frightened. I was in a random strange mansion who knew where, wasn't sure if I could find my way home, and now I was trapped in this room with a gorgeous lunatic. I hadn't even brought my phone with me because stupid Zack had wanted to meet Chelsea and not me! I couldn't call for help because of him!

Zack, you ass hat! Now I'm screwed because of you! And scared!

I swallowed hard.

Mr. G.A. glared. Was he going to screw me?

I mean, not that I'd ever been screwed by a man as handsome as him. But I was very open to the possibility.

Then again, searching body cavities by hand wasn't screwing.

Or was it?

He had said by tongue…

"What's it gonna be, Jane?" A devilish smile played across his full lips and perfect teeth. "Do I chain you up in my sex dungeon and never let you out, or…"

I was afraid to ask what the "or" was. But I sort of wanted to find out. He was *that* hot.

A barrage of images flashed through my mind. In all of them I was tied up naked with leather straps or handcuffs. Yes, I saw the Fifty Shades movie when it came out. Twice. In the theaters. I also own the DVD. And downloaded it to my iPhone. Anyway, all of the images now flashing through my mind included every size and shape of spiked and studded leather S&M weapon you could imagine. In my fantasy, Mr. G.A. was shirtless, looking sexy as hell in tight black leather pants and boots. He had great abs and a great ass. And shoulders. And arms. And chest. On his face he wore a standard black masquerade mask and was tugging stout black leather gloves onto each hand like a kinky sex surgeon. The tuxedoed butler I'd imagined earlier, the one outside carrying a silver tray and a shot glass of water, now stood beside Mr. G.A. with a tray that held several many-tailed whips. The butler said, *Might I suggest the cat of nineteen tails instead of the nine, sir? This young strumpet needs to be taught a lesson she won't forget.*

The real Mr. G.A. flashed a dirty smile that I didn't like at all.

I cringed. Fifty Shades was a movie. A fantasy.

I wasn't a strumpet and I didn't actually like pain. At all. And I certainly didn't need to learn any lessons.

"I should go," I said, my voice quivering. Why hadn't I brought my phone? Or pepper spray? Or a straight jacket for crazy Mr. G.A.?

"You're not going anywhere, you little strumpet."

"Did you just call me a strumpet?"

He smiled an evil smile.

Gulp.

Time to run!

Chapter 8

Mr. G.A. cracked a smile and held out his hand to shake. "I'm just kidding. I don't have a sex dungeon. Name's Wesley. Wesley Callaway. You can call me Wes."

"Wait. Do you or don't you have a sex dungeon?"

"Not here," he winked.

"Wait, do you really have one or not?"

He smiled mysteriously.

"I'll take that as a yes, Wes."

"Take it any way you want."

Reluctantly, I shook his hand. It was much larger than mine and it was very warm, which I found comforting.

I shook it for a long time.

It was SO warm…

And firm…

And I stared at his crotch.

Whoops!

I met his gaze and giggled. "Nice to meet you, Wes."

"You can have the ring if you want. I really don't have any idea where it came from."

"Oh, I don't—" I found myself staring at it where it lay on the vanity. I didn't know why, but I really wanted to keep it. Maybe as a token to remind me of Wes because I knew I would probably never see him again and he was treating me much better than most men ever did. I wanted to remember this moment.

I picked up the ring.

"Put it on," he suggested.

"Okay." I didn't want to put it on my ring finger. That felt too symbolic, like Wes was proposing to me, which he wasn't. I mean, a man like him would never propose to a woman like me. So I tried to put it on my middle finger. Unfortunately, I couldn't get it past the first knuckle. I grinned at Wes. "Sorry." Why was I apologizing?

He was staring straight into my eyes. His blazed with their own mahogany fire. "Try your ring finger."

My heart skipped a beat. "Okay." I felt the oddest sense of hope. My entire chest sizzled like something special was about to happen.

Something that would change my life forever. I slid the ring down past my nail…

Past the first knuckle…

And then—

It stopped well before the second knuckle.

Damn it.

I tried to force it.

I was going to get this ring on my damn ring finger even if I had to grind my skin off!

"I don't think it fits," Wes said.

Was he disappointed? Or was I projecting? I wasn't sure.

"Maybe try your pinky?" he suggested.

"Yeah," I muttered, disappointed for no good reason. Finally it fit. Barely.

I held it up for Wes to inspect.

He smiled, "Looks great."

Those lips… I nearly swooned right then and there. Instead I sighed. "What do I owe you?"

"Owe me?"

"This is an estate sale, isn't it?"

"It is. But I have no idea where that thing came from. You can have it."

"Don't be silly. I can't just take it. How about ten bucks?"

"Sure, okay. I'll take ten."

I winced. "I don't have my purse."

He chuckled, "What am I going to do with you, Jane?"

Anything you want, Sexy Wes. Anything. Yes, I was gaga for Mr. G.A.G.A. *Great Abs, Great Ass.* "Can I bring the money by later?"

"I won't be here later."

"I could bring it by tomorrow."

"I won't be here tomorrow." He put his hand on my shoulder in a brotherly way. "I really don't need the ten dollars, Jane. But thank you anyway."

My fantasy was evaporating before my eyes and I panicked, speaking rapidly, "But you gave me the free water and the ring and all the hospitality. The water alone was worth at least five and—"

"The entire case cost eight bucks at Costco."

"Well the hospitality is worth at least fifty."

He shook his head and smiled. "Forget it, Jane. It's on the house."

But I don't want to forget about you, Wes! Men like you don't talk to me unless they've met my sister and they're trying to get to her through me. They don't care about me, and they certainly don't ever smile at me like you're smiling at me right now. My heart was trying to jump out of my chest with gratitude and excitement. And hope. Sometimes the impossible happened, right?

I didn't know what to do, but I knew I didn't want this moment to end. Whatever came after wouldn't live up to my forever fantasy: wedding bells, the altar, the cheers, wedding cake in the face, the laughter, the love, and the limousine ride to an exotic honeymoon, the beautiful bouncing babies that followed soon after, and last but not least, the happily ever after ending…

Suddenly sad, I stared at the floor. My glasses slid down my nose. I pushed them up. They slid back down. What was the point?

"Jane, I don't mean to rush you, but I have work to do." His voice was gentle, compassionate, and completely comforting.

I was going to cry. But not in front of him. I sniffed, "Oh, right."

"Do you need a ride home?"

"A what?"

"A ride home."

"Uhhh…" Even though my wedding fantasy would never come true, I couldn't believe that a male runway model like Wes was offering me a ride. There was no way I was turning him down, wedding or no wedding. "Sure," I smiled meekly.

He patted my shoulder. "Okay. I'll have my driver take you home." He pulled a phone out of his suit jacket and fired off a text.

"Oh."

Why couldn't Wes be the one to drive?

Because the fantasy is always better than reality.

He walked me out of the master bedroom and down a long hallway. Patterned carpeting with wavy lines ran all the way to the end. A series of framed black and white glamour headshots, large vintage movie posters, and a bunch of really old magazine cosmetics advertisements were mounted between art deco sconces on both walls. The vibe was almost like a golden age movie theater lobby. As we walked, I noticed the same woman was in all the posters, photos, and ads. Her name was featured on most. Helen Callaway.

"Wes, can I ask you a question?"

"Sure."

Will you marry me? I cleared my throat. "Who is Helen Callaway?"

He smiled, "My grandmother. This was her house."

"Was?"

He nodded.

"I'm sorry. Did she pass recently?"

He slowed to a stop, took a deep breath, looked up at the ceiling and sighed. His jaw ticked and he closed his eyes, holding his feelings in.

I could relate. I was always holding my feelings in. "I'm sorry, Wes. I shouldn't have asked."

"No worries. You didn't know." He smiled down at me, his chocolate eyes shimmering. He was really tall, at least 6'2". To me, he was a giant. And not at all an ass.

"Were you and your grandmother close?"

"Very."

"I'm really sorry." I touched his wrist.

"Thanks," he smiled, his voice tight. "She lived a long and full life. It'll be a year next week since her passing."

"Oh. I, uh—"

"We should go." He placed his big hand against the small of my back and I nearly fainted. "Are you okay, Jane?"

"Yeah, I'm..." All choked up.

"Shall we?" He cocked his head.

I couldn't speak. I just nodded.

He led me downstairs, his hand still on my back.

I think I floated the entire way.

Outside, most of the cars from earlier were gone. Two remained: the one I think was a Bentley and the blue Lamborghini. A good looking guy with burly arms, short salt and pepper hair, and distinguished wrinkles in all the right places stood in front of the Bentley with his tan muscled arms clasped in front. He wore a pinstriped polo shirt and khaki slacks.

Wes said, "Gavin, will you please take this beautiful young lady home for me?"

Beautiful?

He didn't mean it, but it was the thought that counted.

"Certainly, sir," Gavin said with a British accent. He was much sexier than the butler I'd pictured earlier. Gavin had an MI5 look about him, or maybe SAS, or like he had once been security for the Queen of England. He opened the back door of the Bentley for me. "Hop in, luv. We'll get you home right quick." He winked at me and smiled.

I almost swooned at Gavin's graciousness and charm. He was very easy on the eyes. I couldn't help but giggle to myself. I'd never been waited on hand and foot by two handsome men before. Not even one handsome man.

But I was far more interested in Wes, who held out his hand for a final shake. "It was nice meeting you, Jane." Despite that hint of danger he'd displayed earlier, he was incredibly polite.

I stared at his hand. I didn't want to just shake it. I wanted to jump in his arms so he could hold me forever. I frowned. I wasn't about to do that. Instead, I shook his hand and savored the feeling of my small hand enveloped in his big one for the last time. I tried to burn the memory of this moment into my brain. "Nice meeting you too, Wes." I wanted to cry again.

I was absolutely certain I would never see him again.

"Enjoy the ring," he winked as I climbed into the car.

"Oh. I will." I sat down on the smooth leather seat. I couldn't resist the urge to look up at him one last time. As usual, my glasses slid down my nose. I reached up to push them in place, but Wes stopped me with a smile.

"Wait," he muttered. "Don't."

"Don't what?"

"I want to see your eyes."

"Oh."

He leaned down and gently removed my glasses. This had suddenly turned into an overwhelmingly romantic moment, even though nothing romantic was actually happening.

Without my glasses on, he was only a handsome blur. I could tell he was looking into my eyes, but to me his were just chocolate smudges. Even so, my heart started pounding. The longer he looked, the more my entire body lit up like fireworks.

"You have beautiful green eyes, Jane. Like emeralds with flecks of gold. They're truly radiant."

Swoon! He called my eyes radiant. And beautiful. No man this attractive had ever paid me such a priceless compliment. I almost passed out and slid out of the leather seat and onto the stone pavers like a puddle of swoon. It took everything I had to stay conscious and drink in this moment.

"You should wear contacts so people can see your eyes." He handed my glasses back and I took them but didn't put them on.

"I wish I could," I cringed, "but I can't. My prescription is too strong." My magic moment faded as fast as it had arrived. I lowered my head and put my glasses back on with a sense of shame.

"No matter. I've seen them and I'll remember them forever."

I looked up into his smiling eyes.

"Goodbye, Jane."

"Bye."

Wes gently closed my door.

That's when I nearly did faint dead away. Wes had just said the most romantic thing any man had ever said to me.

I too would remember this moment forever…

While I swooned in the back seat, Gavin started the engine and Wes watched as we drove down the stone drive.

My pinky was tingling and I was pretty sure my new ring was cutting off my circulation. I twisted it on my finger, trying to relieve the pressure. I'd probably have to soap it off when I got home. It really was just an old piece of junk. But I would treasure it forever. This ring was proof that at least for a moment, a gorgeous man had flirted with me in his mansion, and he'd done his best to make me laugh and feel special, all while treating me with the utmost respect.

Not everyone could be so lucky.

As Gavin drove me home in the Bentley, I tried to tell myself the memory of Wes was enough.

Back at home, I spent three hours on Google Maps trying to retrace my steps using street view, but I couldn't find the entrance to Wes' mansion. I couldn't find its circular driveway with its huge fountain on satellite view either. Nothing turned up. It was almost as if there never had been a mansion. It had disappeared from my life as surely as Wes had.

When I got ready for bed, the ring was really hurting my finger and I did have to soap it off. I couldn't leave it on. I didn't want my finger falling off. I also had to soap off the green ring it had left around the base of my pinky. Like I thought, nothing but junk.

But I clutched it in my hand like it was priceless as I cried myself to sleep.

While I slept, I dreamt that I was in fact married to Wes and we lived in his grandmother's mansion, which was now completely restored, looking like the day it was first built. All the rooms were bright and clean and filled with light, all the colors rich and vibrant. Throughout the house, the laughter of friends and family and children echoed through the hallways. The house had transformed into the most beautiful dream home anyone could ever want.

Too bad everyone knew fantasies like that never came true.

Chapter 9

"Aaaaahhhhhhh!!!!"

I screamed myself awake the next morning, lying on a bed of broken glass, writhing in excruciating pain. Ice picks stabbed every inch of my body. Pain, pain, pain. My skin burned. My bones ached. A dozen jackhammers slammed into my skull. My teeth hurt. My gums were sore. My fingernails and toenails pulsed with pain. My scalp itched. Even my hair hurt. Every part of my body was self destructing.

Was I dying?

I didn't know, but I couldn't move a muscle without more pain.

My agony was so intense, I passed out within minutes.

The next time I woke, I had just enough energy to crawl to the bathroom and pee. Halfway there, I thought I wasn't going to make it. The feeling of my knees and elbows and stomach scraping across my apartment carpet was almost too much to tolerate, like crawling across razor blades. But the need to pee was ten times worse. Crawling onto the toilet was possibly the hardest thing I'd ever done, but I did it.

Worse, peeing burned. Literally burned.

Imagine someone sticking a hot poker up your—

You get the idea.

What was happening to me?

When I finished, I whimpered as I crawled back to bed and passed out.

Horrifying nightmares tormented me while I slept. My body was being invaded by some unstoppable flesh eating bacteria that was killing me. Or twelve kinds of cancer all at once. Or parasitic worms eating me alive from the inside out. Whatever it was, there was no known cure. Doctors and soldiers wearing orange Haz/Mat suits hovered over me, operating on my body while I was wide awake and screaming in pain.

They couldn't figure out what was wrong with me.

But I knew my death was only hours away.

I wanted to wake up from this nightmare, but I couldn't.

I gasped awake into darkness.

The first thing I noticed was that my pain had subsided.

Not completely. My bones still ached, especially the ones in my face. But my skin wasn't burning and my scalp didn't itch. Thank goodness for that much.

But I still felt awful.

My throat was paper dry.

I didn't have to pee but I needed water, so I crawled out of bed. The carpet no longer felt like razorblades on my skin. Just sandpaper. That I could tolerate for a few minutes. When I slid onto the faux parquet wood floor in the kitchenette, I had to slide across on my belly because it hurt my knees and elbows too much to put any weight on them.

I managed to prop myself up in front of the sink and fill a glass with tap water.

I guzzled it down.

Dirty LA tap water had never tasted so incredibly good.

I drank two more glasses before crawling back to bed.

It was light out when I woke again.

My bladder was ready to explode.

I stumbled into my bathroom just in time.

After, I drank more water before falling back into bed.

That's when I realized I heard a rhythmic banging against my bedroom wall. The one that I shared with my new neighbor Blaze, the gorgeous jerk who'd dismissed me the day he'd gouged up my door.

Bang, bang, bang.

Shrill feminine moans drifted through the wall.

Grunting masculine ones followed.

He was having sex and it sounded like he was going to break the bed.

No surprise with a guy like him.

I hoped he broke the floor too, and his bed fell through the ceiling. I just hoped nobody was home downstairs when it happened. I tried to picture Petrak's face when he saw the mess. The bill would be in the thousands and Blaze would have to pay for it. *Serves him right.* With any luck, Petrak would evict him and I'd never have to see his too handsome face again.

"Uh! Uh! Uh!"

Bang. Bang. Bang.

He sure gave new meaning to the term banging.

I tried not to picture Blaze's head hanging over me, his unruly hair swaying with each thrust, his blue eyes on fire as he stared into mine and filled me to the hilt.

"Yes! Yes! Yes!"

Bang! Bang! Bang!

I sneered at the image of whatever bimbo he was boning. I tried to shout, "Stop it!" But my words came out in a thin whispery croak.

If I wasn't still half-dead from whatever disease I had, I would've kicked the wall repeatedly until they stopped.

But I was too tired to do anything.

BANG! BANG! BANG!

A scowl stretched painfully across my face as I drifted off to sleep.

The ringing of my phone woke me.

My headache had faded to a manageable dull thud, but the sound of the phone was killing me. If I could reach it, I would throw it out my bedroom window.

Finally, it stopped ringing.

I slowly realized I was baking in my bed from the heat. The sheets were soaked. I kicked my covers off, welcoming the cool air. It took only a few minutes to realize my apartment was still an oven.

My eyes half shut, I stood up and slid open my bedroom window. I almost punched a hole in the glass because the frame was lower than I remembered. I didn't spend any time thinking about it. I pressed my face against the screen and felt a slight breeze. Not good enough. I turned on the fan in front of the window and cool air blew across my sweaty face.

Relief.

Partially.

I really needed to pee again. I stumbled out of my bedroom, making a beeline toward my bathroom. On my way there, I heard Blaze's front door slam shut. It startled me so much I spun around and saw a woman strutting past my living room window. Probably the one I'd heard him banging. It was hard to see details because of my sheer curtains, but I could see enough. She was tall, impossibly thin. Everything she wore was tight. Her boobs floated on her chest like they were filled with helium. *Yeah, those are real.* The huge pile of platinum blonde hair spilling down her back looked like fake extensions she'd bought at the Barbie factory.

She spun and headed back to Blaze's door and pounded on it, screaming, "Is Brenna one of your clients? Or do you fuck her for free?"

Clients? Free?

Was Blaze a male prostitute?

He was certainly attractive enough.

Whatever he was, he was a prince among men. Ha ha ha.

The blonde screamed again, "Answer me, asshole! Who is Brenna?!"

I waited for the sound of Blaze's front door ripping open, followed by the sound of him groveling. As bimbos went, this one appeared to be at the higher end of the scale. I imagined the men who liked plastic women would want to hold on to this one. But Blaze never opened his door. The least you would expect from a muscular manwhore like Blaze was that he would be man enough to take a tongue lashing from the women he kicked to the curb the morning after banging them. Apparently not.

Oh well. Not my drama.

She pounded several more times. "Oooh!!! You are a worthless piece of shit! I hope Brenna gives you AIDS and your dick falls off!" A second later, she breezed past my window, her heels pistoling off the balcony walkway. Wow, she was really angry. I couldn't imagine why.

Sarcasm.

I waited patiently, hoping Blaze would finally come out of hiding and go chasing after her. I liked the idea of hearing him beg. I was in the mood for a good laugh at his expense.

Plastic Blonde's clicking heels faded into silence.

No sign of Blaze either.

That was a surprise. I was sure he'd grovel.

I smirked to myself, *What an ass brain.*

After I peed, I dug my phone out from behind my nightstand. I must've knocked it off the charger last night. I looked at the screen.

42 missed calls.

9 voicemail messages.

Tons of texts.

What the hell?

How long had I been asleep?

I looked at the date on my phone.

Friday.

It was Friday?

The entire world turned upside down.

The last thing I remembered was… I drew a blank. My memory was foggy. What had happened last?

Wes.

I had been at his house on Sunday.

Sunday.

I counted the days off on my fingers.

Five.

Five days.

Had I just slept five days?

No. That was impossible. I shook my head and looked at my phone again. Friday. Was I losing my mind? How could I have slept five days straight?

I hadn't been that sick, had I?

Or had Wes drugged me? Or poisoned me?

Had that water bottle he'd given me been laced with something? No, that was crazy. I'd taken it from the pack myself. He'd said it was from Costco. He couldn't have drugged each one. That was just ridiculous. What about Gavin, his driver? Had he drugged me? No, Gavin had dropped me off outside my apartment building and had driven off before I'd walked through the front gate. He had no idea which apartment I lived in. It wasn't like my name was on the door. And I knew Petrak wouldn't have told Gavin if he'd come back later and asked. But Gavin did have that MI5 look. Had he spied on me and drugged me in my sleep with a poison blow dart? No, that was crazy.

So what had happened?

I scrolled through my list of missed calls.

Chelsea.

Work. Oh shit.

George Sweet.

My parents.

Work again.

And again.

And again.

I was supposed to work Monday night. And Tuesday. And Wednesday. And Thursday.

Had I just missed the last four days of work without checking in? If I had, I was probably out of a job!

Panic seized me as I listened through my messages.

Chelsea checking in.

George on Monday afternoon apologizing for not hanging out and asking if I wanted to hang out later in the week.

Maria from work asking where I was on Monday. Fricking *Monday*.

Maria again on Tuesday.

Doug Wallace, the general manager from work and my direct boss asking if I was okay and to please call.

Chelsea on Wednesday wondering why I hadn't called her back.

Doug again on Wednesday telling me that Rick Martinez from the Venice store was now covering my shifts but he really needed me to call and let him know what was going on.

On Thursday, Stacy Lewis, the head of HR at the 95 Cent Store corporate offices, warning me that if I didn't call or show up in the next day or two, they would assume I'd quit permanently and replace me.

Shit!

Stacy again today, about two hours ago, informing me that I had been terminated and I could pick up my final check from the store at my convenience.

Triple shit!

I needed my job!

I called corporate, my hands shaking as I punched in the number.

The machine answered, "You have reached the main offices of the 95 Cent Store Incorporated after our regular business hours. If you know your party's extension, please dial it now. For a directory of—"

I punched Stacy's name in and got her voicemail.

"Stacy! It's Jane Johnson. I've been really sick. I had a really bad flu and I couldn't get out of bed for five days. I'm so sorry I never called. I was literally unconscious. I don't know what happened, but I slept all week." I laughed once. "I know it sounds impossible, but that's what happened. Please call me as soon as you get this message."

I ended the call.

I was pretty sure she wouldn't get the message until Monday. I didn't have her personal number. So I called my store. Doug might still be there. I needed to explain. He knew me. He'd understand.

The phone rang and rang. Fridays were always busy. Doug could be on one of the registers helping out, or out on the floor helping stock the shelves. Nobody answered.

My body jittered from all the stress induced adrenalin.

I needed to do something.

I couldn't lose my job. If I did, I wouldn't be able to pay rent next month! *Crap!* Time to jump in the shower and get dressed and hurry down to my store and beg Doug for my job back.

When I ran into the bathroom and saw myself in the mirror, I nearly had a heart attack.

Chapter 10

I had just gone insane.

Or had a stroke.

Or maybe I was still asleep.

Whatever it was, there was no rational explanation for what I saw in the mirror.

Someone else.

Not pudgy little me with bad hair.

Some supermodel I didn't recognize.

I blinked several times.

But I still saw the supermodel.

I was hallucinating.

I squeezed my eyes shut and rubbed them until I saw stars. Then I opened them.

Still seeing a supermodel.

Long flowing blonde hair, a bit messy and bedish, but it was silky and shiny gold and looked good enough for a photo on a box of hair dye.

A finely shaped face with high cheekbones, trim nose, wide full mouth and lush lips. Her lashes were naturally thick. When she smiled, she had perfectly straight white teeth.

The supermodel was taller than my five foot nothing. If I had to guess, I'd say she was almost 5'9" with long and slender arms and legs and an hourglass figure.

Then it hit me. I was looking through a window at another person. It was the only thing that made sense.

So I stuck my head slowly out my bathroom door to see if the blonde supermodel was standing on the other side of the wall, looking at me through a window. Super Blonde matched my movements exactly and, surprise surprise, she wasn't standing behind the wall in my hallway.

Nobody was.

Back in front of the mirror, I scratched my head for a moment and Super Blonde did too.

Wait.

Wait, wait, wait.

Duh.

I wasn't wearing my glasses. I was just imagining all this. The brain can be like that. Wishful thinking and that sort of thing. Probably left over hallucination from my crazy five day flu.

I walked into my bedroom and found my glasses on the nightstand where I always left them before bed. I put them on.

Whoa!

I couldn't see!

My glasses really hurt my eyes.

I yanked them off and looked at them. Were these *my* glasses? They seemed like it. Was it an old pair? Maybe that was it. I put them on again. My entire bedroom squiggled and vibrated and had this magnified quality that made me nauseous. I took them off and searched through my desk for a different pair. Put those on. Same thing. They hurt my eyes too. I went back in the bathroom with my glasses and put them on in front of the mirror. Same result. They hurt my eyes and blurred everything, so I set them on the counter.

Had someone given me LASIK while I was asleep?

I'd think about that later because one thing remained the same, whether I had my glasses on or off.

I was the blonde supermodel in the mirror.

It wasn't my eyes. It had to be something else.

Then I figured it out.

Of course.

Someone, maybe Gavin, had replaced my bathroom mirror with some super high-tech 4K movie screen while I was asleep, and installed hidden cameras in my bathroom. The cameras were filming me so the actress playing Super Blonde could copy my movements, and her movements were being projected on my new 4K bathroom movie screen. She was being filmed at a secret sound stage on a set that looked exactly like my bathroom, which Gavin had taken pictures of. The actress even wore the same My Little Pony T-shirt I slept in, the one with Twilight Sparkle, the one I'd bought at the Bay Area Brony Spectacular convention with George. On me the shirt had always been a loose fit across my chest and a tight fit across my waist. On the supermodel, it was the opposite. Big boobs stretched it out and it hung loose around her trim waist.

Was this some cruel joke?

Had I been Punk'd by my enemies? Were they mocking me with an image of the woman I wished I looked like? The one every woman wished she looked like?

That was absurd.

I didn't have any enemies, except maybe my new neighbor Blaze, but he struck me as too lazy and disinterested to bother. The only people I knew who had the resources to pull off such an elaborate prank were Gavin and Wes. But they wouldn't do that. They were both so nice and they barely knew me anyway. Why would they bother?

I rested my palms on the counter top. It was lower than I was used to. I reached up to touch the mirror.

Super Blonde's hand met the mirror at the exact same moment mine did. The glass was cool to the touch. It looked like a regular mirror to me.

And I noticed that my hand was the exact size and shape as Super Blonde's hand in the mirror.

My chest fluttered with a strange excitement.

I looked down at my hands.

They weren't my hands.

My arms weren't my arms.

The were thin and beautiful. Elegant. They looked sort of like Chelsea's hands. Or Mom's hands.

I slid my palms down my chest.

I had boobs!

Big boobs!

I tore my T-shirt over my head and looked at myself.

I squeezed my breasts. They weren't the boobs I was used to. They were so full and pert, but they *felt* like they were mine.

What had happened to me?

I ran my hands down my flat stomach and over my arched hips.

My waist was now narrow and curvy.

I turned to see my butt in the mirror. My baggy granny panties looked awful. I kicked them off so I could check out my ass. It was… perfect. No cellulite. Nothing.

I was going to faint.

I was going to cry.

I was beautiful.

Undeniably certifiably beautiful.

With the exception of my emerald gold-flecked eyes, which were most definitely the eyes I'd been born with, I looked nothing like me. Well, maybe a beautiful blonde version of myself who may have vaguely resembled Chelsea or Mom.

But better looking.

When I was a little girl, my favorite story for the longest time was The Ugly Duckling. I'd always imagined one day I'd grow into a beautiful swan. But I'd realized some time around junior high school that I'd always be nothing but an ugly duck.

But now?

Now I was finally the most beautiful swan of all.

Tears of joy dribbled down my face while I thought this over. I touched and squeezed every part of my body for twenty minutes before I convinced myself I really had transformed. Even my toes were pretty.

I had swansformed.

I spent another hour pacing my apartment on long legs that took some getting used to. The whole time, I was trying to convince myself this was all just a dream.

But it wasn't.

And if it really wasn't some hallucinatory fever dream, a dream caused by a fever so high it was probably causing permanent damage to my brain, how on earth would I explain all this to my family?

Or my boss Doug at work?

Or to anyone?

I stopped pacing and tried to picture it. Me calling everyone and laughing crazily, "I finally turned into a swan!"

They would all think I was insane.

I would just have to show them.

In person.

Then I pictured an absolute stranger going up to Mom or Dad and saying crazily, *Hey, Mom! Hey, Dad! It's me, your daughter! I know, I don't look anything like her, but you have to believe me! I'm not insane, I really am Jane! And no, I didn't kidnap her or kill her. It's me, Dad! Me!* They would want to know what the insane woman (me) had done to their beloved daughter. With my luck, I'd end up in prison for murdering myself, Jane Johnson.

But I desperately wanted to call everyone I could think of and tell them the amazing news!

I had transformed into a different person!

A beautiful person!

I shook my head. Just thinking the words sounded ridiculous.

I couldn't call anybody.

I was probably still asleep and dreaming.

Once again, I pinched myself. Ouch! I splashed water in my face over the bathroom sink. It was cold and wet. But I was still a supermodel. I jumped into the shower to see if I could wash it off.

Nope. Still beautiful.

When I got out of the shower, two things were on my mind.

One, what was I going to do about my job?

Two, if I stayed like this, what was I going to do in general?

I didn't know the answer to either, but I knew my life was about to change.

Drastically.

Before that happened, I needed to go shopping.

None of my clothes fit my new body. I'd grown almost nine inches in a matter of five days.

As impossible as this all seemed, I was starting to accept it was actually happening. I felt wide awake. In fact, I felt better than ever. I was literally a new person.

I ended up putting on a dress because all my sweats and jeans now looked like Capri pants on my long legs. The only bra I had that fit my new boobs was a sports bra. And my shoes were all too small, so I had to wear flip-flops. My heels hung off the backs, but they would work for now.

When I got in my car, I had to decide between going to work or going for clothes. If I went to work, would anyone believe I was me? No. I'd probably get trucked off to a mental hospital.

Clothes it is.

Since I didn't have much money to spare, I went to the Goodwill store in Santa Monica. I knew Chelsea was right about it. They got all the castoff clothes from the rich women in the neighborhood who went through new clothes like candy, but they sold everything at regular low Goodwill prices. It didn't take me long to find some outfits that looked cute on me because everything that fit looked cute. To be honest, I was marveling at how amazing I looked every time I caught a glimpse of myself in a mirror. No wonder beautiful people were so obsessed with themselves. They were in awe every time they saw their reflections.

I had to laugh at myself.

I would never be like that.

While holding up different tops in the nearest mirror, I noticed two teenaged girls, maybe 15 or 16, rifling through the racks to my left. They were watching me closely while whispering and giggling.

I tried to ignore them.

"Looks like the walk of shame to me," the first girl said just loud enough for me to hear. "Her dress is on backwards."

My dress wasn't on backwards. What were they talking about?

The other one said, "No, she's probably homeless. Look at those dirty flip-flops. They don't even fit. She probably found them in a dumpster."

I frowned in the mirror. My new frown was much prettier than my old frown. I tried to ignore the girls and held up another top.

"I bet she's a coke whore. Fucks random guys for drugs."

"No, heroin. And meth. Total skank."

"I bet she'll be toothless within a year from shooting up."

"Then she can charge more for blowjobs."

They both laughed like hyenas and leaned into each other.

Disgusting.

I sized them up in a second.

They were cheap copies of the mean girls who'd tormented me in high school. I glared at them. I wasn't afraid of two pretty little bitches. As a kid, I'd grown a thick skin early on. Being the number one nerd girl meant constant insults. At first, people made fun of me all the time, but only until they realized I could cut them up worse then they ever could me. By the time I was a sophomore at North Valley High School, the insults had stopped. Thankfully, college and adulthood weren't like high school and I hadn't been treated this badly in years.

But listening to these two girls cut me up now stung like I was 13 all over again. Old wounds.

They hung their clothes up on the rack and walked past me on their way to the shoe section.

As they passed, one muttered, "Dirty slut."

The other said, "Moldy ho bag ."

Teenagers. So full of insecurity and hate. The only law they understood was the law of the jungle, or The Lord of the Flies, or Hunger Games, or whatever it was. Standing tall with my hands on my hips, I said, "When you two narcissistic imbeciles drop out of Santa Monica College because it's too hard, and you can't find jobs because you don't have a single brain cell between the two of you, you're going to realize that all of Daddy's money and all the plastic surgery in the world isn't going to make anybody hate you less. So shut your fucking mouths and keep the insults to yourselves, you ugly little twits." They weren't ugly on the outside. They were better looking than I was. But they were monsters on the inside.

They both stared at me wide eyed, frozen with fear.

One of them started to tear up.

I scowled, "Aww, is da wittle baby butthurt?"

The other girl snarled at me, "Just because you're better looking than us doesn't mean *you're* not a stupid bitch. Let's go, Emily." She pulled her friend by the arm.

Emily's eyes were red and she snuffled at me, "Bitch."

I smirked. "I'm the bitch?"

I watched them walking away.

The second they turned into the shoe aisle, Emily started sobbing.

What was her problem? They started it.

I shook my head and turned back to the mirror and looked at myself. Slowly, the realization that I wasn't a five foot nothing nerd girl with thick glasses sunk in. I looked like a supermodel who was better looking than both of them combined. There was no mistaking it. But, no matter what I looked like on the outside now, I'd been a little nerd girl for 99.9% of my life. One day of being beautiful didn't erase all that. And pardon me if my new reality was a wee bit hard to believe.

I could barely wrap my own head around the idea.

Emily's friend was busy consoling her while glaring at me.

Was it possible they started making fun of me because they assumed I'd been born with the looks they could only dream of? Of course they did. No one on this planet would believe otherwise.

Wow, just wow.

Although I still suspected this was all a dream and I was probably still in my bed, sick with the plague and hallucinating while teetering on the edge of death, I didn't need to be a bitch. Even in my fever dreams. Being mean for no reason was not me.

No matter what the circumstances.

Chapter 11

An hour later, I walked out of Goodwill with five new outfits and two pairs of shoes that cost me a total of $85.00. You had to love Goodwill.

I wore my favorite combo that I'd just purchased: a striped tank top, artfully shredded skinny jeans, a necklace of flower pendants, and white sandals. Nothing fashion blog worthy because to be honest, I didn't really have the knack for dressing that Chelsea and Mom had. I'd never bothered to learn.

But I was happy with my haul.

On my drive home, I reminded myself to be more considerate of other people's feelings. Even if this was a dream, an impossibly realistic HD dream with sight and sound and smell and the heat coming off my steering wheel (it had been baking under the sun in the parking lot), I didn't ever want to treat other people the way I'd been treated.

If none of this was a dream, and I'd actually turned beautiful in a matter of five days, then I *really* needed to be nice to people. Probably nicer and more considerate than usual.

Lost in thought, I thumbed the ring on my finger.

The one I got from Wes.

Which was now on my ring finger.

I didn't remember putting it on. I remembered falling asleep clutching it in my hand. It hadn't fit my ring finger before. It had barely fit on my stubby little finger. But now I had long slender fingers so it fit my ring finger fine.

It made perfect sense.

It made no sense at all.

When I stopped at a red light on Santa Monica Boulevard, I looked at the ring in direct sunlight. It was now shiny gold, not tarnished brass or whatever it had been before. The circle of the ring was also thicker and had a weight to it. If I didn't know better, I'd say it had turned into real gold. It had that authentic yellow color that you couldn't fake. If it was real gold, it could easily be worth thousands of dollars. The obvious conclusion: this was a different ring. But I didn't own any gold rings. And this one had the same two hearts engraved on the top that I remembered, except now the engraving was much nicer, more complex, more dimensional and artful, like a piece of custom jewelry.

Back at my apartment, I jingled my keys into the lock and opened my front door. As I was about to step inside, Blaze's door whipped open. As I stepped through mine, he stepped out of his.

I watched from my open doorway as he passed.

He flicked a glance at me. A sudden grunt escaped his lips as he stumbled to a stop and stared at me. He was just as handsome as the first time I'd seen him (underwear model hot) and just as unattainable. Unlike last time, he wore a tight fitting V-neck shirt that did nothing to hide his muscles and tattoos.

We stared at each other for a long time.

His eyes blazed pure blue, like million dollar sapphires.

My body responded and I tried not to squirm.

His eyes swept over me, bright with desire.

No man had ever looked at me this way.

Not even my two exes Aaron and Harvey, and I'd had sex with both of them.

No. Man. Ever.

Blaze looked… hungry. And hunt ready. He drawled, "Heeeeeeey. What's your name?"

Was this really happening? He stuffed his fingers in the pockets of his tight jeans and leaned against my doorframe. I guess it was.

"Chelsea." I blurted it out without thinking. Was that a bad idea?

"Hey, Chelsea."

Too late to worry about it now. I still held my doorknob and tried not to stare at his bulging muscled arms. "Did you have a name?"

Why was I asking? Probably out of habit. I didn't really want to know this guy.

Did I?

"Brodie." His smile curled into the same sexy dimples I remembered.

"Hey, Brodie." I had to wonder, did it make Brodie a douche that he had ignored me when I was a little nerd girl and was drooling over me now? I wasn't entirely sure. Whatever the case, I had no idea what to say.

"You just move in?"

"Nope. Er, sort of."

"I don't remember seeing you here before. Just some short girl with glasses. You her roommate?"

"Uh, yeah." Despite the unreality of my recent swansformation, I was trying to function like it was really real. And if I now looked like someone else, I needed to be careful about what I said to who. The less the better. I stared at him. "Anything else?"

He ran his hand through his charcoal dark hair. His muscled arm flexed and he blushed. It was hard to tell with his tan, but he *was* blushing.

Because of me.

Will wonders never cease?

I smirked, "My roommate told me what you did to our door."

"Right. That." He smiled and dropped his arm. He was nervous. This hot stud was nervous. Again, because of me.

More wonderment on my part. A sly grin curled across my lips. I could get used to this.

"What?" He chuckled, met my eyes with his, looked away while grinning to himself. Eventually, he looked at my door carefully. "I can probably patch and paint it this weekend. But I'll need to take a color sample down to Home Depot to match it." He ran his fingertips across the scuffed black gouge. "Yeah, I can patch this. I'll have it finished Sunday. That work for you?"

I couldn't believe my ears. Was this what life was like for beautiful women? Beautiful men offering to drop everything and do stuff for you without you asking? I supposed it was. Every fairytale princess I'd ever read about had Sir Lancelots galore slaying dragons for them or fighting wars over them since the beginning of time. It was how the world worked.

How to respond? Did I tell him not to fix my door which he broke? Of course not.

"Sure, Blaze. Sunday is fine." I smiled absently. I couldn't stop staring at his perfect eyes and his perfect everything else.

"Brodie."

"Sorry. I meant Brodie." Wow, I was already acting like a dumb blonde after half a day.

"Who's Blaze?"

"Oh, it's stupid." I giggled. I shouldn't giggle, but I couldn't help myself. "Since I didn't know your name until now, I was calling you Blaze in my head since we met."

He narrowed his eyes, confused. "We just met now. I've never seen you before. I would've remembered you. Believe me," he chuckled. "You're unforgettable."

My anger suddenly flared and I almost barked, *What, did you forget Jane already? You never asked her her name, you shallow shithead! So why do you need to know mine now, you pencil prick! Let me guess, is it because you already forgot about that plastic blonde you fucked last night and kicked to the curb this morning?* I glared pure hatred at him. *Are you so shallow that your dating strategy is to just fuck whichever blonde is closest? And I happen to be standing here?* I hated this guy from head to toe. I tried to hide my scowl, but it wasn't working.

"You okay?" He didn't know why I was angry.

I didn't want to stir up a bunch of drama, so I took a deep breath and calmed myself. "What were we talking about?"

"You were telling me how you knew me before we ever met."

My chest tightened as I remembered I was pretending to be someone else. My preference was to avoid complicating things more than necessary. *Keep it simple, stupid.* I faked a laugh, "Oh, right. I meant my roommate *Jane* was calling you Blaze because she didn't know your name. She told me all about you and your... chair." *And your plastic girlfriend who you treated like trash.*

He chuckled. "Guilty. I was kind of a dick that day." *Yeah you were.* "Had a shit ton to get done. Tell Jane I'm sorry when you see her."

I almost blurted, *You tell her! She was the one who had her feelings hurt by your rude ass!* Then I realized he had just apologized. And I didn't need to be a crazy bitch because his love life was none of my business. The only thing I couldn't decide was whether he was apologizing because he cared or because he wanted supermodel me to like him. Before, he'd acted like the real me wasn't worth a second of his time. Now he was hanging all over my door and it disgusted me. I started to close it in his face. "I've got to go, Bluh—Brodie." My preference at that moment was to never see this manwhore again.

"Hold up," he smirked, leaning his weight against the door so I couldn't close it. "What are you doing tonight?"

Was he serious? I couldn't believe this guy. I smirked, "I have to work."

"Until when?" His eyes traveled up and down my body.

"Until late." Was I turned on? Of course I was. I scowled at myself for being as shallow as Brodie was. To be fair, on a scale from one to ten, Brodie was a perfect ten. Despite having principles, I was still a woman and he was all man. And there was such a thing as hate sex, although I'd never had any. Somehow I imagined hate sex was the only kind Brodie ever had.

"What're you doing after work?"

"Sleeping." I couldn't believe Brodie was practically begging for me to hang out with him. I tried not to gloat because my answer would always be no.

"You sleeping alone?"

I rolled my eyes at him. "Yes. And you?"

"How about I keep your bed warm till you get home, and when you do, we skip the sleeping?"

I rolled my entire head theatrically. "You did not just say that."

"I think I did."

"I think you need to get laid, Brodie. And not by me." I wanted to say something about his plastic blonde girlfriend, but I really just wanted to be done with him. "Now let go of my door so I can close it."

He took a step back. "Suit yourself. But you don't know what you're missing." He still had a hand in his front pocket and he shifted it around suggestively, repositioning himself.

Against my will I glanced down. Only for a second.

Geez, was he hard?

He was hard.

That bulging bulge of his had turned into a full-fledged denim-clad erection. I was not at all surprised that a stud like Brodie had no shame. He was too proud and cocky for shame.

My face turned red. Not because I was blushing. Because I was furious. "Is this your play, Brodie? Show your dick off to whichever woman tickles your fancy and hope she didn't hear you banging some other bimbo through the walls the other night?"

"You heard that?" His face squirmed into a confused smile that was absolutely adorable. Had I turned the tables and thrown Brodie completely off his game? It was sweet. Somewhere inside that cocky bad boy was a decent human being. Or so I told myself. Wishful thinking? Too soon to tell.

"Yeah, I heard. I also heard her shouting at you this morning outside my living room window. Was she mad because you refused to pay her for services rendered?" I immediately regretted saying it. I didn't know the first thing about her.

"Easy, Chelz. She's not a hooker."

"Don't call me Chelz."

"Why not?"

"Because my name is Chel-*see*. Not Chelz." What was I doing? Besides getting angry at Brodie, who wasn't worth my time. Whatever it was, him calling me Chelz was just too weird. It also made me think that if he ever met my sister, he'd shamelessly hit on her too. The last thing I wanted was this ass head dating my sister. Not that she would date him, but still.

"Okay. I'll call you C.C."

"C.C.?"

"Chel-*see*. C.C.?"

I shook my head. "Don't like it." I also didn't like Brodie nicknaming me.

"Fine. Chelsea. Anyway, sorry if we kept you up all night."

Notice how he implied he was having sex for hours? This man had an ego big enough to blot out the sun. "Please. I was so bored I fell asleep inside of five seconds."

"She didn't," he chuckled.

"Was she screaming your name all night long? Brodie, Brodie, Brodie?"

He smirked, "Yeah. If you were in my bed, you would too."

I laughed. "Do you hear yourself? You are easily the most arrogant man I've ever met."

"You love it."

"Really," I said sourly. I glared at him. He was such an ass. I pointed at my face and grimaced. "Does this look like love? How about disgust."

"If I'm so disgusting, why haven't you slammed your door in my face?"

"Maybe because I'm polite. And maybe…" I needed a moment to think. I couldn't let him have the last word. A door slam was an easy exit. I wanted to hand him his balls before politely closing the door in his face. "Maybe I like watching you squirm. Something tells me most women dance for you on command. Not me."

"Not yet."

"Ha! Have you ever seen a cat catch a mouse and play with it before it eats it?"

"You gonna eat me, Chelsea?"

"Oh, wow. Are you sixteen?"

"Cause if you're not, I'll eat you right here. Just give me the word and I'll tear your pants off." He stared at my crotch.

"Eyes up, Brodie."

He stared at mine. "I bet you taste like cherry pie."

"Do you understand how that is the wrong thing to tell a woman on her period?" I wasn't on my period, but he didn't know that.

"I can vampire."

I chuckled, "I'm not sure I want to know what that means."

"It means I will eat every inch of you like you're dessert seven days a week, all year long. Nothing tastes better than a woman coming on my tongue."

"Please," I scowled, trying not to picture him burying his face between my legs and licking me to orgasm.

"Who's begging now, C.C.?"

"Not me, B.B."

"Wait, do you know my last name?"

"Does it start with a B?"

"Yeah."

"Is it Brains?"

"No. So what is B.B.?"

I shrugged, "Butt Brains."

He snickered.

I shook my head. I couldn't believe he found this funny.

Why was I talking to this fool? No man I'd ever known talked this way to women. It was… it was stupid. I felt stupid just for listening. Even stupider that I was responding to his routine. I should've closed the door in his face five minutes ago.

His eyes flashed.

Damn it, they were captivating. Blazing blue. Like his broad shoulders and tattooed arms and the rest of him. I hated that he had any effect on me. So why was I enjoying the attention so much?

I folded my arms defensively across my new boobs. Doing so pushed them up provocatively, so I repositioned my arms until they were covered, making my nipples tingle. Good thing I had my sports bra on under my new tank top, otherwise Brodie probably would've noticed my nipples poking through and jumped to conclusions.

"Nervous?" He reached out and brushed a knuckle across my naked forearm.

My skin fired where he touched it. I needed to put a stop to this. "No. Nauseous."

He chuckled, "You wish." He stepped toward me.

"Stop." I thrust my palm into his rock hard chest. Not necessarily a good idea. I wanted to run my hands all over that chest. Secret moan.

He backed up a step. "Anything you say, C.C."

Despite my new height, he was still taller than I was. I looked up into his eyes and swallowed hard. "What do you want from me, Brodie?"

"Everything."

Wow oh wow. I was on the verge of telling him he could have me, take me, do me, use me, anything he could dream up, as long as it involved his cock inside my—gulp! Sadly, this was an animal attraction my body couldn't deny. Men didn't get any more desirable than him. I desperately needed to mate with this man. Now.

Good thing my brain steered my ship. "Out." I shot my finger over his shoulder. "Go, Brodie. I'm busy."

"For now," he muttered.

I barked, "What?!"

He backed out of my apartment, smiling proudly, like he knew he'd made progress. Had worn me down. Had found a chink in my armor.

Not even close. I growled, "I don't want to see your face again until my door is fixed!" *Crap!* Why had I added that part about my door? I should've said, *I don't want to see your face ever again AND fix my fricking door!* Damn me! I'd just given him an excuse to see me again. Stupid!

"See you later, C.C." His smile spread and his dimples were back and he looked ridiculously cute in the manliest way possible.

"Go, Brodie!" I restrained a nervous giggle and closed my door in his face. Politely, because I wasn't a bitch, not because I was reluctant to close it.

I groaned as I leaned against the inside of my door.

I may have gotten the last word, but that hadn't gone the way I'd planned at all.

Chapter 12

Doug Wallace, my boss and general manager at the 95 Cent Store in West LA, was walking to his car when I pulled into the parking lot. He wasn't usually here this late on a Friday because he had a wife and kids at home. Maybe he'd stayed late to show my new replacement the ropes, whoever that was.

I parked near Doug's car and jumped out of mine. I was fully prepared to get down on my knees and beg for my job back. Doug and I got along great and he knew I was a good manager. He would understand.

I hoped.

I trotted up behind him just as he was sitting down behind the wheel of his Chrysler. "Hey, Doug! Wait a second."

He turned to look at me. His eyes widened. Then they narrowed. He stared right at me, confused. "Do I know you?" He didn't recognize me.

Of course he didn't.

I wasn't me.

"Doug, it's..." What was I going to say? *It's me, Jane. This may sound strange, but I turned into a supermodel. That's why I was out sick for five days and didn't call. Can I have my job back now? Pretty please?*

"Where do I know you from?"

"I..."

"You look familiar." The wheels were turning. He pointed at me casually as recognition set in. "Were you in that new X-Men movie Matthew made me go see?" Matthew was Doug's ten year old son. Loved the kid.

"Uh, no?"

"Oh, I know. You're Matthew's swim coach, right? You're Lauren, right?"

This was not going to work. He would never believe I was me. "You know what? I have you confused with someone else."

He frowned. "You're not Lauren?"

"No, I'm—" I stopped myself. Doug and I weren't BFFs, but I liked him and considered him a friend. I'd even been to his house and met his wife Pam and son Matthew several times. But could I trust him with the truth? No, I didn't know him that well. If I was going to tell somebody, he wasn't first or even tenth on my list. "I'm sorry to bother you, sir." I turned to go.

"Wait, how did you know my name? Did Pam put you up to this?"

"I—I should go." I walked away as fast as I could.

Out of habit, I walked right toward the doors of the 95 Cent Store. I couldn't help glancing back at Doug. His head poked over the roof of his car and he watched me. After a moment, he shook his head, climbed in, and drove off.

I had a sinking feeling that my life was about to get a lot more complicated.

Inside the store, I wandered through the aisles, pretending to shop. I needed to collect my thoughts before I approached anyone else. Something about being in a familiar place helped me focus.

At the moment, Maria was at register 4 and Natalie was at register 6. Unlike Doug, who was my boss, Maria and Natalie were my subordinates. I may have been their manager, but I believed in a very casual management style. I never bossed anyone around, and I was probably more friendly with them than I was with Doug. In my experience, you could accomplish far more by caring than ordering people around. It had worked for me so far.

With Maria, we often talked about our personal lives. She'd been at the 95 Cent Store for two years. I knew about Antonio, her boyfriend. I also knew she was dying for him to finally propose after three years of dating. She was already 20 and didn't want to still be single at 25. She planned on having two kids by then. So sweet.

I didn't feel as close to Natalie because she was a bit shy and mousy and she'd only been working here for six months. But we got along well enough and she'd told me all about her plans to finish classes at LA City and eventually get a business degree at Cal State LA. I was the one who convinced corporate to pay her tuition at LA City, for which she was hugely grateful. It wasn't much but it was something. If she stayed on the job long enough, my plan was to ask corporate to pay for her tuition at Cal State LA.

Standing in the drinks aisle, I grabbed a bottle of Tazo Tea and made my way to the registers. I reached register 6 as Natalie was setting the Closed sign on her conveyor belt. She looked right at me and smiled before turning away.

She didn't recognize me.

That's okay. Maybe she had something else on her mind. Like her new manager, who was standing behind her and holding her cash drawer. I didn't recognize him. He was tall, looked about fiftyish with mostly gray hair, and he reminded me of my high school Math teacher, who was a total perv. I'm sure the resemblance was completely coincidental. Besides, this guy wasn't a math teacher. He wore a blue 95 Cent Store vest over his button down shirt. I'm sure he was nice. Doug wouldn't hire a perv to work the night shift. Neither would corporate.

"Excuse me," Natalie said as she tried to back out of the register area.

If I wasn't mistaken, the new manager was blocking her way. I definitely felt some weirdness.

Manager guy was busy pretending to do something with Natalie's cash drawer. He should've just taken it to the manager's booth to count it. Instead, he held it up above her head, as if suggesting she should squeeze past him.

Was he serious?

More like serious perv.

Natalie glanced at me briefly. She wasn't recognizing me. But it seemed like she was pleading for help. As I was about to speak, she said to the perv, "Can I go please?"

"You've got room," he said. "Squeeze on by."

Was this really happening?

It was.

Natalie winced, afraid to say anything. She wasn't one to stand up for herself.

When manager guy caught me watching, he stepped aside for Natalie, but only slightly. She had to wiggle past him. He had his dick facing her. Probably had a hard on. Natalie pressed her stomach against the bagging counter and bent over it so she didn't have to touch him as she went by. Manager guy stared down at her like he was doing her doggie style. I'm sure he was imagining her naked.

Disgusting.

I couldn't believe what I was seeing. I shook my head in disbelief. When Natalie was gone, I was ready to tear his balls off and remind him that sexual harassment was against the law.

Before I could say anything, he walked back to the manager's booth at the front of the store.

What a depraved dickhead.

I couldn't really do anything about it now. I didn't work here. I'd been fired for disappearing. And I wasn't even me. I was nothing but a random customer.

I walked to register 4 where Maria was busy ringing up an old man who was buying several six packs of Ensure, all of them vanilla because that was the only flavor we ever stocked. Like everything we carried, I'm sure they were six months past their shelf date, hence the 95 cent sticker price. I watched Maria as she rang up everything.

What would she think when she saw me?

What would I say?

I had no idea.

I'd just have to go with the moment.

I set my Tazo Tea bottle on the conveyor belt as Maria bagged up the last of the old man's Ensures and handed him everything. He thanked her and walked away.

Maria turned to me and smiled. She always had a smile for the customers. "Hi." She swiped my tea over the barcode scanner and it beeped. "Anything else?"

I stared into her eyes, willing for her to somehow recognize me.

Still smiling, she frowned. She had no idea who I was.

It hurt. Physically hurt. I wanted to grab her wrist and plead, *Maria! It's me, Jane! Don't you recognize me?!*

She giggled nervously and looked away. "That'll be ninety-five cents."

Please! Maria! It's me! This was very distressing. My hands shook as I pulled a dollar bill out of my purse.

Maria took it and made change. She held out a nickel and my receipt.

I stared at her, verging on shock. I didn't know what to do. This was worse than getting friend dumped. I knew because it had happened many times to me from kindergarten until college. People deciding they didn't like me because I was too nerdy or dorky or weird, and the turned up noses that soon followed. In some cases, people told me straight to my face they didn't like me for one stupid reason or another. That had always hurt the most. I'd never believed people could be so cruel, but they could.

But all that was different from this.

Maria wasn't a jerky high school kid. She liked me.

I knew she did.

I thought she did.

I was suddenly doubting myself.

I had to remind myself she didn't recognize me.

To her, I was a complete stranger.

But on some deep emotional level, it felt exactly the same as if she were shunning me. It hurt so much I wanted to vomit. But I tried to remind myself Maria and I were solid. The last time I'd seen her at work, we'd laughed through half our shift, like always. The only thing that had changed since then was…

Me.

"Your change," Maria said, gesturing with the nickel and my receipt.

"Oh, right." I took them and stuffed them in my purse.

"Lady, are you okay?" Her concern was genuine.

I smiled absently. "Yeah. I'm fine. Thanks." Verging on tears, I hurried past her. On my way toward the exit, I also passed the new manager standing in the elevated manager's booth.

"Find everything okay?" he asked with a smile, eyes roaming all over me.

"Yeah," I said softly, still dealing with my feelings about Maria.

"You get some Tazo?" He leaned over the edge of the manager's booth.

"Huh? Yeah. I guess so." I slowed to a stop, my mental gears shifting to this rapist in training.

"That's great tea." He was staring at me like I was a target for his dick. The only reason he was staring at my tea was because I held the bottle in front of my boobs. He looked like he was ready to dive right in.

Get a good look, dicknose. This guy was too much. I glanced at his name tag. Phil Berger. I leaned an elbow on the manager's booth counter top, something I'd never been tall enough to do before today. I smiled at him, giving him a front row seat to my tits. There wasn't much cleavage because my sports bra covered most of it, but that didn't stop him from drooling.

"Hey, Phil," I said, all friendly.

"Hey." He smiled. "Is there anything I can help you with?"

Like removing my bra? I don't think so. "Tell me, Phil. What's it like being the night manager here?"

"It pays the bills." He shrugged, blushing. Something told me Phil wasn't used to supermodels flirting with him. That didn't stop him from leaning over the counter while his eyes tried to burn a hole through my sports bra.

"That's great, that's great." I nodded earnestly, skimming my fingernail on the counter top lazily. Suggestively. Sexually.

"And I get to meet people like you." He smiled, his thin lips pulling back over crooked nicotine stained teeth. The smell of stale cigarettes on his rank breath was like a punch in the face.

"Like *me*?" I said coquettishly, hiding my disgust and trying not to gag.

"Yeah," he nodded, trying not to drool.

"What do you mean 'like me,' Phil?"

"You know what I mean," he snorted. Translation: *People like you are women I want to eye-fuck, grope, or fondle whether they give me permission or not.*

"I guess I do." I smirked, "Phil, I was just wondering…" I looked up at him with hooded eyes.

"Yeah?" He swallowed hard, ready to jump out of his pants and into mine.

"Is cornering female employees so you can cop a feel part of your job description?" A smug smile spread across my face.

He winced, blinked several times, stood up straight and cleared his throat.

I glared knives at him. "I saw what you did to Natalie. I'm sure Doug Wallace wouldn't be too happy to hear about it. Or Stacy Lewis at corporate."

His eyes narrowed. "Who are you? And how do you know Doug? Or Stacy?"

"I'm your worst nightmare, Phil."

"I'm sorry," he grumbled angrily, shaking his head, "but I have no idea what you're talking about."

I scowled sourly. "I'm sure you don't. But you make damn sure you keep your hands to yourself, Phil. If you want to keep this job and pay your bills, that is. You do want that, don't you, Phil?"

"Miss, I don't know what you're talking about. You need to leave my store."

"Your store?" I laughed. It was my store. I'd worked here for almost five years. "You own the place?"

"Now you listen," he growled in a low voice, furious. "I don't know who you think you are—" *I wasn't entirely sure myself at the moment, but I knew I wasn't a pervy dicknose like him.* "—but I don't appreciate you coming in here and making false accusations about—"

"Please, Phil. I saw you. Should I go ask Natalie if she was comfortable with the way you tried to pin her against the register with your dick?"

His eyes were wide and he squirmed with fright. His mouth wiggled defiantly, but no words came out.

I tapped the countertop of the booth with my fingernails. "If you can manage to keep your hands and your dick to yourself, Phil, you won't have any problems. If you don't," I pointed at him, "I promise you, I will get you fired for sexual harassment." I smiled a friendly smile. "And don't stare at my ass when I walk out of here." I turned and waltzed toward the exit door. Halfway there, I spun around and winked at him. He stared right at me, mouth hanging open. "Remember, Phil. Eyes up and hands to yourself."

Outside, I strolled across the parking lot with a victorious grin on my face.

Chapter 13

"You will never believe what happened at work tonight," I blurted over my iPhone to Chelsea. Because I was driving, this was a voice call. Whenever drama happened, I would always call her without a second thought to vent. She always did the same.

"Slow down, Jane! What's wrong?"

I was driving my Hyundai up Santa Monica Boulevard, heading toward my apartment, screaming at my phone. "Men! I'm telling you, they're all dogs!"

"What happened? And why haven't you called me all week? I was worried about you. And why does your voice sound strange?"

Whoops. I forgot about that. In fact, I hadn't really thought about it at all, but my voice was different. Not a lot. Maybe huskier than it used to be, but it wasn't my voice. "Oh, I was really sick." I faked several coughs. "Still getting over it." Cough, cough.

"Are you at work?"

"No, I mean yeah. I'm on my break."

"Why aren't you on FaceTime?" We almost always used FaceTime. Not using it stood out as strange. In fact, the only time I didn't use it with her was while driving. I suddenly realized, if I hadn't been driving when I'd called her just now, I probably would've FaceTimed her and she would've seen me looking like someone else. Wow, that was a close call. I needed to be more careful.

I took a deep breath, "Oh, uh, I am at work. You know, uh, I didn't want to use up my data." It was the worst explanation ever. I had unlimited data. I hope she didn't call me on it.

"Anyway, what happened?"

"Okay, so this—" I was all set to tell her about what Phil Berger the pervy new night manager had done to Natalie. But then I realized I couldn't tell the story without revealing that I'd lost my job and wasn't the night manager anymore. So I slightly adjusted the truth and made it sound like Phil Berger was just some pervy customer who cornered Natalie in one of the aisles while she was stocking shelves. I was lying through my teeth to my sister, but that didn't change what had happened to Natalie.

When I finished my story, Chelsea said, "What an ass. Did you call the cops on him?"

Whoops. If your boss harassed you, you called HR. If a random customer harassed you, you called the police. I needed to adjust my story!

I said, "No, uh, he didn't actually grope her. Just scared her. Good thing I was there to chase him out of the store before he could do anything serious." More lies. "But I've got my eye out for him if he ever comes in again."

"Did you get any video of him on the security cameras? Maybe you can turn that over to the cops."

"Oh, uh… we did, but, uh… he was wearing a hat and sunglasses and you can't see his face in the video." I cringed. Lies, lies, lies!

"Good for you, Jay. Those girls are lucky to have you as their manager."

I grimaced to myself. "Yeah. Totally." It pained me that I couldn't explain what happened to my sister. I never held things back from her.

Suddenly, a car horn blared right beside my window.

Chelsea asked, "Is someone honking at you? I thought you said you were at work."

"What? No. I mean, yeah. I'm standing outside in the parking lot. By the street. There's a lot of traffic." I cringed again, disgusted with my lying self.

"Gotcha. Oh, hey, did you ever talk to Mom and Dad? Dad called me this afternoon and asked why you hadn't called them back. I think he's worried something happened to you."

Something had happened all right. I wasn't their daughter anymore! Not on the outside. But that counted for everything. If they saw me, Mom and Dad would never believe I was Jane. Never. If I was in their shoes, I wouldn't either. Funny how you only realized the importance of your particular appearance *after* it transformed without warning. I was quickly realizing your face was your fingerprint and every single person who knew you was checking it like a bar bouncer checks IDs. Unlike bouncers who might get to know you over time, your friends and loved ones checked your face every time they saw you. Every single time. If they didn't recognize you, you didn't get their trust. You were a complete outsider and not to be trusted until proven trustworthy.

I said to Chelsea, "No, I'm fine. Did you tell Dad anything?"

"I just said you were probably busy working. But you should call them soon."

"I will." Mom and Dad both had day jobs, so I rarely talked to them during the week. Working was a perfectly plausible explanation.

"Anyway, my break is almost over so I should probably go."

"Sure. Oh, hey, I have some good news."

"Yeah?"

"I'm flying down early for a meeting with a new client. I assume you have room for me to crash?"

"When?"

"Two weeks. Is that okay?"

Oh no. How was I going to explain looking like a supermodel to my sister? I wasn't ready to deal with this! My top priority was finding a job, not trying to convince my family I wasn't a scam artist!

"Jay? You still there?"

"Yeah! Of course! You're always welcome at my apartment, Chelsea!" I ground my teeth together, wanting all of this to go away.

"I can't wait to see you."

"Me too!" I lied.

What the fricka-frack was I going to do in two weeks?

At home, my keys jingled in the lock outside my apartment door. For some reason, I couldn't get it open. Why was this taking so long? Surely not because I kinda sorta maybe wanted Brodie to come out and flirt with me. No, I hated that guy. It was just the stupid lock misbehaving.

"Jane? Is that you?" My other neighbor Mrs. Wiser stuck her head out of her apartment. I'd met her the day I moved in and had known her for years. She was 82 and had lived by herself since her husband died seven years ago. We talked all the time and often had dinner together, what with us both being single gals.

"Hey, Mrs. Wiser," I smiled, happy to see a familiar face.

"Oh! You're not Jane. Sorry, dear. I thought you were someone else." She turned to go back into her apartment.

My heart sank once again. So much for a familiar face. She didn't know the new me. Something told me she would never believe I was me, no matter how I tried to tell her. She'd probably think I was trying to scam her too.

She suddenly stopped and lifted the glasses dangling from a beaded chain around her neck and peered at me. "Are you Chelsea?"

"No," I sighed. Over the years, Mrs. Wiser had spent plenty of time talking to Chelsea. She knew how Chelsea spoke and I didn't think she'd believe I was her. She was very sharp for her age. Better for me to be someone else. But who? Since Brodie knew me as Chelsea, Mrs. Wiser may as well too. I didn't want to risk having them calling me different names in front of each other, so I needed to be a different Chelsea. "Um… I'm Chelsea and Jane's cousin. But my name is Chelsea too."

"Another Chelsea?" She laughed. "How strange."

"Yeah."

"I've never heard of such a thing." She winked, "I may be old, but I don't know everything. Last time I checked, I don't think I even knew the half of it."

"I don't even know a quarter of it," I giggled, happy to be talking to someone who knew me without them treating me like a complete stranger.

"It's so nice to meet you, Chelsea Number Two. I have to ask, how did you know my name?"

Whoops. I told you she was sharp. "Oh, uh…"

"Did Jane tell you?"

"Yeah."

"How is she, by the way? I haven't seen her in almost a week. Is she all right?"

Not even slightly. I laughed nervously, "Yeah. She's fine. She's… on vacation." In my best British accent I added, "Holiday, as we Brits like to say." As usual, I was hiding my anxiety with humor.

"Oh really? Where did she go?"

Great. "Um, Jane went on a road trip."

"How come she didn't take her car? It's still parked in her carport." Sharp as ever.

Yes, I sucked at lying. *Oh what a tangled web we weave, when first we practice to deceive.* "Um, she took mine. I'm using hers. Mine has, uh… better gas mileage."

"Oh, that's nice of you, Chelsea. I'm sure Jane really appreciates the savings. Gas is so expensive these days."

"Sure is," I smiled. Now I was dying to get out of this conversation because I didn't think I could lie my way through the rest of it without Mrs. Wiser catching on.

"You aren't hungry, are you, dear? I was just about to put dinner in the microwave."

"Thanks. I just ate. Maybe next time?"

She waved a hand. "Sure, sure. You probably have plans anyway. It is Friday night. I'm sure a pretty young woman like you has plenty of boyfriends."

I laughed nervously. *Not yet, but that Brodie is sure trying.* "Nice meeting you, Mrs..." I offered my hand, acting like I'd already forgotten her name. I was also hoping she'd forget I already knew it.

"Wiser." She shook it. "You really do look a lot like Jane's sister, you know."

"You think so?"

She lifted her glasses again, examining my face. "Very much so." She lowered them and clucked, "Too cute. Well, have fun tonight with whatever his name is. And don't do anything I wouldn't do," she laughed and tugged my elbow. "In other words, use a condom."

"Mrs. Wiser!" I giggled.

"And don't be afraid to carry your own. We ladies need to take care of ourselves. Can't depend on the men to do it for us. Am I right?" Same old Mrs. Wiser.

"You are."

"Nice to meet you, Chelsea Number Two." She laughed and smiled before shuffling into her apartment.

I went inside mine and closed the door.

At least someone I knew was treating me like they sort of knew me.

Maybe I needed to start telling everybody I was my own cousin.

I ate dinner alone, sitting on my couch while Casablanca played on the TV, wondering what I was going to do about a job. I couldn't go back to the 95 Cent Store. How was I going to convince Doug Wallace and Maria and Natalie and corporate that I was me? I mean, without sounding insane?

Picking up my final paycheck would be bad enough. What was I going to do? Show Doug Wallace my ID and insist I was Jane Johnson? Fat chance. He'd never give me my check.

Maybe I could get corporate to mail it to me. That way I could deposit it at the ATM without the hassle of ID. But how long would it take for corporate to mail it? Would I get it in time to pay rent?

Who knew.

I shook my head. If my rent was late, Petrak would be pissed. He hated late rent payments. He hated them even more when your front door looked like it had been run over by a tractor. Stupid Brodie and his stupid chair. And speaking of stupid jerks who were too hot for their own good, when was he going to fix my fricking door?

DING DONG!

I nearly screamed.

But it was just my doorbell.

Probably Mrs. Wiser. Or maybe Brodie. Unless it was Petrak? I hoped it wasn't Petrak. I didn't want to do anymore impromptu lying tonight. Had Petrak met my sister? I couldn't remember. Should I just tell him I was my cousin Chelsea, like I was everyone else? Whatever I told him, I needed to tell him something. If he kept seeing supermodel me coming and going, and no plain Jane, he would ask questions.

I got up to peek through my peephole. Normally, I always had to stand on my tiptoes to see through it. Now I had to lean down. There were some advantages to being a 5'9" supermodel.

When I saw who was outside, I almost had a heart attack as adrenalin flooded my body with liquid panic.

George Sweet stood outside.

George knew my sister ten times better than Mrs. Wiser did.

George knew me a thousand times better than he did my sister.

George also knew I didn't have a cousin named Chelsea.

George would be instantly suspicious.

He would know something was wrong.

Shit!

He would know!

What was I going to do?

I wasn't ready for more pretending I wasn't me, especially not with George, and I couldn't think of a suitable lie under all this pressure!

DING DONG!

I squealed.

"Jane? Is that you? Are you home?"

My mind raced. I hadn't called George in days. That wasn't normal for us. I'm sure he was worried about me. Should I pretend I wasn't here? I could always text him that I was fine. Or should I open this door and tell him the truth? I'd have to tell someone eventually, wouldn't I?

Maybe George was the best person to tell.

He might actually believe me.

George was a big conspiracy theory believer. Alien abductions, UFOs hidden away in government hangers, Area 51, Roswell, all that stuff. He also believed in ghosts, ball lightning, and every other kind of paranormal activity. If anyone was going to believe me, it would be George.

I hoped.

Should I just tell him?

Unless I planned on cutting all ties with everyone I knew and forging a new life as a woman with no past, I had to tell someone. George was really the perfect person to start with. I had no interest in being some wandering vagabond or heroic loner. No, I needed my friends and family. I knew that fact like I knew my own name.

Was it Jane or was it Chelsea?

Ha, ha.

But not funny.

"Jane?"

Now or never...

I took a deep breath and opened my door slowly, wincing in anticipation of his reaction.

George frowned. "Oh, uhhh, hi, Chel—" He did this little head shake, probably realizing I wasn't Chelsea. "Um... is Jane here?"

I hated this. "Yes. I mean no. You can come in and wait for her if you want."

"Who are you?"

"I'm Jane's cousin." I didn't want to tell him the truth with the door wide open. Mrs. Wiser or Brodie might overhear. "Come in. Jane'll be here soon."

"I don't remember Jane mentioning any cousins."

I grunted, "Will you just come inside, George?"

"How do you know my name?"

"Relax, George. I'm not going to kill you. Jane told me you might come by."

George nibbled his lip. "Uhhh... maybe I'll come back later." George wasn't the bravest guy in town, but he knew how to stay out of trouble. Running always worked for rabbits. They did it all the time when they sensed danger.

"Come in, George." I grabbed his arm and pulled him inside. He stumbled through the door and I closed it behind him before he could escape. Normally, at 5'5", George was the tall one. Now I was. So weird. "Can I get you something to drink?"

"No thanks." He just stood by the door, slightly confused.

"Nice hoodie," I said.

Like me, George had a budget wardrobe that consisted of hoodies, T-shirts, jeans, and whatever shoes he could find at Payless ShoeSource for under $14.99. The one place where he splurged was on his hoodies. The one he wore now was bright sky blue with a silkscreen of Rainbow Dash's butt tattoo over the breast pocket. The tattoo was a cartoon cloud with a rainbow lightning bolt coming out. The hood wasn't up, but I knew it had pony ears sewn on top, a rainbow mane sewn along the seem of the hood, and little wings sewn to the back shoulders. It looked ridiculous, but George loved it and wore it all the time. He may not have been brave when it came to danger, but when it came to his wardrobe, he had no fear.

"George, I need to tell you something."

He put his hands in his hoodie pockets and stared at me. "Do you know where Jane is?"

"Please, sit down." I led him to the couch and pulled a chair over from my kitchen table and sat facing him.

"Um, who are you? And what are you doing in Jane's apartment?"

"Uhhh…" I couldn't quite bring myself to say it.

His eyes suddenly widened. "Is this some kind of ransom thing? Did you kidnap Jane?"

"No, George. This isn't a ransom thing. Jane is fine. Nobody kidnapped her."

George stood up, agitated. "Well where is she? I haven't heard from her since Sunday. Is something wrong? She better be okay, or I swear I'll…" He ran his eyes over me, trying to make sense of the situation.

I was touched that he cared so much. I mean, we'd been close for nine years, but George rarely showed this much emotion when it came to me. "Relax, George. Jane is okay. I promise." I took a deep breath. "George, this is going to sound crazy. Maybe you better sit down."

"Is she dead?" He looked horrified.

"No! She's not dead! She's… Please sit, George."

He didn't. "Just tell me already. Who are you anyway?"

I heaved a sigh. "George, I'm Jane."

He broke into laughter, shaking his head. "What?!"

"George. It's me. Jane. Your friend for nine years."

He snorted denial.

"George, I'm telling you the truth. I'm Jane. The vampire, but not really a vampire. I work the night shift at the 95 Cent Store. The other day I told you I was at a blood rave last Saturday night, dressed like Blade *and* Buffy. But I was at speed dating with Chelsea and you said I should've gone speed skating. The last time Chelsea was in town and I was hanging out with her, I told you afterward that she and I drove to Washington so we could find the town of Forks and kill that stupid Bella from Twilight. Then I was going to marry Edward because I'm already a vampire, and Chelsea would marry Jacob because she likes werewolves and Taylor Lautner, even though he's way younger than her." Considering I'd never told anyone that stuff, not even Chelsea (she hated Twilight and Taylor Lautner), George had to realize I was Jane. Who else would know such specific details about our private conversations?

George looked at me thoughtfully. "Did Jane tell you all that?"

"No, George. I'm Jane. I'm the girl who goes to Brony conventions with you and to San Diego Comic Con. We met in college nine years ago. I don't know how to explain it, but this is me. Something weird happened. I was sick all week. I couldn't get out of bed. When I woke up today, I looked like this."

George scowled. Was he considering it?

I rolled my eyes. "Would it help any if I told you I was abducted by aliens and they did this to me with advanced alien medical technology?"

George frowned, "Uh, no?"

"Okay, see this ring on my finger?" I pointed to it. "It's cursed. Or blessed, or I don't know what. Anyway, I think it may have turned me into this." I gestured at myself with both hands.

He shook his head slowly. "What's your name again?"

"Jane. It's Jane!"

He chewed his lower lip. "Um, are you high on something?"

"George! It's me! Jane Johnson!"

"Okay, okay. Calm down." He looked around thoughtfully. "Okay, if you're Jane, then tell me what the Love Jug is."

I immediately broke out in cackling laughter. It felt so good to laugh so freely. The Love Jug was a secret I'd never told anyone except George. Not even Chelsea. It was too embarrassing and I'd made George swear he would never tell a soul.

Smiling, I locked eyes with George. "Have *you* ever told anyone about the Love Jug?"

"Nope. Never told anyone." He smirked confidently, like he'd just posed an impossible riddle that could never be solved.

Laughing, I said, "The Love Jug is..." I was blushing like crazy. The mere thought of it made me want to hide my head under a pile of blankets. Shame, shame, shame! "Can I start by describing it?"

"Sure."

I took a deep breath, trying not to laugh. "Okay, the Love Jug is this old bottle my parents keep on a bookcase in their guest bedroom. You've seen it." He nodded. He had. "They still have it. It looks like a genie's bottle, like in Aladdin. It's about this wide at the bottom," I held my hands apart, "and about this tall. The neck is shaped kind of like a dick. The entire thing is covered in leather, it has some brass ornaments on the base, and a bulbous leather stopper." Just describing it made my face burn. I searched his eyes. "Well?"

He arched an eyebrow, "That *is* the Love Jug. But why is it *called* that?"

I grabbed a magazine off my coffee table and threw it at him. The pages fluttered open and it landed on the couch cushions. "I'm not going to say it out loud, George! Telling you once was enough!"

George's smile faded and his knee started to bounce and he put his fists in his hoodie pockets. "Did Jane tell you that story?"

I started to panic.

He wasn't believing I was me.

It was entirely possible that no one would ever believe I was me. No matter how many secrets I told them, who would possibly believe I had turned into somebody else while I was sleeping? It was crazy. UFOs were one thing. People all over the world, reputable people, had UFO sitings.

But how many people believed that shapeshifters really existed?

Not even George believed in those conspiracies.

Fear swept over me. I sensed my closest friend was on the verge of disowning me. I grabbed him by the wrist. "No, George! It's me! Jane Johnson! I know you hate Domino's Pizza because you think their cheese tastes like plastic. I know you hate spiders, and every time you have to kill one, you play Seek & Destroy by Metallica. I know you're still obsessed with your LEGO collection. I know you tried LSD once in college, but you never did it again because it scares you too much. I know you blame your mom for giving you asthma because she smoked when you were a baby. I know your dad is an alcoholic but your mom insists he's not. I know he was drunk the first time he taught you how to drive, and he smashed the car into a cement trash can in the parking lot at the mall where he took you to practice, and he broke the headlight and made you tell your mom you did it. And you hated him for it, but you told her anyway." My voice had gone from agitated to quiet as I revealed darker and darker secrets. My hands were folded in my lap and I stared at them.

When I next spoke, my voice was barely a whisper, "I also know you wanted to kill yourself four years ago. When I found the bottle of sedatives you stole from your mom in your medicine cabinet, I flushed them down the toilet."

I was crying when I looked up at him and said, "Please, George. It's me, Jane. I need you to believe me. You're the only one who knows."

His eyes were starting to water.

I felt bad for bringing up so much of his personal pain.

"You're a liar." He stood up and walked to my door.

"George!" I threw myself in front of my door, blocking his way. "George, please! It's really me! Jane Abigail Johnson!" Seeing his tears start to flow made me lose it and I started sobbing. I grabbed the sleeves of his hoodie and held onto them like a life preserver. "I don't know what happened, George! But this is me! You have to believe me!"

He stared at me, his face red as tears dribbled down his cheeks. "Let go of me," he grunted.

Defeated, I dropped my hands and stood aside.

He grabbed the doorknob.

In a small voice I pleaded, "Please, George. Please don't go. It's me. I promise it's me."

He tore the door open and stepped outside.

"Please," I whispered, "I can't do this alone…"

Chapter 14

"You are such a LOSER, Jane!" George shouted in my face an hour later.

I laughed, "No I'm not! I won the last three races!"

"Like that matters," he chuckled. "I won eleven straight before that."

We sat side by side on my couch, both of us holding game controllers attached to the dusty old Super Nintendo console I'd had since I was a girl. We were busy playing Super Mario Kart, something we often did when we talked. It was mindless fun and I think it helped both of us feel more grounded about everything.

While we'd been playing, we'd also been talking.

I explained everything to George, from waking up this way to losing my job. We'd also gone into microscopic detail about every little thing George and I had done together or knew about each other. Finally, it seemed like he believed me.

It was a tremendous relief.

"You know," he said, "if being someone else is such a pain in the A, maybe you should just take the ring off."

"It's not the One Ring, Samwise," I snarked. "If it was, I'd be invisible right now."

"I'm not saying it is, Frodo," he winked at me. "But maybe if you take it off, you'll go back to normal."

"How does that make any sense? The ring has nothing to do with it."

"So take it off and see what happens."

A sense of excitement washed over me. "Maybe you're right." I slid it off without a second thought. Looked at George. "Am I any different?"

"Not yet. Maybe it takes a while?"

"Maybe." I flashed back to all the pain I'd gone through during my swansformation. I wasn't in a hurry to go through that again. After another thirty seconds, I put the ring back on and smiled at George.

He said, "I guess this means you want to stay beautiful?"

"No." *Maybe.* "It just means I'm not ready to go through another five days of torture. You weren't here for all the fun, George." I said it sarcastically. "I felt like I was dying. And if turning beautiful nearly killed me, turning back might *actually* kill me."

"Good point. Maybe wait a few weeks. Or months."

"Yeah."

I realized then that I had no idea what toll the swansformation might have taken on my body. Pain was a signal to your body that something was wrong, and I'd swum through an ocean of pain to get here. The idea that this ring might have the potential to kill me if I wasn't careful with it was enough for me to leave it right where it was. If it ain't broke, don't fix it. Since I didn't have a manual for the ring, maybe it was best to leave it where it was.

For now.

(forever)

Maybe I'd try again in a few weeks like George suggested.

After finishing another Mario Kart race, he looked over at me, his face illuminated by the blue glow of the TV. "You know what I keep thinking, Jay?"

"What?"

"Don't hate me for saying this."

"I won't hate you." I was desperate for him to accept me. Hating was the last thing on my mind. "The next race is starting."

He turned back to the TV. While working his controller, he said, "I keep thinking you look exactly like Sailor Moon." The Japanese anime Sailor Moon was a guilty pleasure for both of us.

"A cartoon?"

"No, I mean in general."

I shook my head, snickering. "I do not look like Sailor Moon. My hair isn't down to my toes and I don't wear a Japanese School Girl outfit twenty-four seven."

"True," he smiled. "But you have the blonde hair. How about a real life Barbie?"

"I don't look like Barbie either!"

"You kinda do," he chuckled, eyes focused on the game. "We need to find you a Ken doll."

"Shut up!" I nudged my knee against his. An image of Brodie popped into my mind. Brodie was better than a Ken doll. He was the bad boy version. And he was real. And he lived next door and he... I didn't want to think about it. Brodie was an arrogant, shallow, self-centered jerk.

George tilted his head while examining my face. "You're hot, Jane. I mean, really hot. You could be one of those hot cosplay models like Violette Threatt."

I knew the model he was talking about. We'd seen Violette Threatt in person at the last San Diego Comic Con. As always, she'd looked gorgeous and had been surrounded by a crowd of fans wherever she went. I remembered being jealous of her confidence and regal air. She had no problem strutting around like a queen while wearing practically nothing. Thousands of comic book nerds had drooled over her and begged her to pose with them for photos, which she'd done with grace and good humor. I wasn't like her. Not even close. I chuckled, "Thanks, George. But somehow I don't think that's my career path."

"Why not? Top cosplay models make serious bank. I would do it if I had those boobs." He was staring right at my chest. Unlike Brodie, who saw me as a sex object, I knew George was probably imagining me in a Sailor Moon costume. George was safe. He continued, "Violette Threatt is like the Lady Gaga of cosplay right now. She's worth almost two million dollars and she's only been doing cosplay seriously for five years. How is that not a career path?"

"Wait, are you serious?"

He shrugged. "That's what I read online."

Sarcastically, "And because you read it on the internet, it must be true."

"Just saying. Violette Threatt does paid appearances at tons of cons, has videos on YouTube and makes ad money from that, and has a Patreon which brings her like $25K a month."

"A month?"

"Yeah."

"That's like three hundred grand a year!"

"I know, right? And guess what? You're way hotter than her. I'm sure you could make double what she does, if you tried. You're already a fan. Now you just need the costumes. And a manager."

"Why do I need a manager?"

He winked, "You need someone you can trust."

"Who, you?"

"Durp. Yeah me. Who else?"

I stared at him, mulling it over. I'd been to enough fan conventions with George to know how hot cosplay was. I'd always thought it would be fun to dress up, but I never had, probably because of my insecurities. And I knew George was right. Women like Violette Threatt (or whatever her real name was) made a living off of it. But I was pretty sure it wasn't any easier to be a top cosplay model than it was to be a rich rockstar. It wasn't a real option. I needed a steady paycheck.

I said, "Let's table the cosplay discussion for now. How are you doing? We haven't talked in a week." I wanted to return our conversation to something vaguely normal, something that would ground me, not put my head back in the clouds. I needed a break from the clouds.

"A lot better than you," he snorted. "What are you gonna do about your job?"

"Look for a new one, I guess. I'm going to be late on rent if I don't find something quick."

"Maybe you should try stripping. They make a ton of money. A lot more than a night manager at a 95 Cent Store."

"Uhhhh... No. I can't be a stripper."

"Why not?"

"First, because I don't know how to dance. Second, because it's just not me."

"It could be you."

"Are you trying to pimp me out, George?"

He laughed. "No. I'm just trying to help you think of options. I mean, if this is really you," he gestured at me, "I mean really *really* you, you don't look like your ID anymore, right?"

"You're right," I sighed.

"So you need a job that pays under the table. Stripping is all cash, right?"

"I don't know. Do you? Or is that something you read on the internet?"

"I'm pretty sure they work for tips. And I'm guessing strippers don't need background checks."

"They need ass-ground checks," I smirked.

"And boob-ground checks," he grinned. "So go be a stripper. You're stripper name can be Sailor." He winked.

I elbowed his arm. "No, George."

"How about Moon?"

"That's worse!" I scowled.

"Barbie? That actually sounds like a stripper name."

"I hate you, George. I hope you wake up one morning looking like a supermodel. No! I know! In an alternate universe where video games and cartoons don't exist! How would you like that, George? Huh? Doesn't sound like fun, does it?"

He smiled at me and searched my face, "You really are J-Chan, aren't you?" Chan was a Japanese honorific used for best friends. George didn't call me J-Chan often. I think it was his way of saying he loved me. Or liked me. Or whatever. Whatever he meant, it was as close as he got to expressing affection toward me. From him, now, it meant a lot.

"Yes, George. It's me." I sighed. It felt so good to have him believe me. "Promise me one thing, George."

"Sure?"

"Don't tell anybody about this. I mean, nobody. I don't want anyone finding out. This is bigger than the Love Jug."

"Yeah it is."

"Can you keep this a secret?"

"Totally. You know I've got your back."

"Please, George. You've gotta promise." I squeezed his wrist.

He nodded. "Okay, okay. I promise."

"Promise?"

"Do you need me to take a blood oath?"

I looked at him for a long time.

He said, "You can count on me, J-Chan."

"All right, G-Chan. I believe you." But I prayed he would stay good to his word.

If there was one thing I'd learned growing up as a little nerd girl, it was that I hated being singled out for being different. I didn't want to be a novelty or a sideshow circus freak. All I could think about was the abnormal amount of attention beautiful people and celebrities already got. Imagine how bad it would be for someone who had transformed from plain to beautiful in five short days? The media scrutiny would be unprecedented. For all intents and purposes, I was a walking miracle. Everyone would want to know my secret, which I wouldn't be able to tell them. A magical ring seemed the least likely explanation. Maybe I was some genetic abnormality. Whatever the cause, if word got out, I'd be all over CNN and TMZ and every other news outlet on the planet. Scientists would want to do experiments on me. Opportunists would want to exploit me.

I didn't want any of that.

I preferred to remain in the background and live my life like a normal person.

The last thing I wanted was people paying any more attention to me than they already did. That meant avoiding jobs like cosplay modeling and stripping.

I needed to find a regular job and keep my head down.

Chapter 15

The next morning, I walked out my front door after breakfast and a shower. While I was locking the deadbolt, Brodie's door opened and he stuck his head out.

"Hey, Chelsea," he drawled.

I didn't even look at him. "Fix my front door, Brodie." Like he'd done to me the first day we'd met, I turned and walked away without looking back, but I was kind enough not to flip him off dismissively.

Was he staring at my ass as I walked?

I didn't turn to check.

But the heat on my backside told me he was.

Whatever.

After I drove off, I spent all of Saturday job hunting.

There had to be somebody in town other than a strip joint who would hire me without checking my ID. The only question was, if someone did hire me, would they ask for my ID when I filled out my W-4, emergency contact info, health insurance, etc.? Some places wouldn't offer health insurance, but what about the other forms?

I'd cross that bridge when I came to it, and if I had to, I'd keep crossing different bridges until I found one without a gatekeeper or whatever.

In the meantime, I needed to find somebody who was actually hiring. This morning while eating breakfast, I had started an online job search, but I quickly realized I needed to create a new email and a fake online presence first. Hot Jane Johnson didn't have a Facebook page or Instagram or any kind of social media. She didn't even have email or a LinkedIn page. I didn't want a potential employer doing a search and coming up with nothing. That would raise more questions. I needed to land a job face to face with a handshake. Not online.

Did that even happen anymore?

I was about to find out.

In preparation, I did doctor up the stack of résumés I carried in my purse. My job for the past five years had been at the 95 Cent Store. They had stores all over LA. Everybody knew the 95 Cent Store with its Walmart ripoff blue awning and uniforms and decor. So I changed my résumé to say I'd worked at Dollar Tree instead. They had stores all over the country, but I didn't say which one on my résumé. The last thing I wanted was a potential employer calling the Dollar Tree down the road in Culver City or Marina Del Rey only to find out I'd never worked there. If someone did ask me which one during an interview, I'd say it was the Dollar Tree in Orange Park, Florida or Little Rock, Arkansas, or Bumfrack, Iowa, and hope they didn't know anything or anyone in Florida or Arkansas or Iowa. Nobody would bother to call Iowa, right?

Fingers crossed.

I started out at the Third Street Promenade, an outdoor mall near the beach in Santa Monica. It was also right next to Santa Monica Place, an indoor mall. I'd hit it up later. Between the two, there were probably a hundred shops and restaurants to choose from. At least one of them had to be hiring, right?

I spent hours going from shop to shop.

It was grueling work.

First, nobody was hiring. Second, I was starting to notice a trend.

Every single male manager I talked to was very friendly and wanted to hire me on the spot, but none of them had any job openings. At first, I thought they were being nice. But eventually I realized most of them were just flirting. They didn't want to give me a job. They just wanted in my pants.

With the female managers, I sensed an undercurrent of cattiness. I knew catty behavior, when I saw it, but I'd never seen so damn much of it directed at me. At least I didn't have to waste time being flirted with. Well, one woman was gay and she definitely flirted, but more cautiously than any of the men. I think she wasn't sure whether I was gay or straight, so she didn't push it.

Several hours later, I was exhausted. What a hassle. I didn't have a job but I did have five applications I didn't want. Several male managers insisted I take one and made me promise to fill it out and submit it so they could keep it on file. On file. Pfft. Yeah, right. I wasn't stupid. They just wanted my phone number. I threw the applications in the trash. Like I said, I needed to get a job with a handshake. Maybe the Promenade was the wrong place to look.

After all the walking and talking, I needed a break and some food. I bought a slice of cheese pizza at Stefano's and sat down on a bench outside, right in front of the Abercrombie & Fitch store. Since it was Saturday, the entire Promenade was packed with people going in and out of the shops, and street performers trying to make a buck from the browsing crowds.

I nibbled on my pizza while watching a street magician do tricks in front of about a hundred people.

"How's your pizza?"

I looked up into the face of some random guy hovering over me. "Uh... just fine. Thanks."

"Looks really good," he said. This guy was reasonably attractive and wore a stylish leather jacket. Had he walked up to me a week ago when I was plain Jane, I would've been shocked he wanted to talk to nerdy little me. But after all the men who'd bugged me today, I was over it.

"Yeah," I muttered, taking another bite.

"Can I ask where you got it?"

I didn't want to be rude. "Stefano's. It's around the corner."

"Which corner?" He looked around like he was really interested. *Please go away.* "That way."

He nodded. "Got it. Hey, if you want another slice, I'll buy one for you. You wanna come with?"

I smiled politely, "No thanks."

"You sure?"

Please take the hint and leave. "Yeah, thanks."

He shrugged. "Whatever." He sounded disgruntled, but he walked away.

I would've thanked him for leaving, but I didn't want to encourage him. That was the other thing about today. Random guys like him were constantly stopping me for the lamest of reasons. At first I was flattered. It didn't take long before I was annoyed. But I remained polite and tried to keep the conversations short. Sadly, it got to a point where I was spending more time being polite to random men than I was job hunting. So I started ignoring them. I felt like a rude bitch, but I needed to find a job.

Now I knew why Chelsea tended to prefer staying in.

Men could be pests.

My big plan to keep a low profile and go unnoticed was backfiring magnificently. Maybe I needed to start wearing a big hat and big sunglasses and a scarf so I would be less conspicuous. As it was, I wasn't wearing any makeup, but it didn't make a difference. The new me was a man magnet. Maybe I needed to shave my head and get a full facial tattoo. I'd probably get less attention that way.

I took the last bite of my pizza.

"For this next trick," the street magician said over his microphone (it was attached to a couple of portable PA speakers on stands), "I need a volunteer."

I wasn't listening. Having finished my pizza, I blotted my lips with my napkin, stood, and dropped it and my paper plate in the nearest trash can.

"Yes, you! Miss! Over here!" The magician waved and caught my eye. He pointed at me and made his way through the spectators watching his show. He hooked a finger at me. "Come on over, miss!"

"Me?" I touched my fingers to my chest. "I can't. I'm late for an appointment." I tapped my wrist and shook my head.

"Come on," he waved me over. "You've got two minutes to help me with my magic trick. Let's hear it for this nice young lady!"

The excited crowd started clapping and hollering at me.

Great. I rolled my eyes. I didn't want to look like a bitch. I reluctantly walked over to join him. So much for fading into the background. Let's just get this over with.

"Give the young lady a hand, everybody!" The magician grabbed my wrist and pulled me into his stage area on the street. He was cute and about my age. If I was him, I would've picked me out of the crowd for sure. Great scam for meeting women.

I snickered to myself while the crowd applauded.

"What?" he said quietly, covering the microphone on his collar with his hand.

"Nothing." What I was thinking was: *I've been beautiful less than twenty-four hours and I'm already sick of it. Since you're a magician, maybe you can change me back to normal?*

He was about to turn to the crowd, so I tapped him on the shoulder.

"Yeah?"

I muttered in his ear, "Hey, do you think you could make me shorter?"

"Huh?"

"And, I don't know, give me bad hair and some glasses?"

He frowned, "Why would you want me to do that?"

"Never mind." I shook my head and my blonde straight hair waved gently around my shoulders. It never did that before. Anyway, asking this guy to change me back was stupid. I knew magicians just did tricks. It was all sleight of hand and misdirection and special props. They weren't really magical. Oh well.

"Okay, everybody," the magician said to the crowd, his microphone amplifying his words through the PA. "How would you like to see me read this young woman's mind?"

Some grungy woman in the crowd yelled out, "Good luck with that! Everybody knows blondes like her are brainless bimbos! Nothing to read!"

Everybody heard her. I scowled. A few people laughed but a few others booed. Were people really this rude? Yes they were.

The magician said, "I doubt she's brainless." He was trying to make me feel better. "Or a bimbo."

I grinned and said loudly, "No. That woman was right. I'd have to be an idiot to come up here and make a fool of myself in front of everybody for free. Maybe you oughta split your tips with me." I smiled at the magician and nodded toward the black silk top hat that sat on the ground near the front of his stage area. A bunch of ones, fives, tens, and a few twenties sprouted out the top. To me it looked like rent money. I could definitely make use of all that cash.

Scattered applause from a few people. Some guy shouted, "She ain't dumb! Give her some money!"

More applause from the crowd and a few whistles.

The magician said, "Okay. How about this? You think of a card. Any card from a normal deck of cards, and I'll try and guess which one. If I *can't* guess what card you're thinking of, I'll give you all the money in that top hat." He looked at the crowd. "Huh? Whaddya say, people? Does that sound like a fair bet?"

More cheering and agreement.

"Wait, wait, wait," I said. "That's not fair. We all know this is just a trick and you can't actually read minds. We also know you're a good magician because you have a big crowd. That means you have some way of tricking me into picking a certain card so you can guess right and look all magical. Otherwise, you'd look like an idiot and wouldn't be out here in the first place. So the safe bet for me is that you will, quote, read my mind, and you will guess which card I picked. In other words, if you guess right, *I* should get paid. Not you."

The crowd was silent. I think they were as confused as I was, but I was pretty sure I'd said it right.

The magician stared at me, also trying to sort out what I'd said.

Some guy yelled out, "What she said!"

A few people clapped and laughed.

"Okay," the magician said, "let me get this straight. If I guess which card you picked, you don't get the money, right?"

"*Don't* get the money?" I shook my head and giggled. "No no no! You're twisting my words. I said, if you guess which card I pick, *I* get paid! Me! Not you! I get the money if you're right! Got it?"

He wobbled his head and stared right in my eyes. He was trying to confuse me again.

I grabbed his collar and spoke into his microphone so my words went out over the PA. "Let me make this simple for you. If you guess right, I get the money in your top hat. If you guess wrong, you get the money." I smiled at him. "Your reputation is on the line, Mr. Magician. You just have to decide if it's worth all the money in your top hat or not."

Now the whole crowd was clapping and cheering.

The magician said, "How about this? I get it right, we split the money. I get it wrong, you get all of it. Deal?" He held out his hand.

"Mmmm. Okay. Deal." I shook it.

"All right, let's get this show on the road!" The magician walked over to a little table near the side of his stage area and grabbed something. "Miss…" He walked back up to me and put his arm around me. "What's your name, miss?"

"Ch-Chelsea." I'd been telling people I was Chelsea all day. No reason to change things now.

"Chelsea. Got it. Lovely, Chelsea. Lovely. Now, I want you to think of a card you would find in a normal deck of cards." He made all these rhythmic hand gestures as he said it. "Any NUMBER," more hand gestures, "or any of the THREE face cards."

"Okay."

"LOVELY. You got it in your mind?" He nodded at me three times.

"Yeah."

"Lovely. Now think of any suit. HEARTS, diamonds, clubs…"

"Okay."

"Think real haaard."

"Thinking," I smiled.

"You got it? Number, face, suit?" As he said it, the fingers of his left hand flicked out, *flick, flick, flick.*

"Yeah."

He handed me a scrap of paper and a black Sharpie pen. "Lovely. Now, I want you to do THREE things. Can you do that for me, love?"

"Sure." I nodded.

"Turn around so I can't see you, write down the card you're thinking of on that paper. And THREE, show it to the crowd so I can't see it. So I *can't* see it."

"Okay." I turned around and did what he asked. Without thinking, I wrote down the three of hearts. "Do I show it to the crowd?"

"Please. But make sure I can't see it. So don't turn around. Got it?"

"Yeah."

He waved a stopping hand at the crowd and shook his head at them, "Please, keep the card to yourself. Do NOT say it out loud."

I capped the Sharpie and handed it to him. Then I held up the paper with both hands carefully, so only a few people in front of me could see it.

Numerous people leaned over to get a good look. I walked from side to side so at least two dozen of them saw it. Right at that moment, I glanced past the crowd and into the eyes of a tall man who slowed down to watch the magic show.

The stranger's eyes locked right on mine.

In response, my chest locked up tight.

It was Wes. From the mansion. Wesley Callaway. *I will remember your eyes forever.* That Wes. I nearly collapsed seeing him here now. After saying goodbye to him the other day, I was convinced I'd never see him again.

Yet here he was, standing twenty feet behind the gathered crowd while more people passed back and forth in front of him. Maybe the stage magician really was magical. He'd summoned my dream man out of thin air.

Wes stared right at me. He wore a white linen shirt with the sleeves rolled up to the elbows, oblivious to the hundreds of people on the Promenade.

For a second, it seemed like the whole world disappeared and it was just me and Wes standing here staring at each other.

All I wanted to do was run and grab him and talk to him. I had no idea what I'd say, but I wanted to talk to him. Badly. Too bad I was stuck in the middle of this stupid magic trick. Could I leave? Could I crawl over the crowd standing between me and Wes and go to him? No, there were too many people. I'd have to step on babies and young children to get to Wes. I could go around the crowd, but what if Wes suddenly left? There were so many people here on the Promenade, I could easily lose him.

My hands started to shake.

The magician said, "Have you people in the front row seen what she wrote down? Don't say it if you have. Just say yes." A bunch of yeses and yeahs from the people in front of me. "Now Chelsea, I want you to carefully fold the paper up so I can't see what's written on it. Can you do that?"

I was afraid to turn around. I didn't want to lose sight of Wes, so I folded up the paper while keeping my eyes on him. "Yuh-yeah."

The magician rattled around behind me. He said, "Okay, as you all can see, I have a fresh unopened pack of pristine playing cards."

I didn't turn to look.

"Chelsea? Can you turn around for me, sweetheart?"

"No!" I blurted. Some of the crowd started laughing. The last thing I cared about was this stupid magic trick. I wanted it over with. I couldn't even remember what card I'd written down. I just stared at

Wes.

The magician chuckled. "Okay. Then I'll come to you." He walked up beside me and held out the pack of cards.

I didn't even look.

He nudged it against my arm. "Chelsea? Can you open the pack of cards?"

"Shuh-sure." I was still watching Wes.

He was still watching me.

"Can you turn and face me?" The magician asked.

"Yeah, whatever." I turned my body but kept my eyes pinned on Wes.

"Can you please unwrap the cards?"

Without looking at what I was doing, I shoved the wadded up slip of paper into my purse and dug my fingernails into the plastic shrink wrap and peeled it off. I looked away from Wes for a split second. When I turned back, Wes was gone.

Oh no!

Oh, wait. It was just an illusion. So many people were walking between me and Wes, it made it seem like he'd gone. But he was still there. My heart rate slowed down to a mere 180 BPM. Yes, I was that nervous. I desperately needed to talk to Wes one last time before he disappeared forever. I wasn't sure why, but it was important. Closure, maybe. I didn't know.

"Do you have the pack open?" The magician asked.

I absently stuffed the balled up shrink wrap into my purse with the slip of paper. "Yeah, yeah."

"Okay, now I want you to look through the deck and find your card."

"Huh?" All I could think at that moment was, *Wes Wes Wes.*

(love love love)

"Please turn around so you're not facing me and look through the deck until you find your card, but don't tell me when you find it."

The last thing I wanted to do was busy myself searching through a deck of cards. Wes could get away! Besides, I couldn't even remember which card I wrote down. I was over this stupid card trick. "Sorry. I have to go." I handed him the deck and pushed through the crowd without looking back.

"Wait! I was gonna give you half my top hat money! But I need that paper you wrote on to finish the trick! Chelsea! Come back!"

I jogged through the throng of people walking back and forth between me and Wes. But I couldn't see him anywhere! I'd been distracted by that stupid magician and his stupid card trick! That jerk had been so busy misdirecting me, he'd just made Wes disappear!

Asshat!

I ran to where Wes had been standing and spun in circles, trying to pick him out of hundreds of people. Panic set in, every cell in my body tingling in disbelief.

He'd been right here!

Right where I was standing!

I balled my fists in frustration, my nails digging into my palms. "No, no, no!" Out of the corner of my eye I saw a flash of white. I twisted around but it was just a woman in a white blouse.

"Shit!"

I spun again and another flash of white disappeared around a building. I ran after it, convinced it was Wes. When I turned the corner, all I saw was more people. But it had to have been Wes! Still running, I pushed my way through the crowd on the sidewalk, bumping people aside. Some yelled at me, others cursed.

"Sorry! I'm really sorry!"

I had to find Wes!

When I reached the next block, I slowed to a stop and swiveled my head from side to side.

Where was he?!

There! Going into one of the parking garages on Second Street. I chased after. Just as I turned into the garage, an elevator door started to close. Someone was inside!

Wes!

"Wait!" I ran up and pounded the UP button repeatedly.

But it was too late.

The doors had closed and Wes was gone.

Again.

I heaved a sigh.

Damn it!

I just missed him!

"Are you stalking me, Sunflower?"

I spun around to face the owner of that familiar and imposing baritone.

Chapter 16

Wes leaned casually against a rectangular cement column, watching me.

He stood with his hands in pockets, looking cover model handsome. His fitted linen shirt revealed a body even more delicious than I'd imagined. Broad shoulders, wide hard pecs pulling against the slightly transparent white material. His abs were hidden but his stomach was obviously washboard flat. The rolled-up cuffs revealed smooth tan forearms with a criss-cross of veins playing over chiseled muscles. A chunky gold bracelet hung from one wrist. His tight slacks told me the bracelet wasn't the only thing about him that hung well. Rippled folds slightly tented a sizable package.

I folded my arms across my chest and shifted my weight to one hip. "Stalking? What makes you think I'm stalking anybody?"

"I heard your flats slapping the sidewalk. Sounded like running to me."

"Maybe I'm late for an appointment."

He smirked, "Then why are you still standing here talking to me?"

"Because I'm trying to figure out why *you* are stalking me."

"Ha! Following me around one corner is a coincidence. Following me around three is stalking. You're stalking me, Sunflower."

"Me?!" I huffed. "You were the one staring at me during the magic show!"

"Oh, that's right," he nodded thoughtfully but his voice dripped with sarcasm. "Me and a hundred other people were watching you and a street magician doing a card trick. Very creepy. All those pervs dying to find out what card you picked. Scandalous. We should all be locked up. And I feel terrible for that magician. He probably hates having people stare at him as much as you do."

"I don't like having people stare at me," I grumbled.

"So, what, you followed me so you could give me a beating for looking at you? Teach me a lesson I'll never forget?" He was smiling now. "You have thin skin, Sunflower."

"Stop calling me Sunflower," I giggled. He could call me Sunflower from now until forever.

His eyes flashed and a dimple curled beneath his cheek. "I can call you anything I want, Sunflower. Since I don't know your name, I'm going to keep calling you Sunflower."

That's right. Wes didn't know I was Jane. That meant I could have fun with him. I smirked, "Okay, Oak Tree. Tell me why you were staring at me?"

He chuckled and muttered, "Oak Tree."

"You weren't watching the magic show. You were watching me, Mr. Oak Tree. I'm not blind."

"What can I say? You're more interesting than the magician." He said it so casually it could almost be interpreted as an insult.

"Gee, thanks."

He snickered.

"Are you enjoying this?" I challenged.

"What's not to enjoy?"

"You're insufferable, you know that?"

His smiled widened. Damn it, he was gorgeous. "So I've been told. Can I ask you something, Sunflower?"

Anything. I rolled my eyes, "What?"

"Aren't you late for your appointment?" He stifled a laugh.

"Shut up, Oak Tree!"

"Stalker."

I reached into my purse and grabbed the first thing I found and threw it at Wes. "Ass." A crumpled up piece of paper bounced off his chest.

"And a litterer too. Tsk, tsk, Sunflower. I should place you under citizen's arrest and haul you off to jail."

I held up my wrists like I was ready to be handcuffed. "Oh, please. Would you? Before I commit some heinous crime against humanity?"

"I'll let you off easy. *If* you pick up your trash." He toed the crumpled paper with his dress shoe.

"You pick it up."

"One. Two. Three…"

"Are you counting, Dad?"

"I'm not your dad." There was a sinful flash in his eyes. "Four. Five…"

"It usually stops at three. A count of three."

"Six. Seven…"

"Do I have until ten?"

"Eight. Nine…"

"What happens if you hit ten?"

"Do you really want to find out the *hard* way, Sunflower?"

"Maybe I do, Oak Tree."

"You know what I love about oak trees?"

"What's that?" I sneered.

"They're so damn thick, from tip to root…"

I laughed. He'd said it so sexually I couldn't help myself. "I knew you were a perv! And a stalker!"

"Make up your mind. And would you pick up your trash already, you dirty litterer?" His words dripped with sexual innuendo once again. He toed the crumpled paper and it wobbled slightly.

I really did hate littering and never did it myself. "Fine." I walked toward him and bent to pick it up, but stopped when I realized that if I bent any lower, or squatted down, his crotch would be in my face. There was no way around it. I hesitated.

"Are you gonna pick it up or not?"

"You'd like that, wouldn't you?"

He grinned a syrupy grin. "I'm already liking it quite a bit."

I stole a glance at his crotch. Was he getting hard? I wasn't going to look long enough to make sure.

"Like what you see?"

"No." It was a lie.

He chuckled, "Who's the perv now, Sunflower?"

"You wish," I snorted, standing back up to my full height. Damn, he was really tall. Even in my new 5'9" body, he was much taller than me.

"Pick it up," he commanded.

"No. You pick it up."

"I wasn't the one who threw it."

I scowled, "Then back up so I can pick it up."

"You've got plenty of room."

I jammed a hand on my hip. "Do you like humiliating women?"

"Nope. Just litterers." He winked and smiled. Why did the stubble on his perfect jawline have to be so damn sexy?

"Okay, okay! Move and I'll pick it up."

"My pleasure." He kicked it and it rolled behind me.

"That's not what I meant!"

"You didn't specify."

"Do you have more than zero friends? Or *any* people who don't hate you?"

"Never really thought about it. Pick up your trash, Sunflower."

I turned to get it, then I realized I'd be showing him my ass if I bent over. So I backed up and started to squat, but he was staring right at my cleavage. So I twisted my shoulder to the side and growled, "Getting a good view?"

"Not as good as I'd like."

I swiped the paper off the ground and stuffed it in my purse.

"So much better. And now I think it's time for you to get to your appointment."

"You are a completely diseased dick, aren't you?" I was now furious.

He laughed happily. "No. Not at all, Sunflower. I even have the papers to prove it."

"Stop calling me Sunflower!"

"Tell me your name and I'll call you that."

"No!"

"Sunflower it is." He smiled a smarmy smile that was frustratingly sexy.

"Seriously, does this approach work with women?"

"You tell me," he chuckled.

My eyes flared with anger. "You know what? I have to go!"

"To your appointment?" He stifled a laugh.

"Yes!"

"Better get moving. You've been standing here all day." He still leaned against the cement column like he was going to stand there gloating until I left. This guy was infuriating.

All he had to do was be the slightest bit polite and I'd be happy to stand and chat with him, but after the way he'd been treating me, I couldn't continue talking to him in good conscience. This guy had the maturity of a fourteen year old. I wouldn't encourage behavior like his by rewarding him with my name. I'd be a disappointment to myself and all of womankind. I turned to go. "Have a nice life, Pine Needle!"

He laughed. "Hey, Sunflower!"

I stopped but kept my back to him. "What?!"

Right at that moment, two young women turned into the parking garage. They were chatting and giggling with each other as they walked past me and hit the button for the elevator. They were both dressed to get attention from men: tight skirts, low cut tops, and slutty high heels. It took a moment, but the two of them slowly noticed Wes. Once they did, they couldn't keep their eyes off him.

The brunette with the salon curls smiled at me briefly.

I smirked back.

The built blonde with the Kate Upton hair and boobs muttered to her friend, "What's that guy doing?"

Salon Curls said, "He looks like a stalker."

"He's too cute to be a stalker."

The brunette giggled, obviously checking out Wes.

I shook my head, scowling. I'm sure these bim-hos were more Wes' speed than I was. They could have him.

The Kate Upton blonde twirled a lock of her hair extensions with her finger and said to me quietly, "Are you with that guy?"

"Pfft," I answered and shook my head. "He's all yours."

Her eyes did a devilish dance as she took Wes in. She bit her plump cherry glossed lower lip and flashed him a look that said, *Your place or mine?* Then her brows furrowed with uncertainty and she said to me, "Are you sure?"

"Help yourself. Really. He's all yours."

Her friend was as confused as she was, glancing between me and Wes.

The elevator dinged and the doors opened. The two bim-hos walked inside somewhat reluctantly. I walked into the elevator without looking back.

"I still didn't catch your name," Wes said behind me.

I didn't want to turn around to face him, but I couldn't stand in the elevator facing the two bim-hos. It would be weird. So I turned facing out and looked everywhere except at Wes. To his credit, he never took his eyes off me.

The elevator doors could close any time they wanted to.

"Your name, Sunflower." Wes' intense stare was making me squirm.

To my annoyance, the blonde with the Kate Upton hair was holding the DOOR OPEN button. She said to me, "I think he's talking to you."

"No, I think he's talking to you."

Upton Hair frowned, then smiled at Wes, arching her eyebrows to say to him, *You're talking to me, right?*

Wes said, "No, I'm talking to the pretty little sunflower standing next to you." His eyes were glued to mine. "The one who's pretending to ignore me."

Upton Hair finally smirked and said quietly enough that Wes couldn't hear, "He's your boyfriend, right? And you guys are having a fight, right?" The thrill I felt that a woman as attractive as her would make that assumption was extremely annoying. She still held the DOOR OPEN button and Wes still stared at me.

I grumbled, "He's not my boyfriend. We're not having a fight."

The brunette with the salon curls snickered, "I bet makeup sex with him is the best ever."

"He's not my boyfriend," I growled.

Wes heard that. "What she said, Sunflower. Makeup sex. You bent over the bed begging for more, me pulling your hair as I fuck you senseless from behind until you come so hard you can't stand up."

The two bim-hos tittered, drooling over Wes.

Salon curls giggled, "Oh my God."

Upton hair also giggled, "You're such a lucky bitch." She was talking about me. "I bet he has a huge cock." Now she was talking about Wes.

Salon curls tittered, "Totally."

Both of them were extremely annoying.

Wes smiled a cocky smile and cocked his cocky head to the side, completely loving this. "Like they said, Sunflower. Best. Makeup sex. Ever." He said it with a perfect California Mean Girl twang, that bottom of the voice clicky thing that Britney Spears popularized years ago and that now drove me crazy whenever I heard women talking like that. In 2016, everybody talked like a pop star.

Salon Curls realized that Wes was mocking her expertly and she scowled at him.

He struggled not to laugh. "Sorry, ladies. Just having fun with you."

Salon Curls couldn't decide if she wanted to smile and flirt with Wes or hate him.

I could relate.

Upton Hair decided now was a good time to take her finger off the DOOR OPEN button.

It took a moment for the doors to start closing, but it was more than enough time for my impulses to take over and walk me right out of the elevator.

As the doors closed behind me, Wes' grin widened into a full, unabashed smile. He opened his mouth to speak.

I glared at him, "Don't."

"Don't what, Sunflower?"

"Don't say what I think you're going to say."

"I was just going to ask your name."

"Do you really want to know?"

"Yes. I really do."

"It's—" I seriously considered not telling him. "It's Chelsea."

"That's my favorite name," he said with total sincerity.

"No it's not."

"It is now." He held out his hand to shake, the one with the chunky gold bracelet. "Wes. Pleasure to meet you, Chelsea."

"I'm not touching you." I stared at his hand, barely restraining my total disgust.

"You know you want to—"

Touch his cock. "No I don't!"

"—shake my hand. Because you're not a bitch."

"I am not a bitch!"

"That's what I just said," he smirked.

"No you didn't! You said… wait! Ugh! Would you stop! You're hurting my brain!" I was getting completely flustered. Wes' animal magnetism was undeniable. They didn't make men any more gorgeous than him. It was killing me that I was so attracted to him. But then I remembered two things. One, he'd basically ignored those two bimhos, and they were sending signals like crazy. Two, when I'd first met Wes, when I was just plain Jane, he'd treated me pretty much the same as he was now. But he'd also been nice and sweet and he'd made a huge impression on me that his current behavior couldn't erase. And I had to respect the fact that he wasn't suddenly kissing up to me now that I looked like a supermodel. He was acting like he genuinely didn't care if I hated him or refused to speak to him ever again, like he was completely unimpressed with my looks. *That* I could completely respect.

I took a deep breath. "Wes, if I shake your hand, will you stop being such an ass?"

He winced. "Mmmmm… maybe?"

"Wes!"

"Shake my hand, Sunflower. I promise I'll be nice."

"Promise?"

"Life is full of risks, Chelsea." He still held his hand out.

Still irritated, I grabbed it and shook it hard before throwing it down. "Happy now?"

"Almost."

"What do you mean almost?"

He slid his hand casually into the pocket of his slacks. "What are you doing tomorrow night, Sunflower?"

"Nothing with you," I grumbled.

"I've got this thing tomorrow and I sort of need a plus one."

"Ha! I'm not going on a date with you."

"Who said anything about a date? I just need arm candy."

"Arm candy? Wes, are you really this shallow?"

"I'm not. But it's a thing. I can't show up alone and I'd rather bring someone entertaining like you."

I scoffed, "Entertaining?"

"What about this isn't amusing?"

I snarled at him.

He smiled and shrugged, "If you don't wanna be my arm candy, I've got plenty of people I can call."

"If you hurry, I'm sure you can take both of the two Chicklets who just got in the elevator. I'm pretty sure they had bubble gum for brains."

He smirked, "No. Not them. Too common. I prefer gourmet."

"So call an escort service." I scowled, "I'm sure you're on a first name basis with every escort service in town."

He just smiled.

"Are you?"

He frowned. "No. Do you think I am?"

"Wes, I don't know what to think. So far the only thing I know about you is that you... you're..." I narrowed my eyes, trying to think of the perfect comeback. "Wes, you are a dirty riddle wrapped in the dickhole of a mystery inside the asshole of an enigma."

He chuckled, "Did you think of that just now, Sunflower?"

"I did."

"I'm impressed."

"At least one of us is."

He chuckled again. "See? This is why I'm asking you out for tomorrow."

"I thought you said it wasn't a date."

"It doesn't have to be."

"You just want to torment me all night, right?"

"I'll make you a deal. If you come as my plus one, I'll torment you all evening. If you *come* as my date, I'll just make you come. But no more than three times. We won't have time for more than that."

"Wes, I don't—" I spun my head in a circle and rolled my eyes and made the tiny mistake of glancing at his crotch. If I wasn't mistaken, he was hard. Which was funny, because I was 99% sure I was wet. And had been for at least the last five minutes. My body was loving every second of Wes' dirty innuendos and arrogant male bravado. I was completely disappointed in myself. I coughed out a laugh. "There will be no coming under any circumstances, Wes."

"So that's a yes?"

"I didn't agree to anything."

"Yet."

"Would you stop?!"

"Not until you say yes."

"Fine!" I threw my hands in the air, completely exasperated. "I'll go with you! To your thing! But no coming!"

"Deal." He pulled his phone out of his pocket. "Give me your number and I'll call you tomorrow morning with more details."

Chapter 17

After leaving Wes, I went back to the Promenade and ran into Victoria's Secret to buy some new bras and panties. If I was going out with Wes tomorrow night, I wasn't doing it wearing a sports bra and baggy granny panties underneath everything. Then I hopped in my car to go look for jobs in a less corporate setting. I drove all over Santa Monica and West LA, hitting up every non-corporate store I could find. Restaurants, coffee shops, health food stores, delis, furniture stores, yoga studios, anything I could find that wasn't a giant national chain.

Several hours later, I gave up and went home. Nobody was hiring and I was ready to drop.

My keys jingled as I walked along the balcony and approached my front door. I was surprised to discover it had been sanded and patched. It wasn't painted, but it was halfway to being fixed. Had Brodie done it, or had Petrak taken the initiative? I'd have to ask.

Thuds echoed inside Brodie's apartment and his door swung open. He leaned his head out, "Hey, Chelsea."

"Hey, Brodie." I said with an irritated sigh.

"How you like the door?" He leaned against the thin column of wall between our two doors, muscled arms folded across his chest and bulging proudly. He wore no shirt. It was nearly impossible not to stare.

Nearly. I inspected the work on my door instead. "Did you do this?"

"Of course I did it. Who else woulda done it?"

"Petrak."

"Right. Anyway, yeah. It was me."

I ran my hand over it and smirked at him, "Nice work. When are you going to paint it?"

"You gonna let me take you out for dinner?" His blue eyes did that hypnotic blazing thing. Not going to work on me.

"Paint my door first."

"The putty has to dry. Can't paint it till tomorrow."

"Not my problem."

"I'll paint it tomorrow. You want dinner after?" He was trying and I could respect that. I wasn't a total hard ass. Even excruciatingly gorgeous men deserved a second chance when they showed some effort.

Although I was actually considering letting Brodie buy me dinner (a girl had to eat and he had broken my door so he owed me), tomorrow I had plans with Wes. But it was difficult to think about Wes when this wall of muscled manhood was staring at me with blazing blue eyes that threatened to burn my clothes off.

Brodie rubbed a big hand casually over his abs. Boy oh boy, he was bold.

I scowled, "Must you?"

"What, this?" He kept rubbing himself. He also smelled faintly of musky cologne. Something that made me think of…

Sex.

Sex, sex, sex.

His scent was only slightly intoxicating but it had the potential to be insanely addictive. His cocky smile grew. He knew what he was doing.

"I have to go, Brodie. Talk to me *after* you paint my door." I pushed inside and slammed my door behind me. Yes, my heart was thudding. I was human and Brodie was a perfect specimen of raging male sexuality. He was also a tease. Although I wasn't sure if that definition fit because tease usually implied the teaser wouldn't put out, but it was obvious putting out was exactly what Brodie wanted to do. Or should I say put in. He'd had that look all over his face.

Let me put it in you, C.C.

Leaning against my front door, I squeezed my shaking knees together and let out a little moan.

"I heard that," Brodie's voice vibrated through the door.

"I stubbed my toe!" I shouted. How the heck had he heard that?

"Yeah, right."

"Will you go away, Brodie?"

"Something tells me that's not what you want me to do."

"Go, Brodie!"

His deep laugh rumbled through my door. "Catch you later, C.C."

After I heard his door close, I considered making a side trip to my bedroom to give myself some much needed sexual release. Between Wes and now Brodie, I was ready to pop. But the idea of masturbating with Brodie right next door was a bit too much. He would definitely be listening for my orgasm while giving himself one. I pushed images of him laying naked on his bed with his fist around his hard-on out of my mind. I would have to take care of myself later, when he wasn't around.

Maybe you could let him take care of you when he was around.

No way.

I knew trouble when I saw it.

What I needed right now was

(*Brodie*)

food because my fridge was empty and I was starving from job hunting all day. Time to go to the grocery store.

"Nice ass," some random guy said as he walked behind me in the produce section of Ralphs a half hour later. "How much to fuck it?"

I groaned loudly. I never thought I'd say it, but I was now officially sick of attention from random men. Flirtation from Brodie and all the guys at the Promenade was one thing, but being propositioned like this was a thousand miles past too much.

I spun around and glared at the owner of the foul mouth. "Really? *Really?* Do you talk to your mother with that mouth?" It wasn't my favorite witty retort, but it was the best I could think of on short notice when I didn't give a damn.

Foul Mouth wasn't a bad looking guy. He was even dressed nice: silver suit, silk shirt, shiny dress shoes. He looked so civilized and presentable. But with an opening like that, forget it.

He smirked, "I fuck with this mouth."

"Stop." I hung my head and shook it while pinching the bridge of my nose. "Just… stop."

"If you need any help squeezing the melons, lemme know." He winked at me.

That's when I remembered I was standing in front of the cantaloupe display, holding the cantaloupe I'd been about to put in my grocery cart.

I glared at him. "Would you go away?"

"Not till you gimme your number."

"My number is 911," I smirked.

"Come on. Gimme your number. I'll take you out and treat you right."

"No, seriously. It's 911. Call it right now and tell them you need an ambulance."

"An ambulance?" he chuckled. "What for?"

"Keep asking me for my number and you'll find out."

"You're a tease, you know that?"

I mimicked, "I'm not interested, you know that?"

He made a creepy duck faced smile. "You know what I'd do with you, little girl?"

"Serial kill me?" I scowled, disgusted. "Would you take a hike already?" For a second, I considered throwing my cantaloupe at his head, but thought better of it. I put it back on the stack and walked away with my grocery cart.

"Yeah, yeah, yeah. You just watch yourself, little girl. You piss off the wrong guy and—"

I was so mad I saw red. I turned around and whipped out my phone. "Fine. You wanna get to know me? Tell me your name and your phone number."

"Really?"

"Really." I arched my eyebrow, waiting.

He wasn't sure what to do.

"Any time," I grumbled, thumbs hovering over my iPhone.

"Lester." *The Molester.* "What's yours?"

"Last name, Lester?" I said it sweet, trying to stay calm.

"Clements."

"Show me your driver's license, Lester Clements."

"Why?"

I smiled seductively. "You wanna get to know me, Lester, this is how it starts."

He snorted a laugh, "I show you my ID, you'll suck my dick, right?"

I scowled, "Sure, Lester, sure."

"You a hooker? I was just joking around."

"No, Lester. I don't fuck for money."

"Okay then," he cackled. "I like free." He flipped open his wallet and pulled out his driver's license. He bit his lower lip and grinned while shaking his head in disbelief. "Easiest piece of ass I ever had."

"You're not supposed to say that out loud, Les."

"Right," he winked.

I snapped a photo of his driver's license with my phone.

"Why you taking a pic of my ID?"

"So I won't forget your name, Lester Clements."

He frowned, "You a cop or something?"

"No, Lester. But you oughta be a detective. Now take a hike and leave me alone."

He stuffed his wallet back in his pocket, his face growing red. "You're a privileged little bitch, you know that?"

"Go away, Lester." I pushed my grocery cart past him, the wheels rattling as I hurried away.

He grabbed my arm hard and squeezed, yanking me to a stop.

"Hey!" I growled, "Let go of me, Lester!" I tried to break free but his grip was too strong.

His voice cut low and dangerous. "You think you can walk around being a cunt and no one's gonna do nothing about it?"

"You started this, Lester. So back the fuck off."

He squeezed my bicep extra hard, fingers biting into my skin. He was going to leave bruises. "What's stopping me from taking you out back and raping the shit outta you, huh, Miss Priss? You think Lester Clements is my real name? You think that's a real ID?"

Was he bluffing? I had no idea. I had no experience with men like him. Was he a criminal or something? Organized crime maybe? I had no idea. But I knew for certain that my swansformation was now a curse after less than twenty-four hours.

"Answer me, sweetheart," he grunted. "GULCK!" Without any warning, Lester's face turned bright red and he suddenly folded over, grabbing for the side of the cantaloupe stand, trying to stop himself from falling to the linoleum floor.

That's right, I just kneed him in the balls.

You didn't go through life being five foot nothing without taking a few self defense classes. But I'd underestimated my new 5'9" strength. I could pack a wallop with my knee.

Oops.

Unfortunately for poor Lester, who now sat an his ass, he'd grabbed at the cantaloupes on his way down. A whole pile of them fell on his head and shoulders, bouncing off and rolling everywhere. Several thumped right on his crotch. He grunted each time one landed.

Poor thing.

Not.

I pushed my cart quickly but calmly around the corner of the produce section and left it and my groceries in the next aisle over. Adrenalin flooded my blood. I was crazy scared. Something about Lester said hardened criminal. I ran outside to the parking lot, my heart racing. My hands shook as I fished for my keys in my purse. Where was my car? I searched for it, unable to remember where I'd parked. The lot wasn't that big. I could see all of it from where I stood near the entrance to Ralphs. But I couldn't see my car anywhere! After what seemed like five minutes of scanning I finally found it and beelined straight for it.

"Watch where you're going!" A random woman shrieked behind me.

Over my shoulder, I saw Lester push past a middle aged woman going into Ralphs and lumber toward me, his face a twisted dark smudge, murder or worse in his eyes.

Oh, shit.

I ran toward my Hyundai, fumbling in my purse for my keys, trying to hit the panic button on the remote. I couldn't find the button so I pulled the whole thing out. Screw the panic button. My new plan was to jump in my car and lock the doors. I fumbled with my key ring and—

Shit!

I dropped them on the ground!

I was so panicked, I ran for it, trying to put distance between me and Lester. He could have my car and my keys. I didn't care. Not even thinking of calling for help, I sprinted past my car toward the exit and —

VROOM!!

Ran right into a black motorcycle turning into the parking lot. The guy on the bike braked hard when he saw me. The nose of it dipped as he stopped an inch from hitting me. I slapped my hands on the little front window to stop myself from slamming into it.

The tall muscled rider with a tight T-shirt flipped up his visor. "Chelsea?" Familiar blue eyes blazed.

"Blaze! I mean, Brodie!" What a relief.

"What are you doing?"

"Running away from that guy." I nodded behind me toward Lester, who slowed to a stop ten paces away. Fury fired from his eyeballs as his gaze danced between me and Brodie.

Brodie leaned to the side and scrutinized Lester. "That your boyfriend?"

"No!" I slapped his motorcycle. "He's some random asshole."

Brodie chuckled, "He looks pissed."

"You think?" I growled.

"What'd you do?" Amusement.

"I didn't do anything! Are you gonna help me or are you gonna get out of my way?"

Brodie's eyes smiled at me. "Get on."

"What?"

"Jump on my bike."

I didn't need to be told a third time. I tried to climb on, but I wasn't sure where to put my feet. Brodie reached back with his big hand, grabbed my thigh, and basically threw me onto the seat behind him.

"Hold on tight. Really tight."

Lester stared at us, planning out his next move, which included reaching into his suit jacket. Did he have a knife or a gun? I didn't know.

Brodie revved the engine. "Ready?"

I wrapped my arms around his waist and squeezed as hard as I could. His entire body was *really* hard. Having a wall of muscle between me and Lester was exactly what I needed right now.

Brodie revved the throttle and this time the motorcycle sped toward Lester. Brodie wasn't going to stop! He was going to run right over Lester!

Oh shit!!

WHAM!!!!

I coughed out a laugh, unable to believe what had just happened. As we'd driven by, Brodie had kicked Lester right in the face with the toe of his motorcycle boot.

In. The. *Face!*

Lester flew backward and landed in a heap with a strangled grunt. He *had* to be dead after that. I couldn't imagine him actually surviving. Unless Brodie had kicked him in the chest? I couldn't be sure.

It all happened so fast.

Brodie blasted the bike across the parking lot. I looked back to see if anyone had witnessed Lester's likely murder. Not yet.

When we hit the street, the bike leaned way over and I swore I was going to fall right off. I squeezed Brodie as tightly as I could. After that, we went really fast for several blocks and turned about twenty times. I just held on and trusted that Brodie wouldn't get us killed.

Suddenly, the bike slowed and I lurched forward, whacking my chin against Brodie's back.

"Fuck," he grunted.

"What happened?"

BRAA-AAH!!

The sound was the buzzing burp from the loudspeaker of the Santa Monica Police cruiser trailing behind us. It was so loud, I nearly let go of Brodie and fell off the back of the motorcycle. Somehow, I managed to hold on, probably because my adrenalin had spiked again. Why? Because someone at Ralphs had probably already discovered dead Lester the Molester, called 911, and now there was an APB out for Brodie and Clyde, a.k.a. Chelsea, a.k.a., I was now an accessory to motorcycle murder!

Fabulous!

Jail, here I come!

Did they still have the death penalty in California?

Yes!

Eek!

Chapter 18

Brodie parked the motorcycle in a red zone in front of a fire hydrant. The police cruiser rolled to a stop and double parked behind us, reds and blues flashing.

Brodie didn't have much choice about parking because the street was narrow and filled on both sides with parallel parked cars. Even though this was a tree-lined suburban neighborhood street, it was still Santa Monica. Eighteen million people and counting in the greater LA area. There was never parking anywhere.

Brodie put his kickstand down and leaned the bike on it.

"Sorry about this," I muttered. My assumption was Brodie had been speeding. Because of me.

He pulled off his helmet and tossed his hair out of his eyes. "Wasn't your fault."

"Yes it was."

"Don't worry about it." He swung his leg over the front of the bike with the grace of an Olympic hurdler or a martial arts master.

"How'd you do that?"

"Practice." He took my hands and helped me off the back of the bike.

A male officer stepped out of the cruiser wearing the standard black uniform and gun belt. His bulky bulletproof vest puffed out the uniform, making him very intimidating. He jabbered something into the radio clipped to his shoulder before walking up to us. He looked right at Brodie and said, "Sir, do you know why I stopped you?"

"Yup."

"I don't," I said, looking between them. "We weren't speeding, were we?" It had felt like we were, but what did I know?

"No, you weren't," the officer said. "Miss, are you aware that California has a helmet law?"

I was now. And I'd just broken it. Great. For the first time in my life, I consciously played dumb and hoped to hell my luxurious blonde hair would sell it. I said to the officer (as stupidly as possible with my voice rising like a little girl), "There is?"

"There is."

"Oh, gosh," I pouted breathlessly. "I'm really sorry, officer. I've never been on a motorcycle before." That was true.

Officer Doubtful smirked at me like I was lying.

"Honest. It was my first time. And we were just going a few blocks. See, we live in the same apartment building and we were—" *Running away from a guy who tried to rape me before Brodie killed him?* I sighed, feeling defeated. Maybe if I showed remorse he'd let us go with a warning or whatever. In a normal voice, I said, "I'm sorry, officer. It was my fault." *About the helmet, not the murder. That was Lester's fault! He was totally asking for it! He deserves to be dead.* "I should've known better than to ride without a helmet."

The officer looked at Brodie, "Do you have a second helmet for your friend?"

"I don't."

"Were you aware the helmet law applies to passengers as well as riders?"

"I was," Brodie said curtly.

The officer's eyes roamed Brodie's face for a moment. "Sir, can I see your license and registration?"

Brodie sighed and pulled his wallet out of his back pocket. "Yeah, yeah." He handed both to the officer.

"Thank you, sir." The officer turned to me and looked me over again.

Oh no.

He was going to ask for my license too.

I froze with fear.

If he did, I was in big trouble. I didn't look anything like the picture of plain Jane on my license. He'd probably think I'd stolen my own ID. But it was the only ID I had. What did they do with people who weren't in the system, because supermodel me didn't actually exist. There were no driver's license pictures of me/her, no college graduation photos, no high school pictures, etc., etc. This was bad, bad, bad.

What would happen then? Would they just lock me up and throw away the key? I didn't know for sure, but I knew things were about to get a whole lot worse.

Officer Doubtful was still staring at me.

He knows! He knows I'm hiding something!

Crap! Crap! Crap!

I swallowed hard and tried not to look scared to death. What happened if Officer Doubtful arrested me? Would he cuff me and stuff me and haul me down to the station to interrogate me for the murder of Lester the Molester? Would the police play good cop bad cop until I broke and told them everything? What would I do then? Call a lawyer I couldn't afford? I'd have to call my parents. What would they think if they came down to the police station and saw me? I knew one thing: they wouldn't think I was their daughter! How would I prove who I was to anybody? I supposedly knew Brodie but he didn't even know who I was! I wouldn't even be able to prove I was a US citizen! I'd probably end up deported to Russia and sold into white slavery!

This was a thousand different kinds of bad!

I cringed, trying to hide my naked fear.

How had this day gone from bad to worse to ass fucked in just one hour?

Then it hit me. I would tell the police I was Chelsea Johnson, my sister. I'd say we'd switched driver's licenses by mistake. That's it! I'd say we got carded at a nightclub last week and mixed up our IDs and now she was up in San Francisco so we were waiting until her next visit to switch them back, rather than risk losing them in the mail. It was perfect! Chelsea would totally back my play! But I'd just have to convince her I was me. No, wait. That wouldn't work. Chelsea didn't look like plain Jane me. Shit.

Shit, shit, shit.

There was no way out of this.

Maybe I'd just tell Officer Doubtful I'd lost my license and tell him I was Chelsea. Yeah, that was my only option. My sister was going to be pissed when—

The officer smiled at me. "Give me a minute." He walked away and climbed in his cruiser and started punching things on the computer screen next to the steering wheel.

I blew out a huge sigh, trying to rid myself of the now toxic levels of anxiety pumping through my system.

"You okay?" Brodie asked.

"Yeah," I lied. "Hey, I'm really sorry about this. This is all my fault."

"No worries. We're good."

"You sure?"

"Yeah, I'm sure." He rubbed his knuckle against my arm affectionately.

That made me feel better. Sadly, I was too stressed to be turned on, but it was nice to know he wasn't mad at me. I shook my head, "If it wasn't for that stupid Lester, none of this would've happened."

"Who?"

"That guy at Ralphs, the one you—"

"Shhh." He flicked his eyes toward the cop car.

"Oh, right." While I tapped my foot nervously, I noticed the officer kept staring at me.

"That cop is checking you out," Brodie grumbled.

"No he's not. He's a cop. He's probably profiling me. Wondering if I'm high on meth."

Brodie snorted. "He's checking you out. Guy has a dick, doesn't he?"

I watched the cop closely. Brodie was right. When I watched the cop, he stopped watching me. "Okay. Maybe you're right." I walked around the motorcycle so it was between me and Officer Wandering Eyeballs.

Brodie smiled. "Told ya. For a hot chick, you're pretty clueless when it comes to dudes."

I frowned, "Hot chick?"

"What? It's not an insult."

"Yeah, but it's still degrading."

"How?"

"If I have to explain, it's definitely degrading."

He chuckled, "That makes no sense."

"Shut up."

Officer Eyeballs stepped out of his car a minute later and handed Brodie his license and registration. "Sorry for the delay, Mr. Bolden."

I muttered, "Your last name is Bolden?"

He nodded.

I snickered to myself. It figured. I said to the cop, "We're neighbors. He just moved in next door the other day."

"Right." The cop nodded, not caring. "Sir, unless you have a helmet for your lady friend, I can't let her back on your motorcycle."

Brodie barked, "How am I supposed to give her a ride home?"

The officer spread his hands and shrugged as if to say he couldn't help.

I groaned. "I guess I'm walking."

Officer Eyeballs said, "I'd be glad to give you a ride, miss. If you need one."

"I bet you would," Brodie smirked. He shot me a side glance that said, *Told ya.*

"Oh, uh…" I stammered. "Do I have to? Or can I just walk?"

The officer said, "It's up to you, miss. But I'd be happy to drive you wherever you need to go."

"You know what?" Brodie blurted. "I'll walk her home. You don't need to give her a ride." He sounded irritated. "What's your name, officer?" He read the man's name tag. "We'll walk. That cool with you?"

Officer Eyeballs smiled an angry smile up at Brodie, who was at least two inches taller. "Fine by me. But you better move your bike. Unless you want me to impound it."

I rolled my eyes. Men.

Brodie glared at Officer Eyeballs, his jaw muscles ticking repeatedly. After a strained moment, Brodie's lips tightened over his teeth like he wanted to punch Eyeballs in the face. Or kick him to death.

Eyeballs was amused, like he was up for whatever Brodie threw at him. "Are we having a problem here, Mr. Bolden?"

Oh, geez. Who was this douche? Was he one of those cops who thought he was above the law?

"Nope," Brodie said. "We're good. All good. Aren't we good, C.C.?"

"Uhhhh…" I stammered.

"Miss, would you like me to give you a ride home? Your friend seems agitated."

"Yeah, *miss*," Brodie said sarcastically. "Do you want Officer Nice Guy to give you a ride home?" If Brodie didn't get himself under control, he was going to get himself arrested.

I grimaced, "Um, I think I can walk, if that's okay with everybody?" I looked between the two men.

Eyeballs arched an eyebrow and looked at me.

"She'll walk," Brodie said victoriously. "You'll walk."

"I'll walk." I forced a smile.

"Oh, you know what?" Brodie said. "I think my bike chain is loose. Okay with you if I walk it home, Officer? On the sidewalk, I mean?"

Eyeballs shrugged, "As long as you push it and don't run the engine, sure."

"Great." Brodie smiled at me, "Wanna help me walk my bike home, miss?" He was mimicking Eyeballs.

"Oh, uh, sure. But don't call me miss." I was getting irritated with Brodie's irritation. Yes, I was flattered he was being protective, but he was taking things a bit too far.

Eyeballs said to me, "You sure you don't want a ride home?"

I rolled my eyes. Officer Overly Chivalrous was getting to be a bit much. "I'm fine. Thanks." I just wanted him to leave.

"Suit yourself," Eyeballs said with a wink. "If you need any help, don't hesitate to call the Santa Monica Police." He pulled a business card out of his breast pocket.

Brodie turned to the side and chuckled, "I can't believe this."

I took Eyeballs's card. "Thanks."

"Call me…" he said and his eyes flashed suggestively. "… if you ever need *anything*."

I blinked my eyes and shook my head in disbelief. "Wait, did you just hit on me?"

Brodie's face turned red and he laughed angrily.

"No, ma'am." Now he was calling me ma'am, covering his ass. "I said, call me if you ever need anything. From the Santa Monica Police."

"That's not how he said it," Brodie grumbled.

"Have a nice day," Eyeballs said before sauntering to his car and climbing inside.

"What the fuck!" Brodie seethed in a whisper. "That guy just made a play for you!"

"What do you care? You're not my boyfriend." Frankly, I was irritated with both men for their bad behavior.

"You want *him* to be your boyfriend?"

"Would you just shut up until he's gone?"

Eyeballs sat in his car, glancing between us and his computer. I didn't want to wait around and give him a chance to arrest either of us.

"Let's go, Brodie."

He stood his motorcycle, toed the kickstand, and rolled it onto the sidewalk.

I followed.

We walked to the end of the block and turned the corner. With Eyeballs out of sight, I felt immediate relief. But neither of us said anything for two more blocks.

"That guy was a fucking cock gobbler," Brodie barked.

I suppressed a laugh. "I don't think that's his thing."

"Right. I forgot. He was interested in you, not me. Unless you have a cock. You don't have a cock, do you?"

I laughed openly now. "No!"

"So he was interested in you. Like I said."

"Jealous?" I smiled at him.

"Me? Jealous? Of that prick? Fuck no."

"You sure?"

"Sure I'm sure. If that guy wasn't a cop, I would've twisted him into a pretzel." Brodie definitely looked strong enough and big enough to have done it.

"Brodie, do you know what denial is? It's this." I gestured at him, my palms raising and lowering like I was one of those Price Is Right models showing off the prizes.

"What are you talking about? Wait, you weren't into that guy, were you?"

"Would it bother you if I was?"

"Shit. Are you one of those women who can't resist a man in

uniform? You are, aren't you?" He laughed. "Some women go crazy for that shit. Don't let the badge fool you. A guy like that is too big a pussy to be an outlaw, so he joins up with a bunch of other pussies so they can harass guys like me."

"Awww, poor little Brodie. Is the thug life too hard for you?"

He smirked, "I'm not a thug. Or an outlaw. But you should be. I saw how you flirted your way out of a citation."

"What?! I did not!"

"You kidding? You're a total outlaw biker babe and you don't even know it."

I scoffed, "I'm not an outlaw biker babe."

"That's what they all say. Wait'll we get you a helmet and some skin tight leathers."

"We?"

He smiled and a sexy dimple popped out. "Yeah, we. I'm picturing you in some tight ass leather pants with the side laces all the way from ankle to hip. And a wrap around zipper. You know, the kind that goes around from front to back like a G-string." His eyes flashed as he stared at me. "You totally have the ass for it. Mmmm, mmmm. I would tear that shit off you in a heartbeat. Unzip that zipper and take a bite out of your wet pussy before I sink my dick into it."

Yes, I was getting turned on. Having a caveman save you then drool over you while suggesting he dress you in trashy biker wear before he fucked you was definitely a guilty pleasure. As frustrating as my swansformation had been, it did have it's perks. This was one.

Trying to hide my blush, I took a deep breath and sighed, "Easy, cowboy. Just because I've ridden on your horse doesn't mean you get to ride me." Okay, maybe I shouldn't have said it quite like that. No, I wanted to say it like that. Let him squirm because he was making me squirm.

He laughed, "Okay, cowgirl." Suddenly his eyes bored into mine. "You do the riding. Regular or reverse, I don't care which."

Against my will, my eyes flared back at him. I pictured me sitting on his cock, hands planted on his hard chest as I ground into him and rode him like the stallion he was.

Oh, wow.

He nodded, "Thought so. You're thinking about it right now." I didn't deny it. "You like to be in control, don't you? You like holding the stick. Am I right?"

Maybe I did. I smiled. And blushed. And looked away. "Oh, shit!"

"What? I say something wrong?"

"No! My keys! And my car! I just remembered they're back at

Ralphs with that guy Lester! What are we gonna do?"

Brodie grunted, "Fuck that guy. If he isn't dead, I'll kill him when we get there."

"No, I'm serious!"

"So am I."

I stopped on the sidewalk. "Are you kidding? You'd murder a guy?" *For me?* Should I be swooning or calling Officer Eyeballs? I'd never known a murderer personally, but sometimes they moved in right next door.

Brodie stared at me. "If he tries to hurt you, yeah I fucking will."

"You're serious?"

"Dead serious."

I winced. "Uhhh..."

"Relax. I'm not gonna kill the guy on sight. But if he makes a move on you? I will end him." The way he said it was so dangerous, I believed he would.

"Let's worry about that later," I said nervously. "I just want to get my keys and my car."

"Yeah, sure. Let's go."

Chapter 19

"Can you describe your keys to me?" The man asking was the curly-haired store manager at Ralphs. He stood in the manager's island between all the registers.

Brodie stood beside me.

I said, "Yeah. There's a key to my Hyundai and a few others, and a Power Puff Girls enamel keychain." George had bought it for me at San Diego Comic Con two years ago.

The manager smiled, "That's them." They jingled when he reached under the counter and pulled them out. Thank goodness he didn't ask for my ID.

"Thank you so much. Can I ask, do you remember who turned them in? I'd like to, uh…" *make sure it wasn't Lester the Murdering Molester.* "…thank them.""

The manager, who seemed nice, looked up thoughtfully. "Let me think… You know, I'm sorry, but so many people have been in and out all day, I honestly can't remember."

"It wasn't a guy wearing a silk shirt, was it?"

He shook his head, "I can't really remember. Sorry."

"Thanks anyways."

I didn't know why I was asking. A guy like Lester probably would've kept them and tried to follow me home so he could sneak in while I was sleeping and try to rape me before killing me. I repressed a shudder.

Brodie and I walked out to my car.

"That was easy," he said.

"Yeah, but what about Lester?"

"Who?"

"The guy who tried to attack me. What happened to him?"

"Well, if he was dead, his body would still be here, the cops would be swarming the parking lot, there'd be yellow crime scene tape everywhere, and a thousand people gawking."

"So he's not dead," I said, disappointed.

"That's a bad thing?"

"What if he's… I don't know. What if he's in his car watching and waiting to follow me home?"

"Let him. I'll break that guy in half."

"I think he had a gun, Brodie."

"Did you see a gun?"

"No. But he looked like the type."

"What type is that?"

"Mafia? I don't know."

"Was he Russian? Italian?"

"I don't think so. He didn't have an accent."

"Doesn't mean he wasn't mafia."

I hated that this had happened. I wanted my plain Jane life back. Speaking of which, if I somehow managed to turn back to my normal self, Lester would never recognize me. The only question was, would I change back to myself if I took the ring off? Maybe it only worked once and I'd stay like this forever. I didn't fucking know.

"What?" Brodie asked.

"Nothing."

"You can tell me."

I smiled at him forcefully, "Trust me, it will sound ridiculous. So let's just focus on Lester, all right?"

"How about we focus on dinner."

"Huh?"

"Wasn't that why you went to Ralphs?"

"Oh yeah. Why the heck were you at Ralphs when I was at Ralphs? It seems a bit stalkerish, don't you think?"

He snorted, "It's the closest grocery store to our building."

"No, Star Market is closer."

"I don't even know what that is."

"It's the Persian deli on Santa Monica Boulevard."

"Whatever. I shop at Ralphs. And you need food. You're turning into a bitch."

"I am not!"

"I said turning into. But we can stop the process with food." He winked.

"Ass." I slapped his muscled arm where his tattoos peeked below the sleeves of his T-shirt. "But I'm not going back into Ralphs."

"No prob. I'll take you out. Anywhere you wanna go, C.C."

"How about takeout?"

"Your place or mine?" He offered a smug smile.

"No sex, Brodie."

"I didn't say anything about sex, C.C."

"You're a man. You didn't have to."

He laughed, "Let's do it."

I glared at him.

He smirked, "I meant, go get food."

"I mean it, Brodie. No sex!"

"When was the last time you got laid, C.C.?" Brodie asked before taking a bite of his burrito.

"Not as recently as you," I laughed and grabbed a warm tortilla chip from the greasy paper bag and dipped it in one of our plastic cups of salsa. We sat at my round dinner table, which stood between my kitchenette and the living room. Several aluminum foil takeout trays of Mexican food were open between us.

"I think you're well past due for an orgasm or five, C.C. You've got that uptight unfucked thing going. The one that says you need to come all over a hard cock so you can ease up a notch."

I sat back in my chair and folded my arms across my breasts, partially out of irritation and partially because this conversation was making my nipples hard, and I didn't want Brodie to notice. "How do you know I'm not a lesbian?"

He shrugged. "Dykes like dicks too. Why you think they use strap ons?"

"Do you have any idea how ignorant that sounds?"

"What? It's true. Everybody likes dick."

"Except yours."

He laughed. "Okay. Whatever you say, C.C."

"Some of us can get through life just fine without dick."

"I don't know if you've heard, but in the twenty-first century, some people enjoy casual sex. Men *and* women."

"Emphasis on casual," I snorted derisively.

"What, do the people in your world have to be married before they're allowed to fuck? Or just engaged?"

"How did we get on the topic of sex again? Oh yeah. Because it's all you ever talk about."

"Just answer the question."

I groaned. "No, they don't have to be married. And no, I'm not a virgin."

"I hope not," he chuckled.

"What's that supposed to mean?"

"I don't do virgins."

"And you won't be doing me, B.B."

He snickered, "Butt brains. Remind me never to tell you what C.C. really means."

"I thought it was short for Chel-*see*."

"That too." He was grinning from ear to ear.

"What else does it mean?" I demanded.

"Not telling."

"Let me guess. It's something sexual."

"You're on the right track," he smiled.

"Brodie, do you ever stop thinking about sex?"

"When you're around? Nope."

"Are you walking Viagra or something?"

"No. You are. One look at you and *BAM!* Punched a hole right through my jeans. Already had to throw out two pairs since I met you."

"Did not," I laughed.

He just grinned and popped another tortilla chip in his mouth.

My iPhone sat on the table beside me. It made a bubbling noise, signaling a new text. A second later, it bubbled twice more.

"You need to get that?" he offered.

"Let me check." I picked it up and swiped over to the messenger.

Wes: Make sure you get plenty of sleep tonight.

Wes: Tomorrow could be late.

Wes: Don't want you falling asleep and missing all the fun.

I texted back: **Okay, Dad. Should I take a nap tomorrow afternoon too?**

Wes: Not a bad idea. We can do it together.

Me: I'm not napping with you.

Wes: You're right. We wouldn't get much sleep.

Me: Dirty pig.

Wes: I knew you loved bacon. Talk to you tomorrow, Sunflower. Oink oink!

Amused, I smiled to myself.

"One of your boyfriends?" Brodie asked while munching on another tortilla chip.

I glared at him, "Why, yes, Brodie. One of my six boyfriends. If you're lucky, you can be lucky number seven."

"No shit?" He didn't sound excited. He sounded disappointed, like he took me seriously.

"No, butt brain. I don't have *any* boyfriends. Or friends with benefits. Geez, are you that gullible?" I wasn't sure why, but I felt like he was assuming I was a slut like him, which made me angry.

"What the fuck, C.C.," he said, slightly offended. "Chicks as hot as you always have a line of guys waiting to be next."

"Are you calling me a slut?" I was ready to lecture him for making assumptions about my nonexistent sex life. I'd been one step above celibate for years.

"Relax. I didn't say you had guys lined up. I said guys *are* lined up. Whether you know it or not, every guy who knows you is constantly wondering when he'll get a shot at you."

"A shot? You mean have sex?" I scowled when I said the word sex.

He rolled his eyes. "Don't be so uptight, C.C. Some guys, yeah. All they want is to fuck you. Other guys want to put a ring on that shit and start making babies so they can send out Christmas cards to their buddies every year with you in them. I would. Anyway, whatever kind of guy we're talking about, I promise you, every guy who knows you wants you."

I couldn't believe my ears. Despite the reality of my swansformation, inside I was still the little nerd girl who couldn't get a single guy from speed dating to call her back. Not even the boring ones like un-extreme Mike. I smiled at Brodie, "So, which guy are you?"

He picked up his burrito, but paused before taking a bite. Then he said, "Not the guy who just texted you."

I rolled my eyes. "Eat your burrito, butt brain."

He laughed before chomping his burrito.

I forked up a bite of my cheese enchilada and chewed it down. "So tell me, Brodie. What do you do when you're not busy fixing broken doors or saving damsels in distress at the local grocery store?"

"You wouldn't believe me." He smiled and took another bite of his burrito.

"Handyman?"

He finished chewing and wiped his mouth with a paper napkin. "Not anymore."

"Don't retire too soon. You still owe me a painted door."

"Don't worry, I *always* finish what I start." He winked, clearly making an allusion to sex.

I ignored it. "Okay, you're not a handyman. Auto mechanic?"

"Used to do that too. Now I just work on my bike or my friends' bikes when they need help."

"Okay, how about drug lord?"

He grinned, "Not that either."

"I'm running out of ideas, Brodie. Help me out."

"Keep guessing."

"Underwear model?"

He arched an eyebrow.

"You are *not* an underwear model."

"Was."

"What? I don't believe you."

"I don't need you to believe me," he laughed. "You gonna eat that second enchilada?"

"Go ahead," I said absently, my iPhone already in my hand. I swiped over to Safari and typed Brodie Bolden into Google. A bunch of black and white photos loaded, all showing Brodie in underwear with the same incredible abs I'd seen in real life. I clicked on a bunch of the photos to enlarge them. "Holy shit! That's you!"

He smirked while forking up my enchilada.

I looked at several more pictures. "Wait, did you pose for Calvin Klein?"

He smiled around a big mouthful of enchilada.

I gasped, "You did not!"

He just grinned and chewed.

"Wow, I live next door to a CK celebrity!"

He shook his head, "No. I'm just a regular guy."

"B.S.! Look at you!" I showed him another photo on my phone.

"That's me," he said, dismissively.

"How did you get into modeling?"

He shrugged. "Met some guys at a gym here in LA who were doing it. They were putting together a beefcake calendar and needed another guy. One thing led to another and the next thing I knew, my abs were everywhere. But it was always more of a side thing. Never did it full time. Always had a regular job."

"Even when you were doing the underwear stuff?"

"Yup."

"Are you still modeling?"

"Nah." He wiped his fingers on his napkin. "I got tired of it. Too much competition. And it got old after a while. People judging you solely on your looks. Seemed like a waste of my life."

"Whoa, who are you? Are you the Brodie I know?"

"Same one."

"Okay, if you're not modeling anymore, what do you do for your regular job now? Or did you retire on all the money you made?"

"It doesn't pay that good. I've got some cash saved up, but I'm not retiring on it. So I'm still working. I've always been working."

"Doing what?"

He took a deep breath. "You really wanna know?"

"That's why I'm asking."

"I teach developmentally challenged adults how to manage their lives."

I laughed in his face for a full ten seconds. "You do not."

He scowled at me, sat back in his chair, and tossed his wadded napkin on the table. "I told you you wouldn't believe me. And, yeah, I do."

"Wait, really?"

"Really."

"Like, what do you do?"

"I've got a bunch of clients. Right now, most of them are young autistic men. Couple have Asperger's. Most are high functioning enough to work regular jobs, but they need a lot of help managing the basics like paying bills or getting around town or remembering to brush their teeth and take a shower. One of my kids, Wyatt, can't even do that."

I felt my heart pinch when he called Wyatt his kid.

"He'll probably never be able to work a job. I'm like his big brother. I pretty much just spend time with him so his parents get some down time. They'll have to take care of him his whole life. See this?" He pointed at a small fading bruise shaped like a crescent moon just below his left eye. "Wyatt clipped me there a couple weeks ago when I took him to the Santa Monica Pier to ride the rides and play all the games. He doesn't like the coasters, just the basic stuff like the merry-go-round or Pacific Plunge. That's the one that bounces you up and down like twenty feet. Pretty chill. He loves that shit. Laughs his ass off the whole time."

"How old is Wyatt?"

"He's seventeen."

I knew the ride and pictured the two of them on the bench seat with their arms in the air, laughing as they bounced. I hid a secret smile.

"Anyway, he got too excited when he was playing that game where you smash all the mechanical gophers with the padded mallet. When he finally hit one, I cheered him for doing a great job, so he hit me with the mallet like I was a gopher."

"Really?"

He grinned. "Yup. Whacked me good. Right in the eye." Brodie chuckled and shook his head as a faraway smile eased onto his face. "Great kid. But I always gotta be on my toes with him. He almost broke my nose a month ago. Tried to hug him and he bashed me with his forehead and gave me a bloody nose. Kid's skull is made of steel."

"Wow, Brodie. How did you ever get into doing this sort of thing?"

He shrugged. "My older brother Brian is autistic. I did the same thing for him growing up. By the time I was sixteen and had a driver's license, and he was twenty-two, I knew more about how to take care of myself than he does now. Back then, I was always showing him stuff because he was my brother. It's just what I did. You ever see that movie Rain Main?"

"No, sorry."

"Rain Main is a movie with Tom Cruise and Dustin Hoffman. They're brothers and Hoffman is autistic. Watch it some time. That's kind of what it's like with me and Brian, except Brian can't count cards in his head like a human computer or hear a song once and play it note for note. He can't do any of that savant stuff. He's just autistic and needs a lot of help. Still lives with my parents down in Garden Grove, but I see him all the time. Anyway, I do the same thing for my clients that I did for Brian growing up. Kind of fell into it, I guess," he smiled.

My jaw dropped. I couldn't believe what I was hearing.

My heart had completely melted for Brodie.

He smiled at me like it was business as usual. "That's what I do these days. Between that and my savings, I get by."

I was suddenly seeing Brodie in an entirely new light. "That is incredible, Brodie."

"Nah. It's just my job."

"Wow. Do you, um, do you ever work with women? Do women even get autism? Sorry if I sound stupid. I'm just curious."

"Nah, you don't sound stupid. But it's funny you say that. Until a few years ago, there's been almost zero research about women with autism, how to diagnose them, treat them, all that. It used to be women on the spectrum would get misdiagnosed with all kinds of *other* mental health problems. Borderline personality, OCD, agoraphobia, bipolar, depression, anxiety, eating disorders, you name it. All kinds of wrong things. Nobody knew it was autism or Asperger's underneath it all."

"Wow." I was partially wowing because I could imagine how hard it must be for women with autism to get the help they needed, but I was mainly wowing because Brodie knew all these facts off the top of his head. I was definitely impressed.

"I know, right? The good news is, nowadays there's all kinds of studies looking into it and the therapy strategies are way more effective."

"Do you know why it took so long for science to realize that women can have autism too? It just seems so bizarre they didn't know."

"One key thing they've worked out is that girls tend to go undiagnosed because they're a lot better at faking social relationships. On the outside, they seem normal. It's what's going on inside that makes all the difference."

"Oh?"

"Yeah. They say for a girl with autism, the social part of her brain can be just as active as the social brain of a normal boy the same age. But they aren't boys. They're girls trying to relate to other girls, and girls are all about relationships and emotions. So girls with autism have to use other parts of their brains to figure out how to act in social situations, which stresses them out because it's hard work. It's like they're pretending they're sociable when they aren't. They force eye contact, force body language, mimic mannerisms, that kind of thing. Some autistic women say it's sort of like doing advanced math to solve every social situation. Math all the time, whenever they're around people. It doesn't come easily or naturally for them. So they end up feeling disconnected from other girls. They'd rather be alone reading books or playing with dolls or whatever. They can't relate to all that gossipy social hierarchy bullshit that normal women love to worry about. Does she like me, does she hate me, are we friends, are we feuding? Shit, I can't even relate to that shit." He smirked and the cutest dimple tugged at the corner of his mouth.

"Me neither," I laughed. "I'd rather read a book or play with dolls."

"You? Nah. I can't picture you sitting around by yourself. Too many guys chasing you around. You probably spend all your time fighting them off."

"Something like that," I smiled absently as memories from my childhood resurfaced. Brodie didn't know I'd been a nerd girl all my life. He didn't know I liked books better than boys or even girls because books never made fun of me or bullied me. He didn't know that walking down the Shopkins aisle at Target or going into the Disney Store felt slightly like heaven to me. Did that make *me* autistic?

"With high-functioning women, they can go completely undiagnosed for years. Well into adulthood. They can go to college, hold down a job, have seemingly functional relationships, everything. We didn't realize my sister had Asperger's until she was thirty."

"Wait, you have a sister too?"

"Yeah."

"How old is she?"

"Now? Brenna is thirty-three."

Brenna.

Where had I heard that name recently? A memory of a woman screaming echoed through my brain. *Is Brenna one of your clients?! Or do you fuck her for free?!* Plastic Blonde had screamed those exact words outside Brodie's door yesterday.

Was she talking about the same Brenna?

It would be rude to ask, but I suspected it was. Brenna wasn't a name you heard every day. Was it possible that whole scene outside yesterday was a misunderstanding? Based on what Brodie had just told me, it seemed entirely possible. Was it also possible that Brodie was a sweetheart underneath his bad boy exterior?

Maybe I could ask him indirectly. "Is Brenna one of your clients?"

He smiled, "She acts like it sometimes, but no. Her work is hanging out with women her age who don't have Asperger's. They do shit like go to the hair salon together or girl's night out. But when she goes out *without* her therapy group, believe me, she asks me a ton of questions afterward. What did it mean when somebody said this, or somebody acted like that?" He laughed. "I can't believe my older sister asks me for advice about how to understand women. What the fuck do I know? It's pure comedy. Anyway, I do my best. But, you know," he shrugged, "I can't really teach her how to be a girl. You know what I mean?"

I was suddenly convinced that Brodie's Brenna was the same one that Plastic Blonde had been shouting about. It had to be some kind of misunderstanding. I had to know for sure.

"Brodie, can I ask you something?"

"Sure."

"Who was that woman yelling outside your apartment yesterday?"

In an instant, his face darkened and hardened. "Ashleigh? Fuck that bitch. Wait, did you hear her?"

"I did," I said with quiet respect. "Was she yelling about your sister? She kept saying Brenna."

Brodie's face soured and he shook his head. "That bitch went through my phone. Saw a picture of me out with Brenna and her friends at one of her ladies night therapy things. I go sometimes. I think Brenna is trying to set me up with her friends. Anyway, Brenna had a few drinks that night and had her arm around me in the pic. Ashleigh thought Brenna was some chick I was fucking on the side. Said all kinds of nasty shit about her. Ahhh, fuck Ashleigh. Total bitch. Do me a favor and don't mention her name again. I can't fucking stand her."

"Didn't you tell her you had a sister?"

"Hell no. Someone like Ashleigh wouldn't understand. Hell, I wouldn't want her to ever meet Brenna. Ashleigh was the same kind of pinhead who tortured Brenna in high school."

Quietly, I said, "Then why were you sleeping with her?"

Brodie looked at me for a long time before shaking his head. "Fuck, I don't know. Because I'm an idiot with a dick for brains?"

"Butt for brains," I grinned.

He smirked, "Right."

I smiled at him, suddenly wondering who this man was beneath his arrogant asshole exterior. He was a mystery to me, but I wanted to find out more. A lot more.

"What," he chuckled, glancing away nervously, so different from the cocky Brodie I thought I knew. The real Brodie could be somewhat shy.

"Nothing," I muttered.

By nothing I meant everything.

My entire body warmed with thoughts of Brodie.

He sure was something else.

"There's no more chips!" I shook the greasy paper bag two hours later. We'd been sitting at my dinner table talking about anything and everything this entire time. "You ate the last one!"

"You did. You took it from me an hour ago."

"Liar," I giggled.

"Whatever you say, tortilla thief." He smiled at me.

I sighed. "I hate to say this, but I should probably get to bed."

"That an invitation?"

"No!" I slapped his rock hard shoulder, hurting my hand more than him. "Ow!" I shook my hand. "Are you made of steel?"

"*Vanadium* steel," he emphasized. "It has a higher tensile strength than regular stainless."

I rolled my eyes. "Nerd."

He laughed and shrugged.

Despite Brodie's over-sexed persona, there was more to him than met the eye and he was a decent guy underneath. During our conversation, he'd shared more stories about growing up with an autistic brother and working with his clients.

"I should probly go anyway," he said, standing up from the table. "I gotta be up pretty early tomorrow. My buddy Alan needs to learn how to ride the Metro. So I'm taking him tomorrow morning when the crowds are light. Gonna show him how to buy tickets, figure out which side of the platform to stand on, how to get on and off the train, where to sit, when to get off. You know, subway basics."

"Really?"

"Yup. Alan asks a thousand questions about every little thing, so I need to be focused. That means sleep." He grabbed the aluminum trays that held the remnants of our Mexican food, wadded everything up, and put it in the plastic bag they'd come in before wandering into my kitchenette. "Where's your trash?"

"Under the sink."

"Found it." He tossed it in and slapped the cupboard door shut. Then he grabbed a sponge from the sink, ran some water on it, and wiped my table down.

"You don't have to do that."

"Now you don't either." He wiped crumbs to the edge of the table and caught them with his cupped hand, then kept wiping with the wet sponge until the entire table glimmered like an ice rink. He smiled when he finished and I smiled back.

Okay, okay. Brodie wasn't even close to being the shallow asshead I'd thought. Sometimes first impressions were wildly inaccurate.

I walked him to my door, which was only five feet from my dinner table, but it felt like the polite thing to do.

"Let me get the door for you," I lunged past him and grabbed for the doorknob.

"I got it," he lunged at the same time and wrapped his hand around mine. His huge body hovered over me like a protective shield. Heat radiated from him in waves.

A fountain of warmth blossomed up my arm from where Brodie's hand touched mine, soaking my entire body. I turned and looked up at him. His eyes smoldered. He swallowed hard. I did too.

Was he nervous?

I didn't know, but I sure was.

"Sorry," he muttered, dropping his hand from mine. He took a step back.

Paralyzed, I still held the doorknob. All I could do was look at him and think, *Social worker, life saver, loving brother, what other amazing qualities did this man have?* Did there need to be more?

Having lost complete control of my body, I could only observe myself as I leaned my back against my door, still clutching the doorknob like a safety valve that I desperately wanted to open but couldn't, no matter how hard I tried to turn it. There was no way for me to open my door and release all the tension in the room. The only other thing I could open at that moment was my heart, but I was afraid to do that.

Brodie mumbled, "I should…" He stepped toward me. I was blocking his way.

I wasn't going to kiss him. I wasn't.

So I grabbed the front of his T-shirt in a fist and twisted it into a knot and pulled.

He didn't move an inch but he stared at my fist. Then stared at me. His eyes burned. My entire body burned. My chest heaved with desire. I narrowed my eyes in an angry challenge because anger was what I felt toward him. Repressed anger from before, for the way he'd treated me as plain Jane, for the way he'd treated Ashleigh before I'd heard the whole story. But more than anything, I felt an undeniable desire to make this man mine.

I growled, "I hate you, Brodie."

The blue embers of his eyes flamed and he grunted once before attacking me, slamming me against the door. His lips were harsh, demanding. His tongue fought its way into my mouth. Once inside, I couldn't resist it no matter how hard I tried. But I fought back anyway, my tongue attacking his.

A hard hand grabbed my breast, squeezing me to the edge of pain before releasing and massaging. Then he pinched my hardened nipple and did the same, twisting and releasing at the edge of intensity.

Still we kissed.

I moaned into his mouth and hooked my ankle around the backs of his legs. Ten fingers dug into my ass and I hopped up, wrapping both legs around his waist, opening myself to him. His hot erection ground against the crotch of my jeans through his. I laced my arms around his neck, our mouths melting together as we swallowed each other alive.

This felt too damn good to continue.

I never wanted it to end.

But I had to stop this. I could never be with a man like Brodie. People didn't change. He may have been a social worker, but he was also a shallow manwhore. He'd just fucked Ashleigh, what, yesterday? And now he was kissing me?

No.

Too soon.

This was about him being horny for hot supermodel Chelsea, not about him wanting me, plain Jane Johnson.

My legs went lax.

I broke our kiss. "Stop, Brodie. Stop—"

He sighed and leaned his forehead against the door. His hands on my ass softened and he lowered me to the floor and he took a step back.

I grabbed the doorknob again, but it wouldn't turn.

We were stuck right here, face to face, undeniable passion burning between us.

I was very disappointed in my part of this passion. His I could understand. But mine was… misplaced. Opportunistic.

"Sorry." He raked a hand through his hair, hiding his eyes, staring at the floor. "I shouldn't have kissed you. I need to go." He reached for the doorknob and I released it. He turned it and opened it and grabbed his motorcycle helmet off the floor by the door before walking out without looking back.

I stood there in my open doorway, feeling the cool night breeze.

He turned left, striding down the balcony away from his apartment. The balcony thudded beneath his boots.

I stepped outside and hissed, "Brodie! Where are you going?" Somehow, this felt like a repeat of the first time I'd met him, when he'd barely noticed I existed. I cringed, expecting him to casually flip me off like an afterthought. I hated myself for being so weak and caring about what he thought. I was better off without him.

Was I?

"Brodie?" I took a step in his direction, but he never looked back.

When he reached the stairwell, he jogged right down. A moment later, the front gate slammed shut.

I was so confused, I just stood there. It was late, so the apartment building was quiet. Only a few scattered lights were on in a handful of windows. Almost all of the light in the courtyard came from the aqua blue pool below.

Outside, Brodie's motorcycle engine revved angrily several times before he took off down the street, the engine screaming, tearing a hole in the silence of the night.

But not my heart. I wouldn't let that happen.

The sound faded into the distance within seconds.

What the hell was he doing?

I shook my head.

What the hell was I doing?

Chapter 20

I couldn't sleep.

I tossed and turned restlessly for hours.

All I could think about was Brodie.

I didn't want to think about him but I couldn't stop myself.

He was terrible.

He was wonderful.

He was a mistake waiting to happen.

I wasn't a supermodel.

I was a little nerd girl.

Brodie didn't want me.

Brodie wanted someone else.

Getting involved with him was a horrible idea.

I needed to forget him.

But I was worried about him and his motorcycle.

What if he did something stupid because of me?

What if he ended up dead?

What if I looked like a supermodel for the rest of my life and had therefore just sabotaged something special?

What if I was an idiot and *all* of this was a dream and I'd wake up tomorrow looking like regular old me?

I flipped onto my stomach and pulled my pillow over my head. My breath quickly heated up my face and I tossed my pillow aside. I didn't remember dreams ever being this vivid.

I was awake.

All of this was real.

Impossible, but still real.

I flopped back onto my back, staring at the dark ceiling.

I imagined Brodie's weight on top of me.

I wanted him grinding between my legs.

Inside me.

Fighting. Thrusting. Grinding.

I wanted…

wanted…

A soft knock at my front door.

Brodie?

I swing my feet onto the floor and stand up.

The knock comes again.

My feet whisper across my carpet. I wear only my Twilight Sparkle night shirt. Not even panties. But I always sleep in panties.

Another soft knock.

I open the door without checking to see who it is.

Brodie.

Shirtless in jeans jet blackened by night. Brodie is always shirtless.

"I need you, C.C." He sweeps into my apartment and whisks me off my feet.

I float into my bedroom, cradled in his muscled arms.

He lays me on the bed gently.

My shirt is off.

His jeans are off.

I open to him.

A cool breeze across my wetness.

He crawls onto the bed, erect.

He hovers over me, his arms muscled pillars on either side of my head.

His hot heavy cock slides against my wetness.

"I need you, C.C. Need you now." His voice is desperate and demanding at the same time. "I need to be inside you right fucking now."

I nod, and moan, biting my lower lip.

He sinks into me, hot, hard, deep, full, and thick.

My body quivers and I moan each time he thrusts.

He slow fucks me until I start to come.

The orgasm is so intense my ears ring—

RING!

My phone tore me out of my dream. I clamped my eyes shut, desperately trying to remain asleep. The intense orgasm that had been building started to fade, despite my circling index finger and my dripping wetness. I think I'd been lucid dreaming and had started masturbating. If I focused, I could easily bring myself to a climax. But I needed to get back into my dream. I tried to relax and recall the fabric of my fantasy.

Brodie had been thrusting into me, his face tight with sexual hunger and predatory desire...

RING!

My phone again.

Damn it.

RING!

I needed to change my ringtone to something more pleasant.

RING!

"What?!" I shouted to the empty room.

RING!

So much for my orgasm.

I answered my phone and yelled at it, "What?!"

"Morning, Sunflower." It was Wes. "Did I wake you?"

"Yes you woke me," I growled, my eyes squeezing shut. "I was…" *having an incredible sex dream which you ruined.* Sudden guilt seized me. Talking to an attractive man seconds after masturbating to thoughts of another man was very… unseemly. At least Wes hadn't seen me going to town with my fingers all up in my ho-ha. That thought only fueled my embarrassment, leaving me speechless.

"You were what?"

"Nothing," I whispered.

"I don't mean to rush you, Sunflower, but can you meet me in Beverly Hills in an hour?"

I opened one eye a crack and looked at the time on my phone. It was 8:30am Sunday morning. I grumbled, "Wes, why the *hell* are you calling me this early? I'm not even awake yet."

"Are you still in bed?"

"No. I'm on the toilet pooping."

"No you're not. It's common knowledge that women as beautiful as you don't poop."

"That's ridiculous," I laughed. "But you're right, I'm not pooping. But I *am* still in bed."

"So tell me what you're wearing."

"A potato sack."

He chuckled. "I bet it looks damn good on you."

"What do you want, Wes?"

"We need to get you a dress."

"You never said anything about a dress."

"I just did."

"Two seconds ago does not count as sufficient warning."

"It does in my book."

"Are you always this irritating first thing in the morning?"

He chuckled. "No. Just today. So, we need to get your dress now. Or you can just show up in your potato sack tonight. I won't mind. But people might stare."

"Ha ha."

"Either way, we need to get a jump on it. So chop chop," he joked.

"This is starting to sound a lot like work, Wes."

"It is. But that doesn't mean it won't be mildly amusing."

"Mildly?"

"We also need time to get your hair and makeup done."

"Whoa. Slow down, Turbo. Who said anything about all that? Can't I just put on some eyeliner?"

"You need to look nice. Hair, makeup, and the dress."

"How nice?" I didn't have any evening dresses that fit my new body, but I could always swing by Goodwill when they opened.

"Nice enough to do justice to the rest of you."

Okay, I was amused by his compliment. "Is a dress from Goodwill out of the question?"

He laughed.

"Wow, Wes. You're an expensive date."

"The dress is on me."

"I can't take your money for a dress, Wes."

"Shut up and listen to me, Sunflower. You'll be borrowing the dress, okay?"

"Are you going to return it after I wear it?"

"No. It doesn't work like that."

"Then I can't—"

"Sunflower, will you just do this as a favor to me? Can you do that?"

After last night with Brodie, I wasn't sure I was ready for a night out with Wes. Things could get confusing very quickly. I didn't do love triangles. But I had promised Wes I'd be his date for his thing, and that was before Brodie had saved me from Lester the Molester and then told me he was a secret sweetheart, and none of that was Wes' fault. I'd made Wes a promise and I felt obliged to keep it. I smeared my hand across my face and grumbled, "Fine. Where are we going again?"

He sighed. "Do you want to do this thing or not? I can always go stag." I was flattered he didn't threaten to take someone else like he had yesterday. "But I'd rather bring you. Arm candy, remember? I'd like to have something a little bit nicer than Lady Godiva on my arm."

"Nicer than Godiva?"

"That would be you, Sunflower."

I grinned to myself. Okay, I could be arm candy for once in my life. But just once. I groaned into the phone. "Fine. Give me the directions and I'll be there."

"Make sure you shower first."

"Geez, Wes! Do I smell or something?"

"I haven't smelled you today. Yesterday you smelled like an angel, but who knows about today? For all I know, you went to hot yoga with a bunch of farting smelly hippies and haven't showered since. You don't smell like farts, do you?"

"Wes!"

He chuckled. "Sorry."

"I didn't go to hot yoga! And I don't smell like farts!"

"I'm sure you don't, Sunflower. Do me a favor and please shower now. You won't have time later."

"How long is this dress thing going to take?"

He sighed. "I should've told you yesterday that today is going to be a long day. If you want to take a rain check, I'll completely understand." He was being irritatingly understanding and calm about this.

"At this point, I'm seriously considering doing my taxes today instead of whatever you have planned. And laundry. And cleaning my toilet."

His voice grinned, "I promise, this will be better than taxes or toilets."

"What could be better than that?"

He chuckled, "Are you in or out, Sunflower?"

I groaned, "You are *very* annoying."

"In or out?"

I stuck my tongue out and grimaced for my own benefit. He was making such a big deal out of whatever today was, and yes I was curious. I couldn't believe I was falling for his Mr. Mystery routine, but I was. "Fine, I'll go. But if this thing turns out to be lame, I'm bailing."

"Deal. If it's lame enough, I'll bail with you."

Worried that Wes would send Gavin to pick me up, I'd told Wes I'd be standing by a stop sign at the end of my street on Broadway. If Gavin showed up, I didn't want him seeing me standing in front of Jane's building. He might ask questions like a good MI5 agent would.

I wore the cheap pleather biker jacket I'd got at Goodwill as part of Friday's haul, a white print shirt with black graphics, and a plaid skirt. Since I'd forgotten to buy sexy heels, I wore the Chuck Taylors I'd bought for five bucks. It was amazing what $85 would get you at the

Santa Monica Goodwill. And I had on black lacy Victoria's Secret underneath. I'd never worn thongs in the past, but now I had the body for it, so why not? And speaking of, when I'd showered, I'd planned on shaving my legs for today, but guess what? My new body didn't seem to need it. My swansformation did have certain benefits I couldn't deny. Even my armpits were silky smooth. Go figure.

A blue Lamborghini rumbled down Broadway and pulled up to the curb with the top down. It was the convertible I remembered from Wes' mansion. He smiled at me over his aviator shades. He looked like he hadn't shaved since yesterday (which meant his stubble was even thicker), he wore a faded Guns N' Roses T-shirt, and jeans with holes in the knees that looked just as genuine as the shirt.

"Damn, woman. Nice potato sack."

I rolled my eyes. "Will you shut up?"

He chuckled.

I stared at him pointedly.

"What?"

"Aren't you supposed to get the door for me?"

He smiled, "I thought you were gonna come around and get the door for me."

"But you're already in the car, genius."

"I meant so you could drive." He stepped out, waving me around. I walked around the car and noticed he wore ratty flip-flops that were on their last days.

"Nice shoes," I quipped. I liked that Wes could dress down and look natural doing it. He didn't look like a rich person pretending to be normal by wearing brand new distressed designer clothes. He wore the real deal.

"Get in," he nodded toward the driver's seat.

"Are you sure about this, Wes?"

"You know how to drive stick, don't you?"

"No!"

He winked, "Don't worry. It's semi-automatic."

"Isn't that a type of gun?"

"Not in this case. It means you don't have a clutch. Don't worry, it's easy."

"I'm not driving your car. What if I crash?"

"You won't crash. Hop in."

"I hope your insurance is paid up." Reluctantly, I climbed in and he closed my door before strolling around to the passenger's side and sliding in beside me.

Now that I was behind the wheel, I really felt out of my element.

This definitely wasn't my Hyundai. Wes explained the basic controls like the buttons on the steering wheel for turn signals and the shifter levers behind the steering wheel on the left and right, within easy reach of my fingers.

I said, "Okay, how do I start it? Where's the key?"

"There is no key. Put your foot on the brake, lift this red cap and press the button." He flipped up a red button cover on the center console and pointed.

"It looks like the launch button for a nuclear missile."

He grinned. "I think six hundred horsepower qualifies as a nuke."

"Six hundred?" Gulp.

"Yeah. Now fire this thing up and let's get rolling."

"If I crash and kill both of us with this nuclear missile of yours, I'm going to kill you a second time. Maybe even a third."

"Relax, Sunflower. Just start it."

I pressed the button and the engine roared. "Geez, it sounds like there's a monster under the hood."

"There is. Don't make her mad. She's a real bitch," he winked at me.

I smirked back. "What's this red button on the bottom of the steering wheel? Is that an ejector seat for you for when you get too annoying?"

"No. That's the driving mode. Just leave it set to *strada*. Street mode. It'll shift for you automatically so you don't have to worry about it."

"So it's *not* an ejector seat for you?"

"No."

"You're sure?" I said it seriously, like a courtroom lawyer.

He smiled, "Yes. You ready to drive?"

I sighed, "As I'll ever be."

"Keep your foot on the brake and pull on the right lever to put it in drive."

I did and the car immediately started to pull so I pushed harder on the brake. Then I signaled, waited for an SUV to drive by, then pulled onto the street. I was so scared, I kept the car at around 15 miles an hour, even though the speed limit was 25. It took a few blocks before I got used to the brakes and the gas, but I figured it out.

At the stop sign for Santa Monica Boulevard, I said, "Where are we going?"

"Head east. Toward Beverly Hills."

"Okay."

When I pulled smoothly into traffic, Wes chuckled, "Watch out Danica Patrick, Sunflower Simmons is behind the wheel!"

"Is Danica Patrick that stock car driver?"

"The same. But at this speed, I think she could outrun you on foot."

We were doing 35, which was the speed limit. I smirked, "Are you *triple sure* this isn't an ejector button?" I clicked my nail lightly on the red button on the wheel.

"Sadly, no." He winked, "You're stuck with me all day, Sunflower."

People stared at us in the Lamborghini at every stoplight, especially after we got to Beverly Hills. Wes didn't seem to notice. I found it a bit nerve wracking, but I managed to get us to our secret destination without an accident.

Wes had me park on a side street near a bunch of shops just off of Santa Monica Boulevard. He jumped out and got my door for me and led me up the sidewalk.

"Where are we going?" I asked.

"You'll see."

"Why all the mystery?"

"Mystery is more interesting."

"More like irritating."

"Are you one of those people who skips to the end of a book so you know how it's gonna turn out?"

"No."

"Yes."

"Maybe. Sometimes."

He smiled and stopped on the sidewalk. "Here we are."

We stood in front of a boutiquey dress shop. It didn't have a sign on the big window and it looked closed.

Wes opened the door. "After you, Sunflower."

I walked inside. The color palette was neutral grays and the decor was very spare without looking empty. Two circular steel gray couches sat in the center of the room. Only a few dresses hung on two short racks on one wall. The dresses were mostly black or white, but a few red dresses gave the neutral room a pop of color. On the other wall stood two spacious shelves with various red and black pumps and high heels. Between them was a glass case holding red and black designer handbags that looked pricey. Throughout the room, track lighting aimed artful spotlights on the displays. The entire effect of the boutique was one of unified design.

Wes and I looked completely out of place in our ratty street clothes.

"This isn't Goodwill," I muttered because it was museum quiet in here.

Right when I said it, a tall woman walked out from the back. She looked sixtyish and wore what looked like a vintage 1950s red couture suit jacket and matching dress. The jacket had a deep V neck and big red buttons. A string of pearls looped twice around her neck. The dress was long, the hem below her knees. Despite the dated silhouette, it was very stylish. And despite her age, she wore it with the finesse and confidence of a runway model. In response to my comment about Goodwill, which she'd heard, she rolled her eyes and snorted, "Hardly."

"Sorry, I didn't mean…" She was so commanding, and at least six feet tall in her two inch pumps, I couldn't help but feel cowed around her. I resisted the urge to curtsy, even though it felt like the right thing to do.

She ignored me and walked up to Wes and air kissed him on both cheeks. "Hello, darling." Despite her height, Wes had to lean down for the air kiss.

"And hello to you, Cruella," Wes said with a huge smile.

Her name couldn't possibly be Cruella. She didn't have the trademarked black and white hair. Hers was silver and pulled up elegantly. And she was regal, not cruel. She turned to me and said loud enough for Wes to hear, "Ignore him. He's a child." Her eyes darted toward him and she suppressed a genuine smile before offering her hand to me to shake. "You can call me Madeline. But he can't. He has to call me Mrs. Kettner."

I shook her hand. "I'm Juh—" I'd almost said Jane. "—just call me Chelsea." Phew, that was close. Being someone else was something you had to stay on top of or you'd risk slipping up. Maybe I needed to stand in front of my mirror every morning saying Chelsea, Chelsea, Chelsea. No, that was way too weird.

Madeline put her hands on her hips. "Shall we get started? We don't have much time."

"Do your worst," Wes said.

She smirked at me, "Don't let his charm fool you. He really is as incorrigible as he's acting." Despite her commanding presence, I couldn't help but like her. "Come with me, Chelsea." She grabbed my hand. "Wes can wait out here." She shot a glare at him. "And don't sit on my couch in those dirty jeans, young man."

"These jeans sat in my Lambo, Madeline."

"I don't care about your car. And stop calling me Madeline. Have you no respect for your elders?"

"Last time I checked, you were only twenty-nine... for the thirtieth time. And that makes me your elder by two years."

She smiled, "And don't you forget it. Now keep your hands to yourself and see if you can't learn some manners while the women are working." As she led me down a long hallway into the back, she whispered, "What did I tell you about his charm?"

"Don't fall for it?"

"You learn quick," she chuckled. "I like you already."

The large back room was a combination fitting room and design studio. Dress forms with and without dresses lined one wall. A long work table took up half the room. Several sewing machines stood in the corner. Tall windows and several skylights let in ample natural light.

A young bald guy with a perfectly trimmed black beard and mustache sat on a stool with a measuring tape draped around his neck. He wore slacks and a suit vest over a white shirt with rolled up sleeves.

Madeline said, "This is Jean-Paul, my tailor."

He stood up and shook my hand, "Pleasure, *mademoiselle*." His accent was very French and it came out as *Pleazhure, mad-mwa-selle*.

"Chelsea," I smiled.

Madeline stood with her hands on her hips, looking at the dresses on the forms. All were evening gowns that draped down to the floor and all looked like classy couture. "Which one do you think, Jean-Paul?"

"On her? *Mon cher*, may we see you without your jacket?" He said it, *zhacket*.

"Sure." I shrugged it off. I would've tossed it on the work table, but I didn't want to be rude, so I held it at my waist.

Jean-Paul walked up and took it, hanging it on the clothing rack behind me. He picked up the hem of my skirt and flounced it from side to side, looking at my hips and ass as he walked around me, then let it drop before taking a step back.

Madeline stood across the room, her arms folded, one finger brushing the bottom of her chin. "Chelsea darling, be a dear and take off that hideous T-shirt and skirt, if you don't mind."

That would leave me in my bra and panties. "Uh..."

"Don't worry about Jean-Paul, he plays for the other team."

"Um..." I wasn't used to stripping for anybody. It didn't matter if Jean-Paul was gay or not. I didn't want Madeline scrutinizing my body either.

She arched her eyebrows to say, *You can strip any time you're ready.*

"Okay," I said nervously. I peeled my T-shirt off and dropped it on the floor before pushing my skirt down and kicking it aside. I reminded myself I wasn't me, I was a supermodel with a perfect body and nothing to pick at, but I still felt like an idiot in nothing but my underwear and my Chuck Taylors.

"Spin for us, darling," Madeline said.

Although I suddenly felt like an object on display, at least I didn't feel like a sexual one. More like an art object, or so I told myself. I spun around slowly.

Jean-Paul said to Madeline, "She has a terrific figure. We shouldn't hide it with the A-line."

"I agree. How about the red trumpet dress?"

"With all that cleavage? She might be a bit much for it."

I couldn't believe they were discussing my boobs like I wasn't even in the room.

Madeline said, "We'll tape her in if we have to. I doubt this town has seen real boobs this nice since Marilyn Monroe."

"Brigitte Bardot," Jean-Paul added.

"Her too."

Marilyn Monroe? Brigitte Bardot? What were they talking about?

"Come here, darling." Madeline waved me over to a red gown on one of the dress forms. "Let's get you into this."

A few minutes later, with the help of Jean-Paul and Madeline, I stood on top of a small six inch stand, wearing the red gown and facing a semi-circle of floor length mirrors. The neckline in front plunged way past my boobs, stopping just above my navel. The open V-back plunged down almost to my ass. It walked that fine line between sexy and trashy without going too far. The gown was form fitting and you could see all of my supermodel curves, but it was still classy.

"Wow," I laughed. "This is really nice."

"Jean-Paul," Madeline said, "do you have time to take in the waist? Chelsea has quite the hourglass figure and I don't want to lose it in the material."

He nodded. "*Oui*."

"Fuck… me," Wes said, startling everyone. He stood in the doorway, hands in the pockets of his jeans, staring at me. "Damn, Sunflower. You look incredible."

"Do I need to go get the soap, young man?" Madeline chortled.

Wes smiled, "You do that while I keep looking at Chelsea. Wow." He shook his head, eyes traveling all over me. "I knew you had a body under your clothes, Sunflower, but this is… this is unreal."

I blushed.

Wes walked past Madeline and strolled around me, eyeing my cleavage. I was practically falling out. He whistled a perfect rising and falling wolf whistle.

Jean-Paul snickered.

Madeline rolled her eyes. "Do I need to have Jean-Paul escort you out of here, Wesley?"

"It's not like she's the bride and we're getting married. I can look all I want." Despite his ratty clothes, he was so damn handsome he could look all day long and I wouldn't mind. The predatory glimmer in his eyes said this wolf was ready to dine.

"Out, Wesley," Madeline commanded, folding her arms over her chest.

Wes smirked as he walked out, stopping at the doorframe. "The only thing is, Madeline, I can't decide which of you is hotter in your red dresses." He ran his eyes all over her. "I could take a bite out of both of you."

"Wesley!!"

Chapter 21

Back in my street clothes, Wes whisked us across Beverly Hills in his Lamborghini. Since we were in a hurry, I thought it better that he drive. We pulled up to a curb and daytime valets ran up to the car, opening our doors.

"What now?" I asked as we stood on the sidewalk.

"Now we get your hair styled."

I looked up at the sign. "This is the Luca Rossi Salon. Haircuts here cost like two hundred bucks."

"Even more when Luca cuts your hair himself."

"What? No, Wes. Can't we just go to Supercuts? They have one in Westwood near UCLA. We could be there in like five minutes."

"Have you ever even been to Supercuts? They're butchers. I wouldn't send my dog there."

"You have a dog?"

"Focus, Sunflower." He pointed at the door. "Haircut. Inside. Now."

"Can't we go some place cheaper?"

"No. Luca is cutting your hair."

"Really?"

"Yes."

"Okay, fine. But do you really mean to tell me the owner of one of the trendiest salons in Beverly Hills works on a Sunday?"

"He does this Sunday."

Wes placed his hand on the small of my back and led me through the doors.

The interior was shades of white with metallic accents. The salon chairs and tables were boxy, the mirrors square. Customers sat in most of the chairs. Their stylists wore silvery gray uniforms and were busy cutting and styling while everyone chatted.

Wes walked us up to the girl sitting behind the cube shaped reception desk and said, "We have an appointment with Luca."

She swiped her finger on an iPad mounted behind the counter. "Are you Mr. Callaway?"

"That's us."

"Have a seat and Luca will be right with you." She stood up. "Would you two like some water?"

Wes deferred to me.

"Sure," I said. "I'm kind of parched. I could use a glass."

The receptionist smiled and walked into a squarish side nook while Wes and I sat down on a boxy white leather couch in the waiting area. A minute later, she returned with a rectangular silver tray that held two square glasses with spherical ice cubes and a square carafe. She set the tray on the low round table in front of us.

When the receptionist went back to her square chair, I said to Wes, "Why are the ice cubes and the table round when everything else in here is square?"

"Contrast," he said.

"Good point."

He poured water into both glasses and handed me one. "Cheers."

We clinked glasses.

Before I took a sip, I said, "How do they make round ice cubes anyway?"

"I think they're the tears of angels. They freeze in the upper atmosphere as they fall from heaven."

"Shut up," I laughed.

"Wes! How good to see you!" A handsome man in his forties with olive skin and black hair walked up to us, arms wide. Unlike the stylists, he wore black.

Wes stood up and hugged him. "Hey, Luca. Good to see you. You ready to cut some hair?"

"Always for you, my friend." Luca had a very Italian accent. He looked at me. "Is this her? She is beautiful."

"You're telling me," Wes chuckled, looking down at me on the couch.

I stood up, embarrassed. Nobody ever talked about me like this. They didn't even talk about Chelsea like this. Well, maybe sometimes. Either way, it was kind of ridiculous.

"*Bella*," Luca said, arms wide.

I nervously stepped into his embrace and he hugged me passionately. I patted his back, not sure what to do, but he released me just as quick. He ran a hand through my blonde hair. "Your hair is nearly perfect, *Bella*. Why are we cutting it, Wes?"

"We need it styled for tonight."

"*Sí, sí, sí*. Is okay with you, *Bella*?"

"It's Chelsea," I giggled.

Wes leaned toward me, "*Bella* is beautiful in Italian." Wes said the word *bella* with the same accent Luca had.

Luca laughed deeply. "Yes, while you are here, we call you *Bella*, no?"

"Uh, yes? No? Bella is fine," I giggled.

Luca beamed. "Shall we get to work?"

Five minutes later, I wore a black silk salon robe belted at my waist and sat back with my head in one of the round salon sinks lined up in the rear of the room. A stylist named Fabiana was busy working shampoo into my wet hair.

"I can handle it from here," Wes said.

"Is okay?" Fabiana asked uncertainly. She sounded Italian too.

My eyes had been closed but they popped open when Fabiana pulled her fingers away.

Wes' face hovered above me.

"I can see your nose hairs," I snarked. I couldn't. He was handsome even from this angle. But I wasn't telling him that.

"No you don't, because I trim them," he said confidently.

"Eww! You have nose hairs?!"

"You do too. I can see them." His eyes were locked on my nose.

I covered it with my hand. "No I don't!"

"Everybody has them, Sunflower. But yours are the sexiest nose hairs I've ever seen," he smiled. "If you're worried, I'm sure we can have Fabiana wax them after I finish washing your hair."

"Do people really do that?"

"In Beverly Hills, people wax everything. Now would you relax so I can shampoo your hair?"

"Fine. But I hope you know what you're doing."

"I do," Wes said confidently.

Fabiana pursed her lips and arched a doubtful eyebrow.

He ignored her. His eyes locked on mine as he worked his fingers into my wet hair, massaging my scalp like a pro, a smug smile on his face the whole time. Any tension I'd had from running around town melted away at the touch of his fingers. My entire face and neck warmed and I relaxed until my eyes closed and I eased into enjoyment.

This was a complete turn on.

"Imagine what it would feel like if this was your pussy," Wes said just loud enough for me to hear.

My face burned red. "Wes!"

He chuckled throatily.

"Listen to him," Fabiana said, shaking her head and grinning.

Wes smiled at her, "Can we have a minute, Fabiana?"

"Of course," she waved her hand and walked away, leaving us the only two people in the sink area.

Wes' hands kneaded and stroked my scalp.

It felt so good I couldn't help but moan.

Wes chuckled, "I like that sound."

I was dripping in his hands. This was the most sexual non-sexual touching I'd ever experienced.

"I bet your head isn't the only thing that's wet," he said.

"You wish," I moaned. He was so right. I did my best not to squirm in the chair. My entire body fluttered with warm gusts of pleasure. "You can do this all day if you want."

"Oh, you'll come long before then."

My eyes popped open.

His twinkled down at me.

My nipples were hard and dying for his touch. My breasts tingled too, and everything south of my navel was throbbing, pulsating in time with his circling fingers.

"You can't make me come like this," I lied.

"Would you like to see me try?"

Yes. "No."

"Too bad." He leaned down until we were cheek to cheek. His earthy scent had a smoky quality that permeated my senses and sent sex signals straight to my clit, which was sizzling with him this close. And, my pussy slowly clenched each time his fingers circled my scalp. He whispered, "You're going to lie here and I'm going to make you rain."

His words whooshed down my chest and stormed between my legs. His thumbs brushed ever so gently along my jawline, then danced across my ears. Every single cell in my body exploded at his touch. I shivered down to my toes. If he didn't stop, I swear I was going to come inside of five seconds.

It occurred to me that we had never kissed or anything even close. Did I really want this gorgeous man that I barely knew getting me off in the back of a hair salon?

Maybe just a little.

Maybe just a lot.

"Are you raining yet?" He murmured in my ear.

"Ohhh," I moaned, on the verge of an orgasm.

"Here comes the rain…"

"Yes," I whispered.

Warm wet water rained down on my head as Wes rinsed my hair with the spray hose. The sound of the water spray echoing in the sink whisked away the mounting sexual tension in my body.

I scrunched my face as my pleasure left me and I giggled, "You ass!"

"Is your pussy pulsing?" he asked innocently as he rinsed away more shampoo, still running his fingers sensually through my hair.

Yes. "Not for you," I sneered.

"But because of me."

Yes. "You wish."

He snickered as he finished with the spray hose. Water dribbled into the sink as he gently squeezed out my hair. When he finished, he shook his hands into the sink and said, "Are you still dripping?"

"What do you think?"

He grabbed a towel and started blotting my hair. "The best way for me to clean up the rest of you is with my tongue." He glanced at my crotch. "But I don't think Luca would appreciate it." He wrapped a fresh warm towel around my head and sat me up.

Now his crotch was right in my face.

He was fully erect in his ratty jeans.

"Are you enjoying yourself?" I snorted.

"Doesn't it show?"

I could easily reach up, unbuckle his belt, pull him out, and go to town. But we were in a crowded salon. So I stared up at him. "Do you have a magnifying glass? I can't really tell."

He was sizable and I was lying.

"Are you finished yet?" Fabiana asked as she walked into the sink area.

"For now…" Wes said suggestively.

"Promises, promises," I whispered.

"Whoa, wait. What?" Wes sounded dumbstruck by my comment. For once, he was out of words.

"Nothing," I smiled flirtatiously over my shoulder as Fabiana led me away.

Wes just stood there staring, slack jawed.

Served him right.

An hour later, I sat in a boxy salon chair with Wes and Luca standing behind me. My hair had been cut and curled and arranged by Luca in an elegant but loose up-do. I couldn't believe how good it looked.

"*Perfetto*," Luca said. "She is like a *cigno*, a swan, this one."

"I agree," Wes said. He ran the back of his fingers down the side of my neck, sending hot chills through my body.

I clamped my eyes shut, trying not to get aroused again. "Thank you so much, Luca. It looks incredible. I've always appreciated a man who can finish what he starts," I said it to Luca but shot a pointed look at Wes.

He smirked at me, "You can't run a marathon without warming up first, Sunflower."

What was it about Wes that said marathon sex sessions? Pretty much everything. I hid a smile as he thanked Luca and we made our way toward the front door.

"Don't we have to pay?" I whispered to Wes.

"Already taken care of." He opened the front door for me. "After you."

We drove back to Madeline's studio with the top up on the Lamborghini and the AC running. Once there, she and Jean-Paul helped me into the red dress, being very careful of my hair.

"*Magnifique*," Jean-Paul said.

"Well done, Jean-Paul," Madeline said. "It fits her like a glove."

"I can't wait to take it off," Wes chuckled.

"Wesley…" Madeline warned sternly. "Out."

Once the dress was off, Wes took me outside and walked me to a bistro up the street from the studio and bought food for us and ordered to go lunches for Madeline and Jean-Paul. We ate ours outside under the shade of a table umbrella and the sidewalk trees. The weather was perfect, not too hot and not too cool. I was a little worried about my hair staying nice, so I tried to keep my head still while eating.

"So, what's this thing we're going to tonight?" I asked as I forked arugula and a piece of roasted chicken off my plate and took a bite.

He shrugged, "Just an industry thing. Same old, same old."

"What industry?"

"You'll find out. Eat your salad. I don't want you fainting later from hunger."

"Do you always give people orders and expect them to follow like sheep?"

He winked, "In my business, yes."

"Too bad I'm not a sheep."

"Your salad says you are."

"Shut up," I laughed. "I'm not eating grass."

"You sure? Looks like it to me," he chuckled.

I rolled my eyes.

"Eat your salad, Sunflower. We have a schedule to keep."

"I hate you."

"I know," he winked. "Just wait until we get where we're going."

"Do I want to know?"

He laughed.

We walked back into Madeline's studio.

A middle-aged guy in a suit sat on one of the gray couches in the front room. A large metal briefcase laid on the table in front of him. A tall imposing guy in a dark suit hovered near the back wall, hands at his sides, watching the front door intently.

The guy on the couch smiled at us and stood up as we walked inside. He kind of reminded me of Neil Lane, the guy who always brought out the engagement rings on The Bachelor and The Bachelorette, but I didn't think it was him. It couldn't be him. No, as I got closer I realized he had more of a Mel Brooks from Spaceballs thing going on. Earthier and mirthier.

"Hey, Abram," Wes said, walking over to shake his hand. "Abram Cohen, meet Chelsea…" He shook his head. "You know what, Sunflower? I don't know your last name."

Abram smiled, "Don't you think you oughta should know the girl's name, Wes? What kind of a *mensch* doesn't know his girlfriend's last name?"

"Yeah," I said accusatorially. "What kind of a mensch are you, Wes?" I wasn't even sure what a mensch was.

Wes ran his hand through his chestnut hair, embarrassed. "I just call her Sunflower."

"She is definitely a Sunflower," Abram said, "but you should know her name if you're shtupping her."

I had a pretty good idea what shtupping meant.

"I'm not shtupping her!" Wes laughed.

"Yet," Abram said, winking at me. To Wes, "What's your girlfriend's last name already? You oughta know by now. Am I right?" He nudged my arm with his elbow. I really liked this guy.

"Slow down, Abram," Wes said. "Chelsea, Sunflower, would you mind telling everyone your last name?"

"Uh… um… Johnson?" I considered making up a name, but Abram and Wes were both staring at me and I couldn't think of one.

"Are you sure?" Abram joked, his eyes shining with mirth.

Giggling, I said, "Yes. One hundred percent."

"Ya got that, Wes?" Abram pinched Wes' forearm and shook it. "Johnson. Say it with me, young man. Johnson. Johnson, Johnson, Johnson."

"Johnson," Wes said, chuckling.

Abram's good humor was infectious. "Now that we've been formally introduced," he said, "lets get down to business." He led us to the couches. Wes and I sat down opposite him.

Abram opened the briefcase and turned it toward us.

"Wow," I gasped, suddenly feeling like I really was on The Bachelor, or in my case, The Bachelorette.

So many diamonds...

"You like?" Abram smiled.

"Um..." I laughed. "Yeah."

"Incredible, Abram," Wes said. "You've really outdone yourself."

Inside the case, lying on royal blue velvet, were two gold necklaces with matching pairs of earrings. Both shimmered with enough diamonds to buy a tropical island. Even the chains were covered with diamonds. Priceless. Both necklaces had shiny gold pendants with even larger diamonds. Each had a unique design. One was spirals and curves, the other geometric lines and planes.

"Which one do you like?" Abram asked.

"Me?" I said, trying not to gasp. "I get to pick?"

Wes said, "I'm not gonna be the one wearing it. It's completely up to you, Sunflower."

"Wow," I laughed. "Really?"

Abram and Wes both nodded.

"How about this one?" I pointed at the geometric one.

"Excellent choice." Abram lifted the necklace out of the case with great care. "Let's try it on." He stepped beside me and draped it around my neck. It hung down past my cleavage.

It didn't look right hanging over my print T-shirt.

Wes said, "It'll go great with Madeline's dress."

"Yeah," I nodded, looking down at it. "This is beautiful, Abram. How much does this thing cost?"

He smiled and shook his head, "You don't wanna know."

"Oh, sorry. I shouldn't have asked. It's just, I'm a little worried about wearing it out. What if it breaks or..." I didn't want to say, *What if someone tries to steal it?* I wasn't used to worrying about expensive jewelry.

"I designed this one myself, *Bubbeleh*. And my jewelers do good work. It won't break."

"Don't worry, Sunflower." Wes rubbed my arm. "I'll keep an eye on you and the necklace all night."

I laughed. "Why? So you can stare at my boobs?"

He grinned big. "Why else?"

"You two," Abram chuckled and waved a dismissive hand. "Wait until I'm gone already!" He lifted the necklace over my head and set it carefully in the case. "I need to take an inch off the chain. It's a bit too long. I'll take it to my shop and have it back in an hour. Will that work for you?"

"Yeah," Wes said. "We still need to do her makeup."

"Good, good. I don't want to stop you two lovebirds from doing what lovebirds do. Right, Sunflower?" He winked at me and nudged my arm again. To the big man who'd been watching over us like a silent soldier, he said, "Let's go, Joseph." I guess Joseph was Abram's security guard?

When they were gone, Wes said, "Sorry about that."

"Sorry about what?" I said.

"Abram. The shtupping, the girlfriend comment, the lovebirds comment."

"Oh, he's sweet. I like him. Does it bother you he called me your girlfriend?"

Wes smiled, "Not at all."

It doesn't bother me either. "Okay then!" I laughed, trying to hide my embarrassment. "You said something about makeup?"

Tori the makeup artist was busy applying primer to my face with her fingers. Her own makeup looked flawless and not overdone, so I assumed she'd do a good job on me. I sat in a chair in Madeline's studio. Her two assistants Karla and Robin were busy giving me a mani and a pedi at the same time. I felt bad for Robin because she had to sit on the floor. She had my feet resting on a towel in her lap while she trimmed and buffed my toes.

Tori said, "You have the smoothest and most even skin I've ever seen." She should've seen it two weeks ago. Blotchy with at least two zits at all times. "You don't wear makeup much, do you?"

"Not really." It wasn't worth the trouble.

"Well," she smiled, "You don't need it."

"Thanks." Not as long as I'm a supermodel, I didn't. I had no idea how long my supernatural beauty would last, but I hoped I'd at least make it through whatever tonight was. I didn't want to do a Cinderella at midnight. In her case, the glass slipper still fit when her prince found her in her rags. I didn't know if I'd get glass slippers from Madeline for tonight, but I did know my feet would shrink whenever I changed back to normal, and that meant whatever shoes Madeline gave me now wouldn't fit me later. Would Prince Wes be able to find me then?

"What kind of look are we going for?" Tori asked the room.

Madeline, who was chatting with Jean-Paul and Wes in the corner, said, "Nothing too garish. Subtle. Just a hint of smoke around the eyes. She doesn't need much. And maybe a nude lip."

Wes snickered, "How about nude everything?"

Madeline grumbled, "Do I have to give you a time out, Wesley?"

"Will it just be me and you alone in a room?" he flirted innocently.

"No, it will be you standing alone in a corner with a dunce cap, young man."

He laughed.

Tori went to work on my face and less than an hour later, she was finished. I couldn't believe how good I looked. She'd followed Madeline's instructions to a T.

"Wow, this looks amazing," I said, examining my reflection in the big hand mirror Tori held.

"Time to get you dressed," Madeline said. "That means you can leave, young man." She glared at Wes.

"Like I said earlier, we're not getting married. I can see her getting into her dress."

"Yes, but every woman likes to make an entrance, Wesley. Wait outside."

"Fine," he chuckled and walked out of the studio. "I need to go change anyway."

While Jean-Paul and Madeline helped me into the dress, Abram returned with the necklace and earrings. Madeline supplied me with a pair of red pumps.

"Don't I get glass slippers?" I joked.

Madeline smiled. "Don't worry about the shoes, darling. No one will see them under your train."

Once I had the dress, the shoes, and the jewelry on, they led me over to the mirrors. I couldn't believe my eyes. Abram's necklace hung down past my boobs, but dangled just above the deep V cut of the cleavage, and the matching earrings sparkled in my ears.

I gasped, "I look like a million bucks." I really did. Almost like a movie star. I fought back impending tears. I didn't want to ruin Tori's makeup. It didn't matter if the glamorous supermodel standing in the mirror wasn't really me and it didn't matter if my swansformation faded by morning.

For tonight, I would own it.

For tonight… I would be gorgeous.

"More like ten million bucks," Abram grinned. I didn't want to ask if that's what the necklace and earrings were worth. "You're gonna turn heads tonight, *Bubbeleh.*"

"She's going to turn *every* head," Madeline said.

My eyes were starting to water. I really couldn't believe what I was seeing. I sniffed, "Can we, uh, get a picture? I want to remember this." I was scared to death that none of this would last much longer. It was all too good to be true. It couldn't possibly last. For all I knew, I might not even make it to midnight looking like this.

"There will be plenty of that later," Madeline said dismissively. "You need to get a move on. It's past three o'clock now." She led me out of the studio.

I walked carefully, trying not to step on the long train of the trumpet dress. It trailed three or four feet behind me on the hallway carpet.

Wes stood with his back to me as I approached. He turned slowly, now dressed in a black tuxedo.

Madeline walked in front. She said to Wes, "Are you sure about that red bow tie, Wesley? It is supposed to be black tie. Or did you forget?"

"Fuck black tie," he chuckled. "And this isn't red. It's dark red."

"Well, it certainly isn't black."

"Whatever. Chelsea is wearing red so I'm wearing red too."

I stepped out of the hallway and into the front room and stopped.

Wes stared at me, speechless. His eyes rolled all over me. "Holy shit, Chelsea. Look at you."

Madeline rolled her eyes and sighed, "When referring to your date, Wesley, never use the word shit in the same sentence."

"How about fuck? Fuck seems appropriate, don't you think?" He winked at me.

Madeline smirked. "Try something else."

He looked at me. "I can't think of anything else. Chelsea, you are…" He shook his head. "There are no words." I felt the same way looking at him. He was dashing and impeccably handsome in his tux. Every woman's fantasy. Tonight, he would be all mine.

He glanced at Madeline, Jean-Paul, Abram, Tori and her girls, all of whom now stood behind me. "Can you guys step out for an hour? I think I need to tear this dress off Chelsea and ravage her six ways to Sunday."

Madeline glared at him, "There will be no ravaging and no tearing,

Wesley. The only people who will be removing my dress from her body are Jean-Paul and myself at the end of the evening. Have I made myself clear?"

"Crystal. But once that dress is off," his mahogany eyes flared, "all bets are off…"

My sentiments exactly.

"Are we taking your Lamborghini?" I asked outside. "If we are, I can't drive in this dress." I held the train carefully off the ground like Madeline had showed me inside. "You'll have to drive."

"Not tonight. Tonight we arrive in style."

A black stretch limo pulled up to the curb. Gavin jumped out wearing a tux. "Afternoon, luv," he said to me, not recognizing me in the slightest as he opened the back door for us. Of course he didn't. I wasn't plain Jane.

Wes held my hand while I climbed in. He slid in after. A moment later, the car started moving.

Wes put his arm casually over the seat back and brushed his fingers up and down the back of my neck. Exquisite chills bloomed under my skin and goosebumps crawled up my arms.

"Would you stop?" I moaned, my eyelids fluttering.

He didn't. "Have you ever been fucked in the back of a limousine, Sunflower?"

"Wes!" I glared at him.

"Have you?"

"No! And you're not going to have sex with me right now, so shut up! We haven't even kissed. Geez!" Despite my anger, I started wondering what it would be like… But no, I didn't want to ruin Madeline's dress. Or my hair.

"You know what kills me, Sunflower?" His voice softened from sexually aggressive to a sensitive sigh.

"What's that?"

"I can't even kiss you because I don't want to mess up your makeup." He said it with such warmth and such sincerity, that's exactly what I wanted him to do right then and there. I was dying to taste his lips. But he was right. Maybe later.

He stroked my neck again.

I shivered, "Wes, if you make me so wet I soak through this dress, not only will I kill you, but I guarantee Madeline will kill you too."

"A price I would happily pay. But perhaps not tonight." He reluctantly put his arm back in his lap. "But if for some reason your panties do get too wet to wear, take them off and give them to me. I'll be glad to hold onto them for you."

"Will I get them back at the end of the night?"

"Mmmmm… no." He grinned.

I narrowed my eyes at him, "You know Wes, you pretend you have manners, but you really don't."

"And you love it." A smug smile stretched across his perfect teeth.

"Where are we going?" I looked out the window. "Somewhere in Hollywood?"

"Hollywood and Highland, to be exact."

A few minutes later, the limo slowed to a stop in the middle of the street. I couldn't see what lay ahead because the privacy screen was up. "Are we stuck in traffic?"

"Probably."

"Why is there traffic at three in the afternoon on a Sunday?"

"There's always traffic in LA."

"Not this much. And what time does this thing start, anyway?"

"We don't have to be there until four-thirty. We have time."

An hour later, we were still sitting in traffic, but we'd moved a fair distance. Outside the limo, people were crowded on the sidewalk ten deep. Hollywood and Highland often had thousands of people walking around to see the Hollywood Walk of Fame, Madame Tussauds Hollywood Wax Museum, Ripley's Believe it Or Not, The Chinese Theatre, The Egyptian Theatre, and all that other touristy stuff. But these people were packed in like sardines and were watching us. And they were all cheering and shouting at the tops of their lungs.

"What the heck is going on?" I asked. "It sounds like a riot outside."

"Good thing I'm with you," Wes grinned.

Our limo started moving again then suddenly stopped. Someone opened the back door and the afternoon sunlight poured in.

The cheering crowd went wild and the sound was deafening.

The guy who opened the door had a blond buzz cut and beefy shoulders, giving him something of a military look. He wasn't Gavin, but like Gavin he wore a tuxedo. He also had a microphone in his ear that had a little coiled wire running down his neck and into his tuxedo jacket.

Buzz Cut said, "Welcome to the Academy Awards."

"What?!" I blurted.

Wes just smiled and nodded.

Holy!

Shit!

Chapter 22

Wes slid off his leather seat and stepped out of the limo. I tried to grab him so I could stab him to death and/or pull him back in the car and make Gavin drive us home, but Wes was too quick.

Buzz Cut leaned into the car and offered me his hand.

"I can handle that," Wes said, shouldering Buzz Cut out of the way. He held his hand for me. "Shall we, Sunflower?"

My jaw hung wide open and I hissed, "Wes! What! The! Fuck! You didn't tell me we were going to the freaking Oscars!"

He curled a suspicious grin. "Didn't I?"

"I think I would've remembered! I can't go out there! It's... the Oscars!" I was only slightly mortified that pretty much the whole world was about to see me walking down the red carpet on international television.

He shrugged. "Now you know. But I did tell you I needed arm candy for tonight."

I laughed in his face. "No, Wes!" I was dying to walk the red carpet with Wes, but I was also not entirely sure this was a good idea. Chances were good that everyone I'd ever known would see me looking like *not* me. There would be a permanent record of me turning into a supermodel. I didn't want the whole world knowing I'd magically swansformed into another freaking person. Then again, how would anyone ever find out? Maybe people would think I was my sister. Then either she'd have to make up lies about being here or I'd have to tell her I wasn't me anymore!

Maybe the safest thing would be to just sit right here in this limo and have Gavin drive me home. Wes could walk the red carpet alone.

I hesitated a moment.

"Something wrong?" Wes asked.

Outside, people screamed. The excitement was contagious.

Fuck it.

I was going to the Oscars.

I climbed out of the limo and the crowd cheered and waved their hands. Wes led me to a security checkpoint under a huge white tent. We waited in line behind Kevin Hart and his wife. She was so much taller than him in her heels. I couldn't believe it was actually him. In front of the two of them stood all of U2: Bono, The Edge, and the other two guys. In front of them stood Matthew McConaughy, his wife, and his mom. Even more celebrities were in line ahead of them.

Part of me wanted to fangirl and beg for everyone's autograph and selfies. Another part of me flatly refused the idea and wanted desperately to play it cool like this was my normal. The celebrities were already acting that way, pretending they all knew each other. They sort of did. I mean, when Leonardo DiCaprio or Angelina Jolie walked up to U2, everybody basically knew everybody already. Or at the very least, knew of.

When it was our turn at the security checkpoint, the beefy guys in tuxes didn't immediately recognize Wes or me, but he didn't seem worried. He gave his name to a woman who typed his name into an iPad. Wes's photo popped up on the screen and she waved us in.

Clinging to Wes' elbow, I whispered, "How come they didn't check me?"

"Because the Academy knows me. Whoever I bring is fine with them."

"Oh."

We walked out of the security area and onto the red carpet proper. The crowd screamed even louder here than they had when I got out of the limo. The sound and this moment were overwhelming. On my right, bleachers were packed with screaming fans waving at all the celebrities. On my left was all the press behind white draped fencing. Life-sized golden Oscar statues were placed intermittently along the red carpet. Hundreds of celebrities strolled along it, the men wearing black tuxedos, the women wearing couture evening gowns.

We walked right past Matt Damon and Ben Affleck. Ben saw Wes and waved us over.

I muttered in Wes' ear, "Do you know Ben Affleck?"

"Yeah. We should stop and talk with him and Matt for a minute."

"What?!" I gasped. I was barely keeping it together as it was and the thought of talking to Matt Damon and Ben Affleck made me want to faint dead away. But that didn't stop Wes. The next thing I knew, I was shaking hands with Matt and Ben while pretending I wasn't about to have a heart attack. I let Wes do all the talking because I couldn't speak. A minute later, George Clooney and his wife walked up from behind and surprised all of us. Everyone laughed and said hello to each other like best friends, and Wes was one of them.

Now I was really dying.

Matt and Ben were busy talking to George so Wes pulled me away.

As we drifted off, I giggled and whispered to Wes, "I can't believe that just happened."

"Get used to it. It's gonna be like this all night."

"Oh, wow." I honestly wasn't sure if I could take it all night.

As we walked past the photographers, Wes encouraged me to keep smiling. My cheeks started to hurt after less than two minutes. I still couldn't believe any of this was really happening.

Halfway down the red carpet, there was a platform where numerous famous actresses were going up the low steps to pose for pictures. Nicole Kidman, Jennifer Lawrence, Eva Longoria, Reese Witherspoon, Sandra Bullock.

"I love your dress!" a woman said to my left.

"Thanks, you too!" I turned and saw a beautiful young brunette smiling at me. I hadn't even registered what she was wearing before I said it. It just seemed like the polite thing to do. I didn't recognize her, but she seemed vaguely familiar, like I'd seen her on the cover of Cosmo or in some Netflix movie recently. There were so many new stars in Hollywood, I couldn't keep track of them all. Considering she was here and dressed in a stunning sequined silver gown, she was probably up for an Academy Award or was one of the presenters. Or both.

"You look great in red," she said as she strolled past me and walked up to the platform stage where the other actresses had posed for the photographers. Flanked by life-sized golden Oscar statues, she struck a pose and the cameras flashed. When she was finished, she started waving at me. "Come on! Come up here!"

"She's talking to you," Wes said in my ear.

"No way."

A guy with a clipboard and a headset standing at the base of the platform saw the woman waving.

She hollered to him, "She needs to come up here too!"

Clipboard Guy looked between me and her before waving at me furiously, signaling me to come over.

"What should I do?" I asked Wes.

"Go up there and get your picture taken."

"I can't!"

Clipboard Guy walked up to me as I approached. "What's your name?"

"Chelsea Johnson?" I wasn't even sure myself, my head was spinning so fast, but it had tumbled right out of my mouth.

Clipboard Guy mumbled into his headset microphone, "Next up, Chelsea Johnson." He put his hand over the microphone and asked me, "How do you spell your first name?"

"C-H-E-L-S-E-A."

He repeated it into his microphone and ushered me toward the steps.

I was too stunned to resist. I just went along with it. Going up the low steps, I was scared to death I was going to trip over my heels or the dress or both, but I made it and walked to the center of the stage and struck a wobbly pose. I wasn't used to heels. Hundreds of cameras flashed, nearly blinding me. My heart was pounding and my head was too. I felt ready to die. A minute later, on the other side of the stage, another guy waved me down.

Wes was waiting for me as I stepped onto the carpet.

"Oh my God! I can't believe this is happening!" I started laughing, I was so overcome with exhilaration. I was also hyperventilating and couldn't catch my breath.

"Relax, Sunflower. I'm right here." Wes squeezed my hand in his.

I was afraid to let go and squeezed back hard. I wasn't sure if I could get through this without him right beside me.

Finally, we made it down to the end of the red carpet where it turned to go up the grand staircase that led into the Dolby Theatre.

Wes leaned into my ear, "Can you do one more thing for me?"

"Sure," I nodded vigorously.

"I need to do a brief interview up on that platform. You just need to stand next to me."

"Okay, sure." I wasn't letting go of his hand, so I guess we were doing the interview.

It took a few minutes while other celebrities were interviewed by the guy in a tux standing on the elevated stage, including Emma Stone and Chris Pine, a.k.a. Captain Kirk from the new Star Trek movies. He I really wanted to have sign an autograph. Because, Captain Kirk. Duh. But I didn't have anything for him to sign, so I let it drop.

Yet another guy in a tux with a headset led Wes and I up the steps to the interview platform. Interview Guy had a handheld microphone. He faced a video camera and said, "I am here tonight with the legendary Wesley Callaway and his beautiful date, Chelsea Johnson. As many of you know, Wesley's grandmother, the late Helen Callaway, was a shining star during the Golden Age of Hollywood, winning numerous awards and making the Callaway family a permanent fixture in the ranks of Hollywood royalty to this day."

Legendary? Royalty? Wow, this was all news to me. But all those posters and headshots of Helen I'd seen at Wesley's mansion said it all.

"Chelsea, I have to ask," Interview Guy said, "Who are you wearing tonight?" He held his microphone up to my face.

"Oh, uh, the dress is Madeline Kettner and the jewelry is Abram Cohen." I looked to Wes for confirmation that I was correct and he smiled proudly and winked, rubbing my back gently.

"Well you look ravishing in red, Chelsea. Wesley, it's been a few years since we've seen you walk the red carpet, but it's so good to have you back."

"Thanks. It's an honor to be here. And an honor to have Chelsea by my side. This is the first time I've walked the red carpet without my grandmother, but I know she would want me to be here tonight, and I know she's smiling down on us right now." He squeezed my hand and lifted it up so he could kiss it on camera. He smiled at me, his chocolate eyes liquid and shimmering in the bright lights.

My heart melted right then and there. My knees also shook and threatened to buckle. I was literally about to faint, but Wes steadied me with a hand around my waist, pulling me against his side.

I leaned against him, no longer on the verge of fainting. But I was truly swooning.

Interview Guy said something else, but my head was spinning and the cheering crowd was so loud, I had no idea what it was.

A moment later, Wes walked me down off the stage and through the giant gold curtain that led up the red-carpeted grand staircase into the Dolby Theatre.

The awards ceremony was a blur.

During it, we sat really close to the stage, maybe the tenth row. Apparently, being a Callaway got you special privileges with the Academy. Wes sat to my left and to my right sat Daniel Craig, a.k.a. the sexiest James Bond ever.

Yeah, we talked.

I acted like I didn't know who he was, so I didn't make a fool of myself. At one point during a commercial break (when the celebrities around us would inevitably chit chat), Wes asked in my ear if I realized I was talking to Daniel Craig. My hushed response was, "Shhh! Don't tell him! He's licensed to kill!" Wes chuckled at that.

The ceremony was quite long, but I didn't notice. I was too excited by it all to care. Everywhere I looked, the most famous movie stars and entertainers on the planet were busy being normal.

It was fascinating.

When everything finally finished, the horde of celebrities migrated out to the big white tent to wait for their limousines. We stood shoulder to shoulder with yet more stars while the fans at the edge of the barricades screamed for autographs. While waiting, I had a brief chat with Scarlett Johansson about how great the ceremony was before she got in her limo with her husband and drove off.

Gavin arrived with our limo and drove us out onto the street to join the slow caravan of limos leaving the Dolby.

"That was awesome!" I squealed inside the quiet car, doing a spastic happy dance while sitting down, kicking my dress train up in red billows.

Wes chuckled, "So I take it you had fun?"

I pinched my thumb and index finger close together, "Maybe this much?" I was giddy with excitement.

"So, are you ready for the Vanity Fair after party, or should I take you home and tear this dress off?"

I put my finger on my lips and looked up thoughtfully. "Hmmm, tough choice. Not! After party!" I laughed.

Wes did too.

The Vanity Fair party was only a few miles away at the Wallis Annenberg Center for the Performing Arts. After getting out of the limo, we had to go through two security checkpoints and present an electronic keycard at each to get in.

After security, we joined the line of celebrities strolling through the gauntlet of reporters. Behind us was a long wood wall with huge cutout letters spelling VANITY FAIR. In front was the press behind low velvet-covered fencing. The press called out to the more famous celebrities like Lady Gaga and Taylor Swift, getting them to stop and pose for photos and answer questions. Thousands of camera flashes popped off the entire time.

Inside, the party proper was set in a trendy ballroom atmosphere. Dim but colorful mood lighting, dance music, comfy leather couches, bartenders behind a long bar pouring drinks, waiters in white jackets circulating through the crowd with trays of champagne.

Celebrities galore clustered together, chatting about everything under the sun. I lost count of all the famous people I talked to that night. I'd never remember all of them. It was one thing to have a celebrity sighting in LA, which happened now and then, but that was usually one or two celebrities at most. Being crammed in a room with hundreds of them socializing was another thing entirely. It seemed like every famous entertainer ever was right here.

If someone dropped a bomb on this building tonight, there

wouldn't be any new movies or TV shows coming out of Hollywood for years.

Wes and I circulated for at least two hours. To my surprise, a bunch of different people told me how much they loved my dress and many said I'd be on the best dressed lists in the tabloids all week long. I couldn't decide if that was fantastic or if having my photo spread far and wide was the worst thing ever. I didn't have time to think about it because the party never stopped.

At one point, while we chatted with Conan O'Brien and his wife Liza, Chris Evans, a.k.a. Captain America, brushed past me. He was ridiculously hot in person. He smiled and said hello.

"Hi," I tittered nervously, barely able to speak.

Wes noticed immediately and leaned past Conan and said to Chris, "She's my date, Chris. And she hates Captain America."

"No I don't!" I laughed. "I love the Avengers movies! And Captain America!"

"Okay, fine," Wes chuckled, "but no flirting with America's first patriot." He winked at me before going back to talking to Conan and his wife.

After introducing ourselves, Chris and I kept it casual. Our conversation revolved around tonight's awards ceremony and the Avengers movies. I allowed myself to slightly fan girl while he told me some on set stories about working with Joss Whedon and Robert Downey Jr.

When Chris wandered off to talk to Scarlett Johansson, Wes put his arm around me and whispered in my ear, "Wanna step outside for some fresh air?"

"Sure," I smiled.

Wes led me out to the smoking patio and found a quiet corner away from the smokers and music and conversation.

"Are you still having fun?" Wes asked, holding a full champagne glass in his hand.

"I think fun is too small a word. Hey, can I have your champagne? I forgot to drink anything."

He took a sip before handing me the glass.

I considered turning the glass so I sipped from the same place he had, but I didn't want to be too obvious. "Would it bother you if I went out on a date with Captain America?"

Wes smiled while frowning. "Do you mean Chris Evans the person or Captain America the character?"

"Do you have a preference?" I asked coyly.

"Yeah. I prefer you only go out with me."

"So possessive," I said theatrically. "We haven't even kissed yet."

He took the champagne glass from my hand and set it on a low table. "Why do you think I took you out here?"

Our eyes flicked back and forth.

"You have the most beautiful eyes I've ever seen, Sunflower."

"You too," I whispered. Swallowed hard. He could kiss me any time. He was so damn handsome, I didn't care what he did next.

He placed his hand firmly on my ass and pulled me into his hips. The straining bulge in his slacks pressed against my bare skin in the deep V neckline. The only thing between him and me was his tuxedo. As pleasure swirled in my breasts, my nipples hardened and poked through the thin material of my dress.

He hadn't even kissed me yet, but I was 90% sure I would let him fuck me if he tried. But I wasn't going to start this thrill ride.

He would have to do it.

He leaned down and our lips touched, igniting a fire within both of us. He wasn't savage, but he was forceful, rhythmic, hypnotic. His tongue was slow yet powerful. His other hand squeezed my ass and I pressed my stomach even harder into his erect cock, grinding against his tuxedo pants. It strained and pulsed against my skin. This was the most sensuous, sexual kiss I'd ever had. I couldn't pin it down, but it drove me wild. A slow burn.

Long, hard, intense, overwhelming.

We kissed for a really long time, grinding against each other like we were trying to fuck with our clothes on.

I couldn't get enough of this man.

He couldn't get enough of me.

But I was ready to give him everything. As long as he kept kissing me like this, he could kiss me forever…

"You gonna come up for air, Callaway?" Some guy hollered to our right in a brassy voice, followed by several other men chuckling.

Barely breaking our kiss, Wes and I both glanced over and saw Chris Rock, Adam Sandler, Seth Rogen, and James Franco. The group of them clapped casually and cheered. It seemed like they knew Wes too.

Stunned, I buried my face in Wes' chest and giggled. "Seriously," I whispered, "Do you know everyone in Hollywood?"

"I grew up in this business," he muttered and kissed the top of my head. "This is just how it is." To the group he said, "Take a hike, boys. Me and my lady are having a moment."

They laughed and left.

Could this night get any more surreal?

By the time midnight rolled around, I was convinced that my Cinderella prediction would come true and all of the glamour would disappear in a magic poof, and I'd go back to being plain Jane Johnson, the little nerd girl. Only instead of my carriage turning into a pumpkin, it would just be me that turned into a pumpkin. Either way, I would make a hasty escape.

But that didn't happen.

I remained the gorgeous supermodel version of myself well past midnight.

As the party wound down, Wes led me out of the building to Santa Monica Boulevard. Random celebrities chatted near the In-N-Out Burger stand on the sidewalk, eating Double-Doubles and fresh cut French fries. At this point, I'd seen so many famous people, I wasn't even noticing them anymore.

"Want a burger?" Wes asked.

"I'm good." I hadn't eaten in hours and my stomach was knotted with hunger, but I didn't want to eat in Madeline's gown and risk dripping melted cheese or grilled onions on it.

Wes peered into my eyes.

"What?" I asked.

"Your eyes. I swear I've seen eyes exactly like yours before. But I can't think of where."

"Emerald with flecks of gold. Truly radiant." I was repeating his words from the day we'd met at his mansion when I was just plain Jane.

"How do you know that?"

Without thinking, I blurted, "Because my sister told me."

"Who's your sister? Do I know her?"

"Does the name Jane ring a bell?"

"Jane? Why do I know that name?"

"Imagine big glasses."

His eyes widened. "No way. You mean that cute girl who barged into my grandmother's mansion during the estate sale?"

Wow. He just called me cute. Not supermodel me. Regular me. Jane me.

"Yeah," I said, all choked up. "She told me all about meeting you." I wanted to ask why he hadn't asked me out then, but I didn't want to burst my bubble just yet.

"I knew I'd seen your eyes before." He searched mine again, his flicking back and forth. "I swear, your eyes are *exactly* the same as your sisters."

Because I am my sister. When I'd woken up beautiful, the only thing about me that hadn't changed was my eyes. "Yeah," I chuckled, "they're pretty similar."

"Like you could be twins." He couldn't possibly mean that. Supermodel me looked nothing like regular me. He just meant we had the same eyes, not the same everything else. "Do twins have the same eyes?" he mused. "Or are they just similar?"

"I don't really know. Anyway, yeah, Jane is my sister." I had no idea why I'd said that. Maybe my unconscious had done it. Maybe deep down I wanted Wes to like plain Jane, not supermodel Jane. Would that be so crazy a thing?

Wes wrapped his arm around my shoulder affectionately. "I really liked your sister. And how strange is it that I bumped into you at the Promenade?"

"Pretty strange," I chuckled, not sure if I'd just made everything worse by lying to him.

"You know what? Now that I think about it, your eyes are why I stopped to watch you yesterday. I kept thinking how familiar they looked, but it wasn't adding up in my head."

"Makes sense," I sighed.

"Well, I can't wait to see your sister again. I really liked her."

I wanted to ask, *Liked* her liked her, or just liked her?

But I didn't.

"Right now," Wes continued, "we need to get you out of this dress." His eyes darkened with hunger.

"Um, ok?" I swallowed my excitement along with a hint of sweet uncertainty.

"Picture me peeling these spaghetti straps off one by one," he hooked his finger through one, "and this dress cascading down your breasts like the sexiest waterfall in the history of the world."

"Here?" I coughed. We were outside, but there were at least a dozen people standing around in the bright lights of the In-N-Out stand.

"Not here. I'm not sharing you with anyone." He still had his finger in my spaghetti strap. "This dress will pool at your feet and you'll be standing in front of me naked, the most beautiful woman in all of creation. Venus stepping out of her half shell has nothing on you, Sunflower. You know what I'm going to do then?"

"Will it involve your dick?" I quipped, trying to keep my head while resisting the urge to grab his… *head.*

"That's up to you. But if you give me the word, I will fill your hot wet pussy with my cock until you come a hundred times."

"A hundred?" I said doubtfully, swallowing hard.

"Two hundred," he smirked confidently. "After that, I will come inside you until I'm drained. Ideally, this night will end with both of us spent and you drenched."

I forced a smirk, trying to hide my total arousal. "Ummm, tempting?" I broke into giggles.

"Just give me the word, Sunflower, and I'll make you mine."

As turned on as I was, I wasn't thinking about how long it would be until Wes got me out of this dress. I was thinking about how long it would be until I was out of this supermodel body, because it wasn't mine. It was reasonable to assume it wouldn't last and I could go back to normal at any time. The pressing question was, how long would it take before I returned to normal?

A year?

A month?

A week?

A day?

An hour from now while I was having sex with Wes?

I had no way of knowing.

I wish I did, because the last thing I wanted to find out was what Wes would do if I suddenly changed into plain Jane while he was inside me. How would he react?

The idea made me want to cry.

It wouldn't be good, I knew that much.

Chapter 23

Although I decided not to have sex with Wes that night (it was easily one of the hardest decisions I'd ever made), he insisted on taking me home and walking me to my door. Since it was nearly four in the morning, I insisted he stay quiet. I had my heels off and walked barefoot along the balcony, holding the train of my dress in one hand, my shoes in the other. My phone and house key were in the shoes. Wes carried my folded street clothes and my purse.

The other reason I was being quiet was because I didn't want to wake up Brodie and have him stick his head out and see me with Wes. I felt a little bit guilty about kissing both of them one day apart. Sure, I hadn't made Brodie any promises, and I wasn't even sure where things were going with Wes, but my behavior was slightly questionable.

At my door, I noticed it had been freshly painted. It still looked a bit tacky, so I was careful not to touch it or let my dress brush against it. Brodie had been true to his word. I'd have to thank him in the morning.

"Thanks again, Wes," I whispered. "I should probably get to sleep. Can I return Madeline's dress tomorrow?"

"You need any help taking it off?" He flashed a dimple.

"No, I think I can manage. I'll be extra careful."

He smiled, "I'm sure it'll be fine. But I should take your necklace and those earrings. Abram would kill me if anything happened to them."

"Oh, right! I totally forgot." Before I could do anything, Wes set my clothes and purse down and lifted the necklace over my head. The pendant trailed up the skin between my boobs. Wes just grinned, staring at my totally exposed cleavage.

"Getting a good view?"

"Best ever." He carefully hung the necklace around his own neck. "How does it look on me?"

"Doesn't work. You're like some kind of priest or something."

"I hear priests are sexy."

"I hear priests are celibate."

"Not this one," he smirked.

"Save it for next time, padre." I chuckled as I unfastened the earrings and handed them over. He slipped them in the pocket of his slacks. He'd left his jacket and bow tie in the limo and wore only the white shirt, which was unbuttoned just enough to reveal the edges of his hard pecs but still tucked in. I resisted the urge to tear his shirt open and run my fingers all over him. I didn't want to start anything I wasn't ready to finish.

"I should go." I nodded toward my apartment.

He heaved a huge sigh. "When do I see you again, Sunflower?"

"Um, soon?" I didn't want to commit to anything until I had a chance to come down from my Oscars high and sort through my feelings about Wes, Brodie, and my swansformation.

"Give me the word and I'll take you out."

"Where? The Golden Globes? Or the Emmys?"

"The Globes were in January. Emmys aren't until September," he grinned. "But the Kids' Choice Awards for Nickelodeon are coming up in March. We can do that if you want."

"You know, I might have to take you up on that. Can I bring my friend George? He would love to go to that. I mean, the three of us."

He narrowed his eyes, "Do I need to be worried about George?"

I snickered to myself. If Wes saw George, he'd laugh. I said, "Depends how insecure you are, Wes."

He smirked, "I'm not sure what that means."

"It means, are you man enough to fight for me?" I was picturing skinny little George and tall muscular Wes standing toe to toe. It would be a David and Goliath moment, but in this case, David (George) would be wearing a My Little Pony hoodie and Goliath (Wes) would be wearing a tuxedo. I giggled to myself.

"What?"

"Nothing. Don't worry about George. He's an old friend from college."

"Who's an old friend?" Brodie asked sleepily, suddenly sticking his head out of his front door. His face was mushed and his hair stood up, but he was no less sexy than always. As usual, he had no shirt on. In fact, all he wore was a pair of black boxer briefs which revealed half a hard on, an impressive one at that. *Oh, Brodie. You truly are the man with no shame.* As he stepped outside barefoot, he grumbled, "Who's this dude?"

Wes asked me innocently, "Is this George?"

I laughed, "No. This is Brodie."

Wes smiled at me, "Do I have to worry about Brodie?"

Brodie sized up Wes, anger in his eyes. "Yeah you fucking do. Who is this prick, C.C.?"

I cringed.

Nothing like a man with a short temper.

Okay, so that happened. I never should've let Wes walk me to my front door. So much for taking my heels off to be sneaky.

Wes put his arm around me possessively, squeezing my shoulder. "This prick is her date this evening. Which prick are you?"

Brodie's face soured and tightened. "Hey, fuck you."

Oh no.

"I don't think so," Wes said, attitude in his voice.

No, no, no.

Brodie stepped right up to Wes. Brodie was less than an inch taller than Wes but slightly more muscular. I didn't want either of them getting hurt.

"Relax, Brodie," I said.

"Do me a favor and take a step back," Wes said calmly to Brodie.

Brodie growled, "I'm not doing shit, buddy."

"Take a step back," Wes warned, his tone icy. "This time I'm not asking."

"And I'm not moving."

"Have it your way."

I gasped.

Wes released his arm from my shoulder and positioned himself between me and Brodie, shielding me, but he stood there calmly.

Phew, that was close.

The two men were now nose to nose and looked like two boxers before a championship bout.

Brodie was getting worked up.

So was Wes.

I hissed, "Stop it, you two."

They ignored me.

"I said stop it! Right—!"

What happened next was a blur. Brodie threw a hooking fist at Wes' jaw. Wes dodged and shot a punch straight up at the bottom of Brodie's chin. Brodie took the shot and staggered back but didn't fall over. The balcony shook under my feet and I shouted at full volume, "Stop!" Brodie charged Wes, slamming him against the balcony railing like he wanted to push him over the edge. I dropped my shoes with my phone and house key, then grabbed for Brodie. Wes fired knuckles into Brodie's throat from the side. Too late, Brodie threw up a protective hand and twisted his body defensively, knocking me backward while taking a hit to his neck. I slammed into my front door loudly, crying out in surprise.

Both men stopped and whirled, facing me.

I wasn't hurt, but I was furious. I glared at both men, seething with rage. Somehow, when Brodie had pushed me away, his hand had caught in my dress and torn one of the straps off. There I stood in a half shredded dress, one strap hanging around my waist with my boob hanging out in the open, nipple and all.

I hissed, *"What the fuck is wrong with you two?!"*

Both men stared at me, shocked looks on their faces.

Brodie took a step forward. "Chelsea, I'm so sorry, I—" He suddenly hunched over and grabbed at his foot. "What the fuck?!" Abram Cohen's priceless necklace was stuck to the sole of his foot like castaway trash. It must've been torn from Wes' neck during the fight.

And Brodie had just stepped on it.

Wes withered with disgust, smearing his hand across his mouth and shaking his head in disbelief.

Brodie peeled the necklace off his foot slowly. "What the fuck is this thing?" he grunted as he cocked his arm back to throw.

"No, don't!" I gasped, reaching out to stop him.

Too late.

Brodie whipped it over the balcony railing without a thought.

"Brodie!" I shrieked and dove for the necklace. But I was too late and slammed into the railing, still reaching for the necklace as it splashed down in the pool.

Stunned, Wes grumbled, "Are you fucking kidding me?"

I fired my finger at Brodie and yelled, *"You go get that necklace right fucking now, or I swear I will never speak to you again, Brodie Bolden!"*

Lights inside the apartments around the courtyard started flicking on, upstairs and down. We had woken people up.

Brodie stared at me, angry.

"Now, Brodie! That is a million dollar necklace!" I tried to keep my yelling down to a whisper. I had no idea of the exact value, but a million dollars was close enough to get the point across.

"What?" Brodie chuckled.

"A million dollars! Get it out of the pool right now!"

"Is everything okay?" Mrs. Wiser stuck her head out of her apartment.

Wes was already walking past her, heading toward the stairs, "Nothing to worry about, ma'am. Just going for a late night swim." As he went, he pulled his shirt off and draped it over the railing without a thought.

Brodie stared at me like a gigantic idiot.

"Go get it, Brodie!"

Wes emerged from the bottom of the stairs. Brodie just stood there watching Wes, trying to piece all of this together.

When Wes reached the gate to the pool, he grabbed the top of it and vaulted over in one smooth motion. His loafers slapped on the cement when he landed on the other side.

Brodie finally figured out what was going on. He glared at me.

I glared back, hating him with everything I had. "Why don't you just stand there and do nothing, asshole?!"

"Fine," Brodie grunted. He climbed onto the balcony railing and half squatted, his bare feet seesawing on the railing as he struggled to keep his balance. He was going to jump like a professional wrestler from the top rope.

"Don't, Brodie!"

The iron railing bowed inward from his weight as he jumped.

Right when Wes was diving into the pool.

They were going to hit each other.

Brodie was going to kill Wes by accident, smashing his face into the bottom of the pool.

There was a huge splash as both men hit the water at the same time.

"Oh my goodness!" Mrs. Wiser gasped.

I ran past her and headed for the pool. By the time I got down to the fence, all I could see was the foaming water fizzing on the surface of the pool. I grabbed the doorknob for the gate and discovered it was locked. Oh yeah. It was always locked and you needed a key. Great. My pool key was in my apartment. I tried climbing over the gate, but with the train of my dress smothering my feet, it wasn't going to happen. I turned to run upstairs for my keys.

Petrak came rushing toward me, his keys already out. "Please move."

I took a step back and he opened the gate.

Right as we both stepped onto the pool deck, Brodie and Wes burst through the surface of the water, fighting over the necklace.

"Stop it, you idiots!" I screamed.

"What's going on here?!" Petrak shouted.

Wes and Brodie kept wrestling and throwing ineffective punches, churning up water in the pool.

I took a huge breath and shrieked at the top of my lungs,

"STOOOOOOOOP!!!"

Finally, the two men separated.

That's when I noticed Petrak held a cordless phone in his hand. He lifted it to his ear. "Yes? 911? Yes. Two men are fighting in my swimming pool. Yes. Okay, yes. The address is…"

Great.

My neighbors stood on the balcony surrounding the pool, leaning on the railing and watching the drama in their bathrobes, or standing on the ground floor outside the fence around the pool.

Two uniformed LAPD officers were interviewing Brodie and Wes separately. Both men were still wet, Wes in his damp tuxedo pants, Brodie in his damp boxers. Both had tousled wet hair and both had towels wrapped around their bare shoulders, towels courtesy of Mrs. Wiser.

I held Abram's necklace. To my surprise, it wasn't broken, except for the clasp, but that was a simple fix, right? Other than that, the only thing wrong with it was the lone diamond missing from the chain. Was it in the pool? On the balcony? In the courtyard bushes?

Who knew?

But I was sure Abram would want an explanation. The fact that only one diamond was missing was testimony to Abram's craftsmanship, a reason for him to be proud and hopefully a reason for him to not make a big deal about this, right? I mean, the necklace had at least a hundred diamonds and only one was missing.

What was one diamond?

If only.

Abram was going to kill somebody.

Or three somebodies.

When the police were finished, nobody wanted to press charges. Not even Petrak. It wasn't like anyone had broken the apartment's property.

Just Abram's.

And Madeline's dress. I'm sure she would love me now, *darling*. She was going to hate me.

Groan.

The officer talking to Brodie told him to go back to his apartment and get some sleep. Brodie nodded and walked past me on his way out, trying to catch my eye.

I refused to look at him.

His shoulders sagged as he trudged up the stairs and across the balcony toward his apartment. He kept looking at me but I kept ignoring him until his door closed and he was gone.

I felt terrible. But I hoped he felt more terrible for what he'd done. I didn't make him attack Wes. That was on him. But I couldn't help but wonder, was I a bad person for kissing them both? Weeks apart was one thing, but kissing them one day apart felt a little bit icky. No, it wasn't like I kissed Brodie last night. He kissed me. I just grabbed his shirt and went along wherever he took me. So what if I liked it? That was his fault. And when Wes kissed me a couple hours ago, Brodie was the furthest thing from my mind. So many things had happened since kissing Brodie, I could hardly be blamed for forgetting. I'd been completely swept away in the moment. I mean, I'd spent the previous sixteen hours assaulted by Madeline Kettner, Abram Cohen, Luca Rossi, and Tori the makeup artist and her assistants as they transformed me into a princess. Then I'd been thrown onto the one and only *real* red carpet to face an onslaught of paparazzi taking my picture while the world's most famous movie stars chatted with me one after the other. I was so overstimulated by the end of the night, there was literally no room left in my brain to think about anything, not even Brodie. I just went with Wes' kiss.

And here we were.

Wes finished talking with the police and came up to me where I sat on the edge of a vinyl lounge chair near the glowing blue pool. I had one of Mrs. Wiser's towels wrapped around my shoulders too.

Although I'd knotted the torn strap of my dress together, it was nice to have the towel for modesty's sake, and for warmth. Now that the intensity of the moment had faded, I was getting cold in the pre-dawn chill.

Wes sat down next to me and rested his elbows on his knees. "Sorry about all this."

"It's not your fault. Brodie attacked you."

"Yeah, but I could've backed down. I didn't have to go all alpha."

I turned and our eyes met. "You're right, you didn't." I closed my eyes and shook my head. "Here's your necklace. One of the diamonds is missing and the clasp is broken. That's probably my fault." *My fault for kissing you the night after I kissed Brodie. My fault for agreeing to go on a date with you in the first place. My fault for letting you walk me to my door when my door is right next to Brodie's. Brilliant idea, Jane.* I rolled my eyes at myself. To be fair, this was the first time I'd ever had two men interested in me at the same time. Heck, this was the first time I'd ever had two men interested in me during the same year. I didn't know how these things worked. Dating multiple men had always been my sister's department, not mine.

Wes patted my knee. "Nah. You weren't the one who stepped on Abram's necklace and threw it in the pool. But don't worry about it. I'll smooth things over."

"No, Wes. I'm as much to blame as you are. Find out how much the missing diamond cost and I'll pay for it."

"No."

"What do you mean no? I said I'll pay for it."

"You were right. I should've backed down. I should have politely walked away when Brodie got in my face. Or at the very least tried to talk things out instead of egging him on." He tilted his head back and looked up at the night sky, sighing. "That was really stupid of me. I'm an adult. I should know better."

"Wes, I'll pay for it."

"Lemme see the necklace."

I handed it to him.

"Where's the missing stone?"

I pointed it out. "See? It's just that one little diamond. And the clasp."

He smirked, "I don't know if you realize this, but this looks to me like a one karat diamond. On the low end, it could be worth three grand. Knowing Abram, it's not the low end. It could be as high as ten or twelve."

"Thousand dollars?" I gasped.

Wes nodded.

I didn't have even three thousand dollars to spare. Especially when I was out of a job. The cost of living in LA would deplete my savings quickly if I wasn't working. And, until I got my identity crisis sorted out, I'd be hard pressed to find a job. Who knew such a simple thing as looking like someone else could create so many problems?

Wes poured the necklace carefully into one hand and cupped it protectively. He rubbed my back with his free hand. "I'll take care of it, Sunflower. None of this was your fault."

If he only knew. I was disgusted with myself. I'd turned into a kissing slut without realizing it. "Maybe you should stop calling me Sunflower," I muttered.

Now it was his turn to give me a look. He just stared at me. "Is there something between you and Brodie?"

I couldn't look at him, so I examined one of my nails carefully. It had been torn down to the quick when I'd grabbed Brodie on the balcony. It stung, but not as painfully as the sting of guilt and embarrassment. "No. Maybe. I don't know. I sort of kissed him last night."

"You kissed him?" He sounded shocked. And maybe a little bit hurt.

"Last night. Before I kissed you. That was a lifetime ago. Anyway, it was the first time. He just moved in a week ago. I don't even really know the guy." I was making weak excuses.

"But you kissed him?" His tone was cold and a little bit disgusted.

"I kissed you and I barely know you. You're not even my neighbor." I scowled at myself. Why had I added that last part about neighbors?

Wes' face died right before my eyes. "Oh, great. What am I then? Third in line? Fourth? Fifth?" He shook his head. "I should've known a woman as beautiful as you would have other men in her life."

"There are no other men, Wes!" I wanted to add, *I'm not a slut who sluts around with five guys at the same time! Only two!* I cringed. There was nothing I could say.

"Except for Brodie," he muttered, saying it for me. He rolled his eyes, refusing to look at me.

I winced. "Maybe this was a bad idea, Wes."

"What, tonight? Or me in general?"

"I don't know," I sighed. I had no idea what to do or say to make this better.

Maybe there was nothing I could do.

Wes slowly stood and ran his hand through his damp hair before staring down at me. "Maybe you need to figure things out. But I'll tell you one thing. Brodie is a bad idea. I'm a good idea." His voice had a quiet conviction, but it was tinged with disappointment and maybe a hint of doubt.

Was he judging me?

Judging Brodie?

For a split second, I wanted to rush to Brodie's defense. I wanted to say he wasn't always like this. He was misunderstood. He helped autistic kids. He'd saved me from Lester Whatever. And he'd fixed my door like he'd promised. But that sounded pathetically naive. I barely knew Brodie. And, he was the one who punched Wes without a second thought. Wes had merely defended himself. Did Brodie think he owned me? After one kiss? And, did he punch his way out of every problem? Or just when it came to women?

I didn't want to think about it.

Confused, I gave Wes a pleading look.

He closed his eyes and said, "I have to go. Don't worry about the diamond. I'll take care of it with Abram." There was sadness in his voice. He sighed and turned away. "Maybe I'll see you around, Chelsea."

He didn't call me Sunflower.

He took a step toward the pool gate.

All of this felt like an ominous and tragic ending.

No, I wouldn't let things end this way. I shot to my feet and reached out for Wes.

At that exact moment, he stopped and spun around to face me. "One other thing."

"Yeah?" I said hopefully, clutching the towel around my shoulders.

"I don't know if you noticed, but there's paint all over the back of your dress."

"What?!" I gasped, twisting to look. He was right. My ass was covered in a thin haze of ass-shaped dried paint. It must've happened when Brodie knocked me into my front door.

"I don't think Madeline will need it back. Do whatever you want with it." He turned and walked toward the pool gate, stopping long enough to fold his towel and hand it to Mrs. Wiser, who he thanked graciously before walking toward the front gate of the apartment building. After he pushed through it, it slammed shut automatically on its spring. A resounding clank rattled the ironwork.

I'd heard that sound a thousand times since moving in.

Never had it sounded so dismally final.

A perfect ending to a perfect evening.

Chapter 24

My phone woke me the next morning.

"Yeah?" I said sleepily.

Chelsea screamed over the phone, "Jane! Did you watch the Oscars last night?! Oh my God! Please tell me you watched the Oscars!"

I was at the Oscars. "No. Why?"

"I tried calling you last night to tell you to turn it on, but you never answered your phone."

"Sorry. I turned it off by accident." Actually, it had been in Wes' tuxedo jacket all night on mute. He'd given it back on the way home in his limo. But thanks to Brodie, I'd dropped it during their fight and the screen was now cracked. Stupid Brodie.

I rubbed my eyes. "What time is it?"

"Nine-thirty."

"Aren't you supposed to be at work?"

"I am at work. I have meetings all day starting at ten, so I called you while I had time. Okay, do a Google search for 'mystery woman in red dress takes Oscars by storm'."

"Do I have to do it now?" I groaned, my eyes still closed. I knew where this was going.

"Yes! You will flip when you see the article. Just do it, Jay! Please! Google it!"

"Okay. Hold on." I typed in what she'd said, being careful of the broken screen. "What do I click on?"

"Click on the Yahoo News article. It should be near the top."

I did. After the page loaded, I scrolled down. Sure enough, a picture of me posing on that red carpet stage alone. Captions saying, Mystery woman Chelsea Johnson, a total unknown, sweeps Wesley Callaway and everyone at the Oscars off their feet. More photos of me with Wes on the red carpet. And at the Vanity Fair after party. Fantastic.

Now there was proof.

And it was all over the internet.

"Did it load yet?" Chelsea asked with high excitement.

"Yeah."

"Aren't you freaking out?"

"Yeah, freaking out," I deadpanned.

"She has *my* name and looks almost exactly like me! Can you believe it?! I have a bona fide real-life double!"

"Doppelgänger."

"Doppel what?"

"Gänger. Your double. Specifically, your evil twin." That was an understatement. Fake Chelsea Johnson had already caused more trouble than an army of evil twins riding through town on a regiment of evil horses while setting fire to every house in sight. What more could Evil Chelsea accomplish by the end of this phone call? I could only imagine.

"Hey, do you still have that cold? Your voice sounds off."

"Oh, right." I faked a cough. *Nope, just have a different voice box in my neck. Nothing to worry about.*

"Anyway, isn't this crazy? Me having a double?"

"Do Mom and Dad know?"

"Yeah! They were the ones who told me to turn on the Oscars! You need to call them, by the way."

"Yeah. I do."

"Who do you think she is?"

"Who?"

"My double. Do you think she's related to us? I mean, how could she not be? Some distant cousin or something?"

Ha ha. Exactly the lie I'd been telling people like Mrs. Wiser. "Do we even have distant cousins?"

"We do now," Chelsea said. "Wouldn't it be cool if we could track her down? I mean, how weird would it be for me to meet her face to face? Like finding out about the long lost twin you never knew you had. I wonder if we have the same birthday?"

"Probably not," I groaned.

"How do you know?"

Because our birthdays aren't the same. "Trust me, Chelz. She doesn't."

Something about her excitement was just too much. I'd had it with all of this. I was tired of the lying. Look where it had gotten me? I was out of a job and had guys attacking each other because of me. Wes, Brodie, and that stalker guy at Ralphs, Lester Whatever. And I wasn't even me! This beautiful thing was for the birds. I was sick of it. After mere days, I didn't want to be a supermodel anymore.

I just wanted to go back to being me.

Chelsea said, "I wonder if she has a Facebook page? Duh! Why didn't I check before? Hold on a second while I do a Facebook search and see what comes up."

"She's me, Chelsea."

"What?"

"I said, she's me."

"Who?"

"Your double. The fake Chelsea Johnson. She's me."

"Very funny," she said absently. "Hold on, I'm searching the Chelsea Johnsons on Facebook right now."

"She's me," I said with some irritation. "The girl on the red carpet is me, Chelsea."

"Uh huh," Chelsea said.

"Put me on FaceTime."

"Hold on. I'm still searching Facebook."

"Chelsea! Put me on FaceTime, God damn it!"

"All right, all right! Relax." A moment later, her face appeared on my iPhone screen. "Hold on. There must be something wrong with my phone. I'm still seeing myself."

"Chelsea! You're looking at me!!!"

She blinked several times. "What?"

I turned my phone around to show my entire bedroom, then back to my face. "See! This is me! You're in your office at work! I'm in my apartment! And I look like your evil twin!"

"Ha!" Chelsea just stared at the phone, not believing it. I could relate. It took a moment or ten to sink in.

"Chelsea, watch my mouth. This is me talking to you. Your sister Jane."

She frown-smiled. "Is this some kind of a prank?"

"Nope."

"Oh, I know. Is this some new app that swaps faces? Because I've used those and they work pretty well."

"Jesus Christ, Chelsea! I'm not an app! This is me! I look like you now!"

"How? That's not even possible, Jay."

"I don't know how! It happened last week! Are you getting it now?"

"Jane, I don't know what's going on."

"Me neither, Chelz. But this is me. I don't look like I used to."

"Wait, are you serious?" She still didn't believe me, but she was starting to consider it.

"I'm deadly serious. I'm also like 5'9". I'm taller than you. And no, I didn't get plastic surgery since you were here a week ago. Nobody heals up to perfect in seven days."

She stared at me through the phone, her eyes searching my face for almost a minute. "No... No." She shook her head, blinking nervously.

"Yes, Chelsea. Yes."

"This is impossible."

"*Was* impossible." I waited while she thought about it.

"But… how?"

"Magic? I don't know. I thought I was dreaming when I first woke up like this. But nope, I turned into…" I half smiled and laughed, "into you. Kind of."

She squinted and brought her phone close to her face, examining my image. So I held my phone closer to my face and moved it around slowly so she could see me from every angle. My phone may have been cracked, but hers wasn't. She could see my image perfectly. "This isn't surgery. It isn't a mask. Or an app. It's me."

"What the hell, Jay?"

"Exactly."

Just like with George, I spent over an hour on FaceTime with Chelsea trying to convince her I had actually changed into someone else. Fortunately, I knew so many details about Chelsea, things going back to when we were little, it wasn't as hard to convince her. Once she finally believed me, I brought her up to speed on how I'd been deathly ill for almost five days before waking up like this, how I'd lost my job, kissed Brodie and Wes, and their fight.

"Have you told Mom and Dad?" Chelz asked.

"Ha! Are you kidding? They'd never believe it. You barely do."

"True. Wow, Jay. It just doesn't make any sense. Like, it's scientifically impossible."

"I know, right. It's like, ever since I woke up with this ring on my finger, I—"

"Wait. What ring?"

"This one." I held it up to the phone.

"Where'd you get that? That looks expensive."

"I thought I told you."

"No."

I took a deep breath. "Remember after speed dating how none of the guys emailed me for my number?"

"Yeah?"

"Well, that's when I went for a walk and stumbled on Wes' grandmother's mansion. That's where I found the ring. In his grandmother's vanity."

"Did you steal it?"

"No! He didn't even want it."

"Let me see it again."

I held it up to the phone.

"Why would he not want that? It looks like it's worth a few grand at least. More if that's twenty-four karat gold."

"I think it is. But it didn't look like this when I got it. It was like, I don't know, some cheap brass ring you'd get at a flea market for fifty cents."

"Huh?"

Memories of Wes' estate sale came flooding back.

The only reason I'd kept the ring was as a memento of the moment when the handsome rich and powerful Wes Callaway had been nice to a little nerd girl who'd lost her way and found his grandmother's mansion in the middle of nowhere. I started to tear up thinking about it. *That* had been a special moment. More special than going to the Oscars looking like a supermodel and meeting all those celebrities and having my picture taken a thousand times just because I was beautiful. That didn't matter. None of it did. What mattered was that moment where a handsome stranger had been nice to little nerdy me. That was real. That was something I wanted back.

I wanted to be me, not beautiful.

I sniffed away tears, "I want to be me again, Chelz."

"Yeah, but how?"

"It's the ring. I think it made me this way."

"How does that make any sense?"

"I don't know. It just does. There's no other possible explanation. It has to be the ring."

"So, what, you take it off and change back?"

"I think so. But I have to leave it off. It took me five days of torture to get to here, so it'll probably take five to get back. That's logical, right?"

"What if you take it off and you don't change back?"

I cringed. "It's possible. But the only way to find out is to try."

"Won't it make you sick again?"

"Probably? But for all I know, this stupid ring is giving me cancer anyway. I'm probably better off without it."

"How do you feel right now?"

"I feel great," I smiled.

A worried look tightened Chelsea's face, "Maybe taking the ring off is a bad idea."

"Only one way to find out."

Chapter 25

Two days later, I woke in excruciating pain. I'd taken the ring off after talking to Chelsea.

In preparation, I'd stocked up on water and extra-strength Tylenol, which I kept near my bed. I'd already taken half the bottle and it hadn't helped. I was starting to worry I'd poison myself on painkillers before this was over.

I'd never been hooked on heroin or painkillers, or been addicted to cigarettes or alcohol, or been through withdrawal symptoms of any kind, but something told me mine were as bad as they could ever get.

For the past two days, every waking moment, (which were few because the pain was as intense this time as it had been the first time), made me want to put the ring back on. Not to be beautiful. Just to make the pain go away. I didn't have the fever and cold sweats that people got with regular withdrawals, but my body felt like it had been run over by an army of charging elephants.

I wasn't exaggerating.

My body literally felt shattered.

My bones, my muscles, my joints, my skin, my hair, my nails, every microscopic inch of me burned with fiery pain.

Was this worth it?

It didn't seem like it.

If being normal meant being in this much pain, why not stay beautiful?

No.

I was seeing this through.

I was going back to being me.

My bedroom was dark when I woke again.

I didn't know what day it was.

The only thing that mattered was my splitting headache and my stabbing need to pee. I crawled to the bathroom, barely making it.

After, I climbed to standing and leaned against my bathroom sink.

I flipped on the lights.

And immediately regretted doing it.

My face looked lopsided. Like it had been crushed in a vise or run over by a dump truck. I didn't look like supermodel me or even regular me. I looked...

Deformed.

I gasped.

Had something gone wrong?

Fear seized me.

Was I going to look like this forever?

What if I did?

Oh no oh no oh no!!

But the reality of it stared right back at me.

I looked horrible.

Tears filled my eyes and I swiped the light switch off. In darkness, I stumbled back to my bed, deeply afraid for the first time since all this started.

As another blast of pure pain exploded in my skull, one thought spun through my head like a washing machine on spin cycle:

Deformed.

—deformed deformed deformed deformed deformed deformed deformed deformed deformed deformed deformed deformed deformed deformed—

Chapter 26

A gentle chime woke me.

The soft light of dawn trickled through my blinds.

I picked up my phone.

The screen was blurred.

I squinted my eyes, trying to see. No use. My good vision was gone. I fumbled around on my nightstand for my glasses and found them right where I'd left them. I slid them on and could read my phone.

A new email.

I didn't want to deal with email right now.

I set my phone down and stared at my bedroom ceiling. Lifted my glasses. Everything blurred. Put my glasses back on. Everything was sharp once again.

My body didn't hurt anymore.

Actually, I felt fine.

But how did I look?

Did I want to know?

What monster might be waiting for me in the mirror?

Considering my self-esteem had never revolved around my looks, I climbed out of bed and walked to my bathroom with purpose. Whatever I looked like, I'd deal with it. I'd made it this far in life looking like an ugly duck, so I could make it the rest of the way.

Standing in the dark bathroom, my hand hovered over the light switch, poised to flip it on. I couldn't bring myself to look.

But I had to look.

Out loud I counted, "Five. Four. Three. Two…" I cringed and squeezed my eyes shut. "Here goes nothing…"

Flipped on the lights.

Peeked through one eye.

Then the other.

My plain old face was the most beautiful thing I'd ever seen.

Relief.

I was me again.

Me!

I smiled big, happier than ever.

My phone chimed again, signaling yet another new email. I walked into my bedroom and picked it up. Read today's date.

Sunday.

Wow.

This time, I'd been out for six days.

Six whole days.

At least I didn't have to worry about losing my job. I'd already lost it. I checked email briefly, but there were too many to deal with. I did notice one from Extreme Speed Dating LA, but that was probably just a sales email for their next event. I'd delete it later.

Scrolling through my unread texts, I saw Chelsea had checked in several times. I texted her back briefly to say everything was fine and I was back to normal. Texts from George. I had told him in advance I was taking the ring off. He had offered to come by to help out, but I had told him I'd do it alone. I texted him that everything went great and I'd call soon. Texts from Wes. A bunch of them. I didn't want to read them. He was texting supermodel me, not plain me. I deleted our entire conversation without looking at his new texts. I really didn't want to know. He had also left me several voicemails. Just as I was about to call my voicemail to delete them, my phone rang.

I gasped, thinking it was Wes.

Nope. Chelsea.

With great relief, I hit the FaceTime button.

"Jane!" Chelsea beamed. "It's you!"

"Yeah," I smiled feeling incredibly happy. "It's me."

"Wow, how are you?"

"I'm great. How are you?"

"Fine. So, was it bad?"

"Changing back? Pretty much the same as before," I lied. I shuddered at the memory of my deformed face. I would never share that moment with anyone. My preference would be to never remember it.

"I still can't believe any of this happened."

"I know, it's beyond weird. But it happened. Now it's all in the past. I'm me!" I smiled, giggling.

"Yes you are. And you've never looked better."

I pushed my glasses up my nose, "Thanks, Chelz."

"I can't wait to see you Friday."

"That's right! You've got your sales meeting or whatever."

"New client. Yeah, it's gonna be great to see you. Oh, you're never going to believe this," she said with high excitement. "People at work think I was at the Oscars!" She laughed.

I was part amused and part worried. "What did you tell them?"

"I just said it was a coincidence."

"Did people believe you?" I had a hard time believing any of the past two weeks had happened to me, and I'd lived it. But you couldn't deny hundreds of photos and videos splashed all over the internet.

"Mostly they thought I was lying. Some of the guys at work went all conspiracy theory and said I had plenty of time to get to LA, go to the Oscars, and be back at work on Monday morning. It was really kind of crazy."

"I bet it was." I hoped this didn't somehow come back to bite both of us in the ass.

"So, now that you're you again, what's next?"

"Look for a job. I got let go, remember?"

"Maybe you can get your old job back."

"Maybe," I said doubtfully.

"You should try. What have you got to lose?"

"Jane. What are you doing here?" Doug Wallace stood in the manager's booth at the 95 Cent Store. It was Monday afternoon, near the end of his shift. "And why are you dressed for work?"

"Hey, Doug," I smiled, wearing my blue 95 Cent Store vest over one of my usual work blouses and slacks. *Dress like you already have the job, right?*

"Did you come for your last check?" he asked.

Or not. "Uhhhh…"

"Jane!"

I turned and saw Maria walking into the store with her purse over her shoulder, her vest already on. The relief I felt when she recognized me was overwhelming. Her arms were wide as she ran around the nearest register and headed straight for me and hugged me tight. I started to tear up and hugged her back.

She gasped, "We were so worried about you! What happened, girl? You disappeared for like two weeks!" She held me by both arms, looking me over. "Are you okay?"

"I'm fine. I was just…" I cast a glance at Doug. "I was really sick. So sick I couldn't call in."

"Really?" Maria asked. "Was it serious?"

"Yes and no. It… it's complicated. What matters is I'm fine now."

She noticed my 95 Cent Store vest. "Why are you dressed for work?

Are you taking over for Doug tonight?" She looked at him hopefully.

I leveled a look at Doug. "Tonight? Aren't you off at five, Doug?"

He smirked, "I'm handling evenings until we can get Rick Martinez back filling in. Hopefully by Friday."

"Rick Martinez?" I said. "From the Venice store? What happened to that guy Phil? What was his name? Phil the Turd Burger?"

"Phil Berger," Doug corrected.

"I like Turd Burger better," Maria giggled. "He grabbed my ass his third day here."

"No way!" I gasped, covering my gaping mouth with my fingers.

"Yeah way. That *hijo de puta* was a perv. Tried to grab Natalie too." She pursed her lips and shook her head. "*Sucio verga.* Anyway, Doug fired his ass, right?"

Doug grimaced, "Language, Maria." Doug spoke Spanish, so he knew everything Maria was saying.

"It's true! Me and Natalie came to work early last Thursday to tell Doug everything. He fired that *pendejo* on Friday and worked his shift that night."

"Maria, please," Doug warned.

"Relaaaaax, *jefe.* I'm just telling Jane what happened, yo."

I gave Doug a long look.

His face wiggled nervously.

"Douuuuuuug," I singsonged. "I bet you'd love to go home to Pam and Matthew right now and have dinner with them."

"I would but—"

I cut in, "But you need a qualified manager to take over for you. Maria, who do we know who can run this store on short notice?"

Maria smirked at Doug. "She's right, *jefe.* Nobody is better than Jane."

Right then, Natalie walked in with her usual quiet presence. She smiled big when she saw me and joined the three of us. We hugged. "Hey, Jane. Did you come back?"

I grinned at Doug. "What's Pam making tonight? Lasagna? Or maybe pasta primavera?" I knew Doug loved Italian food. "Why have cold leftovers after midnight when you can eat it hot right now? If you leave at five, you can be home before your dinner gets cold."

"What she said," Maria grinned.

Natalie just smiled and nodded at Doug.

Doug rolled his eyes, "Will you three stop?"

"Not till you let Jane back," Maria said defiantly.

Doug planted his hands on the counter of the manager's booth and grumbled down at us. "You can stop steamrolling me, ladies. Let me call Stacy Lewis and make sure it's okay."

"Do it!" Maria said hopefully.

Doug frowned at me, "You know, Jane, Stacy is going to want a doctor's note of some kind. You were gone for two weeks without an explanation. A note will go a long way to making me and her feel better about everything."

"I wish I had one, Doug," I pleaded urgently. "But I didn't go to the doctor. I was too sick to get out of bed. You have to believe me." I held my breath. Everything depended on how much Doug trusted me.

He arched a suspicious eyebrow.

"She's telling the truth, *jefe*," Maria said.

"How would you know, Maria?" he asked thoughtfully. "Were you there?"

I cringed, expecting her to start spinning some lie that I would have to somehow corroborate on the spur of the moment.

"When has Jane ever lied to you, *jefe*? Or any of us?"

Natalie shrugged and nodded.

I smiled at Doug. "I'm telling the truth, Doug. Please believe me."

Doug's eyes searched mine. I'd known the guy five years. That had to count for something. His face softened. "Okay, okay! As far as I'm concerned, Jane is back on the job starting tonight. But I still have to smooth things over with corporate first."

"*Toma!*" Maria clapped happily. "I'm so glad you're back, *hermana!*" She hugged me again, jumping up and down.

"Me too, Maria."

Natalie rubbed my shoulder and I turned and hugged her too.

Doug made a phone call to Stacy Lewis. We all listened in while he talked, unsure of how things would turn out. I crossed my fingers and Maria did too. Doug nodded a lot while he spoke, saying things like, "Yes, sure. Of course." When he finally hung up, he turned to me and smiled. "Guess who's back on the job?"

I beamed, "Really?!"

"Really." Doug reached down and shook my hand. "Good to have you back, Jane."

That evening, after Doug was gone and it was just me and Maria and Natalie running things, I'd never been happier to be the night manager at the 95 Cent Store.

It was the simple things that counted.

The next morning, I got out of bed, put my glasses on, and smiled at myself in the bathroom mirror.

My plain old reflection smiled back at me.

I was so happy to be me.

While eating a bowl of organic corn flakes, I thumbed through my emails on my broken iPhone. Mostly junk, including the ones from Extreme Speed Dating LA. I was about to delete them when I noticed the subject line on the latest one read: *Your belated matches.*

Belated?

I opened the email and skimmed it. An apology from the company followed by *Good news! You have one more match!*

One more? How about one only?

It was from Mike.

Who was Mike again? I had only a hazy memory of what he looked like. I'd been wearing my glasses when we'd met that night, but that seemed like a year ago.

I scrolled down and read his note.

Jane—

I am so sorry for taking so long to turn in my scorecard from speed dating. If I had a choice, I would've spent the entire evening with you that night, but rules are rules. You're probably wondering why it took me so long to contact you. Let me explain. Halfway through that night, I got paged for work. I wish I had some super extreme excuse for you, like jumping out of an airplane into enemy territory or rescuing people from a burning building, but I don't. It was just work. Business as usual. Not even an emergency. On the scale of extremes, I wouldn't even give it a 2. But sometimes babies don't like to wait, and I have to drop everything to go and get them. Such is the life of an obstetrician.

Wait, was Mike a doctor? I didn't remember him mentioning it, but we'd only had five minutes and spent most of it flirting.

His email continued:

I should have turned in my scorecard before leaving ReaXion that night, but I put it in my pocket like an absent minded professor, which sounds more romantic than it actually was. I was just thinking about that baby. After the delivery, I couldn't find the scorecard. Believe me, I looked all over everywhere trying to find it, but I'd left it in my blazer pocket like an idiot. I didn't find it until I picked up my dry cleaning yesterday. Good thing they found it and saved it for me!

I scrolled down and there was a picture of him at a dry cleaner's, holding up his navy blazer and his speed dating scorecard. He really had a great smile. And those cute blue eyes. Now I remembered him. Un-extreme Mike.

So, Jane, I would love to take you out some time for more than five minutes. We can have an un-speed date. We can do something more extreme than breathing but less extreme than skydiving. I'll even eat Satan's food cake if you want. Well, maybe just devil's food cake. Don't want to tempt fate by doing something too extreme. LOL

Wow, he remembered everything we'd talked about.

Call me some time, Jane.

It might turn out to be the most extreme thing you've ever done.

Yours,

Mike.

I was smiling from ear to ear when I set my phone down and put my cereal bowl in the sink.

What was not to like about Mike?

Chapter 27

Because of our schedules, the first evening both Mike and I had free was the Saturday a week later.

That evening, I stood outside my apartment building, dressed in my nicest black dress, waiting for him. I didn't want him coming to my door because I didn't want to risk Brodie seeing him and beating him up. Mike was tiny compared to Brodie.

Brodie could go fuck himself.

He hadn't even apologized since attacking Wes and making a mess of things.

Total asshole.

Only later did I realize I didn't need to worry about Brodie because I wasn't Chelsea the supermodel anymore. I was just plain Jane. Oh well. Brodie could still go fuck himself.

A new Lexus four door drove up to the curb. Mike jumped out to get my door. Once we were in the car, he reached over my naked knees and opened the glove box.

"Got something for you." He handed me a thin package not much bigger than an envelope. It was wrapped in white wrapping paper checkered with dozens of red chili peppers and tied with a curly red ribbon.

"What is it?"

"Open it."

I tore it open and smiled. "Dark chocolate with chili peppers. Awww! You remembered!"

He winked, "I told you I was extreme."

"Thank you, Mike." I reached across the center console and hugged him.

He chuckled, his blue eyes sparkling. "Are you gonna open it now? Or is that too extreme?"

"What do you think? Duh." I tore the package open.

"Whoa, Jane! Slow down! I don't think I can handle this much extreme!" He laughed.

I broke off a piece and handed it to him then popped a second one in my mouth. We both chewed on our chocolate.

I nodded thoughtfully as the dark chocolate melted in my mouth and the sweet turned to spicy. "This is good. I really like this."

"I told you. What I'm wondering is, have you ever kissed someone while eating spicy chocolate?" His blue eyes twinkled. He really was cute, despite his pinched face.

"Ummm…" All I could think about was all the trouble I'd gotten into by kissing guys without thinking. "Can I think about it?"

"Sure. But don't forget, I did give you the more extreme option."

"You did," I smiled. "And thank you for offering."

Mike took me to dinner. We really had a great time. Mike was funny. Mike was nice. Mike wasn't nearly as extreme as he wanted to be, unless you considered being an on-call obstetrician extreme.

I liked Mike.

But that was it.

When Mike dropped me off, he walked me to my door. By then, I'd remembered that Brodie wouldn't care if he saw little nerd girl me back from a date with Mike the doctor. Knowing Brodie, if he were to see me, he'd probably ignore me. So I let Mike kiss me when he asked. Yes, he asked. It was so cute. How could I say no? It was his second attempt. I couldn't bear to shoot him down twice. Plain Jane wasn't dating anybody else, so I had no reason to feel guilty and I went for it.

The kiss was… just a kiss.

It wasn't bad. It was just… boring.

He did grab me, but only by the elbow. He was being respectful, but it wasn't exactly sexy.

After, he smiled at me, giddy. "I had a great time tonight, Jane."

"Me too, Mike." Was I lying to him? No, he was fun. I had laughed a lot. That was a great time, right?

"When can I see you again?"

"Maybe next weekend?" Now I was lying. I didn't see a future with Mike. Was I being shallow? Maybe. No, it wasn't his looks. I was fine with his looks. It wasn't his height. He was short, but he was taller than me. It was… things just weren't clicking. Maybe I was a bitch. Maybe I needed to give him a second chance. "You know what? Next weekend might be great." *Might be great. Might.* I forced a smile.

He didn't. His smile was wide and genuine. "Okay then. Next weekend we'll do something slightly more extreme than dinner."

"Promise?"

"Promise." He stood there waiting, looking at me and smiling. Smiling and looking. Looking and smiling.

I hope he didn't want me asking him inside for cocktails.

He stuffed his hands into his pockets. "Hey, um—"

"I should probably get inside and get to bed."

"Oh, sure. Right. Hey, you aren't, uh, free tomorrow, are you? I mean, it's Sunday and... you know..."

"My sister's in town." She was. She had flown in Thursday night, but she had decided to stay at Mom and Dad's for the past two nights because she hadn't seen them in so long. "I have plans with her tomorrow." We didn't, but maybe it was time for me to drive out to Mom and Dad's for a visit. They probably felt like I'd been avoiding them, which was sort of true. So I wasn't really lying to Mike.

"Oh, okay." He pecked my cheek. "G'night."

"Good night, Mike. Thanks again. Really. I'll call you next week, okay?"

"Okay."

When I closed my front door behind me, I felt like an ass.

Was I ever going to call Mike again?

Or was I just leading him on?

Who knew.

The next afternoon, a knock at my front door startled me. I hopped up from the couch and dropped the library copy of Gone Girl I'd been reading. It was probably George. He'd be surprised seeing me back to normal, but he'd probably be relieved.

I knew I was.

I stood on my tip toes so I could see through the peephole. I had a moment to think about how I hadn't needed to use tiptoes when I was a tall and leggy supermodel. Now I did. That meant things were back to normal. I liked normal.

Through the fisheye lens I saw Brodie.

My face soured.

What did he want?

Despite my irritation, my heart beat faster at the thought of him coming in. I hoped he was wearing a shirt. I really didn't want to see his abs today.

I opened the door.

No shirt. Abs all over the place and sexy as always.

Brodie looked down at me, confused. "Hey, uh, what was your name again?" Here was Brodie showing his true colors. If I wasn't a supermodel, he didn't give a shit about me.

My face sagged. "Jane."

He half-smiled, "Hey, Jane. Uh, how are you?"

Did he really want to know or was he just being polite? I heaved a sighed. "I'm fine, Brodie. Can I help you with something?"

"Have you seen Chelsea around?"

"Nope."

"You know when she's gonna be back? It's been like a week since she was here. She okay?"

"You'd have to ask her." I really didn't care whether Brodie was worried or not. Besides, what was I going to tell him? Chelsea the supermodel was effectively dead. If I told him that, he'd ask all kinds of stupid questions I wasn't going to answer.

"If you see her, can you tell her I'm looking for her?"

I stared at him for a long time. Was I disappointed? No. I already knew what kind of man Brodie was. People only disappointed you when they didn't meet your expectations. Brodie had met mine. Shallow manwhore. It didn't matter what he did for a living.

But I refused to be rude for no reason.

I sighed, "I'll make sure she knows you were looking for her."

"Thanks."

"Anything else?" *Chelsea isn't going to show up, so you can leave.*

"Nah." He just stood there. Was he going away or not?

"You know what, Brodie?"

"Yeah?"

"Chelsea moved to Milan to pursue runway modeling." It seemed reasonable, and with any luck, this would be the last time he ever knocked on my door.

"Milan?"

"It's in Italy."

"I know where it is. I've been there before."

"Oh." I considered telling him to buy a plane ticket and chase after her, but I wasn't that spiteful. I couldn't send him on a wild goose chase, or in this case a wild swan chase, that would cost thousands of dollars and probably drive him crazy in the process. Maybe I should've told him she'd moved to Laos to work on a fishing boat, or given up all her worldly possessions and moved to India to join an ashram.

Oh well. Too late now.

"Do you have her email or something? I don't even have her phone number. I really need to talk to her."

Could I tell him no without sounding like a spiteful jealous bitch, which I wasn't? I mean, how could I be jealous of a nonexistent person? For all intents and purposes, Chelsea the supermodel was dead, and when she'd been alive, she was me anyway, so what was there to be jealous about?

Yeah, I was jealous. Sort of. Not really.

Maybe a little.

"Please, Jane. I have to talk to Chelsea. It's really important. I... I need to apologize to her. I was a total dick the other night. I messed up everything. I was... I was a total jealous prick. I acted like an ass. Like a fucking two year old. I don't know why. Seeing her with that fucking guy..." He shook his head. "Fuck. I don't know. I was a douche." He was staring over my head, not talking to me. It's like he was sending his apology straight out to fake Chelsea.

He didn't know it, but he was giving me the apology I wish he'd given me a week ago. My heart started to melt. Damn him. He was making me like him all over again. But beautiful Brodie Bolden would never want plain Jane Johnson, the little nerd girl standing right in front of him.

His apology wasn't for me.

It was for super Chelsea.

I wasn't her.

I was done with her.

Brodie finally looked me in the eyes, his face pained, "Can you tell her I'm sorry, Jane? Please?"

I hated him so bad I wanted to cry.

He didn't deserve my tears.

He deserved my door slammed in his face.

The sound of boot heels echoed up the stairwell at the end of the balcony. Brodie turned to look. His eyes widened and a smile erased his sadness in an instant. He completely forgot I was standing here.

He took a step toward the moving boot heels as they walked along the balcony. I stood inside my apartment, so I couldn't see who it was. But Brodie could. He was ecstatic. The boots passed Mrs. Wiser's apartment and were just about to reach mine. Still staring at whoever it was, Brodie said, "Chelsea?"

Oh, shit.

I leaned out my front door.

My sister walked toward us and waved at me, smiling. "Hey, Jane!" As always, she looked gorgeous. Movie star black sunglasses and black blazer over a white mesh dress and knee high black boots. You could see flashes of her white bra and panties through the mesh as she walked. She also wore a black scarf twisted around her neck. It was thin linen and it gave her outfit a subtle BDSM vibe without being slutty. She was sex hot.

As she approached, Brodie gawked at her, his jaw hanging against his chest. She gave him a polite smile as she passed. She didn't know him, but I bet she could figure out who he was.

Brodie reached out and gently tugged the arm of her black blazer, trying to slow her to a stop. "Hey, C.C., where are you going?" he muttered, somewhat confused. Of course he was confused. He thought the real Chelsea was *me* Chelsea, a.k.a. C.C., and she was ignoring him!

Yes, watching my sexy sister ignore him gave me plenty of smug satisfaction. Maybe now he would know what it felt like to be ignored.

Chelz lowered her movie star sunglasses and glared at Brodie over the frames. "Would you let go of my coat?" Her voice was firm and wasn't taking no for an answer.

I hid a smile, loving every moment of this.

Brodie dropped his arm, chastened. "Sorry," he muttered. "C.C., it's me. Brodie." He was begging her to recognize him, but it wasn't going to happen.

Chelz flashed me a confused look.

I said, "Brodie, this is my sister Chelsea."

Brodie's own confusion was obvious. "Sister? I thought you were cousins."

I said, "You're thinking of our *cousin* Chelsea, the one who moved to Milan to be a model. Yes, she does look a lot like my *sister* Chelsea." I nodded at her. "But I promise, they're two different people."

Chelz pulled her sunglasses off and put her arm around me. "We're sisters."

Brodie looked at Chelz for a long time. "You really look a lot like your cousin."

Chelz shrugged. "So I've heard."

"Like you could be twins…" Brodie mused.

Twins?

Shit, if he made a move on Chelz, the real Chelsea, my sister, I would shoot him dead where he stood. I'd have to buy a gun first, but I would go get one post haste and track him down, then shoot him wherever he stood.

"…but you're not her," Brodie finished, distraught. He heaved a sad sigh.

I released my own silent sigh of relief. The last place I wanted to end up was in prison for first degree murdering Brodie.

He looked at Chelz, "If either of you talk to your cousin, can you tell her I'm sorry?" He hung his head and walked back into his apartment and closed the door softly.

It was the saddest sounding door close I'd ever heard.

Chapter 28

"Was that Brodie?" Chelz asked inside my apartment.

"Yeah."

"Wow, he's really hot. Did you see those abs?"

I scowled, "Don't remind me. He doesn't even know I exist."

"He was acting like he knew you. Didn't you say you met him before you turned into me?"

I smirked, "I didn't turn into you."

"You know what I mean."

It bummed me out that Brodie would've asked my sister out if he'd met her first. But he'd met me first. Twice. But he was only interested in supermodels. Suddenly, all my usual insecurities were back. My sister got guys like Brodie and Wes. I got guys like un-extreme Mike the doctor.

"I know what you're thinking, Jay. So stop. You're beautiful."

"You're blind. Maybe I should've left the ring on."

Chelsea looked at me for a long time. "You yourself said it might be giving you cancer."

I frowned, "What do I know? Nothing about what happened to me when I put that ring on was normal. For all I know, wearing that ring might make me disease free and live to the ripe old age of a hundred and twenty. Or longer. But I'll never find out now because I took it off."

"Do you still have it?"

"It's around here somewhere." I knew exactly where it was but I wasn't telling her. I didn't want her or anyone knowing where it was. I wouldn't want it disappearing. Not that Chelsea would try and steal it. She didn't need to be beautiful. She already was and had more hot men than she knew what to do with.

"Maybe you should put it back on," she sighed.

"Really?"

"Yeah. I don't know what Mom and Dad will say, but why not? If it makes you happy, maybe you should. Who am I to say how you should live your life?"

My entire body suddenly tingled with possibilities. I could. I could go back to being beautiful. At least I assumed I could. Would it work? It seemed like it had taken longer to change me back to normal than it had to make me beautiful. Was it running out of gas or power or whatever magic it ran on? Would it work at all if I put it back on? Or would it only work halfway and leave me looking…

Deformed.

I cringed.

Geez, was this even a good idea? Or was I just playing with fire?

Maybe I needed to get rid of it. Drop it in the ocean or something.

No, I didn't want to do that.

Did I?

I needed to distract myself with something more frivolous than this. "So, Chelz. Who do you think is hotter? Brodie or Wes?"

"Well, I only saw pictures and videos of Wes at the Oscars. But it's pretty close. Which one is taller?"

"Brodie. Barely. Maybe an inch."

"I don't know, Jay. They're both fine men. Either one looks like the total package. On the outside, anyway. Brodie seems like he might be a bit too immature. But it's too soon to tell."

"I know, right?"

Suddenly I was thrilled to be having this discussion with my sister. For the first time in my life, we were talking about men and comparing notes. Not her speaking from deep experience while giving me advice because I didn't have any experience to draw from. The opposite. When it came to Brodie and Wes, I was the one with all the experience, not her. Frankly, it made me giddy.

"You know what, Chelz? Let's go out. Just you and me. I could really use a drink with my sister."

She smiled, "Sounds like a plan, Stan."

What a mistake.

Never go out with your supermodel sister after changing back into a nerd girl. Especially not in LA where the men are hot and plentiful.

Everywhere we went, guys hit on her, not me.

Credit to Chelsea: she suggested we call it a night long before I did. She saw the dynamic from the beginning while I was busy ignoring it.

She also saw me getting drunk.

I never got drunk.

But tonight seemed like the right night for getting hammered.

<<<<<<<<>>>>>>>

Monday morning I woke with a horrible hangover.

Chelsea took an Uber car to the airport so I didn't have to drive her. Thank goodness I didn't have to work until five. I didn't formally get out of bed until noon. If it had been my choice, I would've slept until tomorrow.

I dragged myself into the living room and sat on my couch, placed the stupid ring on my coffee table, and stared at it for over an hour.

Should I put it on?

Throw it away?

Now it was just a tarnished piece of junk, just like me. I didn't need to save it.

A walk to the ocean might make me feel better. Then I could chuck the ring off the end of the Santa Monica Pier and never see it again.

Yeah, that's exactly what I needed to do. When I stood up, I sat right back down.

Hello, hangover.

I'd be lucky if I felt up to working in four hours.

Remind me never to drink that many shots ever again.

How many had I had? Six? Eight? Whatever the number, it was way past my limit.

I looked at the ring again.

It was so unassuming now.

I leaned forward and picked it up with the intention of hiding it in my bedroom until I figured out what to do with it. The second my fingers closed around it, my doorbell dinged.

I hoped it wasn't Brodie. I didn't want to see him today or any day. Groaning, I tiptoed up to peer through the peephole.

It was Wes.

What was he doing here?

I opened the door.

He wore his old jeans, flip-flops, and a T-shirt that had the old Nintendo logo on it. He also had on his aviator shades and plenty of stubble. This was casual Wes, accessible Wes, a mere mortal compared to his godlike red-carpet ready self. He pulled his aviators down with a smile. "Hey, Jane. Good to see you. I didn't realize you lived with Chelsea."

"Yeah," I smirked.

"How have you been? You look great, by the way." Was he serious or just being charming? I could never tell with Wes. One thing was for sure: unlike Brodie, Wes projected total interest in me. Whether it was sexual or platonic was impossible to tell, but that made him all the more charming.

"I'm good."

"Mind if I come in?"

I almost blurted yes like a desperate thirteen year old. "Uh, Chelsea isn't here."

"And?" He raised his eyebrows. "Aren't you going to invite me in anyway?"

Okay, that was not what I was expecting. "Sure. Come in." I closed the door behind him, still clutching the ring in my hand. Why did this moment feel so familiar? It wasn't, but somehow it was. Like the day we'd first met, charged with possibility.

Wes dropped on my couch like he owned the place. Or like an old friend who'd been here a thousand times before.

"Can I get you something to drink?" I offered.

He frowned, "You look a little tired. Are you feeling okay?"

I laughed guiltily. "I sort of drank too much last night."

He grinned. "Been there, done that." He jumped up from the couch and took my free hand. "Sit down. You look like you need it. I'll get us something to drink."

Confused, I sat and watched Wes open my refrigerator in the kitchenette and lean over it. "You want this raspberry smoothie thing, apple juice, or water?"

"Water is fine."

He searched my cabinets for glasses.

"Next to the stove."

"Thanks." He pulled out two and opened the freezer.

"I don't need ice."

"Ice for one," he smiled and dropped two cubes in his glass. "You don't have a filter pitcher anywhere do you?"

"No, just tap."

"My favorite."

I couldn't believe this was happening. "What are you doing here, Wes?" He shrugged at me while filling the glasses under the tap. I said, "If you're waiting for Chelsea, she's not here. She's… in Milan."

"Milan? What's she doing there?"

"Traveling." I didn't want to spin up a big lie for Wes.

He nodded. "Milan is great. I haven't been in a while. The weather is nice this time of year. Not too hot during the day, not too cold at night. You ever been?"

"No."

"Then why didn't you go with Chelsea?"

"Oh, uh. I have to work."

He nodded sympathetically. "That's work for you." He walked to the couch and handed me my glass of water before sitting down next to me.

I sipped my water before setting it on the coffee table. I still clutched the brass ring in my hand. I swear it was vibrating against my skin. I took a deep breath and looked at Wes. "You don't have to do this, Wes."

"Do what?"

"Make nice with me so you can... I don't know, get Chelsea's email or whatever."

"Why would I need her email? I have her phone number."

Oh shit! If Wes ever called my number and I answered accidentally, he might start asking questions. If for some crazy reason he called or texted her right now, he would hear my iPhone ringing! Then he'd definitely start asking questions. I needed a good cover story quick. "Oh, uh, Chelsea left her phone with me. She couldn't use it in Milan, so... you know."

"That's funny. My phone works fine in Milan."

I shrugged, not wanting to say more.

"Well, she knows how to reach me. If she wants to, she will. I already left her plenty of messages." He sighed. "If she'd told me she'd gone to Milan, I would've taken the hint and stopped calling." As he said all this, his voice faded from casual to disappointed.

I felt terrible. Wes really hadn't done anything to deserve all the Brodie fall out on Oscar night, nor did he deserve the disappointing ending to our evening. But he did deserve an explanation from fake Chelsea, a.k.a. me. I just wasn't sure I could give it to him in a way that made any sense.

I reached out to touch Wes' wrist. He wore that chunky gold bracelet of his. My fingers touched mostly it, but my pinky touched his skin. It was warm and made me tingle.

There was no denying it.

I wanted Wes.

But I couldn't have him.

Oh well. I was a big girl.

But Wes deserved some kind of explanation, no matter how feeble. I said, "Wes, Chelsea is... She's not stable." I was making all this up as I went along. "She tends to be flighty."

"Literally," he smirked. "Unless she took a rowboat across the

Atlantic?" He winked.

"Yeah," I smiled. "She flew. Anyway, it's not really my place to say this, but, for what it's worth, she…" I wanted to tell him she liked him. A lot. But I didn't want to string Wes along. Fake Chelsea the supermodel was gone for good. "She thought very highly of you, Wes. *Very* highly."

He smiled.

"Anyway, she told me what happened and said she felt bad you blamed yourself. I don't know why she didn't tell you herself, but I thought you should know."

He patted my hand. "Thanks, Jane. I appreciate that." His brown eyes flickered, their mahogany fire slowly dying. I pulled my hand away and he sighed, "Women like Chelsea are… special." That was an understatement. "But they're often temperamental and require a lot of work."

I wanted to add, *Plain Jane Johnson isn't temperamental and doesn't require any work.* I was the queen of low maintenance. Ironically, the supermodel version of myself had already started showing signs of being high maintenance after only a few days. I was thinking of the drama I caused between Brodie and Wes. But none of that mattered now.

I raised my eyebrows, not knowing what else to say.

Wes swallowed the last of his ice water. Stared across the room at my TV. He would probably make an excuse to leave in the next two minutes.

Desperate for him to stay, I racked my brains for something to keep him here.

"Wes, can I ask you something?"

"Anything." He set his empty glass down on the coffee table, moments away from standing and leaving forever.

"Ummm…" I wanted to ask, if he'd never met Chelsea the supermodel, would he have considered dating me? But I was too scared to find out the answer. I just couldn't do it.

"Hold up," Wes said, scooting forward onto the edge of the couch. "Is that what I think it is?"

"What?" I followed his gaze to my TV.

"Is that… Is that a Super Nintendo under your TV?"

"Yeah, why?" My TV stood on an old plastic milk crate. Inside the crate, was my dusty old Super Nintendo console.

"What do you mean why?" He smiled big, "Because I grew up playing Super NES, that's why. Mario, Legend of Zelda, Super Metroid. All those games. They were a big part of my childhood."

"Really?"

"Hell yeah. Why didn't you tell me you had an S-NES, Jane?" He was grinning.

I giggled, "I don't know. Do you want to play now?"

His eyes shimmered like Christmas day at a chocolate factory. I wanted to swim in those chocolate eyes of his.

"Let's fire up this bad boy!" He stood and walked to the TV, crouching down in front. He searched through the pile of cartridges beside the console. "We gotta play Zelda. You have it, right?"

"It's in there somewhere." I would've gotten up to help look, but I was too stunned to stand up, so I picked up the remote from the couch and turned on the TV.

"Here it is." He held up the Zelda cartridge. "You have no idea how much I love this game!" He was so damn happy, I wanted to cry. He pulled out the Super Mario Kart cartridge that was still in the machine. I'd left it there after George and I had last played. Then he powered up the machine with the Zelda cartridge inside and unwound one of the controllers. "I hope you don't mind, but we have to play this through to the end."

"That'll take hours, Wes! I have to go to work tonight!" I would love nothing more than to skip work and spend hours and hours playing video games with Wes, but I really needed to keep my job.

"When do you have to be at work?"

"Five."

"We've got plenty of time. If we skip all the bonus items, I bet we can finish before then." He sat down next to me on the couch.

I couldn't believe this was happening. "You don't have to, Wes. You probably have something more important to do than this. And I have to work anyway, so—"

"More important than saving the princess? Are you kidding? We have to save Zelda!" The startup screen loaded and the familiar music played. "Man, there's a real magic to these pixelated old 16 bit games that I really love."

"Yeah," I sighed. *I really love something too...* Wes was the most magical thing in the room, but I wasn't going to say it out loud.

"We'll share a game. Switch back and forth. Do you want to go first or should I?" Zelda was a one player game, so sharing was the only option. He offered me the controller.

"You go first." I wanted to see if he knew what he was doing or if all this was some crazy dream. I couldn't believe Wes actually knew how to play Zelda. Or any video game. He didn't seem like the type, but what did I know?

He clutched the controller in both hands as the introduction finished. "All right, here goes nothing."

The second he started playing and was focused on the game, I stuffed my brass ring between the couch cushions behind me. I knew it would be safe there for now.

And I was wrong about Wes.

He was a pro at 16 bit Zelda.

Chapter 29

Three hours later, I gasped. "Shit! I'm going to be late for work!"

"But we're almost finished!"

Wes and I had been laughing and giggling and sitting shoulder to shoulder playing Zelda the entire time. While one of us was on the controller navigating Link through the dungeons, the other would get up as needed to get more water or snacks or go to the bathroom. An empty bag of Fritos corn chips lay on the coffee table in front of us. Next to it were the two empty plates I'd used for the cheese sandwiches I'd made for us an hour ago. It felt sort of like a date but not a date. I couldn't decide which because I wasn't supermodel Chelsea, I was just plain old me. Either way, Wes and I were having plenty of fun.

"Wes, I really have to shower and change for work."

"Okay, you shower. I'll keep playing."

"Okay, okay!" Giggling, I ran into my bedroom and grabbed clothes for work before jumping in the shower. I still couldn't believe Wes was actually in my living room playing my Super NES. I also didn't believe he would still be there when I finished in the bathroom. When I came out, he'd be gone because all of this had to be a dream.

But it wasn't.

When I emerged from my bathroom in my blouse and work slacks, he was busy playing, his eyes glued to the TV. I wasn't wearing my work vest because I was embarrassed to wear it in front of him. There was nothing sexy or glamorous about a blue canvas 95 Cent Store vest, night manager or no night manager.

"You look nice," he smiled, glancing away from the game for a few seconds to really look at me.

I smiled back. "Thanks."

He was just being nice. I knew this moment we were having was a one time thing, much like that first day we'd met at his grandmother's mansion. After he left tonight, I would have to be content with the memory of this moment. I was okay with that. Unlike most relationships, memories lasted forever.

The beeps and boops of the game resumed. Wes' eyes were back on the TV.

I sighed, "Are you still playing?"

"Of course I am. Do you want to pause this for now? We can finish it later if you leave the machine on."

"Oh, we don't have to."

"You sure? We spent three hours on it. I'd hate for that to go to waste."

"Maybe?" What was I doing? Why was I turning down a second Nintendo date with Wes when he was offering? This was the greatest day in the history of my life! I couldn't say no!

Wes was now fully absorbed in the game.

He was so incredibly handsome.

And I was the opposite.

I sighed softly.

I was old enough to know Wes and I could never be anything more than friends. Even if I had him over for marathon Nintendo sessions from here until eternity, I knew he would never look at me like he had looked at supermodel me. We would always just be friends.

Did I want to put myself through that? No. I knew better. I knew if I did, it would eventually drive me crazy. The reality was that I'd never have Wes.

I said softly, "Maybe some other time." *Maybe as in never.*

"Huh? Sorry. I got distracted by the game."

I cleared my throat, fighting back tears. "I said, maybe we can play again... some other time." My words turned to mumbles toward the end.

His smile slowly sagged. He got the message. "Yeah, sure." He set the controller down absently, without bothering to pause the game, and stood up slowly, his sudden discomfort filling the room. He held his hand out to shake.

See?

A handshake.

He didn't try for the kiss.

I reached forward to shake his hand, but to my surprise, Wes opened his arms at the last second and came in for a hug. He bent down and squeezed me hard and rubbed my back vigorously. "I had a blast, Jane. We'll do this again." He sounded reserved and a little bit guarded.

"Yeah," I said, all choked up, drowning in impending disappointment.

Did he mean it or was he just being polite?

I didn't want to know.

No, I knew.

I showed him out as quick as I could.

After closing my front door, I waited while his footsteps faded on the balcony outside, and I waited until the front gate banged shut.

Then I started crying.

Not sobbing.

Just quiet crying.

Good thing I wasn't wearing any makeup. After a few minutes on the couch with a box of tissues, I realized I was going to be late for work if I didn't get a move on. I'd only been back on the job for a week and I didn't want to give Doug or anybody at corporate a reason to doubt me.

I needed my job.

I put on my blue work vest and pocketed my phone before heading toward my front door. I couldn't bear to turn the TV and Zelda off just yet, so I left everything on. When I grabbed the doorknob, I stopped cold, staring at the corner of the couch where I'd shoved the brass ring earlier.

Like a desperate madwoman (or relapsing addict), I started tearing cushions off the couch. The ring was gone! It wasn't where I'd stuffed it! I started to panic and tore off the rest of the cushions, but I couldn't find it! Shit! I shook with fear and felt the powerful urge to vomit. I needed to find that ring! I would die without that ring! My life would be over if I didn't find that *stupid fucking ring!!!*

A dark hole in the corner seam of the couch caught my eye. Had the ring fallen in there? I grabbed the edge of it and tore the fabric back without a second thought. When the hole was big enough, I jammed my hand inside and felt around.

No!

The ring wasn't inside either!

It had disappeared!

I yanked my hand out and leaned under the couch, but all I saw was carpet. I felt around just in case it was lost in the pile, but there was nothing there!

Starting to cry, I stood up and jammed my hand back inside the couch like a deranged heroin junkie, going all the way up to my elbow, my palm slapping around at the fabric bottom inside the couch as I literally frothed at the mouth. My spittle flew everywhere as I grunted like a lunatic.

"*Where did you go, you scummy motherfucker?! If you're not here, I'm going to kill somebody! Kill everybody! Aaaaaahhh!!!*"

I growled like a rabid dog.

My arm flailed inside the couch, now up to my shoulder. I was either going to die or go insane if the ring wasn't in my *God damned couch!!*

My fingers closed around it.

The world ground to a halt.

The ring was now cool to the touch, having been here for hours. I pulled it out and held it close to my face. It glimmered darkly in the flickering light of the TV.

Breathing hard from my exertion, I cried silently as I examined it. My glasses had nearly fallen off from all my flailing around, so I pushed them up my sweaty nose and gazed upon perfection.

The ring.

The ring.

I held it over my little finger, poised to slide it on.

What was it about the word poised that reminded me so much of poison?

Was this a bad idea?

No! It's the best idea ever!

Would this ring *really* poison me? Or give me cancer? Or just poison my heart and soul to the core?

No! Never! It'll make me happy! Happy happy happy!!!

Would I become addicted to being beautiful if I put it back on, never satisfied unless I was a youthful supermodel?

No! It's perfection! It's everything I ever wanted!

If I put it on and kept it on day after day, would my incredible beauty last forever, or would it fade a few years from now, leaving me a disappointed heartbroken wreck, abandoned by whoever had known me and wanted me when I was beautiful?

Or would the ring simply malfunction halfway through my swansformation and leave me deformed forever?

Deformed.

Deformed...

I shuddered.

No! It'll work! It WILL work!!!

With shaky hands, I held the ring above the tip of my ring finger.

Poised.

Don't do it, Jane. The voice in my head was Chelsea. The real Chelsea. My sister. The one who'd been beautiful her entire life. *It's not worth it. Haven't you figured that out yet?*

Sighing, I slowly closed my left hand into a fist. My right still held the ring poised to put on, like it was determined to make me beautiful no matter what. Yes, I was torn. What should I do? I pressed my empty left hand against my heart. This was stupid. All of it was stupid. I didn't want to be beautiful. I just wanted to be me.

I wanted to be loved for being me.

Me.

It didn't matter if Wes or Brodie or anybody else didn't like me the way I was.

I just needed to find somebody who did. Somebody like George Sweet or—

Knock! Knock! Knock!

"Jesus!" Surprised, I threw the ring in the air. It bounced off the ceiling before clattering on the square of fake parquet wood in front of the door. I dropped to my knees and scrambled to pick it up, afraid it might disappear under the couch or worse, fall through a crack between the walls and into the bowels of the apartment building, never to be seen again.

Would that be so bad?

KNOCK! KNOCK! KNOCK!

The ring lay motionless where it had landed. I folded my fingers around it before standing and opening the door. It was probably Mrs. Wiser. "Yeah?"

Wes stood there, staring at me, eyes smoldering, impossibly handsome and completely out of my league. The man that plain Jane Johnson would never ever have.

"What do you want, Wes?"

"We need to talk, Sunflower." His eyes sparkled, chocolate bright.

Sunflower? Fake Chelsea was Sunflower, not me.

He arched an expectant eyebrow. "Can I come in?"

Gulp. "Sure."

Chapter 30

"How did you know, Wes?" I asked. We sat on my couch, knees touching. The ring lay on the middle of my coffee table in plain view, a tarnished reminder of something that once was, but would never be.

"I always knew, Sunflower." Wes held my hand in his, his thumb stroking the back of it. He'd been stroking it for all of one minute, but I was already having trouble focusing on his words. The sensation was mesmerizing.

Hypnotizing.

Circling, circling, circling.

My body flushed with pent up heat.

I was getting wet.

The dark fire in Wes' eyes made it impossible for me to do otherwise.

Was I setting myself up for disappointment? Should I give his ring back and ask him politely to leave and never come back? I didn't know because my body was swimming in the ecstasy of his soothing touch.

I cleared my throat, trying to stay focused. "When—" my voice caught and I cleared my throat again. "When did you realize I was Chelsea?"

His smile widened pleasantly, reassuringly. "I always knew it was you, Sunflower."

"When? That first time you saw me at the Promenade and that magician was doing his card trick?"

He shook his head, still smiling. "That first day at my grandmother's house. When you took her ring."

"Took? I didn't take it! I offered to give it back! When you didn't want it, I offered to pay for it."

He chuckled, "If I recall, you asked for a ten dollar loan."

"Yeah, yeah," I giggled, remembering the moment. "I can pay for it now. I'm sure I have ten dollars around here somewhere. Here," I twisted to grab my purse, which lay on the couch beside me.

"No, Sunflower. You don't owe me anything. The ring picked you."

"Picked me?" I frowned, "How does that make any sense? It's just a ring."

"How does a ring that turns you beautiful make any sense?"

I opened my mouth to argue, but I couldn't because he was right.

He arched an eyebrow. "It's yours, Jane. The ring is yours until you're done with it."

"Done? What does that mean?"

"I'm not entirely sure. Nobody really knows how or why it works. It just does what it wants to do."

I squeezed my eyes shut, confused. "So, what am I supposed to do, Wes?"

"I don't know. That's up to you. But I can tell you what my grandmother did."

"Huh?"

"It was her ring until it became yours. She wore it until her death."

Morbid images of Wes pulling it off her finger while her body was at the mortuary, or on display at an open casket funeral, flickered through my mind. "You didn't take it from her, did you?"

He smirked, "No. When she was in the hospital during her final days, she took it off and gave it to me for safe keeping."

"Oh, good. Did you, um, did you know what it did? I mean, that it made people beautiful? Or wait, does it make everybody who wears it beautiful? Or just nerdy girls like me?"

He smiled and his eyes searched mine, "This is why I like you so much, Jane."

Like like me? Or just like me? I wasn't going to ask. All of this was too confusing.

He continued, "To answer your question, no. I don't think it makes everybody who wears it beautiful. Only the person it picks."

"And it picked me?"

"Yes."

"Why?"

"Because it knew you were the one."

I frowned, "Which one?"

"The one for me."

"That's ridiculous, Wes!" I laughed. For a long time. Wes just smiled. I kept laughing. "You're joking, right?"

He shook his head, smiling that delicious smile of his.

"Really?"

"Really."

I laughed again, not believing any of this. I hung my head, giggling to myself, examining the carpet. "Ridiculous," I muttered.

"Maybe," he murmured, squeezing my hand. "But it worked for my grandmother."

I looked at him. "What do you mean?"

"It made her beautiful too. And it made her a star."

"It did?"

"Yes. Let me tell you a story." He took a deep breath. "My grandmother, the late great golden age movie icon Helen Callaway, wasn't born a star. She was born Helen Klueber. In 1937, when she was just a teenager, she took a bus from Nebraska to Los Angeles. She dreamed of being a movie star, just like every young woman her age. Like most, she quickly learned how hard Hollywood could be on aspiring young starlets. She spent several years chasing auditions, trying to be seen, flirting with directors, agents, producers, whoever she thought might cut her a break. But she never got anywhere. Until she found the ring. Or, as she used to tell it, the ring found her."

I smirked, "Are you making all this up?"

"Not a word of it." He squeezed my hand. "When the ring found her, she was working as a coat check girl at the Mocambo."

"The Mocambo? What's that?"

"Have you ever watched that old show I Love Lucy?"

"Yeah. I used to watch the reruns with my mom and my sister when I was a kid. My mom still watches them."

"It's a great show. Do you remember that club Lucy and Desi used to go to on the show? The Tropicana? It's where Desi's character Ricky was the band leader."

"That's right." I smiled, remembering the countless times my mom, my sister, and I laughed at all of Lucy's ridiculousness.

"The Tropicana was based on the Mocambo. Lucille Ball and Desi Arnaz were regulars there, and they were friends with the owner. "

"I didn't know that."

"It's true."

"And your grandmother worked there in real life?"

"She did," he nodded. "And, like many coat check girls in the 1940s, she was hoping to get discovered while at work. The night she found the ring, she was getting the coat of a handsome and notorious talent agent by the name of Walter Callaway, a proven star-maker. She had recognized him the moment he'd handed her his claim check for his coat. Gramms knew that a man like him had the power to get her a screen test at a major studio like MGM or Paramount or Twentieth Century Fox. He could make her career. All she had to do was make an impression on him. When she went to grab his coat off the rack, she said the ring literally jumped into her hand."

"Jumped?"

"That's how she described it."

I grinned, "Sounds familiar."

Wes grinned back. "Her first thought was she could use the ring as an excuse to call on Walter at his office, but she changed her mind at the last second, afraid he might accuse her of stealing it. She needed to keep her job at the Mocambo more than she needed an interview. So she decided to give it to him with his coat, hoping her honesty would impress him enough for him to at least ask for her name."

"Did it work?"

"When she showed him the ring and explained that it must've fallen through a hole in the coat pocket, Walter Callaway told her he'd never seen it before and she could keep it." Wes paused to wink at me.

"You are such a shameless imitator," I chuckled.

He grinned, "Maybe so. After he left, Gramms said she'd shown the ring to a hundred people that night. She didn't want anyone coming back and accusing her of stealing. But nobody wanted it. I mean, who would want a cheap brass ring?"

I smirked at him.

"At the end of the night, she decided to keep it."

"Gee whiz. What a surprise. Let me guess what happened next. She put it on."

He tapped the tip of his nose.

"And did your grandma turn beautiful too?"

"She did. She said it was the most painful experience of her life, but a week later, she said she'd never felt better. Or looked better. The first thing she did was ask around town until she got the address for the Walter Callaway Talent Agency. Then she put on her best dress and her only veiled birdcage hat, hopped on a bus, and sat in his waiting room all day with her purse on her knees, like a good little lady. When he finally called her into his office... well, the rest is history."

"What happened, Wes?" I begged, on the edge of my seat.

"What do you think happened? They fell in love. Got married. Helen Klueber became Helen Callaway, and Gramps made her a star. Eventually they had children. And grandchildren, including me." Wes' chocolate brown eyes bored into mine.

All I could do was stare back blankly.

"Is this making any sense, Sunflower? Or do I need to connect the rest of the dots?"

He didn't. I knew exactly where this was going, but I couldn't believe he was taking it there. My heart raced. The way Wes was looking at me was melting me into a puddle of naked desire. I wanted all of this to be absolutely true, but I couldn't believe any of it. "Uhh, what are you saying, Wes?"

"You tell me, Sunflower."

Damn it, why did he have to be so incredibly handsome? Who said no to a man as perfect as Wes? Nobody did. "Wes, are you…" I was afraid to say it. But I had to say it. "Do you want me to wear the ring so you can marry me?"

"No, I'm saying I want you, Sunflower. You and only you. Whether or not you wear the ring is up to you."

"What happens if I wear it? Will it… you know, give me cancer or something? Or…" (−deformed deformed deformed−) I swallowed hard. "…I don't know, make me look worse?"

"I don't think so. Gramms made it almost to one hundred, and she wore the ring most of her life."

"Most?" I asked, curious.

"She took it off when she wanted to go out in public and not be recognized. It was a painful transition, as you know, but she always told me it was worth it to be normal again, even if only for a few weeks at a time. Outside of Hollywood, nobody knew who Walter Callaway was, and they definitely didn't spare a glance for an aging farm girl named Helen Klueber. My grandparents loved to travel and they always left the ring at home when they did. Gramms said it allowed her and Gramps to focus on each other rather than being famous and signing autographs everywhere they went."

"Wow, Wes. This is an incredible story." I wouldn't have believed him if I hadn't already lived a piece of it myself.

"It is. Witnessing her transformation first hand several times over the years made it no less incredible for me either."

"You saw your grandmother change from normal to beautiful?"

"Not directly, and definitely not when I was young," he grinned. "You don't want a little kid going around blabbing about his magic grandmother."

"I know, right?" I laughed. "So, did you ever actually see her change? I mean, while it was happening?"

"No. The only person she ever let watch was Gramps. It was hard on him every time, believe me. And her."

"I know. I lived it," I muttered.

"Yeah," he said softly. "Not something I would ever want to go through alone…" An obvious hint that he wanted to be there for me.

I ignored it. It was too much to think about right now. "But you saw her before and after her transformation, right?"

"Yes. As an adult. Even then, Gramms was very careful about who she let see her when she wasn't wearing the ring. She was scared to death word might get out. She knew what the tabloids would do if it ever did. Being a celebrity is hard enough. But being a freak of nature?

Nobody wants that."

"Yeah," I nodded thoughtfully. "Wow. Just, wow. All of this is beyond words. I don't know what to say, Wes." I smiled at him.

His eyes locked onto mine. "I know what I want you to say, Jane."

"Did you just call me Jane?" I was avoiding the obvious.

"I did. Before I proceed, I have one question for you."

"What's that?" I was afraid of where this was going because I was afraid I'd go along with whatever he said, no matter how crazy it was.

He narrowed his eyes, "Is your last name really Johnson?"

That was a question I could answer. "Yes. Why?"

"How would you like to change it to Callaway?"

Oh wow oh wow oh wow. He went and did it. I couldn't believe this was happening.

He took my left hand in his. Grabbed his grandmother's ring off my coffee table. Held it a half inch away from the tip of my ring finger. My *wedding* ring finger. And speaking of wedding rings, the ring was no longer a tarnished brass trinket. It was solid gold and covered in a circle of diamonds.

"It changed," I gasped, "How did that happen so fast?"

"I have no idea, but this is how it looked whenever Gramms wore it." He kneeled on the carpet in front of my couch.

"Oh my God!"

"Jane Johnson, will you marry me?"

Time stopped. Or seemed to stop. The only signal that time continued moving forward was the twinkling of Wes' eyes as they searched mine earnestly. But my heart had definitely stopped from the shock.

Yes! Yes! Yes! I wanted to scream those words, but I wasn't crazy. Despite all the fantastic events in my life that had transpired over the past several weeks, I knew that relationships weren't built on fantasy. They were built on reality. The truth was, Wes and I had shared almost zero reality since the day we'd met.

I pulled my left hand away reluctantly and folded it in my lap. I took a deep breath, staring at my hands, trying to make sense of this. When I finally spoke, my voice was even and calm, but I couldn't hide my disappointment. "You've known me for less than a month, Wes. We've been out on *one* date."

"It was a long date," he grinned, "at the Oscars."

I snorted a laugh, followed by a heaving sigh. "We can't get married, Wes. We barely know each other. I don't see how it could possibly last."

"My grandparents knew each other for one week before my

Gramps proposed and Gramms said yes. On the spot, as Gramps liked to tell everyone." Wes smiled to himself wistfully. "They were married for sixty years before he passed."

"That was a different time, Wes. People did things differently."

"People are still people. And staying together is still a choice, Sunflower."

I knew that was the truth. Whenever anyone's relationship got difficult, you either chose to work on it or you chose to give up. I'd never given up on my boyfriends. They'd given up on me. It wasn't me I was worried about. It was Wes. I didn't really know him, and he definitely didn't know me. "But we've spent so little time together, Wes. And most of it you weren't spending with me. You were spending it with Fake Chelsea. How do I know you'll like me for me?"

"You were always you, Sunflower. You may have looked different on the outside, but you were the same person on the inside. Tell me I'm wrong."

"I can't." I shook my head. He was right. But this still felt wrong. "But what if... what if things still don't work out? I don't have the best history with men." I was old enough to know that my love, no matter how strong, couldn't make a man stay if he didn't want to. And on that note, I wasn't even sure I loved Wes. It was too damn soon. Who knew they were truly in love after one official date? Nobody I'd ever met. "I don't know, Wes. Things are moving too quickly."

"Sunflower, the last two weeks have been the most miserable weeks of my life. When you told me I was a bad idea the night of the Oscars, after the swimming pool... *incident*," he grumbled, "I wanted to wither and die. You crushed my world, Jane." His voice was strained. Genuine pain flickered in his eyes.

I had caused that pain.

"Sunflower, I tried to forget you, but I couldn't. Deep in my heart, I always knew there was something about you. From the first moment I heard your annoying voice over the intercom at my grandmother's house," he grinned, "I knew it was you."

I smirked back at him. "Me annoying? What about you, Mr. Giant Asshead?"

He chuckled, "I have my moments. Tell me you don't love them."

Tell me I don't love you, I thought suddenly. Maybe I did love him. But I didn't want to rush into anything. I was happy to take things slowly. Just to make sure. "Maybe we should date for a while, Wes. That's not crazy is it? It's what normal people do."

"I'm not normal," Wes smiled, "and neither are you, Sunflower. More importantly, when you know, you know. Why drag it out?"

"So no one gets hurt? Especially me. If we did this, and I'm not saying we are, I wouldn't want to mess things up. Am I making any sense?" I was being cautious and I knew it. If I got into something with Wes and it didn't work out, I'd be the one whose world got crushed, and I wasn't sure I could pull myself back together again after losing a man like Wes. Losing those losers Aaron Gross and Harvey Pews was one thing. Losing Wes was... unthinkable. Better not to try, right? I gave Wes a pleading look that was a mixture of, *Please don't ask me to do this* and *Please do this but promise me you won't ruin me in the process.*

He squeezed my knee. "I plan for success, Jane. Not failure. I want you to be my success. Correction, I want *us* to be *our* success. What'll it be, Jane Johnson? Can I make you a Callaway?"

"We haven't even had sex, Wes," I pleaded, not entirely sure why I was arguing.

He winked, "If you say yes, we'll be having plenty of sex."

I blurted, "We can't get married if we haven't had sex! What if we're no good in bed?"

"Trust me when I say you have nothing to worry about. Unless you don't like oak trees?" *Thick from tip to root...*

I shivered all over. "Wes, we can't..."

"Excuse me." Still kneeling, he reached down and adjusted his crotch. "Sorry, my jeans are suddenly too fucking tight." He grunted a raspy laugh.

Fucking...

I gasped, "Are you hard?"

"What can I say, Jane? True love makes me want to fuck the woman I love." He seemed slightly embarrassed. It was so cute I couldn't stand it.

Also, I barely registered he'd used the word love because I was too shocked by the idea of short little nerdy me having sex with tall gorgeous perfect Wes. It scared the living crap out of me.

His eyes drilled into mine and he looked ready to pounce.

Every muscle below my belt clenched in anticipation. I gasped, "Wait, do you want to have sex right now? This second?"

"Why not? You said we can't get married without having sex first. I concur. Sex before we make the engagement official, to set your mind at ease."

"Mine? What about yours? Do you really want to have sex with me? Like this?" I gestured at myself.

"What about my hard cock says I have any doubts about fucking you silly, just the way you are right now?"

I stared at his crotch. He was most definitely hard.

And huge.

And pointing right at me.

Me, plain Jane Johnson.

Oh, God, I was so damn wet. Pleasure flamed up from my toes to the top of my head. The thought of having sex with Wes was literally threatening to blow my mind. How could I say no to him? Or that cock?

"Well, Sunflower? Do I have to fuck you into submission before you'll say yes?"

"Is that a threat?"

"It's a promise, Sunflower."

Oh wow. I had been ready to have sex with Wes the night of the Oscars. But that was when I was a supermodel. Now was a different story. Despite his huge erection, I was still afraid to take my clothes off in front of him or even leave the lights on during sex.

"Well?" His grandmother's gold and diamond ring shimmered in his hands before my eyes.

"What about the ring? Shouldn't I put it on and we wait until I'm beautiful again?"

"Who says you aren't beautiful right now?" His voice was soft and sincere.

My heart opened wide to him in that moment. I lowered my eyes and whispered, "I'm scared, Wes."

"Scared of what? Sex or marrying me?"

My entire body shook with fear as I looked him in the eyes. "Of everything, Wes."

"I understand." A hungry smile flickered onto his face. "How about we make a deal?"

"What kind of deal?"

"We fuck first, just to put you at ease. If you have anything less than the most mind blowing orgasm of your entire life, we can go our separate ways." He hastily added, "Not that that would be my preference, but if giving you an escape hatch will make you feel better, I can accept that."

I took my time thinking about it. When I'd made up my mind, I smirked, "Only one orgasm?" Just the thought of coming with Wes inside me made me squirm in my seat.

He smiled, "Make it three. Three mind blowing orgasms, each one more earth-shattering than the last."

"And if I don't have an earth-shattering orgasm?" I was half joking, half serious.

"Then we'll keep fucking until you do. I don't care if it takes days of fucking, or weeks, or months. Fucking all day and all night long until we get it right."

I quivered happily at the thought.

"I'm not letting you go, Sunflower. Do we have a deal?"

My eyes suddenly popped and I jumped up from the couch. "Oh shit! I'm going to be late for work! I have to go, Wes!"

"If you marry me, you'll never have to work again. Unless you want to, that is. I'm loaded."

I giggled, "With money or come?"

"Both," he chuckled. "So, do we have a deal, Sunflower?"

I took a deep breath and held it, afraid that if I spoke, I'd ruin everything. But I had to say something. "Wes, I have people at work depending on me. As tempting as your offer is, can we discuss it later? Is that okay?"

"How much later?"

"I don't know." I knew I was dragging this out, but I didn't want to be forced into a decision. Things never worked out when they were forced.

His face started to harden into the same mask I'd seen at the pool the night of the Oscars, the night when I'd feared that Wes had decided to walk away forever, all because I couldn't make up my mind then either.

Now I wanted to say yes so badly it hurt, but I needed time. It was the smart thing to do. "Wes, please. I have to go to work. I hope you understand."

"Yeah," he nodded, staring at his grandmother's ring for several moments. Eventually, he set it softly on my coffee table like a goodbye. He stood up slowly, gearing up to walk out of my apartment and my life forever.

I wanted to grab the ring and jam it on my finger and jump into his arms and be with him for the rest of our lives, but I knew that was just wishful thinking. Any potential relationship we might have in the future was currently balanced on the knife edge of impossibility. If there was any chance of us lasting, I needed to think things over.

Wes hung his head.

My apartment suddenly felt gigantic, like Wes and I had suddenly drifted continents apart and the distance between us was growing bigger by the second. Soon, the distance would be infinite and permanent.

I was going to lose him if I didn't do something right now.

Say yes, say yes, say yes!!!!

Wes slowly turned his head away.

I opened my mouth to speak, ready to beg him to stay, but I just couldn't do it. I needed time.

The TV flickered with our Zelda game.

His eyes drifted toward it. He sighed heavily, watching the screen longingly. He took a deep breath.

I needed to say goodbye before he did. "I have to go, Wes." My voice quivered with disappointment.

"Right," he muttered. Any second, he was going to say, *See you around* or *Have a nice life*.

I steeled myself for it.

He scratched the back of his head like a lost little boy. "Uhhh, do you mind if I stay here while you're gone and play Zelda?"

"Huh?"

"Someone has to rescue the princess, right?" His hopeful smile was my life preserver.

"Yes. Yeah, sure," I smiled back, nodding vigorously. "But I won't be home until after midnight. Is that okay?"

Relief eased his features. "Midnight is fine. Take your time."

"I mean, if you need to go or whatever. Eight hours is a lot to ask." I was testing him, but I couldn't help myself. I still doubted all of this. I hated my insecurity, but I couldn't pretend it wasn't there.

"I'll wait."

"Are you sure?"

"Yes, Sunflower, I'm sure." He smiled, his voice gaining strength and determination, the frightened little boy disappearing into the confident man Wes was. "There's no place I'd rather be."

"Okay," I said, starting to hope. "Make yourself at home."

"I'll do that," he grinned and walked to the door, opening it for me.

"Oh, can I take your grandmother's ring with me?"

"It's your ring now, Sunflower."

I snatched it off the coffee table and hurried out the door.

Chapter 31

I was only twenty minutes late to the 95 Cent Store. I made a hasty apology to Doug and promised him it was a one time thing. Thankfully, he didn't make a big deal of it because he was still counting a cash drawer from the afternoon shift.

After he left, the store was busy long after the sun went down. It was for the best. Otherwise, I probably would've spent the entire evening analyzing and re-analyzing every last moment I'd spent with Wes since we'd met, trying to find a hole in it, a catch, a flaw, until I'd convinced myself we couldn't possibly work long term. Then, I would prepare a goodbye speech to be delivered to Wes when I got home. Assuming he was still there.

Fortunately, the store was way too busy and I didn't have time to think about anything other than work. But whenever I had a spare moment, I pulled his grandmother's ring out of my pocket to gaze at it.

Yet another rush of late night bargain hunters forced me to focus on work for the next hour. I opened register 3 so I could help Maria and Natalie, who were already on registers 2 and 5. When the steady flow of customers finally dwindled to nothing, I pulled the ring out for the ninth time.

"What's that, *jefe?*" Maria asked as she strolled over from her register.

"Oh, nothing." I stuffed the ring back in my front pocket.

"Looked like an engagement ring to me. Lemme see it."

Reluctantly, I pulled it out and showed her.

"Wow, *jefe!* Are those real diamonds?"

"I think so."

"That must've cost a fortune! Where'd you get it?"

"Somebody gave it to me."

She smirked, "A man somebody, or just anybody somebody?"

"A man."

"Anybody I know?"

I smiled meekly and shook my head, "I just met him a few weeks ago."

"And he gave you that? Already?"

I nodded.

"Did he propose too?"

"Yeah. Tonight."

She frowned, "Why aren't you wearing it?"

I shrugged, not wanting to explain why I didn't want to put this magical beauty ring on my finger.

"Did you tell him no or something?"

"I told him I'd think about it." That was the real reason, not because I was worried about swansforming while at work, although that was as good a reason not to as any. I shivered thinking about it before stuffing the ring back in my pocket. "I just met him a month ago. I barely know him."

"Is he a player?"

"No."

"A thug?"

"No," I snorted.

"Does he have a job?"

Rather than explain Wes was rich, I said, "Yes."

"Then you say yes too, *jefe*. If Antonio ever gave me a ring like that," she shook her head, biting her lip with obvious jealousy, "I'd say yes for sure."

"But you've known Antonio for years."

"So? He never gave me nothing that nice. Hey, Natalie!" Maria called, leaning around the magazine racks so she could see Natalie standing at register 5, where she was flipping through a copy of People magazine. "Come over here girl! You gotta see *jefe's* engagement ring!"

"Her what?!" Natalie hurried over, a big smile lighting up her face.

"Show her, *jefe*," Maria said.

Feeling like a teenager, I pulled the ring out again so they could both gawk at it. It was embarrassing. And surprisingly fun. Who didn't like having everyone fawn over their new engagement ring?

"Wow, Jane," Natalie said. "That is so beautiful! Who gave it to you?"

I gave her the same vague rundown I'd given Maria.

"Is he cute?" Natalie asked shyly.

Maria smirked, "She means, how big is his *chode*? Is it like a *taquito* —" she pinched her thumb and finger close together, "—or a *burrito*?" She held her hands a foot apart.

I giggled, "Maria!"

"Or is it a Coke can?" Natalie asked quietly.

Maria barked laughter. "Ha! Ha! Ha! Two Coke cans, *hermana!* One stacked on the other!" She nudged Natalie, "Right?"

Natalie nodded, blushing and covering her mouth while giggling.

"You guys!" I hissed, thinking some customers must be overhearing us, but the store was currently empty. I spent the next few minutes describing Wes in a bit more detail, avoiding any discussion of his dick size.

Maria smiled, "He sounds hot, *jefe*. And he has a job, right? A good one?"

"Yeah," I nodded.

"Is he nice?" Natalie asked.

"Yeah. Very nice."

"Not too nice," Maria grumbled. "A man needs to act like a man, you know? No sissies."

I rolled my eyes, remembering the way Wes had flirted with me at the Promenade elevators when I was a supermodel (while he ignored those two bim-hos), and the way he'd stood up to Brodie without a second thought. "He's not a sissy. And he can be very manly, Maria. Believe me." I must've moaned it, because Maria started snickering.

"How manly, *jefe?*"

Natalie muttered, "Coke canly manly."

We all got the giggles again and laughed for a long time, finally letting it all out with a communal high-pitched sigh.

Followed by a few more scattered giggles.

Eventually, I said, "What should I do, you guys?"

"Marry him already, *jefe*."

Natalie nodded her agreement.

For the rest of my shift, all I could think about was the simple conviction of both Maria and Natalie. They were both right. There was really nothing wrong with Wes.

I didn't know why I was ever worried.

<<<<<<<<>>>>>>>

It was well past midnight when I stuck my keys in my front door. For a brief moment, I imagined that I'd walk inside, my dark apartment would be empty, the TV would be off, and Wes' ring would no longer be in my pocket or anywhere to be found. All of the craziness of the past month would turn out to be a dream, because really, everybody knew there was no such thing as a magical beauty ring.

Eyes squinched shut, I twisted the knob and walked inside.

"What took you so long, Sunflower? I've been lying here with Zelda on pause for the last two hours, waiting for you so you could watch me save the princess." He looked perfect laying spread out on my couch with his hands folded behind his head, lit only by the blue glow of the game coming from the TV. A half-empty glass of juice and an empty plate with a crumpled paper napkin on top sat on the coffee table.

I closed the door behind me and let out a big tired sigh. I smiled, "How about you save *this* princess?"

"Gladly." He jumped up from the couch, eyes bright.

I dropped my purse on the corner cushion. "So, Mr. Sex Machine, do we still have a deal?"

"Absolutely." His smile spread as quickly as I hoped my legs soon would. "At least three earth-shattering orgasms."

"At least," I chuckled. "So let's get started. My feet are killing me. I've been standing on them all night." I toed my shoes off and flipped each one into the corner by the door with a flick of each foot. They landed beside his flip-flops, which where already neatly stacked on the fake parquet. Kind of like he lived here and we always put our shoes by the door together. Mine landed randomly. He could be the neat one. I didn't mind.

"Shall we start with a foot massage first?" he offered.

I smirked, "No. Let's start with a fuck massage. If you do it right, I'll forget all about my sore feet."

A huge grin spread across his perfect face. He winked at me, "If you're not careful, I'll make your pussy twice as sore, Sunflower."

"You talk a big talk, Wes."

"Everything about me is big, Sunflower."

I looked down at his crotch.

Sure enough, he was right.

It was like a big top circus tent in his jeans.

Was he too big? I wasn't sure, but I was excited to find out.

He peeled his T-shirt over his head, revealing perfect abs, perfect shoulders, a perfect chest… perfect everything. He tossed his shirt on the couch without a second thought and stalked toward me until his chest was inches from my face. I could feel the heat coming off his skin.

Coming…

He was so damn tall, I had to crane my neck to see into his eyes. With liquid swiftness, he scooped me up by my ass. I wrapped my legs around his waist just as quick, like we'd done this a thousand times before.

His cock was rock fucking hard between my legs.

He touched his forehead against mine.

We were nose to nose.

"If we do this, Sunflower, you're mine forever."

"I thought you had to give me three earth-shattering orgasms first."

"That's a foregone conclusion, Sunflower." My name slid off his tongue like a weapon.

A weapon I was powerless to resist.

So I did what any damsel would. I looped my arms around the neck of my Prince Charming and stared into his eyes. "Then do it already, Wes. Take me into my bedroom and… take me." I hissed the words. They dripped with the same sexual desire that dripped from me.

"Your wish is my command, Sunflower."

Two hours and three earth-shattering orgasms later, Wes finally emptied himself inside me.

He wasn't wearing a condom.

Neither of us seemed to care.

When he came, he came hard, grunting and growling with every thrust, firing into me.

Filling me.

On his final forceful thrust, he pushed into me as deeply as he could, burying himself to the hilt, his entire body quivering with needy release. Inspired by his desire, my body launched into a fourth and final orgasm. Not as big as the first, second, or third he'd given me (the third was legendary and definitely planet-shattering), but this one was still more intense than any I'd ever had before today.

This was far and away the best sex of my life.

After, Wes collapsed on top of me and we both gasped for breath. He was still inside me, still pulsing. His head rested on the mattress beside mine, his shoulders heaving and heaving, his face dark with fulfilled desire.

I ran my hands lazily through his hair for several minutes before eventually circling my fingertip lightly around his ear.

He groaned, "You want me to fuck you again, don't you, Sunflower?"

"Maybe," I teased.

"Keep doing that and I will. In about five minutes. I need to rest first." When his breathing calmed, he gently kissed my cheek and whispered, "So, what do you say, Mrs. Callaway? Is it a yes or no?"

I murmured in his ear, "Yes, Wes. Yes. Forever yes."

"Three times is the charm, or so they say."

"It is. It definitely is."
His inviting smile was a miracle.

AND THEY LIVED HAPPILY EVER AFTER…
In the Callaway family mansion, which they renovated (while preserving its historical Hollywood golden age charm), and filled it with children over the years.
Once again, the Callaway home was full of life.
If you listen, you can hear them all laughing in the backyard garden and splashing in the jeweled pool under the shimmering sun like the ghosts of summer.

Are you wondering about the ring?
Did Jane ever wear it again?
She did. And had many exciting adventures because of it, but that is another story.
More importantly, Wesley Callaway loved Jane Callaway no matter what she looked like, because he knew that true love is a transcendent thing that has nothing to do with looks.

THE END

What about Brodie?

He wasn't so bad, was he? Do you think he deserves true love? Do you think he deserves his own
Happily Ever After?

If you want to read a book about Brodie,

tell me: here:

www.devonhartford.com/i-want-brodie

Please leave a review!

Personal thanks from Devon Hartford:

Thank you for taking the time to live with Jane Johnson and all the hot men in her life! If you enjoyed If I Were Beautiful, please leave a review online wherever you purchased this book, Goodreads, or any book blogs you frequent. Be sure to tell your friends about it!

If you want to drop me a line, you can find me at any of the links below. I love to hear what you have to say, and I love to talk books!

Devon

Connect with me on my Facebook fan group:

Devon Hartford's Heartbreakers

If you're not on Facebook, visit me at:

devonhartford.com

ABOUT THE AUTHOR

Devon Hartford spent most of his life in Southern California frequenting many of the locations in Cover Model. Devon is an artist and musician, and drew upon his experiences with both while writing his previous romance series The Story of Samantha Smith and The Story of Victory Payne.

OTHER BOOKS BY DEVON HARTFORD:

COLLEGE ROMANTIC COMEDY:
Fearless (The Story of Samantha Smith #1)
Reckless (The Story of Samantha Smith #2)
Painless (The Story of Samantha Smith #3)

NEW ADULT ROMANTIC COMEDY
Cover Model
Stealing Chastity

HIGH SCHOOL ROMANTIC COMEDY
Stepbrother Obsessed

ADULT ROMANTIC COMEDY
Taking Back Beautiful
Broken Lion

SLIGHTLY PARANORMAL ROMANCE
If I Were Beautiful (If I Were… #1)

BILLIONAIRE ROMANCE:
ONE YEAR LOVE - Collected Edition (Parts 1-4)

ROCKER ROMANCE:
Victory RUN 1-2-3 (The Story of Victory Payne - Collecting Parts 1-2-3)

ACKNOWLEDGMENTS

A HUGE thanks to:

Jackie Barnett for her usual genius

Her Highness Samantha Sheeley, Queen of All Typos and Ouster of Oopsies!

Bethanie "The Typo Hammer" Melander for killing those typos

An even HUGER thanks to all my passionate and fantastic beta readers:

Emaleth Morrigan (mermaid), The REAL Julie England, Rosanne Triegaardt, Sarah Frost, Always Handy Mandy Jamerson, Wendy Boyer, Nicki Hewitt-Hart, Natasha Slater, Megan C Christmas, Maria Combee, Juliana the Blue Bombah, Julie Clarke, and The Ever Special Mel Bushell for invaluable feedback and encouragement! You guys rock the typo sauce!

Jessie Duchannes for her awesome reviews and Sailor Moon.

Kelsey Burns for always backing my play.

Hayley Picknell for slick Brit Pimpin' and awesome reviews everywhere!

Michele McKenzie for equally all-star pimpin' and typo-snyping.

Amy Cossio for always rocking the Awesome Saucio.

And last but not least, for last minute typo-snyping of the highest order and in the face of great personal danger, I award a Typo Heart to **Colonel Melanie Starr**, the one and only **Comma Bomber**, who saved this mission from certain disaster at the 11th hour, but not without significant personal sacrifice on her part. Colonel, I salute you!

Thanks to everybody else who has helped make this book a reality!